THE SON OF GOD

SHARON LINDSAY

Healing In His Wings

THE SON OF GOD

Series: Book 4

TATE PUBLISHING
AND ENTERPRISES, LLC

The Son of God Series: Book 4

Published by Tate Publishing & Enterprises, LLC
127 E. Trade Center Terrace | Mustang, Oklahoma 73064 USA
1.888.361.9473 | www.tatepublishing.com

Tate Publishing is committed to excellence in the publishing industry. The company reflects the philosophy established by the founders, based on Psalm 68:11,
"The Lord gave the word and great was the company of those who published it."

Cover design by Nino Carlo Suico
Interior design by Jomel Pepito

Published in the United States of America

ISBN: 978-1-68028-154-5
1. Religion / General
2. Fiction / Religious
15.03.24

To Benji and Don Greenwalt,
They have been lifetime friends through good and bad times. They are sensitive to the Holy Spirit, opening their hearts and their home for the Kingdom of God. Benji has graciously read and reread my manuscripts. Her suggestions have been invaluable.

Contents

Introduction

But for you who revere my name, the sun of righteousness will rise with healing in its wings. And you will go out and leap like calves released from the stall.

—Malachi 4:2

One of the last Old Testament prophets compares the promised Deliverer to the sun, a ball of fire that rises on a dark world. It sends out golden rays that kiss each man, woman, and child, bringing them into the fullness of a new and joyous day.

In my mind, I see the fulfillment of this prophecy. It is Jesus resting on a rugged hilltop just before dawn. All night, he has been praying. Then suddenly, the sun bursts over the horizon, quickly climbing to burn behind the rock-strewn crest.

Jesus stands, silhouetted in heaven's brilliant glory. Even though it is early, he sees people coming from every direction. Immediately, Jesus tangles the fringes of his prayer shawl in his fingers and raises his arms. The white linen cloth catches the morning breeze, and for a moment, it seems that Jesus is about to take flight. With outstretched arms, he beckons to the crowd that is now pushing up the mountain to meet him. In a loud voice, he calls, "*Come to me, all you who are weary and burdened, and I will give you rest.*"[1] Then, as they come, one-by-one, brushing their fingers across the fabric of his outstretched prayer shawl, healing power is released. For a moment, each person looks deeply into the eyes of their Creator-in-human-form. It is a transformational experience.

Healing in His Wings is about the ministry years in the life of Jesus when his compassionate response was to touch and heal.

This fourth volume in the *Son of God Series* contains the stories of Matthew, Mark, Luke, and John set in the time and culture that was first century Judea. The stories have been expanded to include imagined names, relationships, and motivations only for the purpose of allowing the reader to identify more fully with Jesus and the life that he lived while on Earth. Each character is listed in the index of characters at the end of the book so you can easily know whether it is an addition to the Bible stories or a person who lived and interacted with Yeshua-Jesus.

Now, live those years with Jesus as you read *Healing in His Wings.*

Prologue

Incident at Shechem

Now Dinah, the daughter Leah had borne to Jacob, went out to visit the women of the land. When Shechem son of Hamor the Hivite, the ruler of that area, saw her, he took her and violated her. His heart was drawn to Dinah daughter of Jacob, and he loved the girl and spoke tenderly to her. And Shechem said to his father Hamor, "Get me this girl as my wife."

—Genesis 34:1–4

Shechem, son of Hamor, placed his hand protectively over his groin area as he carefully shifted his weight and changed his position on the bed. It had been three days since he had handed a clean flint knife to a trusted servant and ordered that his own foreskin be cut off. Now, the pain of that event seemed insignificant compared to the pain from the swelling and inflammation that seemed to be part of the healing process.

Settling into the most comfortable position possible, Shechem listened to the sounds of his father's household. He could hear light footsteps outside the curtain over his doorway. He knew it had to be one of the women in the family because every man in the city of Shechem was lying in the same painful condition as he.

The curtain over his door moved a little. "May I come in?"

He knew that voice. It was beautiful, gracious Dinah. Shechem sighed. The daughter of Jacob— he remembered the evening when he had first seen her. She was standing with the young women of the town, watching the spring fertility rituals. He knew now she had been unprepared for the climax of thc fcstivities. Innocently, she had believed it was all about the new crops. She had not expected the young men of the town to suddenly rush upon the maidens, forcing them into dark corners where fertility rites became a human experience. Maybe he should have listened to her protests, but the wine and the way she made his body throb with passion had clouded his judgment. "Forget the past," Shechem spoke to himself. Dinah had forgiven him, and soon, she would be his wife. Her father, Jacob, had agreed to their union.

"Shechem?" Dinah called again through the curtain. "I brought you water from my father's well. It is the best water in the valley. A cool drink will make you feel better."

"Come in, Dinah," Shechem responded as he made sure the lower half of his body was discreetly covered.

Coming through the curtain, a little alarmed cry escaped Dinah's lips. "You are red with fever! Sweat is soaking your bed!" She hurriedly filled a cup from the earthenware vessel she had carried from her father's well. Then she quickly moved to the bedside of her future husband. "Your father and your brothers are also suffering," Dinah commented.

"The whole city is groaning, Dinah." Shechem looked deeply into the dark eyes of the girl he had roughly taken and then tenderly loved. He drank from the cup she offered him. "This water is still cool—amazing." Shechem gave the cup back to Dinah. "If my father had known that water this cool and delicious was on the land he sold to your father, he would never have sold it."

Dinah laughed lightly as she responded, "You don't understand. God speaks to Jacob, my father. He tells him things other men do not know. God told my father what land to purchase. He told him where to dig for water. My brothers and the servants complained because they had to dig far deeper than most men dig for water, but my father insisted. He knows God is never wrong."

"So, instead of calling it Jacob's Well, we should call it the Well of the God of Jacob?" Shechem sank back into the cushions on his bed. "And this pain, is it also a mandate from your God?"

"It is the sign that is placed on every male descendant of Abraham. It is the symbol that we live in covenant with God, the Creator of the Universe," Dinah answered. "My parents have taught me God will send a Deliverer who will bring us back into the perfect home we once shared with God. This Deliverer will come through the reproductive process. This cutting is God's way of reminding us to respect that process and to expect our Deliverer."

Shechem shook his head. He did not understand such nonsense. "My people have their own fables and superstitions."

Dinah cautioned, "Your traditions are not the same. They come from the imaginations of men. Ours come from the mouth of the only real God."

Shechem raised a silencing finger. "I am in no condition to engage in a vigorous discussion."

Dinah responded, "Your discomfort will soon pass. Remember, without this cutting on your body and on the body of each of our male children, our offspring can never inherit from the line of Jacob."

"I hope you realize this is the highest bride price that has ever been paid. Every man in the city has allowed himself to be exposed and cut."

"Every man in the city does not love me like you do," Dinah responded.

"I know. They love your father's wealth. They want to marry his daughters and granddaughters. They want to merge the wealth of Jacob with the wealth of this city," Shechem answered.

"Men will make great sacrifices for wealth," Dinah commented.

"And even greater sacrifices for love." Shechem reached out to touch Dinah's face.

A scream from somewhere in the house froze his hand in midair. The curtain covering the doorway was suddenly ripped away.

"Levi! Simeon!" Dinah gasped the names of her brothers. They stood shoulder-to-shoulder between the doorposts. Blood dripped from the swords in their hands. "What are you doing? What have you done?" Dinah screamed.

Neither brother responded to her frantic questions.

Levi raged, "So this is where we find you—in the bedchamber of your Canaanite lover!"

"We are going to be married," Dinah verbally defended herself.

"But you have not been given to this man in marriage," Levi shouted. "He is not a descendant of Shem. He does not carry the blessing or the seed of the Name too holy to be spoken."

Simeon disgustedly added, "The promises God gave to Abraham belong to the pure seed. We will not allow you to pollute the seed of our inheritance."

Dinah stood to face her brothers. Simeon roughly brushed her aside.

"The curse of Ham and his son Canaan is on this man." Levi stepped toward the bed, his sword poised to kill.

"Wait!" Shechem pleaded as he painfully pulled himself up into a sitting position. "Your father set the bride price. It has been paid."

"You did not spill enough blood to pay for our sister," Levi answered as he brought the edge of his sword swiftly across Shechem's throat.

Screaming hysterically, Dinah threw herself across her lover's bleeding body.

"Stay here," Simeon ordered. "We will come back for you."

"What are you going to do?" Dinah demanded through her sobs.

"We're going to kill every man in this city," Levi answered. "There will be no one left to avenge the killing of Hamor and his son Shechem."

"No!" Dinah then collapsed into more sobbing.

Neither brother responded; both turned to continue on their bloody mission. In the doorway, Simeon paused. He turned back to his sister. "Do not leave this room!"

It was well past noon when Levi and Simeon returned to the room where Dinah had sobbed herself into dry gasps of horror. Throughout the day, she had followed the deadly progress of her brothers as the wails and screams of the town's women had risen from each section of town. They were the terrified cries of her friends, the young women she had come to visit. Again and again, Dinah's heart broke. All she had wanted was a social life that reached beyond her large, male-dominated family encampment. In the city of Shechem, she had experienced life and love.

How could she live with this knowledge—she had brought such carnage upon a whole population? If it had only been just her own life destroyed, not the lives of all her friends.

Dinah looked up. Her two brothers stood in the gaping doorway. Grim, splattered with dried blood, they were men who had completed the task they had begun.

"Let's go." Simeon grabbed his sister by the arm and pulled her to her feet.

Levi picked up her mantel and threw it at her feet.

Dinah understood her face must be covered. Numb with grief, she picked up the fabric and wrapped it around her head leaving the smallest slit, just enough so she could see to follow her brothers.

The trio walked in silence until they came to Jacob's Well. There, Levi drew jar after jar of water. He poured it over himself. He poured it over his brother, and then he thrust a full jar into

Dinah's hands. "Wash yourself, woman. Remove the filth of that Canaanite dog from your body."

Simeon warned, "Do not ever speak the name of Shechem again."

"And pray to God you do not carry his offspring because we cannot allow it to live," Levi added.

Both men turned their backs and guarded the entrance to the covered well so their sister could wash in privacy. Only the spirit of Shame slipped past their post. It attached itself to the grieving girl. It sucked up all the joys of her past. Then it threw her hopes and her dreams into the dark depths of the well. Within her heart, Dinah heard them hit the water and sink to a place where they could never be retrieved.

Brokenhearted and modestly veiled, Dinah stepped out of the well's enclosure. Her tearful gaze was on the ground. Without speaking, she followed her brothers back to Jacob's encampment. They left her at her mother's tent.

Chapter 1

Water from Jacob's Well

Jacob's well was there, and Jesus, tired as he was from the journey, sat down by the well. It was about noon.

—John 4:6

Jesus briskly led the way along the dusty road from Jerusalem to Galilee. His companions trailed behind in conversational groups of twos and threes. As the men entered the valley between the rolling slopes of Mount Ebal and Mount Gerizim, Jesus paused. With his eyes, he scanned the rock-strewn land along both sides of the road. Then he stepped decisively off the road, walking directly toward a small grove of oaks. His friends also paused, and then they followed him.

"Are you tired?" Peter asked as he caught up with the long-legged stride of his teacher. "Do you want to rest under these trees?"

"This is not the place to rest," Jesus answered. "It is the place to remember."

The men who had followed him from the springs east of the Jordan gathered around their teacher.

They watched as Jesus nudged several stones with his foot. Then he bent to examine a few more stones before he chose a specific rock. He held it up, level with his own face. "The rocks in this place speak to me. They repeat the words Joshua spoke to the twelve tribes as they stood on these mountain slopes, '*Long ago your ancestor…lived beyond the Euphrates River and worshiped other gods. But I took your father Abraham from the land beyond the Euphrates and led him throughout Canaan and gave him many descendants.'"*[1]

Jesus looked directly at the men who had been with John the Baptist near the Jordan and who had left John to immerse themselves in his life and his instruction. "It is good to know where you have come from," Jesus emphatically stated.

"We come from Abraham," Peter quickly proclaimed their heritage.

"Yes," Jesus replied. "When our father Abraham first entered the land, there was one large oak where these oaks now grow. He pitched his tent here, and he built an altar."

Nathanael spoke up, "At that altar, the Lord spoke to Abram, promising him this land and an heir."

Simon called the Zealot gruffly asserted, "So, why is this land occupied by Samaritans and ruled by Romans?"

Jesus responded, "When our father Abraham came to this land, it was occupied by Canaanites. This road ran directly through the Canaanite city of Shechem."

"I know the history," Nathanael spoke up again. "Abraham did not remain near the city of Shechem. He moved on to Bethel, but later, his grandson Jacob made his home in this valley within sight of Shechem."

"Yes." Jesus turned. He slowly walked back to the road. The Holy Spirit was making available to him his own heavenly memory as Yeshua the Creator. And Jesus shared what he was seeing as he walked. "Once, this valley was full of flocks tended by the sons and servants of Jacob. Over there"—Jesus pointed to a dusty patch of ground—"Jacob pitched his tent. Each wife, Leah, Rachel, Zilpah, and Bilhah, had her own tent. There was an altar. Jesus looked around before pointing to an indistinct pile of rubble. "Jacob named the altar. He called it the God of Israel because he had wrestled with God and received his name,

Israel. At that place, the God of his grandfather and his father reaffirmed the promises."

"Joseph's tomb is nearby," Nathanael mentioned.

"Yes, this is the land Joseph inherited from his father. When Joseph's bones were brought out of Egypt, they were placed here so it would be remembered forever that this land is the inheritance of the descendants of Jacob," Jesus added.

"Jacob's Well is just ahead!" James informed.

"And the town of Sychar is nearby," Peter added. "We can stop there and get some food."

"If you want to eat Samaritan food," Simon objected.

"I just want to eat food," Peter hotly responded.

"We do not think twice about selling them our fish," James pointed out. "Why shouldn't we buy their food?"

Philip then asked Jesus, "Isn't the correct procedure to purchase food in their city but not to eat that food in the city?"

"Yes," Nathanael concurred. "The food will not make us impure, but associating with the people will certainly require several days of purification."

Conversation stopped as the men looked to Jesus to affirm or clarify the point that was being made, but it appeared Jesus was not listening.

Approaching the well, Jesus broke his silence. "I will wait here under the thatched roof that covers this well. You can go into the town to make your purchases and then return to me."

With shrugging shoulders and nods all around, the men hurried down the road. Jesus watched them go. So far, seven men had attached themselves to him. James and John were his cousins. Their father was Zebedee who was married to Aunt Salome. Peter and Andrew were brothers. Their family had a fishing partnership with Zebedee. Simon called the Zealot was a childhood friend who now had a blacksmith shop in the town of Cana. His father had also been a Zealot, a man who had died on a Roman cross. Jesus had become acquainted with Philip and

Nathanael at the oasis beyond the Jordan where John the Baptist preached repentance and immersed those who believed. His eyes left the men, and he glanced upward, "Father, they are working men. They have good hearts, but their minds are confused by years of tradition and mixed up teaching. Can they change?"

"Their transformation will be gradual," God answered. "At first, they will see dimly, but as they stay with you, the light you shine on each activity, and event will sharpen their vision and their understanding."

Jesus replied, "You have told me one day, these men will go to the farthest corners of the world to call men and women into your kingdom. But today, a small excursion into a Samaritan city seems like a huge task."

"They will learn," God assured.

Photina threw a plain coarse mantel over her head. Quickly, she wrapped it around her face so it covered her thick dark hair as well as the fine features of her face. Only her black eyes could be seen. Casually, she glanced at the man who was sleeping on the couch. This was his house, and he expected certain services in exchange for providing her this home—water from the well, meals, and the comfort a wife usually offers. Photina sighed as she lifted the large earthenware water jar and balanced it on her shoulder. She did not mind cooking, and the touch of this man was not unpleasant, but going to Jacob's well—she could do without the sneering stares of the respectable women in this town.

Determined to do this task quickly before the other women came for their evening water, Photina stepped out into the hot afternoon sun. Looking both ways, it seemed the street was deserted. Yet Shame was lurking in the shadows, waiting to join her simply for the pleasure of presenting his own twisted truths.

Without hesitation, the condemning spirit matched his step to Photina's. Immediately, he pointed to a young man returning from the fields that surrounded the town. "Turn your head, Photina. Don't look that man in the eye. He knows his brother took you by force, and you did not scream or resist. For that incident, you bear the responsibility. You were not properly veiled. You were walking alone across his property. That man knows you looked at his brother with seducing eyes."

Photina quickly looked up and away. She made her eyes follow the smoothly sloping outline of Mount Ebal. Her gaze stopped at the ancient pile of stones where legend had it that Joshua had built an altar and set up a monument with the law of the Lord written on plaster-covered stones. Those old broken stones seemed to shout at her, "*This day I call heaven and earth as witnesses against you that I have set before you life and death, blessings and curses.*"[2]

Quickly, Photina moved her eyes to Mount Gerizim on the other side of the valley. That was the mountain of blessing, the place where her people made their sacrifices to the God of the Jews.

Shame would not let her hope in the blessings. Instead, the evil spirit began to quote the words of Moses that Joshua had spoken at this mountain, "*See, I am setting before you today a blessing and a curse- the blessing if you obey the commands of the LORD your God that I am giving you today; the curse if you disobey the commands of the LORD your God.*"[3] There is no blessing for the sexually impure. You can be certain God does not forgive a woman who finds herself with child and then tricks another man into marrying her."

In her youth before her first marriage, Photina had memorized Joshua's words. Now, they taunted her. Stinging from the reprimand, Photina lowered her gaze so she only saw the little clouds of dust made by her sandaled feet.

Approaching the well, Photina paused to shift her water jar to her other arm. At that moment, she looked up, and to her dismay, she saw a man sitting in the shade of the covered well. He was alone, just gazing out toward Joseph's tomb. For a long moment, she studied the man. When she had determined he was a stranger, most likely a Jewish traveler who would ignore her, she approached the well.

The man did not seem disturbed by her approach; he did not even turn his head.

Just as well, Photina thought as she tied her water jar to the long rope attached to an overhead pulley system. This Jew does not wish to speak to me, and I do not wish to speak to him! That is the way of those people. They think they are better than us Samaritans. They think— Her thought was suddenly interrupted.

"Woman?"

Photina's hands froze on the ropes, and she snapped her head around to see the man looking directly at her.

"Will you give me a drink?"[4]

Defensively, she replied, *"You are a Jew and I am a Samaritan woman. How can you ask me for a drink?"*[5]

Jesus answered her, "If you knew the gift of God and who it is that asks you for a drink, you would have asked me for a drink *and* I *would have given you living water."*[6]

Momentarily, Photina was speechless. Then she found her tongue. "You speak like a crazy man. Are you going to give me water? *Sir,"* Photina *said, "you have nothing to draw with and the well is deep. Where can you get this living water?"*[7]

Jesus did not comment. He just smiled at Photina's logic and waited.

Photina suddenly exploded, "Why are you looking at me like that? Who do you think you are—a man who has better water than the water in this well? *Are you greater than our father Jacob, who gave us the well and drank from it himself, as did also his sons and his flocks and herds?"*

Jesus answered, "Everyone who drinks this water will be thirsty again, but whoever drinks the water I give him will never thirst. Indeed, the water I give him will become in him a spring of water welling up to eternal life."[8]

"I do not want to ever come to this well again," Photina replied.

"I know," Jesus answered.

There was an unusual certainty in his tone. It made Photina pause while a little shiver ran the length of her spine. Then, regaining her composure, Photina challenged, "So, if you are able, *Sir, give me this water so that I won't get thirsty and have to keep coming here to draw water."*[9]

Jesus returned her look with confidence. "I know why you want this living water."

"You do?" Photina started to back away.

"Go, call your husband and come back."[10] Jesus directed. "Then I will tell you everything you need to know about this living water."

Photina dropped her gaze to the ground. *"I have no husband."*

Jesus said to her, "You are right when you say you have no husband. The fact is, you have had five husbands, and the man you now have is not your husband."[11]

Photina gasped. *"What you have just said is quite true."* She fidgeted, wondering what else this man might know. Then, cleverly she moved the conversation away from herself, *"Sir…I can see that you are a prophet. Our fathers worshiped on this mountain."* She pointed across the road to Mount Gerizim. *"But you Jews claim that the place where we must worship is in Jerusalem."*[12]

"You have brought up an unimportant issue. Arrogant religious leaders debate it, but it has no bearing on eternity." Looking directly into Photina's dark eyes, *Jesus declared, "Believe me, woman, a time is coming when you will worship the Father neither on this mountain nor in Jerusalem…A time is coming and has now come when the true worshipers will worship the Father in spirit and truth, for they are the kind of worshipers the Father seeks.*[13] The Father is not interested in a place of worship. He is seeking the hearts of all men in all locations."

For a few moments, Photina struggled to turn the conversation to a safe topic. Then she said, *"I know that the Messiah…is coming. When he comes, he will explain everything to us."*

Then Jesus declared, "I…am he."[14]

Photina's eyes widened. She released her grip on the rope, and her water jar quickly dropped to the water that flowed far below the ground.

"I will take care of your water jar," Jesus offered. "Go get the man you live with. He is sleeping on the cushions beneath the window."

Just then, Jesus's *disciples returned and were surprised to find him talking with a woman.* The men exchanged questioning glances. With their eyes, they asked each other, Who is this woman? Why would Jesus speak to one so obviously beneath him?

The men challenged Photina by looking sharply at her. *But, no one asked, "What do you want?"*

James, the eldest son of Zebedee, looked directly at Jesus. His eyes spoke for all of the men, *"Why are you talking with her?"*[15]

Photina did not respond to the men who were obviously somehow associated with the stranger with whom she had been talking. Instead, she turned, walking swiftly and then breaking into a run as she headed home to find her partner.

When she reached the city gate, she began speaking to individuals, and when she had gathered a crowd, she boldly announced, "There is a man at the well. He knows everything about my life! He speaks like a prophet—possibly the Messiah!"

Quickly, Photina's news spread from mouth-to-mouth. Curious, the people of the town emerged from their homes and their shops. They came out of their houses and their shops. Filled with curiosity, they hurried to hear the stranger who sat under the thatched roof of Jacob's Well.

Meanwhile Jesus's disciples returned to the well. Simon offered him a piece of flat bread wrapped around a pile of mashed chick peas, but Jesus brushed it aside with a casual wave of his hand.

Jesus seemed to be looking beyond the seven men who had attached themselves to him and his teaching. He was watching the road that passed through the city gate of Sychar. Jesus spoke to his friends, *"I have food to eat that you know nothing about.* And more food, a great banquet, is on its way!"

His disciples looked at each other quizzically. *Then* they *said to each other, "Could someone have brought him food?"*[16]

Jesus could now see the people hurrying out of the city gate, running toward the well. Photina was leading them, turning back again and again shouting encouragement. He could not hear her, but he knew what she was saying. "Come meet a man, a prophet who knows the secrets of each person. He told me that he is the Messiah, the one we have been waiting for!"

As Jesus watched, he saw the spirit of Shame remove itself from Photina's side. It lifted and fled in the direction of the wilderness.

Jesus returned his attention to his disciples. They were eating the food they had purchased in the town. Their backs were to the crowd, and they did not know what was about to happen. *"My food," said Jesus, "is to do the will of him who sent me and to finish his work."* Jesus pointed beyond the men to the road that was filled with people and to the fields that surrounded the town, Jesus said, "*Do you not say, 'Four months more and then the harvest'? I tell you, open your eyes and look at the fields! They are ripe for harvest."*[17]

Curiously, the men turned.

Alarmed, John exclaimed, "Jesus, we did not do anything in this city to disturb these people!"

Peter choked on his bread and sputtered crumbs as he shouted, "Master, we have to leave this place at once. A mob is upon us!"

"No," Jesus responded. "You see the harvest. It is coming to us, and we will spend several days gathering it in."

Andrew, forever logical, looked beyond the people. "The harvest? Those are wheat fields. They will not be ready for the reapers until after the summer."

James muttered to Peter, "Why is Andrew concerned with crops? We are about to be overrun by Samaritans!"

"I have my sword." Peter reached under the folds of his long robe and grasped the hilt of his weapon.

"I'm sure our friend the Zealot has one also,"James commented.

The men and women from Sychar were nearly upon them. Jesus stood to welcome Photina and the elders of the city. In a voice that only those disciples who stood beside him could hear, he said, "*Even now the reaper draws his wages, even now he harvests the crop for eternal life, so that the sower and the reaper may be glad together.*"[18]

Photina approached and bowed respectfully before introducing the elders of Sychar.

Stepping back and observing, the disciples were amazed. "I have never seen a Samaritan bow to a Jew," Philip whispered to Nathanael as they watched each elder kneel before their teacher.

"Be seated. Be seated,"Jesus invited everyone to be comfortable.

The people of the city brushed the small rocks aside and found places to sit. The men who were with Jesus remained standing. They were not comfortable with so many Samaritans.

Jesus began by saying, "About seven hundred years ago, the northern tribes of Israel were attacked, defeated, and deported from this land. A few individuals managed to escape and remain. Then foreigners from other nations were brought to this land, and it was given to them. They inhabited the towns of Samaria, replacing the Israelites. These foreigners did not worship the God of Israel.

"Tragedy befell them. Many were killed by the lions that roamed this region. Soon, it was reported to the king of Assyria, "The God of the Israelites is sending lions to devour the people you have settled in that region.

"Then the king responded by sending a priest of the Most High God to teach the people how to live. He set up a house of worship. He taught your ancestors the Law of Moses. He told them the story of Adam and Eve, and he promised that God would send a Deliverer not just for the Jews but for all of mankind."

"Not just for the Jews?"Philip repeated in shocked amazement.

Jesus heard him and turned from speaking to the crowd. Looking directly at Philip, he said, "*Thus the saying 'One sows and another reaps' is true.*' Over the next few days, as you hear these people repent and as you immerse them in water, you will see *I sent you to reap what you have not worked for. Others have done the hard work, and you have reaped the benefits of their labor.*"[19]

"Tell us more about our heritage," someone shouted.

Jesus responded, "This land is the inheritance of Joseph. Close to this well, Jacob set out his pots of dye. With water from this well, he colored the yarn he would use to make a special coat for his favorite son, Joseph—blue for the rivers his grandfather Abraham had crossed to reach this land, red for the blood of the lambs that connected their family with the God of heaven, green for the land God was giving them, and many shades of gray and brown for the numerous descendants God had promised.

"It was a beautiful coat. When it was presented to Joseph, it brought out all the ugliness living in the hearts of the other sons of Israel.

"A day came when Jacob said to Joseph, 'Go to your brothers who are grazing the flocks near Shechem. See how they are doing and bring a report back to me.' 'I will,' Joseph replied.

"When Joseph arrived at Shechem, he was wearing his beautiful coat. That beautiful coat was the tangible representation of his heritage and his future. The entire story of mankind was woven together by those many colored threads."

The people nodded as they listened. This man was speaking about their Jewish ancestor. He was treating them with the same respect that would be given to a group of Jews.

Jesus continued, "Joseph sat in the shade of this well and drank the water. Then he went off to find his brothers. They had moved on to another town, to another well. They were no longer satisfying their thirst with the water of their heritage."

"Our heritage is in that well," an elder emphatically stated.

Photina asserted, "This man told me he could give us living water, and we would not thirst again."

Jesus responded, "The living water is in your heritage and in your future. It is in the stories of this well and the deeper meaning attached to the stories."

"Stop interrupting!" another shouted.

Jesus just smiled and returned to the story. "When the sons of Israel saw their younger brother and when they saw he was wearing the favor of their father, they ripped the coat from his back. They sold him into slavery. It will be the same for the Messiah. He will come to his people, the sons of Israel. He will come wearing the favor of Father God. Evil men will rip the favor from him. They will sell him for some pieces of silver.

"Joseph's brothers took that beautiful coat, the coat that told the story of Israel and everyone who is attached to Israel. They covered it with blood. Then they presented that blood-covered garment to their father. I tell you today, the blood of the Messiah will cover all Israel and everyone else who believes. The blood of the Messiah will be presented to Father God not for the destruction of mankind but so all men will have an opportunity to believe and be saved.

"For centuries, the Jews have told you the way to God is only through the Temple services in Jerusalem. I am here to tell you the way to God is through repentance from sin and belief in the One God has sent. He comes wearing the favor of Father God like a beautiful coat. He comes to fall into the hands of evil men. He comes to triumph over evil.

"Do you believe? Do you want to show your belief by being immersed in water?"

"Yes!" The people came to their feet as one body.

"The purification pools are in the city," someone shouted.

"My disciples will baptize you there," Jesus replied as he stood to lead the crowd back into the city.

As they began walking, Jesus glanced at the seven men who were with him. He knew their thoughts. How could it be? Yesterday, we were baptizing Jews in the springs near the Jordan, and today we will be baptizing Samaritans!

Chapter 2

Judas Joins the Disciples

Judas was one of us and shared in the ministry with us.

—Acts 1:17

"Stinky camels are everywhere!" Peter complained to his brother Andrew. Both men dropped their armloads of sticks and branches and then set to work building a small fire.

Andrew concurred, "I don't know why Jesus chose a caravan way station to spend the night. There are three caravans here and drovers from every nation."

Peter continued, "He's wandering among the caravans now. James and John are with him."

Andrew straightened up from placing the sticks. "I don't want to light this fire until Philip, Nathanael, and the Zealot return from buying food"

"Let's find Jesus," Peter suggested, and both men headed for the closest caravan.

The camels were kneeling and chewing. As Peter walked by the rows of resting animals, he kept a healthy distance. "Every camel I walk past looks like it wants to kick my shin and spit in my eye," he muttered. "I prefer fish."

"There's Jesus!" Andrew exclaimed as he pointed past the piled-up baskets of merchandise. "And I know the man he is talking to."

Peter took a close look. "That man is from Jesus's family. He's Joseph's cousin who lives in Bethlehem. His name is Toma."

Both men hurried over to where their teacher stood with the owner of the caravan and a few other men. Without disrupting the conversation, they found places beside their fishing partners, James and John.

"So, you have taken over Kheti's caravan?" Jesus asked Toma.

"Kheti is setting up a small shop in Jerusalem that will specialize in imports," Toma replied. "He insists he is too old for the road."

"What about Nodab?" Jesus asked about the younger brother of Lazarus, who also worked the caravan routes.

"Right now, he is on his way to Petra. He has the youngest and strongest camels in his caravan," Toma answered as he placed his hand on the back of the nearest camel. "These are the older camels. Kheti and I decided these animals were not up to the rough desert trek, so we are using them just on the standard routes between cities."

Jesus reached over and rubbed the rough flank of the camel that Toma was touching. "This is an old camel, but there is still a lot of work in her joints," he announced.

"If your touch will do for this animal what it did for me when my body wouldn't recover from the beating I had taken, she will walk these roads for another ten years," Toma emphatically stated.

"You know I only do what I hear the Spirit of God telling me to do." Jesus smiled. "I hear the Holy Spirit telling me to touch every one of your animals." With that statement fresh in the air, Jesus began walking from camel to camel. Curiously, the men followed him, wondering why he was taking a long moment with his hand on each animal. Standing beside one camel, Jesus stopped and asked, "Toma, did you know that this animal is pregnant?"

Shaking his head in amazement, Toma stepped up to take a closer look at the resting camel. "This animal is at least thirty years old. I thought she was too old to have another calf." Another man stepped into the group, and Toma turned to introduce him. "Jesus, have you met Judas Iscariot?"

"No." Jesus looked directly into the man's eyes.

Judas took a step backward as if such an intense stare made him uncomfortable.

Toma continued the introduction. "Judas comes from a family of money lenders in the Temple. He wants to learn about buying and selling merchandise on the caravan routes, so he has joined us. He has quite a head for making a deal."

"I recognize the family name," John muttered to Peter. "His family is known for their relentless haggling. Every time we bring fish to their estate, they don't want to pay a fair price."

Jesus moved on to the next kneeling camel. Before touching the animal, he turned to Judas and asked, "Do you know much about camels?"

"I just know their market value," Judas confidently replied.

"How about this animal?" Jesus asked. "What is its market value?"

Judas pulled on his beard as he studied the animal. Obviously, this was another one of the older camels. The animal turned its head and looked directly at the men. Flies were swarming around its eyes. Judas bent in for a closer examination of the camel's eyes.

James whispered to Peter, "That animal has an infection."

Peter responded, "That camel is going to spit in that rich man's face, if he gets any closer!"

Again, Jesus asked, "What is a good price for this animal?"

"Worthless," Judas replied. "It will soon lose its eyesight, and what good is a blind camel?"

With the fringes of his prayer shawl entwined in his fingers, Jesus reached out and brushed the flies away from the animal's eyes.

Gasps of amazement suddenly spread from man to man. "Look, the eyes are now clear! Even the flies have gone!"

Obviously amazed, Judas leaned forward to get another close look, and the camel, which was the center of attention, suddenly spit her smelly brown cud all over the front of his robe.

"I must be a prophet!" Peter proclaimed as he slapped James on the back. Both men could hardly contain their laughter.

Judas ignored thc antics of the fishermen. He ignored the smelly mess on the front of his clothing. He was focused on calculating the value of a man who could touch a sick and used up animal, restoring it to usefulness.

Judas then turned to Jesus. "Originally, my family was from a small town near Hebron. Camels are important in that desert region. A man who can restore the sight and health of a used up animal like this one would be invaluable in that part of the country."

"This is a small thing," Jesus responded. "Do not be impressed with me. Be impressed with God, who cares deeply about every creature on Earth. I touched the animal at his command. He provided the healing power."

Judas could not just accept Jesus's statement and move on. He was still totally fascinated with the financial potential of this man. He had to know more. Taking a step closer he asked, "Jesus, where do you come from?"

"Nazareth," Jesus answered.

"Where are you going?" Judas asked.

"Wherever the Spirit of God leads me," Jesus answered as he turned to move down the caravan.

Impulsively, Judas grabbed the sleeve of his robe. "Wait!"

Jesus stopped and turned. "What do you want with me?"

"I want to see more miracles. I want to go with you and learn. I have never seen such an amazing display."

Toma leaned into the conversation. "Judas does come from a very prominent family. His connections in the Temple could be beneficial."

A slight shadow passed over Jesus's face. Then he gestured toward the fishermen who were with him. "These men often travel with me, and they listen to my teaching."

"I can become one of your students," Judas offered. There was a hint of desperation in his voice.

Standing nearby, making their own jokes about the wealthy man with camel cud all over his clothing, Peter and Andrew, James and John suddenly focused on the conversation Jesus was having with this Judas Iscariot. The lighthearted banter of the fishermen abruptly stopped. Dark scowls quickly replaced their carefree smiles.

Jesus looked at his disciples and then back at Judas. "I already have a relationship with these men. They have been living with me, working with me, and learning from me for the past six months. I am not sure you will fit in."

Peter stepped forward and gave Judas an intimidating look. "We don't sleep in fancy houses like your family home in Jerusalem's upper city," he challenged.

Judas rose to the bait and countered, "For the past month, I've been sleeping on the ground with the stench of camel dung in my nostrils. I'll just trade that smell for the odor of week-old fish. You are fishermen, aren't you?"

"Yes," Peter stormed, "and fishing is an honest trade! We know how to count our catch accurately."

James spoke up, "It seems the counting of coins at the Temple money exchange is always a little inaccurate."

Peter added, "In favor of the lenders."

"Galileans," Judas spoke the word with distain.

Everyone understood his implication. Judas was just letting them know that he, along with many people in Jerusalem, considered themselves better than people from any other region in the land, especially Galilee.

Nathanael, Philip, and Simon the Zealot joined the group. Peter moved his hand so it obviously rested on the hilt of his sword. "Yes, we are Galileans and proud of it!"

Without hesitation, the Zealot stepped up beside Peter. Brashly, he swept the folds of his robe aside revealing the fact that he also carried a sword. "If there is ever going to be freedom from the Romans, it will be because the Galileans begin the revolt."

"Nonsense," Judas retorted. Confidently, he folded his arms across his chest. "The only way we will get our government totally back into the hands of the Sanhedrin will be to purchase that privilege from Rome. The emperor of Rome can be bought."

Jesus stepped in. "As you can see, my friends have strong opinions. Are you sure you want to join us?" Jesus then turned and walked toward the fire that was waiting to be lit.

Nathanael and Philip approached Judas. "We know you come from a good family. Don't let our companions intimidate you. Join us. We will be eating around the fire, and while we eat, Jesus will be teaching."

Chapter 3

The Healing Word from Cana

When he arrived in Galilee, the Galileans welcomed him. They had seen all that he had done in Jerusalem at the Passover Feast, for they also had been there. Once more he visited Cana in Galilee, where he had turned the water into wine.

—John 4:45–46

Dry desert air drifted into the financial offices at Herod's palace-fortress called Machaerus. Cuza, the chief financial officer for the royal family, and Manaen, a lifelong companion and counselor for Herod Antipas, struggled to put an acceptable quarterly report together for the king.

After looking at scroll after scroll of financial ledgers and calculating on numerous parchments, Cuza tossed his writing tool on the table and sat back. He looked directly at Manaen. "The royal family has spent more money than it has taken in this quarter. There is no nice way to say this to Antipas." Cuza laid his hand on a stack of parchments. "There are debts to be paid, and presently, there is no money in the treasury."

"Exactly what is the problem?" Manaen asked. "Are we not collecting enough taxes or is the royal family spending too much?"

"Both," Cuza answered. "Revenue from the fishing industry around Galilee is unusually low. Most of the debts that need to be paid are for materials and craftsmen that Herodias has hired to remodel all the living quarters in all the royal residences."

"All the residences?" Manaen raise his eyebrows in amazement as he repeated the phrase.

"It seems she wants to remove every memory of Phasaelis, the former royal wife," Cuza stated.

"We can raise taxes on the fishermen. We can increase the fees for fishing permits, but who is going to tell Herodias her money is limited?" Manaen asked.

Both men felt an involuntary shiver run through their bodies as they imagined the reaction they could expect from the new wife of Herod Antipas.

"Facts are facts," Cuza stated. "We will give the bad news to Antipas, and he will have to put limits on his wife."

"There is more bad news for Antipas." Manaen tossed a rolled parchment with a broken Roman seal on the table. "This message is from Longinus, the commander of the Antonia Fortress in Jerusalem. The caravan merchants have informed him that the Nabataeans are preparing to go to war. Specifically, King Arteas is getting ready to attack Herod Antipas to avenge the honor of his daughter, the divorced queen."

"But we have a treaty with the Nabataeans," Cuza protested. "We have been good neighbors and trading partners for over twenty years!"

"That treaty, as well as the trade agreement, was part of the marriage contract that Antipas signed so Phasaelis could become his wife. Longinus has been informed that caravans from the territories ruled by Antipas are being turned away. They are not allowed to buy and sell in Petra."

"This is serious," Cuza shook his head. "Why didn't you tell Antipas as soon as you received this message?"

"Antipas would not discuss any state business. He was having an audience with the preacher who never cuts or combs his hair," Manaen informed.

"The Nazirite—that man called John the Baptist?" Cuza asked.

"Yes, Herodias finally talked the king into arresting the man. He is being kept in the dungeon of this palace." Manaen paced a little as he talked. "Antipas seems to be fascinated with him. Every day, he has the preacher brought before him, and every day, that unkempt man tells him to send Herodias back to her first husband or face the wrath of God." Manaen stopped pacing and turned to face Cuza. "I cannot believe what I am seeing! This son of Herod the Great fears both his wife and a wild-haired man from the desert. He cannot decide what to do with either of them." After a pause, Manaen stated, "His father would have killed them both."

Cuza countered, "It is not the preacher that our king fears. It is the people. Thousands of people believe that John the Baptist is either a prophet like Elijah or the Messiah."

"We both listened to this man. We saw him baptizing people in the Jordan," Manaen challenged. "What do you think?"

"I cannot make decisions about such things," Cuza protested. "I deal in numbers and facts. This man, his message, his followers, his connection with God—it is far too speculative for me."

"I have heard several reports about another man." Manaen began gathering the documents he would need to take to the king. "During the last Passover in Jerusalem, a man was healing the sick and teaching in the Temple."

Cuza brushed the information aside with a wave of his hand. "Tell Antipas I will personally visit each tax collector in the region of Galilee. I will audit their books and adjust their fees to cover the short fall." Then Cuza paused; a little smile lifted the corners of his mouth. "Joanna and I have not seen our little boy, Casper, in months. He has been staying with my mother on the family estate near Capernaum. I will take Joanna to him. She will be very happy to step out of palace life for a while. And I will take a few days just to enjoy my childhood home."

Freshly mended nets dried in the heat of the Middle Eastern sun. The fishermen of Capernaum slept the afternoon away while their boats rocked against crude wooden moorings. Matthew bent over his ledgers, calculating the size of each family's catch and the amount each family was required to contribute to the coffers of Herod Antipas.

An unexpected shadow fell across his ledger. Capernaum's tax collector looked up to see the chief financial officer for Herod Antipas looking down at his accounts.

"Cuza! I was not expecting to see you until fall." As he spoke, Matthew jumped to his feet to show proper respect.

"Income from this region has not been as high as usual," Cuza responded. "I've come to check your entries and to research the cause for such low funds."

"It seems that fish are not as plentiful as they have been in the past." Matthew defended the monthly deposits that he made to the royal treasury. "Every morning, I meet the fishing boats. Every morning, I count each fish. I tax each fishing family the total purchase price of the first forty out of one hundred fish that they catch."

"How many boats have you licensed for this season?" Cuza asked.

Immediately, Matthew scurried into the small building behind his outdoor table, looking for his ledger of fishing licenses.

Cuza followed him, remaining in the doorway, scanning the rows of cubicles filled with dusty records from previous years. He took another step into the dim room and bent to pick up a scroll that had fallen to the floor. He was about to make a comment about the need for a more orderly system for these records when he heard someone outside calling his name. There was something in the man's tone that was alarming.

Turning quickly, Cuza stepped back into the sunlight. "I'm here!" he responded loudly.

A servant from his mother's home appeared from behind the building. "I have been looking everywhere for you." The servant was a little breathless. "Your wife and your mother are terribly concerned. Your little boy, Casper, is very ill."

"What are the symptoms?" Cuza anxiously asked.

"He has a high fever with painful muscle spasms," the servant replied. "The muscle spasms are spreading throughout Casper's body."

Cuza covered his face with his hands. He remembered a childhood friend, his sudden illness and his agonizing death. Through his fingers, he asked, "Is Casper's back arching like a bow?"

"Yes," the servant softly answered.

Cuza choked back a sob as he asked, "Is my little boy screaming in pain?"

"Not so much," the servant replied. "His neck and facial muscles are becoming rigid. He is not talking or drinking."

"I have seen this sickness before," Cuza moaned. "It is always fatal." For a moment, he looked up at the servant. "The physicians?" he asked.

"They said the boy is now in the hands of God. They have done all they know how to do," the servant answered. "But your mother says there is a man who is a carpenter. Sometimes he repairs ships on the shore near the home of Zebedee. She has heard he has a special relationship with God. It is even said that he has the gift of healing. She wants you to find him."

Matthew stepped out with the proper records in his hands.

Cuza turned abruptly to face him. "Matthew, do you know anything about a man who repairs fishing boats and heals the sick?" Cuza quickly added, "Why do they say he is a healer?"

"His name is Jesus," Matthew replied. "After the last Passover and after the fall feasts, people returned to this town with amazing stories. Jesus speaks a few words and the deaf hear. He touches sores with the fringes of his prayer shawl, and there is instant healing. He did these things in Jerusalem. People are still talking about the things they have seen this man do."

"Did you see him?" Cuza pressed. "Did you see him heal?"

"At Passover, I was in the men's purification pool. I saw a man with an ugly running sore on the calf of his leg. After Jesus touched it, I could not see where the sore had been. It was just healthy skin," Matthew said.

With a look that screamed both belief and unbelief Cuza asked, "Where is this man?"

Matthew answered, "Presently, he is not in town, but his Uncle Zebedee might know where he is."

"Go!" With a frantic wave of his hand, Cuza directed the servant to find Zebedee and the answer to his question.

"I cannot look at your records now," Cuza waved Matthew's armful of parchments aside. "Prepare for an audit. I will return soon." Quickly, Cuza turned away, striding, then running toward his childhood home, an estate on the outskirts of the town.

Joanna met her husband at the gate. "I cannot stay by Casper's bed another moment. He is in pain. His six-year-old eyes beg for help, and I cannot help him." Joanna collapsed into sobs at Cuza's feet.

Cuza left his wife in a crumpled, sobbing heap. He ran to his son's room. His mother was there with several servants.

His mother looked up. Her eyes had already cried every tear that was in her body. "When you wrote that you and Joanna were able to leave your duties in the palace and come to Capernaum, Casper was fine and healthy. I never dreamed you would find him like this."

Cuza knelt by his son's bed. With just two fingers, he lightly touched the boy's arm and watched him go into more painful spasms.

"Have you found the healer?" Cuza's mother asked. There was desperate hope in her voice.

"Your servant is looking for him," Cuza answered while choking on his own words. Then he directed, "Don't let anyone touch my son. Each touch starts the spasms again. I will find the healer."

"Shalom!" Jesus called the typical greeting as he approached the home of his younger brother Jose, a carpenter in the town of Cana.

Deborah, Jose's wife, came to open the gate.

Simon the Zealot shouted a farewell shalom and then walked on to his own wife and family. The rest of the men entered with Jesus.

"Let's see, how long has it been since the wedding?" Jesus asked.

"Nearly a year," Peter answered before Deborah could respond. "I'll never forget that wedding. You ran out of wine, and Jesus turned water into wine." Peter walked over to the six stone water jars that stood near the entrance to the courtyard. Curiously, he peered inside each one. Then he put a finger in one jar, bringing out a drop of water. "Just water," he said with a little disappointment.

"I heard the story from your mother," Deborah spoke to Jesus. "But I never understood."

Jesus laughed softly to himself before he responded. "It's simple. God loves you. He touched your back. He blessed your wedding with more wine than all the guests could drink in a week, and now, I see he is about to bless your home with children."

Deborah blushed as she said, "Yes, Jose and I are hoping for a son." Then she hurried to place cushions on the floor around a low table. "Jose will be home soon. He went to get a load of lumber for the shop. I know he will want you and your friends to spend the night."

As the evening came to an end, Jesus leaned back away from the remains of a delicious meal. He briefly studied the men who were with him. Peter and Andrew as well as James and John had been exchanging veiled threats with Judas Iscariot ever since he had joined them two days ago. Jesus looked directly at Judas and said, *"Do not judge, and you will not be judged."* Then he looked at the other four men who were traveling with him and he said, "*Do not condemn, and you will not be condemned. Forgive, and you will be forgiven.*"[1] Turning back to Judas, he admonished, "The Temple lenders and money changers have taught you to save money and only to let it leave your hands when there is a profit to be made, but this is the teaching that I have for you. *Give, and it will be given to you. A good measure, pressed down, shaken together and running over, will be poured into your lap. For with the measure you use, it will be measured to you.*"[2]

Judas squirmed uncomfortably. Then he got up and left the table.

Jose quickly stood and followed him. Jesus could hear his brother giving his guest directions to the toilet facilities behind the house. He could see Deborah moving around the room placing little lamps where they would give the most light so her guests would be comfortable.

Returning his attention to his disciples, Jesus continued his after-dinner instruction. "No one puts a lighted lamp in a jar or under a bed. Lamps are always elevated and placed near reflective surfaces so there are no dark places."

The disciples glanced at Deborah and nodded. Judas returned to the room and silently took his place at the table.

Jesus continued. His words seemed to be especially for Judas. "*For there is nothing hidden that will not be disclosed, and nothing concealed that will not be known or brought out into the open. Therefore consider carefully how you listen. Whoever has will be given more; whoever does not have, even what he thinks he has will be taken from him.*"[3]

"Jesus, your teaching always gives me much to think about," Jose said as he stood and stretched. "This has been a long day, and in the morning, I have to unload the wagon I borrowed to get this load of lumber."

"We will make your job easy," Jesus declared. "There must be a number of jobs we can do to help you."

Deborah spoke up before Jose could reply. "The winter rains have softened the ground, but Jose has not had time to prepare the soil so I can plant a garden.

"Six good men could remove all the rocks and break up the soil in one morning!" Peter exclaimed.

The others concurred with nods and smiles except for Judas, who sat in stone-faced amazement that he had been volunteered for manual labor in the morning.

Andrew jovially slapped him on the back. "That's the way we do things in Galilee. We don't have servants. We just work together and help each other."

Judas didn't respond. Stoically, he moved with the others to lay the cushions and pallets on the floor. He could see that everyone would be sleeping in close quarters tonight.

The sun was low on the horizon when Cuza set out for Cana. As rapidly as possible, he walked from one Roman mile marker to the next. His feet moved, but his heart was not in the journey. It stayed beside little Casper's bed, beating a father's will for his son to live.

Dusk turned into darkness. Fear and Doubt were his traveling companions. Cuza lit a little handheld lamp. Never pausing, he hurried on through the night. The blackness of night turned gray; dawn finally broke into early morning.

In Cuza's mind, logic struggled with the illogical. Why was he chasing after a man who most likely could do nothing for his son? Still, if there was anyone, anywhere who could save Casper's life—tormented by his own vacillating thoughts—Cuza hurried on.

About midday, he entered the town of Cana, and after a few inquiries, he found the home of Jose the carpenter. At the gate, he tried to call the typical greeting, but shalom got stuck in his throat. Miraculously, the gate opened anyway, and a young mother asked if she could be of assistance.

"I'm looking for the carpenter who works in Capernaum. I have heard that he heals people." Cuza listened to himself, and he knew he sounded crazy.

"You want Jesus. I will get him for you," Deborah offered.

Moments later, Cuza found himself surrounded by a group of sweaty working men. One of them stepped forward and said, "I am the one you are looking for."

"Sir," Cuza dropped to his knees. "My son is dying. Come back to Capernaum and restore him."

"Do you believe I can do such a thing?" Jesus asked.

"I don't know," Cuza truthfully answered. Then Cuza looked up into the face of Jesus. "I am willing to believe. I am willing to do anything so my son will live. Help me believe so my son can be healed."

Reaching out with his strong forearms, Jesus lifted Cuza to his feet.

At that moment, Cuza felt a tingling sensation travel from the grip of the carpenter's hands up his own arms. That strange sensation lodged deep within his chest, completely displacing every fear and all concern for his son.

Then Jesus said, "Return to Capernaum with peace in your heart. Your son will live."

Immediately, the spirit of Doubt that had traveled with Cuza, tormenting him throughout his all-night journey, fled. The gift of faith came in like a flood, and Cuza gratefully accepted the words of Jesus. He turned and hurried back to Capernaum.

Hurrying back along the route he had traveled, Cuza tried to make sense of his new state of mind. He had no objective knowledge about the condition of his son, but within his heart, he was certain his son was out of danger. There was nothing he could think or imagine that would bring back the fear and worry that had plagued him throughout the night. Logic could not explain the feelings that filled him.

Before the gates of Capernaum came into view, two servants from his family estate met him on the road. "Your son lives! He is completely recovered."

"When?" Cuza asked. "And how did this happen?"

One of the servants answered, "Yesterday, a little past noon, Casper suddenly sat up and asked for water. After he drank, he hopped out of bed and ran to the kitchen, looking for something to eat."

The other servant added, "He has been running and playing ever since."

"Just past noon," Cuza repeated. "That is when the healer took hold of my hands and said that Casper would live." For a long moment, Cuza stood in the middle of the road, weak with relief and dumb with amazement. Then he said to the servants, "Now, I really believe this man is a healer sent from God."

Chapter 4

A Riot in Nazareth

He went to Nazareth, where he had been brought up, and on the Sabbath day he went into the synagogue, as was his custom. And he stood up to read.

—Luke 4:16

At the family home in Nazareth, Jesus called shalom as he pulled the latch and opened the gate. With his right hand, he touched his lips and then touched the mezuzah attached to the entry. Seven of his followers were with him. Each man in turn respectfully touched the mezuzah as he entered the courtyard.

Mary was the first to greet them. She ran from the cooking area, wiping her hands and bowing to her visitors. "You have come for the last night of the Feast of Dedication," she exclaimed. Possessively, she reached up and held the face of Jesus with both hands. Then she gave him that hard-examining look that only a mother can give. After a moment, she kissed him on both cheeks. "I am glad you have brought your cousins and your friends. I have been cooking. I will cook a little more. Your brothers are working in Sepphoris, but they will be home before sunset. Tonight, the whole family is gathering—it will be wonderful!"

Mary turned to the men. "James and John, how are your parents? I have not seen them since Jose was married."

"They are well," John answered.

"And you two?" Mary moved to where Peter and Andrew were standing. "I remember you were at the wedding. Is my boy, Jesus, staying out of trouble?"

"Well, in the Temple at Passover…" Peter glanced at Jesus as he started to tell the story of the money changers. Then he detected that Jesus was giving him a slight negative nod. "Jesus has been teaching," he finished his sentence a little lamely.

"Once, when he was only twelve years old, I found him in one of the inner rooms of the Temple. He was instructing the great Rabbi Hillel. The room was packed, and everyone wanted to hear Jesus interpret the scriptures," Mary recalled.

"Mother!" Jesus exclaimed. "I thought you were displeased with me."

Mary shrugged and tossed her hands in the air. "Secretly, I was very proud."

Then with a questioning look on her face, Mary turned to the men she had not met.

Jesus responded, "Mother, this is Judas Iscariot. He left Toma's caravan to follow me and listen to my teaching." Then Jesus turned to Philip and Nathanael. "These two are fishermen, originally from Bethsaida. They were sitting under the teaching of our cousin, John the son of Zechariah and Elizabeth."

"Have you heard about John?" Mary asked with concern.

"Yes," Jesus answered. "We left Judea soon after we received word that Herod Antipas had sent soldiers to arrest him. I have prayed to my Father for him," Jesus added. Then, on a lighter note, he said, "We have come from Cana. Jose and Deborah are fine. I left Simon the Zealot with his family."

Mary pointed to the part of the courtyard where a large old sycamore tree cast its shadow over the wall. "Wash your feet. Drink some water. Rest in the shade. We will light the lamps at sunset." With that, Mary turned back to her preparations.

"Come! Come! Everyone gather outside the gate." Mary hurried her extended family and guests to the area where she had placed a long wooden bench. She passed out the small oil lamps—one to her second son James, one to his eldest son Enos. The others were given to her other two sons, Simon and Jude, then to their cousins James and John. Finally, there were two more for Peter and Andrew. Then she lined everyone up.

Peter whispered to John, "The director of the Levitical choir at the Temple could not do a better job than this woman."

John laughed. "My aunt Mary has always been a take charge woman!"

Mary handed a lamp that was already lit, along with a long thin stick, to Jesus. "You will be the servant tonight," she directed as she stepped back for a final look.

When everyone appeared ready, Mary pointed to James's wife, who chanted the first blessing. "Blessed are you, Lord, our God, king of the universe, who has sanctified us with his commandments and commanded us to light the lights of Hanukkah."

Mary then pointed toward her daughter, Ruth, who said the second blessing, "Blessed are you, Lord, our God, king of the universe, who performed miracles for our ancestors in those days in this winter season."

Then Jesus placed his lamp on the bench. From it, he lit the thin piece of wood. Mary started one of the songs for the season.

Everyone sang as Jesus stepped toward his brother James to light the first lamp.

May God be gracious to us and bless us
and make his face shine upon us,
that your ways may be known on earth,
your salvation among all nations.

James placed his lamp on the bench. Its tiny flame flickered, and the light it made dimly reflected on the limestone wall. Jesus moved on to the next two lamps. He lit those, and they were added to the ones on the bench. The family continued to sing.

May the peoples praise you, O God;
may all the peoples praise you.

Lamp after lamp, Jesus applied fire to each wick, and one by one, they were lined up on the bench.

May the nations be glad and sing for joy,
for you rule the peoples justly
and guide the nations of the earth.

Nine oil lamps, their golden flames reflected on the off-white stones of the courtyard wall, recalled for each person the stories of the season. Everyone watched the flames. Each person sang and remembered they were the special people, set apart by God.

May the peoples praise you, O God;
may all the peoples praise you.
Then the land will yield its harvest,
and God, our God, will bless us.

Those nine little flames told the story of a deliverer from long ago who drove a cruel ruler out of their land. Now they whispered hope that another Deliverer would come and reestablish the throne of David. The song ended.

God will bless us, and all the ends of the earth will fear him.[1]

Immediately, Mary motioned for the men to sit on the pallets she had spread on the ground. She and the women of her family began serving cups of wine, bread with pungent goat cheese, honey, and almonds. Jesus sat with his friends and his brothers.

In the Antonia Fortress in Jerusalem, Pontius Pilate strode into his wife's sitting room. "Procila, come walk with me. I want to know what you have learned about this feast that has been going on for the past eight days. I also want to know if the gods have shown you anything." Pilate cleared his throat, then he added, "There are rumors from Rome that Sejanus, my benefactor, the man who appointed me to this post, is ruthlessly trying to move himself into a position of such power that he could become the next emperor."

"Wouldn't it be good for you if Sejanus became more powerful?" Procila asked as she picked up a small scroll and prepared to stroll with her husband.

"I am not sure where I stand with Sejanus," Pilate admitted. "Isolated in this desert province, I am afraid I have been forgotten in Rome."

"Forgotten until Herod Antipas or the Jewish leaders send a complaint to the emperor," Procila admonished.

"Ah, yes—the complaints. I fear there have been too many." Pilate held the heavy draperies to one side so his wife could exit the governor's quarters. The guard at their doorway saluted, fist to chest, and Pilate returned the courtesy.

"Let's go to the tower that overlooks the city," Procila suggested.

As they walked, Procila said, "I have been studying the people of this land, their culture, and their religion. This eight day feast is a patriotic celebration, a reminder that about one hundred fifty years ago a small force of men defeated the great Syrian general Antiochus Epiphanes. They restored this Temple and its services."

"I know. My spies have reported much talk of overthrowing Rome with the help of their God, just like Judah Maccabee overthrew the Syrians." Pilate shook his head. "Why would this little nation that does not even have an army consider overthrowing Rome?"

Procila replied, "This nation has a very long history. It is recorded in their scriptures. With the help of their God, they have defeated many great nations. In their hearts, they believe it could happen again."

Slowly, the couple climbed the steps to one of the corner towers. At one of the windows, they paused and looked out over the city. "If I did not know better, I would think all of Jerusalem was on fire," Pilatc commented.

"Every house in the city has at least nine oil lamps burning so they can be seen from the street, and some homes have many more burning," Procila informed. "You are right to be concerned. The fire of nationalism burns in every Jewish heart. Every morning in this Temple, they repeat the words of Moses, '*Rise up, O Lord! May your enemies be scattered; may your foes flee before you.*'"[2]

"This Temple"—Pilate pointed to the magnificent structure that was lit by four huge burning cauldrons of oil—"is a center of treason. One day, Rome is going to have to destroy it."

Procila sighed, "I hope that does not happen in my lifetime. Every time I come to Jerusalem with you, I am fascinated by their rituals."

"What should I know about the rituals of this feast?" Pilate pragmatically asked.

Procila answered, "You should know that the insignificant traditions of this season are laced with danger. In every home, the people are eating cheese and drinking wine. It is a symbolic reminder that once there was a Jewish heroine named Judith. She entered the tent of a famous general. She fed him cheese and wine. When he had fallen asleep, she cut off his head. That one act rallied the Jews and made them victorious over a much stronger force." Procila placed the small scroll in her husband's hand. "This is the Book of Judith. Read it."

"I will keep a safe distance from all the Jewish women in this land," Pilate quipped as he affectionately brushed his hand across Procila's cheek.

For a quiet moment, Pilate and Procila gazed at each other, and then they turned to look out over the city of Jerusalem. After a time, Pilate spoke, "When I left Rome, I expected to rule over a benign desert province. I expected them to cower at the sight of Roman troops."

Procila responded, *"Not by might nor by power, but by my Spirit,' says the LORD Almighty."*[3]

Pilate turned and looked at his wife quizzically.

"It is one of their sayings. It is the reason that the Jews do not fear Rome," Procila explained.

"Where is the amulet you usually wear close to your heart?" Pilate asked as with one finger, he lightly touched the place where her amulet typically hung."

"It is always wise to respect the god of the land," Procila explained. "When I began studying the ways of the Jews with Susanna, I found out the Jewish god is totally intolerant of all other gods. To show my respect and not incur his wrath, I took off my amulet, and I have not brought any of my small gods into this city."

"Does the Jewish god tell you anything?" Pilate soberly asked.

Procila paused and thoughtfully listened to her heart. Then she answered her husband, "My sense is that you should keep your distance from the politics of the empire, especially from Sejanus. As much as possible, hide out in this desert province until the political storms have blown away from Rome."

"You are wise," Pilate responded. "I am fortunate to have a wife who knows how to seek guidance from the gods."

The oil lamps in the city were burning out. Whole areas were now engulfed in darkness. Pilate took his wife's hand. "Will you stay with me, no matter what?"

Procila squeezed the strong hand of the man she had been married to many years before. "My allegiance is to you and no other," she replied.

Pilate pulled her close. It was a rare, private moment between a man and a woman, all titles laid aside. It passed quickly, and both resumed their dignified stance as they strode past the guards, back to the governor's chambers in the Antonia Fortress.

It was a chilly morning after the final night of Hanukkah. A small fire burned in the courtyard. Jesus and his friends sat around the tiny circle of flames. "We need to get in at least a month or more of fishing," Peter stated while the men ate their morning meal.

"He just wants to get back to his wife," Nathanael teased.

"Really," John spoke up. "We do need to get back to our boats and nets. If we get a good catch and then dry them before Passover, we can travel from town to town selling them."

"I know my father," James added. "He is probably shaking his fist at the wind and bellowing, "I need my good-for-nothing sons and their friends to come home and man my boats!"

Jesus smiled as he pictured his uncle. "Would Uncle Zebedee act like that?" he rhetorically asked.

All six fishermen nodded affirmatively.

"Then have a safe and blessed journey," Jesus said as he walked them to the road and sent them on their way. When they had gone a little way, Jesus called after them, "I'll see you in Capernaum, soon."

Jesus then turned back to Judas. "You could go with them. Capernaum is a more exciting town than Nazareth."

"I want to stay with you," Judas answered.

Looking directly into Judas's eyes, Jesus saw the spirit of Greed staring back at him.

The Holy Spirit confirmed what Jesus saw. "This man wants to sell you and your miracles like a broker who sells entertainment to the wealthy."

In his mind, Jesus responded to the Holy Spirit, Greed is a spirit that has been in his family for generations. If he chooses, he can throw it off. If he learns to care more about others than about money or himself, he will break its power.

Jesus turned his attention back to Judas. "When I come to town, I visit the widows. I gather their firewood. I repair their houses. I know a woman who has not been able to plant her garden. We will do it for her today."

"How much will she pay us?" Judas asked.

"Nothing," Jesus replied. "But I have a coin. I will give it to her for the privilege of serving her."

For a moment, Judas looked stunned.

Then Jesus slapped him on the back and said, "Let's go. We must earn our noontime rest."

"Another garden?" Judas mumbled to himself. "Why do these Galileans always want to get their hands dirty?"

Chebar, the president of the synagogue at Nazareth, stood outside the doorway watching the men of the town as they came for the Sabbath morning Torah service. Salmon, the wealthiest man in the town, stopped to have a word. "Chebar, you know, Jesus, the son of Mary and Joseph, is in town."

"Why are you telling me this?" Chebar gruffly responded as he nodded to Moshe and his two grown sons.

"I want to hear him read," Salmon replied.

"I have heard things about Jesus that make me uncomfortable," Chebar rejoined. "You know he upset the Temple authorities." Chebar pasted a soft smile on his face as he nodded at Alon, the cheesemaker, but he did not look at his wife and daughters who were going into the women's section.

"I have also heard things," Salmon argued. "I have heard he has healed people in Jerusalem and in Capernaum, and that he teaches more powerfully than most of the rabbis in Jerusalem. The things I have heard excite me! And I want him to read from the scriptures today!"

Chebar looked at the addition that had been built on to the synagogue just the year before. He knew Salmon had made a substantial contribution. Reluctantly, Chebar nodded his head in the affirmative. "No doubt, the whole town has heard the stories about Jesus. They will expect me to call him to the bema."

"You can ask him now," Salmon urged. "He is coming with his brothers and a friend from Judea."

Chebar greeted Simon as well as James, who walked with his son Enos. Jude and Jesus stopped to introduce Judas. After the introductions, Chebar cleared his throat. "Jesus, would you read from the prophets today?"

There was an uncomfortable pause, and then Jesus agreed.

Taking their places on one of the benches, Judas said, "It is an honor to be asked to read in the synagogue. Why did you hesitate?"

Jesus adjusted his prayer shawl so it covered his head, and then he answered, "I only do the things that please God. First, I had to be sure it was his desire that I read today.""But the president of the synagogue made the request," Judas protested.

"He is a man, and the plans of men do not concern me," Jesus answered. Then he turned his body slightly away from Judas and began to daven. He joined his voice with the cantor and sang.

> *How beautiful are your tents, O Jacob;*
> *how lovely are your homes, O Israel!*[4]
> *Because of your unfailing love, I can enter your house;*
> *I will worship…with deepest awe.*[5]

At that moment, a little tremor seemed to roll through the synagogue.

Judas looked around the room. He sensed an uneasy stirring, but he could see nothing amiss.

Jesus did not open his eyes or concern himself with the movement taking place in the spiritual atmosphere of the building. He knew that Satan was rallying his demonic forces. Obviously, an attack was eminent.

The usual Sabbath chants ended and the Torah reading began. His younger brother, James, was called forward to read from the third book of Moses. The reading ended, and Jesus was called forward to read from one of the prophets. As James came down to take his seat and Jesus rose to take his place at the table in the center of the synagogue, James whispered, "Just read. Keep your comments short."

Jesus merely nodded his head, acknowledging that his brother had spoken to him. At the same time, he looked directly at the two spirits who had initiated the comment, Jealousy and Fear of Man.

Taking his place behind the table, Jesus waited while the scroll of Isaiah was brought forward and laid upon the table. Then he assisted as Chebar and Lemuel found the reading for that day.

The room was quiet, every man waiting to hear one more reading. For a long moment, Jesus paused and studied the men of Nazareth. Each man had his own demonic spirits. With eyes enabled by the Holy Spirit, Jesus could see that every spirit stood ready to challenge his divine authority.

Jesus touched the scroll with the fringes of his prayer shawl. He kissed the fringes. Then with amazing authority, his voice rang out. "*The Spirit of the Lord is on me, because he has anointed me to preach good news to the poor. He has sent me to proclaim freedom for the prisoners and recovery of sight for the blind, to release the oppressed to proclaim the year of the Lord's favor.*"[6]

Jesus stopped reading. He rolled up the scroll and gave it back to the attendant. Very deliberately, he made his way back to his seat. The eyes of everyone in the synagogue were fastened on him. Instead of sitting, he turned and faced them. "These words from the prophet Isaiah have been fulfilled today." As he spoke, he gestured toward himself.

There was a surprised stirring throughout the room. Comments flew from person to person. "When did the carpenter become a rabbi?"

James and the other sons of Mary remained silent, uncomfortably enduring the amazed remarks that seemed to come from every corner of the synagogue.

"He read so well! I didn't know that this son of Mary was so well educated."

"Could it be that the stories we have heard are true?"

"He healed a man in Jerusalem and a boy in Capernaum."

Then Jesus said to them, "I know what you are thinking. 'Will this man entertain us? Will he dazzle us with a miracle?' When I refuse to amuse you, then you will mock me. You will get angry and demand that I do in Nazareth the things I have done in other places. But I do nothing except the things I hear from heaven."

Jesus looked into the faces of the men he had known for most of his life. He saw their expressions change from expectation to resentment, but he continued his commentary as the Spirit directed.

"Let me speak about the history of this nation. We have had many prophets, and none have been accepted, especially in their own hometowns, so the Spirit of God has guided each prophet to another place or to another people to disperse his blessing. Elijah went to the widow who lived in Zarephath, bringing her relief from the famine while many in Israel starved. The lepers of Israel remained outcasts, but God directed Elisha to heal Naaman the Syrian general.

Today, God is not leaving his blessing in the town of Nazareth."

As Jesus turned to take his seat, the people rose in anger.

Chebar shouted, "Enough of your insults!" He grabbed Jesus by the front of his robe and spat in his face. "Who do you think you are? Elijah returned to Earth from heaven? Elisha raised from the dead? Or the One we have been waiting for?"

"It is blasphemy to pretend to be a prophet or the One sent from God," someone shouted.

"You are not better than us!" another man shouted.

"And you do not have some special relationship with God."

Jesus looked up to see it was his own brother, James, who had made the last accusation.

From every section of the synagogue, the demonic spirits rallied, and chaos ensued. Men now possessed with a mob mentality pushed and shoved to get their hands on Jesus.

Judas and Simon, Jesus's brother, tried to intervene, but they were quickly swept aside. From the women's section, Jesus could hear his mother screaming, but no one was listening.

Firmly in the grasp of satanically-inspired men, Jesus found himself propelled out the door, down the road and out of town. The mob carried him to the brow of a hill, determined to throw him down its steep side. When his body hit the hard dirt below, they planned to finish him off by pelting him with stones until he was dead.

Immediately, in the midst of the melee, for Jesus, there was an island of calm. Warrior angels surrounded him, shielding him from the buffeting and from the vision of the demonically incensed men. Totally unruffled, Jesus then walked with his angelic escort through the crowd.

At the edge of the mob, Jesus found Judas helplessly standing with his brother Simon. Throwing his arm around Simon's shoulders, he led both men away from the frantic scene at the cliff. Quickly, Jesus instructed Simon, "Tell our mother that the words of King David are true. '*For he will command his angels concerning you to guard you in all your ways; they will lift you up in their hands, so that you will not strike your foot against a stone.'*[7]

"Also, tell her I have gone to Capernaum. She can visit me there."

Giving Judas a light push from behind, Jesus then said, "Let's go!" With that, both men hurried out of town.

They could still hear the confused shouts of angry men when Judas asked Jesus, "Aren't you afraid they will come after us?"

Jesus chuckled as he answered, "My life is in the hands of my Father God. There is no reason to fear. Behind us, there is a wall of angels. Neither demons nor angry men can penetrate that barrier."

"What kind of man are you?" Judas asked.

"If you stay with me, you will find out," Jesus responded.

For the remainder of the journey, Judas was quiet. In his mind, he considered and reconsidered all he had seen and heard since he met this man called Jesus of Nazareth.

Chapter 5

Fishers of Men

"Come, follow me," Jesus said, "and I will send you out to fish for people."

—Mark 1:17

It was late afternoon. There was no work in the little makeshift carpentry shop where Jesus occasionally repaired fishing implements for the citizens of Capernaum. Jesus looked at the tools of his trade. Without a job to do, they were useless.

At that moment, the Holy Spirit broke into his thoughts with a clear directive. "Yeshua-Jesus, this part of your life has now ended. It is your Father's desire that you travel with your disciples from town to town and city to city telling everyone the good news that the Kingdom of God has invaded the Earth. It is beginning right here in Capernaum, and it will spread to Jerusalem. From there, it will fill the Roman Empire, and finally, the whole Earth. Mighty and massive will be the miracles that accompany your teaching. I am with you, and I will direct your every word and action. Now, go and call the fishermen to leave their nets and follow you."

Without hesitation, Jesus began walking toward his uncle's fishing boats. They were close to the shore to facilitate preparations for a night of fishing. He could see the Holy Spirit moving ahead of him and settling over Peter and Andrew like a glowing mantle.

He watched as both men worked together to assemble panels of netting, making double-layered sections. Then they threw their nets into the water, section after section, observing to make sure each would fall correctly during their night on the lake. Jesus could see they were satisfied and were now pulling the nets back into their boat. He called to them, "Leave your nets in the boat. *Come, follow me…and I will make you fishers of men." At once they left their nets and followed him.*[1]

While Peter and Andrew were wading ashore, Jesus continued walking to the place where he could see the Holy Spirit hovering over his cousins as they worked with their father to mend the nets that would be used that evening. "James, John!"

Both men looked up.

"The time has come to fish for men. Join me. We will prepare to spread the good news of the Kingdom of God," Jesus announced.

Without even glancing at their father, both men immediately left the unfinished nets and joined Jesus. To the amazement of all four men, Zebedee raised his hand in blessing as the five walked off to find Philip and Nathanael as well as Judas.

The Sabbath came. Jesus, with his companions, entered the synagogue at Capernaum. For a moment, Jesus stood in the doorway, observing the people and the spiritual atmosphere within the building.

Peter gave Jesus a little nudge. "Teacher, there are men behind us waiting to enter."

Jesus stepped aside as he responded softly to Peter, "Yes, and their demons came with them."

After the entrance cleared, Jesus and his friends found a bench where they could sit together. Peter squeezed in, pushing John to the side so he could sit close to Jesus. Then Peter leaned over and whispered, "This is the house of God. How can demons be present?"

"You will see," Jesus responded.

All the men stood as the opening chant began. They swayed with the ancient melodic recitation of words.

> O Lord, you are the mighty One who lives eternally.
> You sustain all mankind.
> You heal the sick and set free those who are held in captivity.
> You send men to their graves and you raise them again.
> Blessed is your holy name.

As the Sabbath chants continued, Jesus's voice soared over those around him. With hands lifted and ready to receive from God, he lost himself in the timeless prayers of his people.

The opening chants ended when Jairus, the president of the synagogue, came forward to call. "Jesus, son of Joseph of Nazareth, come forward to receive the blessing that comes with reading from the Torah."

Respectfully, Jesus came to the table where the Torah scroll was already open to the second book of Moses. With the fringes of his prayer shawl, Jesus touched the beginning of the portion he was about to read. Then he brought those fringes to his lips. It was a traditional act practiced in every synagogue each time the words of Moses were read. But for Jesus, it was much more than a required ritual. For him, it was a sincere demonstration of his reverence for both the word and the author. "Bless the Lord the blessed one," Jesus chanted.

The congregation responded, "Blessed is the Lord for all eternity."

With poise and clarity, Jesus began to read. *"Now Moses was tending the flock of Jethro his father-in-law...and he led the flock to... the mountain of God. There the angel of the LORD appeared to him in flames of fire from within a bush. Moses saw that though the bush was on fire it did not burn up. So Moses thought, 'I will go over and see this strange sight.'"*[2]

At that point, Jesus moved into the dialog of the story, emphasizing the inflection and tone so that it seemed to the men in the synagogue that God was speaking audibly, and Moses was fearfully trembling before their eyes.

"When the LORD saw that Moses *had gone over to look, God called to him from within the bush, 'Moses! Moses!'*

"And Moses said, 'Here I am.'

"'Do not come any closer,' God said. 'Take off your sandals, for the place where you are standing is holy ground.' Then he said, 'I am the God of your father, the God of Abraham, the God of Isaac and the God of Jacob.' At this, Moses hid his face, because he was afraid to look at God."[3]

At that point, a warm breeze swirled around the room. Some men looked startled; others appeared refreshed. Jesus could see the presence of the Holy Spirit had entered the room in a greater measure than any of the men of Capernaum had ever experienced before. He could see his own companions reverently covering their faces, while Peter slipped off his sandals. For those in the room who were attached to strong demons, the sensations became obviously uncomfortable. They wrapped themselves protectively in their prayer shawls and avoided making eye contact with anyone in the room.

Briefly, Jesus paused. He raised both arms, welcoming and appreciating the companionship of the Holy Spirit. "Bless the Lord, the blessed one, and bless his Spirit. The Spirit of the Eternal God is with us, today."

Jesus then returned to the Torah reading. *"The LORD said, 'I have indeed seen the misery of my people in Egypt…So I have come down to rescue them from the hand of the Egyptians and to bring them up out of that land into a good and spacious land, a land flowing with milk and honey… So now, go. I am sending you to Pharaoh to bring my people the Israelites out of Egypt.'*

"But Moses said to God, 'Who am I, that I should go to Pharaoh and bring the Israelites out of Egypt?'

"And God said, 'I will be with you.'

"Moses said to God, 'Suppose I go to the Israelites and say to them, "The God of your fathers has sent me to you," and they ask me, "What is his name?" Then what shall I tell them?'"[4]

As he read, Jesus felt the power of the Holy Spirit increasing. It was like a pressure pushing from the center of his back into his chest. His own voice took on a crescendoing authority that he did not possess under normal circumstances. *"God said to Moses, 'I am who I am. This is what you are to say to the Israelites: "I am has sent me to you."'"* [5]

Jesus paused and looked at his audience. He now felt the Spirit in his chest like a ball of fire. Looking into the congregation, he could see the Spirit of God moving from man to man fixing their attention on the One who had come from heaven.

Now, heads were no longer bowed. Every eye, both human and demonic, was fixed on Jesus. Jesus read the final line. "*This is my name forever, the name by which I am to be remembered from generation to generation,* [6] I Am."

Immediately, Jesus sensed a stirring among the demonic spirits, and a man possessed by an evil spirit began shouting at Jesus. *He cried out at the top of his voice, "Ha! What do you want with us, Jesus of Nazareth? Have you come to destroy us? I know who you are—the Holy One of God!"*[7]

"The Holy One?" All over the room the people began to repeat the words they had heard. Jesus's companions, and especially Judas, hardly knew what to think. Their heads kept turning back and forth from the man to Jesus and then to those who had come to worship.

"Be quiet!" Jesus said sternly. Everyone understood Jesus was speaking directly to the demon. *"Come out of him!"*

Then the demon threw the man down before them all.[8]

Jesus left his place behind the reader's table and came to the man who was writhing on the stone floor. As Jesus bent over the man, he reached out to gently touch his forehead. With a howl, the spirit released the man and fled.

Amazed whispers spread throughout the room. "The carpenter has authority over demons!"

But Jesus was not listening to the people. His focus was on the man. "Are you all right?" he asked. "How do you feel?" Looking deeply into his eyes, he checked for other evil spirits that might falsely believe they had a right to inhabit this man.

With shaky legs, the man got to his feet. Kindly, Jesus supported him until he made his way back to his seat.

"We have to keep those spirits from returning," Jesus sat down beside the man and spoke softly. Only those sitting close by could hear the conversation.

"How do I do that?" the man asked.

"First, you must renounce the sin that allowed their entrance," Jesus said.

Instantly, the man knew. The Holy Spirit spoke truth and conviction within his heart.

Jesus heard what the Spirit said, but he did not make that information public.

"What do you say?' Jesus pressed.

"I repent," the man emphatically stated. "Never again will I—"

Jesus cut him off with an upraised hand. "Only God is your judge," Jesus said as he lightly touched the man's forehead and blew his breath in the man's face. "Be filled with the Spirit of God. Let his law be the only guide for your life, and the evil ones cannot return to torment you."

There was no order left in the Sabbath service. Everyone had to express his own thoughts to his neighbor. At first, Jairus tried to fulfill his duty as president of the synagogue. He returned to the bema in a futile attempt to bring the men of the town back into the prescribed program of readings and chants. Finally, he just pronounced, "*The* L*ORD* *bless you and keep you.*"[9] Then he joined a group of men to discuss and digest all that had happened in their synagogue that morning.

While everyone was still talking, Jesus gestured to Peter, James, and John. The four of them slipped out the door going to the closest house, which was the home of Peter and Andrew. At the door, Peter raised a cautioning hand, "My mother-in-law is very ill."

Before he could say more, Jesus heard a directive from his Father, "Touch the woman and heal her."

"Take me to her bedside," Jesus said.

After what they had seen in the synagogue, all three men were anxious to see what Jesus could do for a feverish old woman.

Coming into the small room off the courtyard that had been built especially for Peter's mother-in-law, Jesus bowed and respectfully said, "Woman, do you know me?"

Peter's mother-in-law answered weakly, "I have never met you, but I have heard many things about you."

"He heals the sick and commands evil spirits to leave," Peter asserted.

Jesus ignored Peter's enthusiasm. He bent down over the low bed and took the woman's hand. "You do feel very warm," he acknowledged. "Let me help you sit up."

As Peter's mother-in-law pulled herself up, that little act of faith drew on the healing power of heaven. Jesus felt it flow from the Holy Spirit into his own body and out through his hand into hers.

Immediately, her eyes became wide. "I feel something!" She swung her feet onto the floor and sat for a moment, checking herself. "My weakness is gone, and my body does not ache!" she exclaimed. "I'm hungry!" she suddenly announced. "You men must be hungry too!"

She waved her hands at Jesus and the other men, shooing them away. "Get out of here so I can get dressed. Then I will put some food out." She was laughing as she sent the men on their way. From behind the curtain that was her doorway, she called to Peter, "Tell my daughter to get the flat bread out of the basket in the corner of the cooking area. I will be out to help her shortly."

"The Israelites are to observe the Sabbath, celebrating it for the generations to come as a lasting covenant."[10] In the courtyard of Peter's home, Jesus and his disciples faced Jerusalem and chanted as the sun set and the first three stars appeared in the sky.

"It is now the first day of the week," John announced as he watched darkness slowly overtake the sky.

"Shalom!"

Everyone looked surprised that someone would be at their gate just as the Sabbath ended.

Peter gave his brother Andrew that "I wonder who it could be" look, and then he hurried to pull the latch.

Peter's wife also hurried to the gate. The men heard her gasp. Then Peter called, "Jesus, there are people out here—sick people, wild people, curious people!"

Andrew hurried to the gate. "I've never seen so many people. It must be the entire town!"

Jesus did not hurry. He was listening to the Holy Spirit who said, "I have brought all these people to you so the words of the prophet Isaiah will be fulfilled. '*In that day the deaf will hear the words of the scroll, and out of gloom and darkness the eyes of the blind will see. Once more the humble will rejoice in the LORD; the needy will rejoice in the Holy One of Israel.*'"[11]

When Jesus arrived at the gate, a very well-dressed child was the first to greet him. Jesus came down on one knee so he could be at face-level with the young boy.

The boy smiled, "My name is Casper. My father said you healed me."

Jesus looked up and standing behind the boy he recognized Cuza, the finance minister from the court of Herod Antipas.

"We came to show our gratitude," Cuza stated.

His wife, Joanna, interrupted. Dropping to her knees she said, "You saved my son. He was dying."

"I want to give you a gift." Cuza pressed a large bag of coins into Jesus's hands. "And anything you need, let me know. I speak to our king daily." Cuza looked at the gathering crowd. "Do you want me to have these people sent away?"

"No," Jesus answered as he stood and casually tossed the bag of coins into the hands of his nearest follower, Judas. "I want you to see how much God loves all his children."

Then Jesus turned to Judas. "You're in charge of distributing that money. Find the poorest people and give it all away."

Choking on his words, Judas protested, "But we may need this to travel and teach."

"My Father owns the cattle on a thousand hills," Jesus lightly answered. "I need nothing. The provision of God is always sufficient."

Pointing to John and James, Peter and Andrew, Jesus directed, "Organize these people, like you did for John so he could baptize them. Then bring them to me, one person at a time, so I can lay my hands on them. The power of the Holy Spirit will flow through me, and they will be healed."

Cuza, Joanna, and Casper stood nearby, captivated by the outrageous scene. Groups and lines were formed. Peter's mother-in-law came out and encouraged group after group with her own story. And, one by one, each person received a personal touch from Jesus.

All evening and well into the night, Cuza and his family watched healing after healing. The lame were walking. The feverish were restored. The mute spoke. The deaf could hear, and the blind could see. Infected lesions became perfect skin. Even rotted and abscessed teeth were totally restored.

Matthew joined Cuza to watch the spectacle. "This is amazing," Matthew commented. "Every person he touches is totally cured."

"Were you in the synagogue this morning?" Cuza rejoined.

"Yes," Matthew replied.

"I am returning to the palace next week," Cuza commented. "I will give Herod a full report."

"How can you give a full report?" Matthew asked. "How can you explain the look on Jesus's face as each person is brought to him? Can you describe to King Herod the incredible sadness that seems to flow over the man when he sees the condition of the person before him? Then, notice how he touches. There is such compassion in every gesture. At that point, Jesus appears to be overcome by a supernatural power. I do not know where it comes from. The power takes hold. Sometimes, Jesus and the person he is touching are shaking from the force of that power. Next, there is indescribable relief and joy. Will Herod believe you?"

"Truthfully"—Cuza turned to Matthew—"if I had not personally experienced all you have just described, I would not believe."

Zebedee and his wife Salome were also in the crowd, watching. Salome looked up at her husband, the tough fisherman. She saw tears in his eyes. Salome said, "Do you hear what the demons are saying as they come out?"

Zebedee answered with emotion in his voice, "You are the Son of God!"

Salome responded, "I must tell my sister to come to Capernaum. She must see for herself that the Spirit of God is really upon her son. He is the Messiah. The story about her visit from the angel was definitely true."

Zebedee turned to his wife. "You doubted?"

"Well, there was always a little question," Salome admitted.

"I have always believed in Joseph's boy," Zebedee stated. "He silences those demons because he knows it is dangerous to admit to being the Messiah, but look at this"—Zebedee swept his hand inclusively over the mass of people—"words are unnecessary."

Just then, Philip and Nathanael came running into the crowd. Philip saw John, and he called out, "What can we do to help?"

"Help Judas!" John answered as he pointed toward a shoving, shouting crowd just to the left of where Jesus was healing. "He's giving money to the poor, and the needs of the people are about to overwhelm him."

Nathanael laughed and gestured toward the scene John had described. "That's a first for anyone from the family of Iscariot!"

"Let's help him," Philip offered as both men hurried over to organize the crowd.

It was well after midnight when Jesus wearily sat down on a bench, watching as his disciples sent the last of the curious and the healed back to their homes.

"I'm ready to sleep," Andrew announced as he led everyone back into the courtyard where the women of the house had spread pallets for the men.

"I feel like I have fished all night," Peter stated.

And Jesus responded, "You have."

Early the next morning, before sunrise, Jesus slipped out of the house. Beckoned by the Holy Spirit, he climbed the hills until he found a solitary place to pray.

Later that morning, Peter and his companions became concerned, and they went to look for Jesus, walking up and down those same hills around Capernaum.

When they found him, Peter was the first to say what was on everyone's mind. "Jesus, if you had told us you were coming to this place to pray, we would not have been distressed for your safety."

Casually, Jesus replied. "This time has been well-spent and the same Spirit that called me to this place brought you here also. My Father has plans for us to travel and teach, to heal and cast out demons. Today, we are going to begin walking from town to town in the region of Galilee. So hurry, put a traveling bag together and meet me by Peter's boat."

Chapter 6

The Nets Are Full and Breaking!

Yet the news about him spread all the more, so that crowds of people came to hear him and to be healed of their sicknesses. But Jesus often withdrew to lonely places and prayed.

—Luke 5:15–16

In the early morning hours, Jesus sat alone on the rocky shore some distance from the village of Capernaum. He looked up into the grayness of an overcast sky and called out, "My Father? My Father?"

God answered, "Yeshua, I am here."

"I am alone on Earth," Jesus cried. "No human is truly with me. I have called men to listen to your kingdom instruction. I have healed, and I have cast out demons. Several times, I have offered those you have indicated the opportunity to exchange their ordinary lives for a life that is totally directed by your Spirit. But they are caught up in their families and their professions, like fish tangled in a net."

Jesus looked out over the misty sea. His eyes could not make out the fishing boats, but he knew they were there, sailing homeward, ready to tie up at their usual moorings. His companions, his closest friends, the men who called themselves his followers had fished all night instead of praying. "Father, you know these men—James and John, Peter and Andrew, Philip and Nathanael. They stay with me for a few days, maybe a week or two, but then they return to their boats and the lives they have always known. Judas seems to be the only one I can count on. He follows me like an afternoon shadow. He is a man filled with curiosity and greed instead of generosity and light. What can I do with such men?"

Like the prophet Elijah, Jesus put his head between his knees and continued to push the burden of his heart heavenward. "Father, my so-called companions don't see that all of humanity is about to be consumed by evil. They are so totally unaware that there is a raging conflict between your angels of light and the fallen angels who obey Satan. These fishermen see the sick and the demon possessed, but they do not see the Evil One, who delights in destroying the beautiful people you have created. Open their eyes! Show them people are more precious than fish. Show them *our struggle is not against flesh and blood,* Romans officials or Temple authorities, *but...against the powers of this dark world and against the spiritual forces of evil in the heavenly realms.*"[1]

"Isn't that the way it is with most men?" God answered. "They rely on what their physical senses tell them about the natural world. They don't even try to see beyond the obvious into the reality of the spiritual realm."

"How? How can I reach them?" Jesus asked.

"Begin with what they know," God responded. "Move their thinking from their own world of fishing into our world of the kingdom. My Spirit will tell you what to say."

Later that morning, Jesus walked back into town. He approached the area where all the fishermen were washing their nets. Someone shouted, "Jesus, tell us a story!"

Another person called out, "Jesus, touch the cut on my foot."

"My mother has been coughing all night. Can you come to the house to see her?"

Slowly, Jesus moved through the gathering crowd, touching person after person, often pausing to offer an encouraging word. Finally, when all seemed to be satisfied, he stood on the stones close to the moorings, and he began to teach. "*But I tell you who hear me: Love your enemies, do good to those who hate you, bless those who curse you, pray for those who mistreat you.*"[2]

Three young boys ran to the front of the crowd, squeezing their way into the first row of listeners. They looked up and Jesus, the master teacher, made eye contact. With one finger, he motioned for the boy who had an outstanding black eye to step up beside him. With four fingers close together, Jesus lightly covered that bruised eye. A moment later, he removed his hand.

The crowd gasped.

The boy's eye was completely normal.

Then Jesus bent and spoke to the boy, "*If someone strikes you on one cheek, turn to him the other also. If someone takes your cloak, do not stop him from taking your tunic.*"[3] Straightening up and looking out at the crowd, Jesus continued, "*Give to everyone who asks you, and if anyone takes what belongs to you, do not demand it back.*" Jesus focused on the other boys in the front row, but his voice was loud enough for all to hear. "*Do to others as you would have them do to you.*"[4]

The crowd was growing, pressing Jesus to the edge of the stones that made the harbor's wall. Jesus looked over his shoulder. He could see several fishing boats, bobbing just a step beyond the wall. Peter and Andrew were in one boat, carefully folding and piling each section of their heavy dragnets so they would be ready for the evening. Turning his back on the crowd, Jesus took one giant step into the bow of Peter's boat.

Surprised, Peter and Andrew looked up from their task. Both men quickly broke into welcoming grins, lightly joking about the addition to their crew.

"Move out into deeper water," Jesus directed.

Without question, Andrew quickly slipped the mooring lines from the stake that held their boat close to the shore. Peter grabbed the long steering oar and pushed off. The boat skittered across the wavelets, stopping when Andrew threw a stone anchor overboard.

Then, settling himself in the bow of the boat, Jesus let his gaze move over the crowd. Here and there were faces that the Holy Spirit highlighted. Judas was standing with Matthew. The two men whose lives were most involved with money had found each other. Zebedee was paying close attention. He saw Joanna and her mother-in-law with little Casper. Jesus gave the boy a wave and a smile. Jairus, the president of the synagogue, had come from his shop. His wife and his daughter joined him to listen to the carpenter who had become their favorite teacher. Jesus recognized many of the men from the synagogue. He knew their wives from the market. Near the back of the crowd, there was a new face, a Roman centurion.

The Holy Spirit moved through the growing crowd, and Jesus began to teach again. *"Do not judge, and you will not be judged."* Jesus could see Zebedee nodding. He knew the Holy Spirit was adding conviction to his words. *"Do not condemn, and you will not be condemned."* Jesus caught the eye of Judas.

Judas quickly looked down. He could not stand to connect with the piercing, all-knowing gaze of the teacher.

"Forgive, and you will be forgiven."[5] Jesus looked at Matthew who was standing beside Judas.

Matthew shifted a little, and Jesus knew he was remembering a personal incident, but he did not remove his eyes from the face of the teacher.

Morning was turning into noon. The Holy Spirit spoke to Jesus, "The fishermen have been working all night. The people on shore began their day before sunup. They need to eat and rest. Provide fish for them."

Without hesitation, Jesus turned to Peter and Andrew.

Both men were sitting on their nets, and their body language spoke exhaustion.

Jesus said to Peter, "Raise the anchor. Sail into deeper water where we can cast this net and bring in a catch."

This time, the men did not respond eagerly. Instead, Peter answered, "Jesus, you know we worked hard throughout the night, and you saw that our boats returned to shore, empty. Andrew and I have not slept since yesterday. If we cast this double net, we will have to take it apart, wash, dry, and refold each section before evening. Then there will be no time to sleep before we must take this boat out again."

Andrew joined his brother's protest. Standing up, he pointed to the nets he had been sitting on. "Jesus, you have been with us for several years. You know these nets are only used at night. In the daylight, the fish will not swim into them, even if we beat the water."

Jesus responded, "Everything you say is true in the natural world, but in my Father's kingdom the impossible is possible. Cast the nets."

For another moment, Peter hesitated. He thought about all the miracles he had already seen. Then with a resigned sigh, he said, "I will do it, just for you."

Without further objection, Andrew put up the sail while Peter manned the long oar in the back of the boat that served as a rudder. When they reached the deep water, Jesus stood and helped them drop the nets. Weights dragged the double curtain of netting into two long, semicircular mesh walls.

For a long silent moment, all three men stood in the boat studying the surface of the sea and the placement of the nets. They could see both nets stretching evenly from the silty bottom up to the sun-washed wavelets. Heavy flax lines attached the nets to the bow and the stern of their fishing boat. The water was calm. The drag lines floated freely. Nothing disturbed the nets.

"See, I told—" Peter started to protest.

Jesus held up his hand, and Peter became silent. Then Jesus prayed, "God, you said to call the fish. Your servants have set the net. We are now ready to bring them in."

At once, there was a sudden churning along the net. Fins and tails, flashes of silver scales—the water was boiling with sea life.

"Haul in the nets!" Peter yelled.

"Jesus, grab the stern line!" Andrew directed as all three men set their muscles to the task of closing the net and pulling it close to the side of their fishing boat.

"We need help!" Andrew announced. "One boat can't hold this net!"

Peter called across the water, "James, John, Zebedee! We're tipping! Bring another boat!"

On shore, there was another scurry of activity as a sail was raised and another boat with more fishermen came to add their muscle and their craft to the task of supporting two tons of fish.

As both boats secured the overloaded net so it would not sink, Philip and Nathanael climbed over the side of Zebedee's boat and dove into the water. Each man grabbed one of the sturdy lines that extended from the net. At first, they swam. Then they waded until they met the additional men coming from the dock, each man found a place to grab one of the lines.

From Peter's boat, Jesus jumped into the cold water. He found a handhold, and to the count that Philip called, Jesus pulled with the rest of the men.

Slowly and surely, the fishermen worked together, heaving, dragging, guiding the net up to the stone seawall where women with baskets scooped up the fish and young boys tossed aside those fish that did not have both scales and fins.

From where he worked, Jesus could see Matthew running to get his ledger. He could hear him shouting, "Judas, you have to help me count. I've never seen so many fish!"

Jesus glanced back. He saw both fishing boats were now anchored. Peter and Andrew were in the water, swimming then wading toward the commotion on shore. At the stone breakwater, they pulled themselves up on the dock.

For a long moment, Peter stared in dumbfounded amazement. He watched as basket after basket was heaped full of fish. Fish were everywhere along the dock. They had brought in two weeks' worth of fish in just the length of time it would take to prepare a meal.

Peter saw Jesus pull himself out of the water, up onto the stones that prevented the waves from washing ashore. Jesus stood there in a dripping tunic, looking like all the other men.

The Holy Spirit spoke to Peter's heart. "Can a mere man do such a thing as you are now seeing? Look at all these fish. Do you need to fish tomorrow or the next day? Can't Jesus fill the nets anytime your family needs to sell fish? He has been asking you to take a break from the fishing business, to travel with him and help with the crowds that always come."

Peter did not wait another moment. He started running to the place where Jesus stood. He fell on his knees, covering his face. "Lord, I am a man full of sin and doubt. You should leave me and find someone else to help with your mission. I did not believe. I was afraid to leave my fishing business for more than a few short periods of time."

Jesus knelt beside Peter and put his hand on Peter's shoulder. With great understanding Jesus said, "How can you expect to understand unless you see with your own eyes and experience with your own hands?"

By this time Zebedee, with his sons James and John had also come to the place where Jesus was kneeling with Peter. Standing, Jesus pulled Peter to his feet. Then he spoke to the men who were closest to him. "Trust in the provision of my Father for your families. From this day forward, you will throw nets that bring men into the Kingdom of God."

So Peter and Andrew, James and John, Philip and Nathanael pulled their boats on shore. They left their nets and their gear with relatives. Day and night, they sat under the instruction of Rabbi Jesus of Nazareth, and often they traveled with him throughout Galilee and Judea.

The road to Chorazin wound around the hills and cut through the green fields of wheat. Beyond the fields, Jesus sensed demonic eyes were following every step he took and every word he spoke. Silently, Jesus prayed, "Father, our enemy is waiting for an opportunity. I have faced him, but these men you have given to assist me are so unaware of the incredible evil that is stalking us."

"Teach them," God responded.

Then Jesus gestured toward the fields of wheat as he asked his companions, "Will the harvest be good?"

Philip answered, "The plants look healthy and well watered."

"Are there weeds among the healthy plants?" Jesus pressed.

Philip replied, "At this point, it is difficult to tell. The plants will have to grow up together. Closer to the harvest, it will be easy to identify the weeds."

"You are correct, Jesus responded. "When the Creator made man and woman and placed them in the garden that was their home, it was like a good man who prepared and sowed his wheat field. In the night, an evil neighbor slipped into the field and spread weed seeds over the freshly planted field. Later, when the seeds sprouted and grew heads appeared, and the work of the evil neighbor became apparent." Jesus paused and walked to the edge of the road. With his hand he separated the stalks, looking carefully until he found one weed. He pulled it up and showed it to his disciples as he continued his story.

"As the grain matured, the servants noticed an abundance of weeds throughout the field. They came to the owner of the field and said, 'Didn't you sow good seed during the planting season?'

"The owner replied, 'My enemy snuck into my field and left bad seeds.'

"'Should we go through the fields and pull every weed we see?' the servants asked.

"'No,' the owner replied. 'So early in the growing season, you will destroy both the good and the bad plants. Let them grow together until the harvest. At that time, we will separate the produce from the weeds.'"

"What kind of man would deliberately damage his neighbor's crop?" Nathanael exclaimed.

"I am not talking about a man," Jesus answered. "I am talking about the Evil One also called Satan. He has filled the hearts and minds of men with his own self-centered ideas. He has brought disease and poverty to the wonderful beings that God created in his own image; so now, they no longer resemble their Creator. He has filled the field of God with weeds."

Andrew spoke up, "John the Baptist used to preach about the harvest. He said it would take place when the Messiah comes."

Peter recalled, "I heard the prophet say, 'The One we are waiting for *will baptize you with the Holy Spirit and with fire. His winnowing fork is in his hand to clear his threshing floor and to gather the wheat into his barn, but he will burn up the chaff with unquenchable fire.*'"[6]

"Right now," Jesus said, "you are standing with me against our enemy, Satan. Stalk by stalk, person by person, we are removing the curse so in the end, there will be a great harvest and only a few weeds will need to be burned."

Ahead, the disciples could see the city of Chorazin. Beside its gray basalt walls, a hovel of unsightly huts caught their attention. "Lepers," Peter said the word that had gone through the mind of each man.

"Should they be so close to the city?" James nervously questioned.

"How else will they get food?" John responded.

"Look, one is sitting right beside the road!" Peter exclaimed. "We will have to walk within an arm's distance of the man!"

Waving his arms in a shooing motion, Peter called to the man, "Move back! Move back from the road!"

"He cannot move easily," Jesus responded with compassion. "He has been afflicted for most of his life, and this disease has taken a great toll. It is not just on the surface of his skin. It goes deeper, into the muscles and nerves."

As the men continued toward the city gate, John gasped, "The man's face is grotesque!"

"He cannot walk. Look, he is just scooting!" Andrew added.

The men were now close to the leper. All but Jesus were hugging the opposite edge of the dirt road.

"Is this a weed, meant for the fire? Or, is this a man, created in the image of God?" Jesus asked. Jesus did not wait for a response. His own compassion was drawing him to this mutilated shadow of humanity.

Peter, John, and the rest of the disciples stopped in their tracks. They could not believe their eyes. Jesus kept steadily approaching the leper.

"Alms for the unclean," the man whined without lifting his eyes to see who stood in front of him. His body rocked back and forth and with one pitiful rag-bound arm, he gestured toward a chipped piece of pottery that held just two coins. As if he sensed that the shadow of a man had fallen across him, the leper scooted back while mumbling the mandatory chant of the unclean. Then he stopped.

In the spiritual, Jesus could see the Holy Spirit highlighting and preparing this man for healing.

"Who are you?" the leper hesitantly asked.

"Jesus of Nazareth," Jesus softly answered.

Suddenly, the man became excited. "I have heard of you." Awkwardly, he bowed. "Healer, I know you can give me a new life and freedom from this curse. Please, make me clean."

Behind him, Jesus knew that the forces of evil were working to infiltrate the minds of those men who were with him. He could feel their horror and repulsion.

He responded to it by silently praying, "Father, change their hearts."

Then without hesitation, Jesus reached out and placed his own hand on the man's shoulder. He said, "It is my Father's desire to restore all men to his perfect image. Be clean!" "

From the other side of the road, Jesus heard his disciples shudder. Judas gasped, "The teacher is touching—"

Then there was silence. For a long stunned moment, Jesus's disciples could not tear their eyes away. They could scarcely breathe. It was as if they could see wave after wave of healing power as it moved through Jesus into the man who was now screaming, "My feet! My fingers! I can feel them! I can see them!"

Instantly, the man jumped to his feet, old rags falling from his limbs.

"He has a normal face!" John broke the silence on the other side of road.

"And a name," Jesus smiled broadly, never taking his hand from the man's shoulder. "What is your name?"

"Abidan of Chorazin," the man answered.

"How does everything feel?" Jesus touched each finger. He looked at the man's feet, at his perfect smile, and into his eyes. "This sickness will never come upon you again," Jesus stated. "But you must be faithful to the Law of Moses. Follow all of its regulations."

Then with unusual sternness, Jesus admonished, "Do not tell anyone that healing came through my touch or through my words. Just go to the priest and do everything that the Law of Moses requires. Then you will be able to return to your family and your normal life."

Before Jesus had finished speaking, Abidan was running through the city gate. Jesus could hear him yelling at the top his lungs, "I have been healed! Look, no more leprosy! It was Jesus! Jesus of Nazareth! He touched me!"

A crowd quickly gathered, surging out of the gate toward Jesus and his disciples. So many people were coming out of the gate that entering the city was now impossible.

With resignation, Jesus moved away from the road, climbing a nearby hill. The people gathered around him. His disciples organized the crowd so everyone could be healed. Then Jesus told the people to be seated, and he began to speak about the Kingdom of God, a place for all to grow into the image of God.

In the spiritual, he felt a shudder like thunder. He knew that terror and dismay were rolling through the camp of his enemy. One by one, the captives were being freed and the image of God was being restored in the sons of Adam.

Chapter 7

Miracles in Capernaum and Magdela

Some men brought to him a paralytic, lying on a mat. When Jesus saw their faith, he said to the paralytic, "Take heart, son; your sins are forgiven."

—Matthew 9:2

Jairus closed his shop for the day. He turned and looked up and down the main road of Capernaum. The town was quiet. Satisfied that all was as it should be, Jairus turned toward his home only to stop short in his tracks. To his surprise, he saw four men walking into town. Flowing robes and elaborate prayer shawls, he knew they had to be scholars associated with the Temple or the synagogue system.

Quickly, Jairus brushed off his own robes, hoping his shopkeeping attire would be suitable. As president of the synagogue, he knew it was his duty to entertain any religious scholars who might come to town but rarely had anyone ever come. With a final check on his appearance, Jairus hurried forward to bow and greet the men.

"Shalom, my esteemed friends." Jairus was now close enough to identify the men. Yonatan, he recognized as a scholar who lived in the hill country of Galilee. With him was Gamaliel from Jerusalem, a well-known rabbi whose grandfather was the great Hillel. There were two other men from Nazareth, Chebar, the president of the synagogue in that town, and Lemuel, their local rabbi.

Chebar, with whom Jairus was well acquainted, puffed himself up a little, and then he spoke, "Lemuel and I were in Jerusalem for the Feast of Esther, when we were unexpectedly called before a small group of Temple authorities."

Lemuel abruptly stepped in front of Chebar to face Jairus, "The authorities want to know about Jesus of Nazareth. Last Passover, there was an incident with the money changers, and stories are flying about healings and large crowds."

Chebar put out a restraining arm as he stepped back in front of Lemuel, getting close to the face of his colleague in Capernaum. "I told them the carpenter has been driven out of our synagogue and out of our town. He may call himself Jesus of Nazareth, but Nazareth wants no part of him."

Lemuel spoke up again, "His brother James told me he has made his home here in Capernaum."

Jairus just stared at the men in stunned silence. He didn't know how to respond to such intense emotions regarding a simple but amazing man.

Gamaliel motioned for Chebar to step back; then with composure and tact, he said, "Jairus, Yonatan and I are just here to gather a few facts for the Sanhedrin. We hear great crowds follow this man. We know he is an especially gifted teacher. We want to be sure he is not stirring up trouble with the Roman authorities."

"We've had no problems with the Romans," Jairus quickly responded.

"I have heard him speak," Yonatan inserted. "He has amazing skill with parables."

"He heals?" Gamaliel lifted his eyebrows quizzically.

"There are many in this town who have been healed," Jairus answered. "That includes the son of Cuza, the finance minister for Herod Antipas."

"My friend Nicodemus tells me this Jesus of Nazareth has tremendous knowledge of the scriptures. Have you found that to be true?" Yonaton asked.

"He often reads in our synagogue. Then he explains what he has read," Jairus replied. Straightforwardly, Jairus added, "We are always blessed on those Sabbaths."

Yonaton glanced questioningly at Chebar, who responded in an angry tone, "The carpenter just stirs up trouble in the Synagogue of Nazareth."

"Is Jesus in town now?" Gamaliel calmly asked.

"No," Jairus answered. He gestured toward an area where several fishing boats were tied to their moorings. "If Jesus was in town, the entire wharf area would be filled with people."

"Do you know where he is?" Gamaliel patiently probed.

"He went with the fishermen, the sons of Zebedee and their partners. I believe they went to Magdela on the first day of this week."

Manaen and Cuza stood in the bow of one of the many barges belonging to Herod Antipas. Slowly, the crew brought their vessel to a safe mooring among the many fishing boats in the harbor of Magdela.

Both men, the highest officials in charge of procurements for the king of this region, stepped onto the busy dock. "We're looking for the sailmaker." Manaen spoke to a passing fisherman.

"At the end of the wharf area, near the construction site for new vessels," the fisherman responded.

Cuza and Manaen followed the man's directions. Strolling the length of the waterfront, they eyed the activity of the fishing industry while silently calculating the expected tax revenue. Thoughtfully, Cuza commented, "I believe we should be getting more tax money from this city."

"A surprise audit might be a good idea," Manaen replied.

When they arrived at the sailmaker's shop, they could see the proprietor had many workers cutting, measuring, and stitching. "This is a busy place," Manaen observed as both men stepped inside the small building from which all the activity originated.

A group of fishermen huddled around a table, haggling over the price and quality of a new sail. "I know those men," Cuza stated. "They are from Capernaum. They fish for Zebedee, and—" Cuza paused. He looked directly at a tall man standing a little detached from the bargain-hunting fishermen. Then he turned to his companion. "That is Jesus of Nazareth. He is the one who healed my little boy, Casper."

"He looks very ordinary," Manaen commented.

A woman walked into the shop. Her mantel was pulled across her face so only her eyes could be seen. She walked directly over to the haggling men, coming right up to the table. Suddenly, she brought her hand down on the table with a smack that got the attention of every man in the room. "The price for this sail is fixed. Pay or leave without your sail!"

Ignoring the muttered protests about women doing men's business, she turned her back on the table where coins were being counted and the transaction was now concluding. She moved over to where Cuza and Manaen were standing. "Are you here to purchase sails?" she asked.

"Yes," Manaen replied. "Is this your family business?"

"It is," the woman answered.

"May we speak with your husband?"

There was a moment of angry silence before the woman responded, "If you want to do business here, you will do it with me."

Cuza was the first of the pair to recover from the woman's shocking response. Adapting quickly, he composed a reply. "We represent Herod Antipas. We are here to purchase eight new sails for his barges."

The woman held out her left hand. "I'll need the dimensions."

"I've brought the plans," Manaen stepped over to a table and unrolled the schematics for a barge.

"Yeshua?" Father God was calling his son.

Jesus looked away from the business transaction that James and John had just concluded. He focused on the word his Father was speaking through the Holy Spirit.

"Assist the woman who owns this business," the Holy Spirit directed.

Unobtrusively, Jesus took a few steps toward the table. He recognized Cuza. He could see a parchment scroll was open on the table, and he could see the woman who had been so dominant and controlling a few moments ago was now hesitant and floundering.

Uncertainly, she glanced at the blueprint. Then she looked back at Manaen. "Where are the dimensions for the sails? I need to know length and breadth."

"Woman!" Manaen's voice was laced with exasperation. "You are the sailmaker. You should be able to look at these plans and tell me the required length and breadth."

At that moment, Jesus stepped up to the table. He greeted Cuza. "How is your little boy?" The question fell from Jesus's lips with such sincerity that for a moment, the problem of sizing the sails was forgotten while Cuza bragged about the health and intelligence of his son.

Jesus then turned his attention to the detailed drawing on the table. Without being asked, he began to comment on the design. "These are the plans for a beautiful and functional vessel," he said. Looking at Manaen, he continued, "I am a carpenter by trade, but for the past few years, I have been working mostly on boats."

Cuza nodded, adding, "He is the only man the fishermen of Capernaum trust to work on their boats."

"Did you know there is a formula for calculating the correct size of the sail for each vessel?" Jesus lightly asked. Then he turned to the woman. "Do you have a small parchment and something I can write with?"

Pointing to the lines indicating the size of the barge, Jesus explained the relationship between the size of a vessel's haul and the required sail. He scratched a few figures on the scrap of parchment and handed it to the woman. "Here are the dimensions."

With that piece of paper in her hand, the woman regained her authority. In the spiritual, Jesus could see her authority came from the demonic spirits that rallied to support her aggressive behavior.

"Tell King Herod the sails for his barges will be ready in two weeks. I require total payment now," she boldly announced.

Stepping back from the table, Jesus removed himself from the transaction. Still, he remained focused on the woman, who was accepting a bag of coins and asking a subordinate to make out a receipt. He saw her put the bag of coins under her robe and then slip out the back door.

"Yeshua, follow her," the Holy Spirit directed.

Without hesitation, Jesus walked out the door behind her, entering a small courtyard.

Suddenly, the woman spun around. A knife was in her right hand, a badly scarred hand. "Have you come to rob me?" she challenged while taking an intimidating step toward him. Her mantel slipped away from her face, revealing that the right side of her face was also badly scarred.

"No," Jesus responded. He carefully took a step backward and sat on a nearby bench.

Then he watched as the woman responded by lowering her knife. He could see she was flanked by demonic companions, but those aggressive spirits were now trembling in his presence.

"I wanted to speak with your husband," Jesus politely pressed.

"I can tell that you know about the construction of ships, but if you are looking for a job, you will have to talk to me." The woman also took a seat, gathering her robes and rewrapping her mantel. Then she looked Jesus in the eyes and told him what she seldom ever said, "I am the owner of this business."

"That is most unusual," Jesus responded. "Most women do not have the freedom to own and make decisions about such an important business. What is your name?"

"I am called Mary of Magdela." Then the woman chuckled to herself as she added, "The men I do business with have many other names for me. To them, I am just a female dog! But they had better beware—this dog has teeth."

Above her head, the Holy Spirit unrolled a living scroll. On it, Jesus saw Mary as a young woman expecting a child. In her home, she was approached by a fisherman who had obviously had too much to drink. Words were exchanged. Then the man hit her. She fell into the fire. The scroll closed.

"Mary?" Jesus spoke her name with tenderness.

The Holy Spirit carried that tenderness to the hardest part of Mary's heart and a little crack formed.

Tears pooled in Mary's eyes.

Jesus watched as she blinked and struggled to keep them from falling.

"I don't understand," Mary spluttered as she used a corner of her mantel to wipe her eyes. "I never get emotional."

Jesus nodded, kindly accepting her statement without challenge or contradiction. "May I touch your hand, the scarred one?" Jesus asked. "I have touched many people and through the power of God, they have been healed."

At first, Mary hesitated, and then she gave a shrug that was meant to indicate the past was the past. With her stoic mask back in place, Mary thrust her hand toward the stranger so he could see the gray ridges of deformed flesh. "It is already healed," she pragmatically stated. "There is no more pain. It is just ugly."

"I see pain," Jesus responded as he reached out to place his own hand over the back of her hand.

The tingly warmth of the man's touch took Mary by surprise. Tears returned and spilled from her eyes. "I don't know."

Behind him, James and John came through the back door that led to the little courtyard. They stood quietly, not interrupting, feeling that holy presence they called the healing power of God.

Mary felt so disturbed. Her notorious composure was crumbling. She didn't know how to respond. Quickly, she pulled her hand away. Then she stopped. A gasp and a cry of amazement escaped between her alarmed sobs. Her hand had become beautiful and smooth, the perfect hand of a young woman.

Through a flood of tears, Mary stared at her hand. She moved her fingers. The stiffness had disappeared.

Before she could say a coherent word, Jesus brushed her mantel aside and put his hand under the fabric, gently touching her face, and speaking so softly that James and John could hardly hear the words he said.

"I speak to the evil ones who have been your companions. Shame and Ugliness, I demand you leave this woman. Abuse, you are no longer attached to her life. Bitterness, you are now replaced with love and openness." Jesus removed his hand from her face. His fingertips were wet with Mary's tears. Carefully, he took her own hand in his and brought it up to her face so she could feel her new smooth skin.

Jesus then asked, "What happened to your child?"

"I lost him," Mary sobbed. "He was born too soon." Her body was now shaking with a flood of both new and remembered emotions.

"And the man who was your husband?" Jesus sympathetically asked.

"The elders of the city granted him a divorce because of the severity of my injuries and the loss of our child. He told them he could not stand to look at my face. As compensation for the injuries he had inflicted, I was given the business my father had turned over to him at the time of our marriage." Mary used a corner of her mantel to wipe her tears. She looked up at Jesus.

"Except for testifying before the city elders, I have never told that story. It has always seemed too shameful. Most of the town thinks I am just an angry woman."

Jesus moved Mary's hand to her abdomen and said, "Now I speak to this empty place. It should have been filled with the joy of motherhood. Be filled with the joy of the Lord! This entrance to your pain is now shut and sealed. The Evil One has no more access. And I speak to the wall you have erected between yourself and others. Be destroyed. Lying spirit of Fear, I send you far away. Distrust, you must also leave this daughter of Abraham."

Jesus looked into Mary's eyes, and he could see one remaining demon looking out at him. "Mary, what do you feel guilty about?" The question was spoken so softly. It was just a whisper.

"I am a sharp-tongued woman," Mary answered between small sobs. "I use words to make men feel small." She sighed. "That is what I did to my husband. So he drank, and he came home angry."

"You are forgiven," Jesus stated.

"How? How can you say I am forgiven?" Mary asked.

"I am one with my Father who lives in heaven," Jesus answered. "Whoever or whatever I forgive on Earth, he forgives in heaven." Jesus then took a commanding stance and spoke to the one remaining demon. "Guilt, remove yourself from this woman."

Suddenly, Mary slumped over.

John and James hurried forward to catch the owner of the sailmaking establishment before she fell off the bench and hit the ground.

It was only a brief weakness. Mary quickly regained her strength. She sat up on her own, laughing and looking into the kindest face she had ever seen. She turned around to see the men who had been supporting her, and she said the most unusual words. "Thank you." There was a brief silence and then Mary began laughing again. Between her joyous peals, she managed to say, "I cannot believe I just said thank-you! I never thank anyone. What has happened to me?"

"I cast seven demons out of you," Jesus informed.

"Seven!" John repeated as he and James exchanged wide-eyed glances.

"Demons?" Mary restated in wide-eyed wonder.

"Most people don't know where their demons come from, but they often attach themselves to the victims of abuse and abandonment," Jesus informed. "You are no longer a victim. Those evil spirits will never bother you again."

"Where do you stay?" Mary asked.

"Capernaum," Jesus answered. Then he added, "I stay with the fishermen. You can come see me there. At every feast, I usually teach in the Temple. You can find me there."

With another nod and a reassuring smile, Jesus turned and left to sail back across the lake with James and John, the sons of Zebedee.

Returning to Capernaum, Jesus went to stay in the home of his friends Peter and Andrew. It wasn't long before the people of the town heard that he had come home.

Matthew pushed through the gathering crowd to find Judas. "Come with me. I need to bring my friend, Sebastian to Jesus. Hurry!" Matthew tapped two other young men and the four of them ran to a tumbled down house at the edge of the town. They did not bother to politely call shalom. The men just barged into the house, nearly falling over each other in their excitement. They rushed past an older woman who was heating some water. Again without announcing themselves, they pulled back a thread-bare curtain to see Matthew's friend since childhood lying on a soiled pallet.

Sebastian looked at them with a little disgust and then said, "If you would send a messenger first, then I would have my mother clean me up. The odor in here is so bad I want to vomit. You know I don't have any control over what comes out of my body ever since we climbed those rocks and"—Sebastian looked directly at Matthew—"your brother pushed me."

"It was an accident," Matthew protested. "My brother would give anything if you had not fallen."

Judas spoke up. "We've come to take you to Jesus."

"The carpenter who often reads in the synagogue?" Sebastian asked. "I can't go into the synagogue. There is a running sore on my backside, and I stink! I cannot wash myself. I cannot move or feel anything below my chest."

"Jesus heals people," Matthew interrupted. "I have seen him do it."

"With my own eyes, I saw him bring a half-blinded camel back to usefulness. That camel is still walking the caravan routes," Judas asserted.

"A camel?" Sebastian incredulously repeated.

"When a camel is nearly blind, recovery is hopeless," Judas said. "Animals can't pretend to be healed. What I saw was real!"

"I'll wash you," Matthew offered.

"No," Sebastian protested. "Call my mother. She will do it."

Jesus began by healing all who were brought to him. First, the sick gathered inside Peter's home. As more people pressed in to receive a healing touch, they filled the courtyard. Finally, the gates were forced open. People crowded against the entrance and pressed against the outer walls. Some even climbed to sit on the walls and rooftops of surrounding buildings.

Jairus came, pushing through the crowd making a path so his important friends could get close to Jesus. Jesus saw them. He knew their names and their positions, but he did not go beyond an acknowledging nod to his friend, Jairus. The Holy Spirit was not highlighting these men, so they were not his concern.

Jesus had already healed all those who were close, so he pressed into the message the Holy Spirit was giving him. "*You have heard that it was said to the people long ago, 'Do not murder, and anyone who murders will be subject to judgment.' But I tell you that anyone who is angry with his brother will be subject to judgment.*"[1]

As soon as Jesus had spoken those words, he felt some dirt fall from the ceiling onto his head. He brushed it away, but another larger clump fell. Curiously, he looked up.

James shouted, "Peter! Someone is putting a hole in your roof."

"A hole in my roof!" Peter exploded. "Stop them!"

Jesus placed a calming hand on Peter's shoulder. "We can repair your roof. Look!"

Four pairs of hands were now visible and dirt was falling everywhere. In a short time, the hole was enlarged. Everyone could then see four faces. Dirt-covered hands tore away more and more of the thick sod and supporting limbs that held the roof in place.

All eyes were on the widening hole. For a moment, a mat of some kind seemed to fill the opening. Then it broke through. Held by sturdy ropes, the mat descended through the hole and settled on the floor. Most people stepped back to make room, but the visiting scholars pressed in for a closer look.

"Sebastian!" Someone recognized the man on the mat. "I didn't know you were still alive. We heard about the accident."

"I haven't been able to move since the fall," Sebastian stated as his eyes moved from face to face. He was looking for the carpenter.

Jesus stepped forward, and then he knelt down beside the mat. He looked directly into the eyes of the man and asked, "How long have you been like this?"

"A week before Passover, my friends and I were climbing the rocks not far from here, and a man pushed me," Sebastian answered.

"A planned act or a slip of the hand?" Jesus responded.

Before Sebastian could formulate an answer, the Holy Spirit showed Jesus that Bitterness had distorted his memory. Blame had become the primary controller of Sebastian's thoughts. Imagined Revenge was quickly becoming his dominant spirit.

Jesus turned away from the man and began teaching again, *"You have heard that it was said, 'Eye for eye, and tooth for tooth.'*[2] *But I tell you: Love your enemies and pray for those who persecute you, that you may be sons of your Father in heaven. He causes his sun to rise on the evil and the good, and sends rain on the righteous and the unrighteous."*[3]

Gamaliel turned to Yonatan. "This man's teaching is good. He is not talking about violence or resistance."

Yonatan thoughtfully nodded.

Jesus turned back to the young man. "Your friends have great faith. So now, I say to you, '*Son, your sins are forgiven.*'[4] I must instruct you, if you are to be free and totally recovered, you must let go of all the feelings you have about the event that caused your paralysis."

The teachers from Jerusalem and Nazareth immediately became alarmed. "How can this man say, 'Your sins are forgiven?'"

"Blasphemy! By those words, Jesus is elevating himself to the level of God in heaven."

"Only God can forgive sins."

Immediately, the Spirit of God revealed to Jesus the critical thoughts of those men. Jesus turned to Jairus and his visitors. "Why does my statement concern you?"

Jesus then stood and faced Chebar. "Which is easier to say, 'Your sins are forgiven' or 'Get up and walk'?" Jesus took a few more steps so he now faced Gamaliel and Yonatan. Looking both men squarely in the eyes, Jesus said, "But just so you may know that my Father has given me this authority."

Jesus turned back to Sebastian. He reached down and took his hand. Then he said to the paralyzed man, "Stand up. Take your mat and return to your home."

A big grin suddenly spread across Sebastian's face. He called up to his friends who were peering curiously through the hole in the roof, "I can feel my feet!" Pulling against the resistance of Jesus's hand, Sebastian stood up, rolled his mat, and then hurried away.

As Sebastian passed Yonatan, the scholar reached out and touched his leg. "It is flesh." Yonatan announced. "He is a man and not a spirit."

Gamaliel stood and followed Sebastian. "I want to ask some questions."

Sebastian brushed the dignitary from the Sanhedrin aside. He was looking for someone. Suddenly, Matthew broke through the crowd. His brother was with him.

Sebastian ran to his estranged friend. "I'm sorry."

"I was so sorry that you fell. I should have been more cautious," Matthew's brother responded.

Both men hugged and wept while the officials from the Temple and from the town of Nazareth watched and considered all they had seen and heard.

Often, Jesus went out to the grassy hillside near Galilee. One day, a large crowd gathered and he began to teach. *"Do not store up for yourselves treasures on earth, where moth and rust destroy, and where thieves break in and steal."*[5] Jesus saw the Holy Spirit moving over his listeners. It stopped, over Matthew, illuminating the local tax official, so Jesus could see this message was especially for him.

Making eye contact with Matthew, Jesus continued with the words the Spirit had given him for this moment. *"But store up for yourselves treasures in heaven, where moth and rust do not destroy, and where thieves do not break in and steal. For where your treasure is, there your heart will be also…No one can serve two masters. Either he will hate the one and love the other, or he will be devoted to the one and despise the other. You cannot serve both God and Money."*[6]

Money. Jesus could also see that demon. Here and there in the crowd, it was losing its grip on people. He watched as Matthew brushed it aside. Then he saw the Holy Spirit rush to occupy those places in the heart and mind of the tax collector that had once been the home of Money.

Not everyone was responding so positively. Jesus glanced at Judas, who stood beside Matthew. He could see Money still had a very strong hold on his disciple from Judea.

Then, from behind, Jesus heard a gloating voice that he recognized. It was the Evil One taunting the Spirit of God. "If a person wants their demon, the Creator-in-the-flesh cannot cast it out." Satan then laughed. "How foolish you were when you gave created beings the right of free choice!"

The Holy Spirit answered, "Man is made in the image of God; therefore, he must be free to make choices."

There was a brief pause while Satan looked over the crowd. Some were frantically pressing to get close enough for Jesus to heal them. Others were going away, tired of listening. The Evil One turned back to the Holy Spirit. In a mocking tone, he said, "Look at these people, disinterested in the message, begging for a healing touch. Do they resemble God?"

"Do not get haughty with me," the Holy Spirit responded. "The Creator has come to restore his beautiful creation. Listen to the promises he is making."

"Blessed are the poor in spirit, for theirs is the kingdom of heaven. Blessed are those who mourn, for they will be comforted. Blessed are the meek, for they will inherit the earth. Blessed are those who hunger and thirst for righteousness, for they will be filled. Blessed are the merciful, for they will be shown mercy. Blessed are the pure in heart, for they will see God. Blessed are the peacemakers, for they will be called sons of God. Blessed are those who are persecuted because of righteousness, for theirs is the kingdom of heaven."[7]

Confidently, the Holy Spirit stated, "Because these are the words of the one who was known in heaven as Yeshua the Creator, they will be honored by God forever."

In angry silence, Satan withdrew to brood and consider his next attack.

Jesus ended his teaching. He began moving through the press of people, touching each person. Sores were immediately healed. Coughs and fevers disappeared. His body quivered as a constant current of healing power poured through him.

No one was unimportant. Jesus's eyes met the eyes of each individual, and he did not move on to the next person until he saw illness and emotional bondage released. Then when emotional and physical pain turned into joy, Jesus laughed. He hugged each one like a he would hug a member of his own family. Jesus did not show any weariness until every person had been touched.

By then, darkness had fallen. All the people, even the disciples, had returned to their homes. Jesus stood on the beach alone. Slowly, he walked away from the shore, stopping when he found a grassy spot. He threw his cloak on the ground. It would be his bed for the night and his prayer rug before dawn.

In the morning, Jesus walked back into Capernaum. As he entered the town, he saw Matthew sitting in his tax collector's booth. The Holy Spirit settled over the man, and their eyes locked. Then Jesus approached with an outstretched hand and a gentle invitation. "Join me. Leave this job and become one of my followers."

Immediately, Matthew stepped out of his booth and fell into step with Jesus.

Chapter 8

At the Pool of Bethesda

Now there is in Jerusalem near the Sheep Gate a pool, which in Aramaic is called Bethesda and which is surrounded by five covered colonnades.

—John 5:2

Longinus, highest-ranking centurion under governor Pontus Pilate, paced a little as he waited with his subordinate centurions from the various regions of the Jewish territories. Pilate had ordered a report from each region. The governor had to know whether those other rulers, Herod Antipas and his half-brother Philip, were keeping the interests of Rome uppermost.

The quick click of military sandals on the stone floor tiles alerted the waiting officers. With military precision, they stood and saluted as the governor of Judea strode into the dining hall of the Antonia Fortress in Jerusalem. Pilate returned their salute, and then he motioned for his centurions to be seated.

"You men have pledged loyalty to Rome and to the emperor." Pilate looked each man squarely in the eye. "This supersedes any commitment you have to Herod Antipas or Herod Philip. At this time, I want a full report on any movements, charismatic characters, or unlawful activities in your area."

He nodded for Longinus to take over. Longinus announced, "Cornelius, recently from Italy and now overseeing troops in Caesarea."

Cornelius stood. "I maintain a legion in that city. We protect your palace. We patrol the waterfront. Ships from every nation in the empire come into the harbor. It is predominantly a non-Jewish city. There have been no major incidents."

Pilate indicated that he accepted this report, and then Longinus pointed to the next centurion.

He stood. "I am Flavius, senior Roman centurion over the troops maintained by Herod Antipas. All the soldiers under my command are Syrian. They have a strong dislike for the Jewish population."

Pilate leaned forward in his chair. "What trouble is the Old Fox stirring up among the Jews who live in the region of Perea?"

Flavius replied, "The people are stirred up because Antipas has imprisoned a very popular prophet."

"The man who was baptizing people in the springs at Bethany, beyond the Jordan?" Longinus asked.

"Ah yes." Pilate nodded a little smugly. "The man who spoke so publically against Antipas taking his half- brother's wife."

"He is the one," Flavius replied.

"What is the charge against this man?" Pilate asked.

"So far, there is no official charge." Flavius answered. "Several times a week, Antipas calls him to stand and speak in his presence, but he never pronounces the man innocent or guilty."

Longinus interrupted, "What do you hear about the Nabataeans? Are they still preparing to attack Herod Antipas because he divorced the daughter of their king?"

"I have been ordered to prepare my men for a possible battle. We are fortifying the palace at Machaeraus and the surrounding villages."

"Hadrien?" Longinus pointed to another centurion. "What is happening in the region of Galilee? Antipas also governs that region."

"Tax revenue is low." Hadrien shrugged and then added, "But I do not think that is important."

"What is important?" Pilate growled.

"There is a man named Jesus of Nazareth. He travels from town to town and huge crowds follow him."

"Is he a troublemaker? One of those anti-taxation Jewish rebels?" Pilate asked.

"Neither," Hadrien answered. "He is a healer and a teacher. I have listened to him many times. I have never heard him mention matters that concern the Roman Empire. He talks about how people should treat each other. He speaks about inner purity." For a moment, Hadrien hesitated. Then he added, "I find the man fascinating."

Longinius spoke up, "During this Passover week, a man named Rabbi Jesus has been sitting in the place of instruction in the Temple. Every day, he has a larger audience than any other teacher." Longinus looked up at Pilate. "Your wife and her friend Susanna spent hours at the tower window, listening to the man. You should ask her about him."

Pilate turned to the last centurion. "How is Herod Philip doing north of Galilee?"

"He is collecting taxes and living quietly," the centurion answered.

"If he keeps himself out of the torchlight of Rome, then he is wiser than his half-brother," Pilate commented.

Pilate then turned back to Hadrien and Longinus. "I want regular reports on this man, Rabbi Jesus, especially when he is in Jerusalem."

All over the Mt. of Olives, people ate their last pieces of unleavened bread. They packed up their camping areas to begin their journeys back to the towns and villages of the land. Slightly removed from the men with whom he had shared the Passover experience, Jesus continued his all-night conversation with his Father, undisturbed until—

"Jesus! Jesus!"

Jesus opened his eyes to see Mary, the sister of Lazarus and the new wife of Jonathan the perfumer, running toward him.

"I have been looking all over the mountainside for you. We went back to Bethany for the Passover meal, but now, we have returned to Jerusalem." She held out a basket. "I made fresh yeast bread this morning so you and your disciples could have a meal. There is also some dried fish and some raisins."

Jesus took the basket and carried it over to where his disciples and some of John's disciples were stirring.

Peter was the first to begin eating. John, Judas, and Matthew were quick to follow. After eight days of unleavened bread, fresh yeasty loaves were especially delicious.

Jesus took the basket over to John's disciples who did not quickly help themselves to the morning meal. "Don't you know it is the fourth day of the week?" one asked.

Another quickly chimed in, "Those of us who follow the teachings of John and those who follow the teachings of the Pharisees are careful to fast on both the second and fourth days of each week. Why don't you teach your followers to fast?"

With crumbs flying out of his mouth, Peter was quick to inform, "In Galilee, we fish six out of seven days each week, and we eat every day of the week except for the Day of Atonement. A man who is weak from fasting cannot pull in the nets."

Jesus then answered John's disciples with more thought. "The Pharisees are in mourning for the tragedies that are part of the history of our people. But now, the hope of our people, the heir to David's throne has arrived. My disciples are full of joy and expectation, like the guests at a wedding celebration. As long as the celebration lasts, there will be no fasting. But when the bridegroom is separated from his bride, there will be sorrow and fasting."

John looked puzzled so Jesus added, "I am the bridegroom. You are all here for my betrothal celebration. I promise you will also be present for the wedding."

Mary got Jesus's attention once more. "I want you to come to the shop." She beamed with pride, and Jesus knew she wanted to share her newly-wed happiness with him. "We had a storage room added on. Jonathan's older brother Simon arranged for the workmen and the supplies."

"Is your husband satisfied with the work?" Jesus asked.

Mary hesitated, "He said many carpenters would have done a better job, but for now, it is satisfactory."

Jesus nodded with a little concern. Then he advised, "Tell Jonathan, not to overload the shelves. The walls may not be up to the weight." Then Jesus added, "I will stop by before the Sabbath begins."

Late on the preparation day, Jesus and his disciples entered the perfumer's shop. As they walked through the open door of the small business, conversation momentarily ceased. Middle Eastern aromas barraged their senses. Peter breathed deeply the sweet, heavy aromas of cinnamon, myrrh, and spikenard. Then he let his breath out in one long satisfied sigh.

Andrew playfully slapped Peter on the back. "Smells better than a basket of dried fish, brother. We were born into the wrong business."

At that moment, Jonathan, the owner, hurried from the back of the shop, bowing and greeting Jesus and his friends. He called Mary, who came from the living quarters, excited and ready to show Jesus her new home and her husband's business.

Jonathan's was a small establishment. The tour did not take long. In the back, Jesus looked carefully at the new storage room. With a trained eye, he examined the supporting timbers, and then he motioned for Jonathan to come take a close look with him.

Jesus pointed to where one of the main beams was just resting on the surface of the hard-packed earth instead of being planted in a rock-supported hole. "When your brother and I spoke about the cost of your supply room, I warned him that paying less than the standard price might result in poor workmanship."

Jonathan shook his head. "My brother insisted I use the carpenter he had found."

"Well, do not put any weight on this wall," Jesus advised. "Store your burial spices and oils in the center of the room."

Both men stepped away from the poorly placed beam, just as Mary came rushing in. "There is a messenger in the shop from the Fortress of Antonia. The governor's wife wants ointment for a skin rash!"

"We'll get out of here so you can finish this business before sundown," Jesus responded as he and the men with him left the building and continued down the road to buy the food they would eat over the Sabbath day.

In the privacy of the governor's apartments within the Antonia Fortress, Procila helped her husband apply the ointment of myrrh mixed with balm.

"I cannot return to Caesarea until this skin condition heals," Pilate complained. "To ride a horse would be complete misery. If we were in Rome, I would go to the healing bath at the Shrine of Asclepius and spend the night soaking in its medicinal waters."

"There is a similar place in Jerusalem," Procila informed. "It has no priests or statues of Asclepius with his staff and coiled snake, but it has an abundance of fresh spring water that is believed to have healing properties. There is a tradition among the locals. When the waters mysteriously move, it is by the hand of an angel. They believe if you can get in the water before the movement ceases, you will be healed."

"I don't know that I believe in angels," Pilate stated, "but soaking in cool spring water sounds wonderful. Where is this place?"

"It is the Pool of Bethesda, near the Sheep Gate," Procila answered.

"I will ask Longinus to determine how I can safely use the facility without instigating a national incident."

The first three stars could be seen in the evening sky. The streets of Jerusalem were empty. Sabbath had officially begun. Throughout the city, a woman in each home had finished lighting the lamps. Families were eating together before hurrying to synagogue services.

Very quietly, a sedan chair was carried out of the Antonia Fortress. Longinus, with a small guard, led the way to the Pool of Bethesda. Entering by torchlight, the centurion noted there were five porches surrounding a double pool. Here and there, people were camped out, but only a few. The very sick and extremely crippled were the only ones spending the night in this place.

Longinus moved his detail to a deserted porch. The bearers lowered the sedan chair and Pilate stepped out. Without ceremony, he stripped and walked down the stone steps into the black coolness of the water. When he was neck deep, he let his body relax and float. Prepared for the night, Longinus set a guard and then allowed the rest of the men to rest, leaning against the columns that supported a portico.

From across the pool, Talmon observed as one by one the burning torches were extinguished, until only one torch was left to burn throughout the night. This was a curious scene. For thirty-eight years, he had been living beside this pool, and Romans had never used this facility.

Torch light reflected on the ripples of the water. For a moment, Talmon tensed, ready to propel himself into the pool with both arms. Then he thought better. This was not a shallow pool, and in the darkness, who would help him out of the water if this was not his healing moment?

The cripple moved his beggar's pot and then lay back down. He thought about all the times he had pulled himself over the edge and into the water—just a little too late. He thought about all the times he had prayed to God, to the angel of the pool, and even to Asclepius, the Roman god of healing who carried a rod with a coiled snake not unlike the bronze serpent that Moses had raised in the wilderness.

His familiar spirit of Bitterness spoke into his heart. "Life has been so unfair. God has been so unjust. You were a healthy child until the day of the fever. After that sickness, you never walked again. It would have been better if you had died."

Another familiar spirit chimed in, "There must be someone you can blame. Your mother? Your father? Are you paying for their sins?"

Occasionally, thoughts of suicide filled his head, voices that offered the oblivion of drowning in the night waters of the pool. So far, Talmon had resisted.

This night, to silence the voices, Talmon said one simple prayer, "God, on this Sabbath, remember Talmon who sleeps beside the Pool of Bethesda."

Before dawn, Talmon was up and scooting around using his strong arms to drag his lifeless legs as he prepared for the day. Across the pool, torches were being lit. A man wearing a simple Roman toga entered the sedan chair. Quickly, the soldiers moved into formation. The bearers lifted the chair and the military detachment moved out.

Very soon after the Romans left, the sick began to arrive. Then the devout men of the city who did not have their own private pools of water came for their morning purification. This was a daily occurrence, but on Sabbath the men took longer. Some dipped beneath the water seven times instead of just three.

Jesus came with his disciples. They needed to wash before they could go to the Temple. Quickly, they removed their garments. Jesus, with Judas and Matthew, walked down the steps into the water. The fishermen who were with Jesus just jumped off the side of the pool, immediately submerging in the deep water. After several dives beneath the water, they easily paddled back to the edge and pulled themselves up and out.

While they were drying and dressing, the Holy Spirit singled out one man among all the suffering individuals that lined the porches of the pools. In the spiritual, Jesus saw the Spirit go to that man and remain there. And in his heart, he heard the voice of Father God. "Thirty-eight years is long enough."

Walking directly over to the man, Jesus made eye contact and then asked, "Would you like to walk and move normally?" With his foot, Jesus nudged the beggar's pot. "For many years, you have supported yourself on the pity of others. A healthy man must earn his own living and has no one to blame but himself if he is not successful." Looking deeply into the man's eyes, it was easy for Jesus to see the spirits that had made a home in his life. So Jesus asked again, "Do you want to live as healthy men live?"

"Sir," the cripple replied with a self-pitying whine, "There is no one to assist me when the water is stirred, so while I try to be the first to touch the water of this pool, someone always gets in ahead of me."

"You do not need to wait for an angel to stir the water. Neither is there power in any Greek myth that has intertwined itself with the serpent Moses raised in the wilderness. Only through the power and compassion of God will you be healed." Then Jesus looked directly into the eyes of the cripple. "Stand up! Roll up your mat, and carry it to your house." Immediately, Talmon jumped to his feet. He bent over, rolled his mat, and tucked it beneath one arm. Then he took the first steps since his childhood.

Turning to his disciples who were watching in wide-eyed amazement, Jesus said, "It is time for us to leave this place." And quickly, they walked away before a crowd could form.

Since it was the Sabbath day, many of the very observant had come to the pool for their daily purification. Some of these men stopped Talmon before he reached the street. They surrounded him, pointed to his rolled mat, and said, "It is the Sabbath! Why are you transporting a load?"

Excited, Talmon replied, "A man spoke to me. He said, 'If you want to be healed, pick up your mat and walk.' I did as he said. And look! I am walking for the first time in thirty-eight years. Surely, any man who can heal should be obeyed."

Agitated and incensed, the devout men continued to press for information. "Who is this man that told you to break the Sabbath commandment?"

Talmon looked around, scanning the crowded porches for the face of the man who spoke and instantly recreated muscles with functioning nerves in both legs. "I do not know his name, and I do not see his face," Talmon answered. "But if my mat concerns you, I will leave it and return for it later." Then turning his back on the amazed and muttering men, Talmon sprinted out of the pool area. He was going to the Temple, a place he had never before entered.

Jesus and his disciples were already at the Temple listening to the Levitical choir, hearing selective teachers when Peter suddenly exclaimed, "Jesus, isn't that the man you healed at the pool this morning?"

Jesus replied, "Yes, I have been waiting for him." Moving quickly through the milling people, Jesus approached the man.

"Sir, I am glad to see you found your way to the Temple." Before the surprised man could speak, Jesus added a message from the Holy Spirit, "Now that you have been healed, stop sinning. A worse condition could come upon you. Guard your thoughts. Do not allow yourself to consider any resentment. Remember to worship only God and to honor your father and mother."

There was an uncomfortable tension as if Talmon feared this man who seemed to know his private thoughts. He almost wished he had never been healed. With a slight acknowledging nod, he turned away.

Jesus watched as Talmon hurried directly over to some of the men who had been questioning him at the pool. Observing their gestures and the turning of their heads, it was easy to know that Talmon was identifying Jesus as the man who had healed and then instructed him to break the Sabbath regulations.

A few of the Pharisees who had gathered around Talmon broke away from the group and approached Jesus. "Is it true, what this man tells us? On the Sabbath, you spoke healing words and then told him to carry his bed?"

Jesus replied, "Does God the Father of all mankind turn away from Earth every seventh day? No, he continues his watchful care over the sons and daughters of Abraham. He sends rain and sunshine. He encourages the processes of nature to continue. Animals find food and plants grow. My Father's good work never ceases so my good works never cease."

For Jesus, it was easy to know their response even before they spoke. He could see spirits of Religion and Murder infiltrating their thoughts.

"Are you trying to claim some elevated relationship with God?" one man accused.

Another jumped in, "Did you say you are the son of God, like you possess some kind of divinity equal to his?"

"Kill him! Kill him!" Jesus could hear the spirits of Religion and Murder planting the seeds of his destruction in the minds of these men. At the same time, he could see an army of angels and the restraining sword of the Spirit. Today was not the day he would die.

A crowd began to gather, and Jesus began to teach. "When I went to the Pool of Bethesda this morning, there were many sick and disabled in that place, but my Father, God, singled out one man to receive his healing touch through the words I spoke. I do nothing by my own thought processes. I follow the directions of heaven. Does that anger you?"

Gamaliel and Yonatan joined the crowd. Nicodemus ended his own teaching and came with his disciples.

Jesus continued, *"I tell you the truth, whoever hears my word and believes him who sent me has eternal life and will not be condemned; he has crossed over from death to life. I tell you the truth, a time is coming and has now come when the dead will hear the voice of the Son of God and those who hear will live. For as the Father has life in himself, so he has granted the Son to have life in himself. And he has given him authority to judge because he is the Son of Man."*[1]

Joseph of Arimathea stepped up beside his friend Nicodemus. "Is this the Messiah?"

"I don't know," Nicodemus replied. "But my heart burns with excitement when I hear him speak."

Several priests joined the crowd. One of them exclaimed, "This man speaks as if he considers himself to be greater than Moses!"

Another challenged, "Let us see you raise the dead!"

From the midst of the crowd, an angry Pharisee shouted, "When did God make you judge over us?"

In response Jesus said, *"You diligently study the Scriptures because you think that by them you possess eternal life. These are the Scriptures that testify about me, yet you refuse to come to me to have life*[2] *Your accuser is Moses, on whom your hopes are set. If you believed Moses, you would believe me, for he wrote about me. But since you do not believe what he wrote, how are you going to believe what I say?"*[3]

Looking down from the Fortress of Antonia, Longinus noted the agitated crowd. He quickly sent a message to the captain of the Temple guard. "Who is at the center of this gathering, and what is his message? The Passover has ended. I expect you to limit the size of the gatherings in your courts, so I do not need to bring my soldiers down there and disperse crowds for you."

Jesus glanced up. He saw the Holy Spirit indicating it was time for him to leave. "For now, I have finished speaking," Jesus announced.

The muscle-bound fishermen who were his companions broke a path through the crowd, and Jesus walked out of the Temple through the Beautiful Gate. Because it was a Sabbath day, his friend the beggar was not there.

Chapter 9

The Sabbath Controversy

Then he said to them, "The Sabbath was made for man, not man for the Sabbath."

—Mark 2:27

Again, Peter turned around, looking behind his own group of companions steadily walking returning to their homes in Capernaum. With a little exasperation in his step, he hurried forward to match his stride to the smooth stride of Jesus. "Master, I know we left Jerusalem four days ago, but Jerusalem has not left us. They are following us! Some of the same men who argued against you in the Temple have been walking behind us for four days! I cannot believe they all have homes or business in Galilee."

Jesus shrugged it off. "Everywhere I go, I am followed. The Holy Spirit is always with me. The angels of God are my front and rear guard. The Evil One is always lurking and hoping for an opportunity. Now, people are added to my royal court attendants. Some are merely curious. Some are desperate for my help, but those you are most concerned with are agents of Satan. They are controlled by the Evil One, and they have their hearts set on destroying me."

"Well, what are we going to do about it?" Peter asked with a hint of agitation.

Casually, Jesus answered, "I'm just going to continue following the instructions of the Holy Spirit. My life is totally in my Father's hands." Then Jesus added, "The Sabbath is approaching, and there is a small town just ahead. We will take our Sabbath rest there. Maybe the slow pace and the simple amenities of that little town will be punishment enough for those who have followed us all the way from the Temple."

For a moment, Peter thought about the town they were approaching. A little smile played across his lips as he pictured the Temple elite in their pristine, flowing robes and elaborate prayer shawls sleeping on beds of hay. "Those men may be sleeping in barns tonight!" Peter made the statement with satisfaction.

Jesus responded, "My comfort in this situation is that all the promises of God belong to me. *The arrogant mock me without restraint, but I do not turn from* God's *law. I remember* his *ancient laws… and I find comfort in them.*[1]

A few field mice scurried around, making the hay rustle. Their little squeals and squeaks woke Jesus. He was surprised that he noticed such small sounds over the raspy snores of his companions.

"Yeshua?"

Jesus recognized the voice of the Holy Spirit calling him by his heavenly name.

"Do you remember the day you created these little creatures?" As he spoke, the Holy Spirit pulled back the veil that hung between the heavenly and the earthly.

And Jesus, for that moment, had his own heavenly memory. "It was the sixth day," Jesus answered. "I made every land animal, large and small. Then I formed Adam from the dust of the earth. We named the animals, and I gave Adam his wonderful companion, Eve.

"Then as Earth rotated into sunset, I declared, 'In six days, I have finished my work of creation. Earth, and all that is in it, is good! So the seventh day is my day of rest and celebration. As long as there is day and night, the seventh day will remain set apart, holy and blessed for the pleasure of the men and women I have created.'"

"How did you spend that first Sabbath?" the Holy Spirit asked.

Jesus answered, "It was a wonderful day. From sundown to sundown, I strolled through the garden with Adam and Eve. In the darkness of the night, we named the stars. At dawn, we found ourselves standing in a field of wheat. I showed them how to pick the ripe kernels, rub off the husk, and then enjoy the chewy grain. I said, '*I give you every seed-bearing plant on the face of the whole earth and every tree that has fruit with seed in it. They will be yours for food.*'[2] All through that first Sabbath day, we walked and tasted the great variety of edible plants that I had made for man."

Jesus let out a long sigh as he silently savored his delicious memory. Then he stood and stretched, shaking the loose hay from his robe.

The first dull gray wisps of morning light were pushing through the cracks in the barn's wooden door. Jesus went out to find a pool of water and to prepare himself for a morning in the synagogue.

For a while, Jesus was alone at the pool where all the men dipped beneath the surface to complete the required washing. Soon, his disciples joined him, and then the men of the town came. Finally, the visitors from Jerusalem made their way to the pool, looking slightly rumpled and somewhat grumpy.

Without engaging anyone in conversation, Jesus led his companions away from the pool, through a wheat field, toward the synagogue in the center of town.

Peter glanced over his shoulder, and then he hurried up to Jesus. "Those Pharisees from Jerusalem are following us again."

Jesus merely shrugged and continued walking. Behind him, the disciples were wondering about their morning meal. James broke off a few heads of grain, rubbed the husks off and began eating. Andrew and Peter saw him do it and they thought it was a good idea. They grabbed some grain also. Soon, everyone who was with Jesus had either a handful or a mouthful of wheat kernels.

Peter glanced over his shoulder one more time. He saw several of the men from Jerusalem struggling not to trip over their flowing robes as they ran across the rough ground, trying to intersect with Jesus and his disciples. Peter called ahead, "Master, they are coming!"

Jesus stopped and turned, graciously waiting for the red-faced Pharisees to catch up.

"Look," the self-appointed spokesman huffed as he pointed toward Jesus's disciples. "Your disciples are harvesting grain on the Sabbath!"

Jesus answered, "When there is need for daily food, the law can be interpreted more generously. Remember when David and his lawless companions were hungry. They went to Abiathar the high priest. He gave them the consecrated bread from the table of show bread in the Holy Place in the Temple. There is no scriptural condemnation for that act."

"This man is delusional! "One of the Pharisees exclaimed. "He thinks he is the great King David and these fishermen are David's mighty men!"

The rest of the Pharisees responded with mocking laughter.

Then the spokesman held up a restraining hand and the laughter stopped. "Does your reference to King David mean you plan to reestablish the throne of David?"

"Defeat the Romans?"

"Are you another Messiah?"

Jesus then lifted his hand to silence every one of them. "I believe your question was about the Sabbath. You will find the creation story in the first book of Moses. From the first to the seventh day, everything that God created was made for the pleasure of man. *The Sabbath was made for man, not man for the Sabbath. So the Son of Man is Lord even of the Sabbath.*[3] It is a gift and not a set of fetters for the descendants of Adam."

In the Spirit, Jesus could see that he had silenced both the men and their demons, but only for the moment. Without another word, Jesus turned and began walking again. His disciples followed him, still eating freshly plucked wheat and totally amazed that these men from the Temple in Jerusalem had followed them all the way to this obscure town on the edge of Galilee.

Leaving the field and the flustered Pharisees, Jesus and the men who were with him went into the synagogue. Right away, the Holy Spirit indicated a specific man with a shriveled hand who sat on a front row bench waiting for the service to begin.

The Pharisees from Jerusalem also entered the synagogue, and they were still hoping for another occasion to accuse Jesus. They also noticed the man with the withered hand. It was drawn up close to his chest. Obviously, it could not be straightened.

The spokesman for the Pharisees turned to his companions. "We heard that this man performed a healing miracle on the Sabbath day when he was with us in Jerusalem. Let's see if he dares to do it again!"

Puffed up and filled with self-importance, the visitors from Jerusalem walked up to the bench where Jesus was seated with his disciples. They asked him, "Do you keep the Sabbath holy by healing the sick or should you refrain from that activity until the Sabbath has ended?"

It was easy for Jesus to see the question was not their own. It came from the Religious spirits that clung to their flowing robes and extravagant prayer shawls.

Comfortably, Jesus replied. "Let me answer your question with a question. If your donkey becomes entangled in briars or your prize ewe falls into a pit on the Sabbath day, are you going to just leave it?"

Every head in the synagogue nodded negatively.

Jesus then said what every man was thinking. "No, you will pull that animal to safety."

At this point, everyone in the synagogue moved to better hear this confrontation. They stood and leaned into the conversation.

Jesus did not disappoint his audience. He also stood, and then he stepped to the center of the room so all could see and hear. Filled with Holy Spirit authority, Jesus began to teach. "Aren't men and women more valuable than animals? Therefore, it must be lawful to bring them relief on the Sabbath."

Without hesitation, Jesus beckoned to the man with the shriveled hand, "Stand here, beside me."

So the man got up and stood there, a little hesitant at first. Then Peter got up and stood behind him. The other men who were with Jesus—Andrew, James and John, Philip and Nathanael as well as Matthew and Judas—also came to the front. Like a wall of support, they stood shoulder to shoulder behind Jesus and the man. Peter leaned forward and placed his thick fisherman's hand on the man's shoulder. "You are about to be healed," he confidently announced.

There was an unusual tension in the air. Every person was silent. Only Jesus could hear the taunting demons, "If you heal this man, you will only bring trouble upon yourself and your friends."

Looking around the room, he could read the questions on every face. Who is this man? Can he really heal?

Then, the Holy Spirit poured into Jesus the words for that moment. Jesus said to the men of the town and to the visitors from Jerusalem, "This is the Sabbath day. Should I do a good deed and save a struggling man or should I coldly turn my back on his plight, doing nothing, allowing his torment to continue?" There was righteous anger in his question. Unhurried and immovable, Jesus took the time to look each man in the eye and to allow the Spirit of God to challenge their thoughts.

Then Jesus looked directly at the man with eyes of compassion. "Extend your arm." His voice was filled with confidence.

And the man responded without hesitation.

Immediately, the disciples broke into bawdy cheers.

Stunned and thrilled, the man studied his hand and outstretched arm. He flexed his fingers. Then he held his arm high in the air, taking his fingers and wrist through a complete range of motion so everyone could see.

Peter clapped the man on the back and then held his own hand out. "Squeeze my hand. I want to see what kind of a grip you have."

Every head bent toward Peter and the man. The man grasped Peter's hand. He gave it a firm squeeze and a hard shake. Then everyone broke into excited laughter.

It was time for the service to begin. The president of that synagogue called Jesus up to read, but the Pharisees haughtily grabbed the fringes of their prayer shawls, pulling them close to their bodies as they stormed out of the service. For the remainder of the day, they waited in the small town, plotting a bloody end for the teacher who dared to love people above the minutia of the law.

As the Sabbath ended, the angry Pharisees, along with their demons, were on the road, making their way back to Jerusalem by the light of the moon.

Jesus watched them go. He was very aware of their evil plans. Following the directions of the Holy Spirit, Jesus then left that town. But many people from that region followed him down the road. Graciously, he paused again and again, healing their sick and warning them not to spread the word that the Messiah was now among them.

The next day, Jesus and his disciples arrived back in their hometown of Capernaum. But they were not alone. The story of the healing in the synagogue seemed to travel faster than they could walk, and from every village along their route, people were coming with their sick and infirmed.

"Master?" Peter looked alarmed. "There are so many people following us."

"There is not enough room in the town," Andrew commented.

Looking ahead, Jesus could see the Holy Spirit indicating a bare hillside close to the lake. So Jesus led his disciples to that place and the crowd followed. At the base of the hill, Jesus pointed to one of the fishing boats. His disciples immediately pushed it away from the rocky beach and climbed aboard, ready to quickly launch into deep water. Then they waited while Jesus moved through the crowd healing and casting out demons.

The sun moved across the sky. The crowd kept growing, desperate people, pushing and clamoring for his touch. Most of the disciples climbed out of the boat, hurrying to stand beside Jesus as he worked the crowd.

Each time a joyful shout of release was heard, more people pressed forward. Peter set himself between Jesus and the crowd. James and John began funneling the people toward Jesus so they would not overwhelm him. The other men actually formed a human barricade to hold back the frantic masses. Throughout the desperate sea of humanity, there were individuals whose minds had been captured by evil spirits. Even from a distance when those spirits saw Jesus, the people who were possessed fell down and shrieked, "We know you are the Son of God!"

Whenever that happened, Jesus would stop what he was doing and point directly at that person. With a commanding voice, Jesus would shout over the crowd, "Say no more! Remove yourself from this individual. You may never return!"

Then that person would roll on the ground and scream. Sometimes, he would convulse. But the reaction would be brief. Within moments, the individual would be up on two feet, laughing and normal in every way.

When everyone had been healed, Philip and Nathanael pulled the boat very close to the shore. Jesus waded out and then climbed over the side. Before the crowd could splash through the shallow water after him, the fishermen moved their boat into deeper water. The rest of the disciples climbed into another boat, and they also pushed away from the shore.

Then Jesus stood in the bow of his boat and began to teach. "*Do not think that I have come to abolish the Law or the Prophets; I have not come to abolish them but to fulfill them.*[4] Every week, I enter into the rest of the Sabbath. It is a restorative rest, meant to allow men and women to stop working like animals, and for that period of time, to move back into the image of God. Everything I do on the Sabbath is directed toward restoring man to the image of God.

"I am not writing a new set of laws. Moses wrote the laws as God spoke them to him. *I tell you the truth, until heaven and earth disappear, not the smallest letter, not the least stroke of a pen, will by any means disappear from the Law until everything is accomplished.*[5]

"So do not ignore the things that Moses wrote. *Anyone who breaks one of the least of these commandments and teaches others to do the same will be called least in the kingdom of heaven, but whoever practices and teaches these commands will be called great in the kingdom of heaven.*[6] I challenge you to check your hearts and your motives when you apply the requirements that were actually written by Moses as well as when you apply those regulations that have been added. Every act of obedience must come from a heart totally devoted to pleasing God and to restoring people to the image of God. You must understand, unless you can keep all the laws of Moses with greater piety and precision than the Pharisees and teachers in the Temple, you will not qualify to enter the kingdom of heaven."

The sun was beginning to set. Jesus signaled the other boat to put out into deeper water. Philip raised the sail in the boat where Jesus sat, and it quickly caught the evening breeze. Both boats were soon far from shore.

Jesus asked Philip to pull up close to a deserted peninsula. Nimbly, Jesus jumped over the side and waded to shore. Lifting his hands to his mouth, he called to his friends in both boats, "Return to Capernaum. I'll meet you there within a day or two." Then he went off, climbing the rugged hills to be alone with his heavenly companions.

Chapter 10

He Chose Twelve

One of those days Jesus went out to a mountainside to pray, and spent the night praying to God. When morning came, he called his disciples to him and chose twelve of them, whom he also designated apostles.

—Luke 6:12–13

Manaen and Cuza straightened their banquet robes as they walked toward the open gate at the estate of Matthew, the tax collector of Capernaum. "I understand this festive occasion is Matthew's retirement celebration," Manaen commented.

Cuza responded, "Yes, I am looking for his replacement now. I'm hoping someone from his family will want to step into his position." Cuza paused and let his gaze sweep over the large walled compound they were about to enter. "A man can do very well collecting taxes."

"He can also become very criticized and ostracized." As Manaen spoke, he gestured toward the local synagogue.

Cuza glanced toward the meeting house. Three men were standing in the doorway. Cuza recognized Jairus, the president of the synagogue, with two other men, obviously devout Pharisees. "It seems we are being watched," Cuza observed.

"I believe they are making a list of all the sinners in town," Manaen wryly quipped. "Because only sinners would drink fine wine and eat well-prepared food in the home of a tax collector."

Cuza chuckled. "If those men knew how many sinners we associate with on a daily basis in the service of our king, Herod Antipas, they would hurry away for fear of becoming unclean."

Both financial officials shrugged off the concerns of the men at the synagogue. They entered the courtyard, greeted by servants and directed to the stone jars that contained water for washing. Manaen and Cuza looked around. The elaborate courtyard with its beautiful mosaic floor was filled with men, mostly fishermen from the town, reclining around a U-shaped table. Colorful draperies provided shade. Servants were pouring the wine.

After washing their feet and hands, both men were escorted to their cushions close to the guest of honor, Jesus the teacher and healer.

Cuza greeted Jesus with a bow. He was forever grateful that this man had healed his son.

Matthew stood. "I have called all my friends and partners in the business of collecting taxes together to celebrate a change in my life." He looked at Cuza and Manaen and announced, "No longer will I be sending money to the king's treasury." Then he turned to Zebedee and all his fishing partners. "And I won't be running to the docks to count your fish." Matthew stepped over beside Jesus. "I am becoming a student of the scriptures. My teacher is Rabbi Jesus of Nazareth."

Zebedee quickly stood, raising his glass of wine. "It is more honorable to be a student than a tax collector. I give you my blessing."

"Blessings to you!" everyone shouted. Then they chanted the traditional blessing over the wine and drank their first cup.

Manaen rolled back on his comfortable cushions. His stomach was full. The food had been as good as anything he had ever eaten in Herod's palace. For a moment, he thought it would be nice to just fall asleep, but that was impossible. Beside him, a loudmouthed fisherman was complaining about the Pharisees from Jerusalem and the region of Galilee. It seemed some religious zealots had started following this new teacher named Jesus from town to town. They were spying on him, criticizing him, picking arguments with him.

In the midst of his complaint, Peter suddenly turned to Jesus. "Teacher, how long are we going to let these men from the Temple continue to harass us?"

Jesus answered, "We are going to demonstrate our response by treating them as we want to be treated.

Manaen looked at Peter's face. The fisherman's disappointment was obvious. Manaen leaned over and spoke confidentially to Cuza. "I grew up in the court of Herod the Great. This Jesus could never have been one of his advisors."

Cuza responded, "I believe the teacher is a man of peace. I feel certain he would rather help someone than protect himself."

Manaen thoughtfully studied the new teacher. He thought about Jesus's statements in the practical sphere of everyday court life. Then he said to Cuza, "I do not believe this man will be a political problem."

Cuza answered, "I hope he is wise enough not to accuse either the king or his wife. I would not like him to end up in prison like the prophet who was baptizing near the Jordan."

Manaen nodded in agreement. "It does not appear Antipas plans to release that prophet anytime soon."

It was late. Jesus stood by the gate saying a personal word to each man who had attended the banquet. Peter was the last to leave. He turned to Jesus. "Are you sleeping in Zebedee's home tonight, or will you stay here with Matthew?"

Jesus answered, "Neither. I am going up on the mountain. My Father, through his Holy Spirit, is calling me." Jesus paused and then he said, "Tell the others to meet me at the foot of the mountain in the morning."

Peter agreed, and then he walked on to his home.

Matthew said, "Master, I would go with you, but there is much to do now that the banquet is over."

Jesus waved his offer aside. "Another time." He smiled and nodded his assurance that all was well. With a proper bow to his host and a warm embrace, Jesus left Matthew's estate, walking into the night.

There was enough moonlight to see the windy footpath that led to the summit of the large rolling hill close to Capernaum that the locals called "the mountain." Jesus walked the path with his eyes on the Spirit. Like a glowing cloud, it led him higher and higher until it rested on a clump of gray boulders sheltered by the long limbs of solid ancient trees.

Making himself comfortable on the hard, flat surface of one of the rocks, Jesus pushed the events and concerns of everyday life from his mind and opened himself to heaven.

"I waited patiently for the Lord; he turned to me and heard my cry."[1]

In a clear rich baritone, Jesus began to sing.

Here I am, I have come—
it is written about me in the scroll.
I desire to do your will, O my God;
your law is within my heart.
I proclaim righteousness in the great assembly;
I do not seal my lips, as you know, O Lord."[2]

The Holy Spirit responded, "You have not sealed your lips. You have spoken every word I have given you. Your name is recorded in the books of heaven as Faithful."

God then spoke.

The great trees sheltering Jesus trembled as the audible voice of the Master of the Universe shook the ground that encased their mighty root systems.

"Yeshua, my son, it is my desire that you gain the attention of the religious establishment in Jerusalem by becoming like them in one small way. Their great rabbis have students called disciples. Three are very close, personal assistants to their teacher. These three are privileged to learn the secrets of their master. Then there are nine others who also receive direct instruction from their master. In addition, there will be a multitude of followers who receive general instruction at large gatherings. After you return to rule with me, these disciples will spread the message of our kingdom throughout the world."

For a moment, Jesus was thoughtful. Then he responded, "I have read the scriptures, and I have been taught by your Holy Spirit. I understand the symbolism of the Passover lamb. I know the price I will pay to establish our kingdom—but what about my disciples? Our enemy, Satan, is vicious and violent. What will he do to them? Will they be able to overcome him?"

Jesus paused again. Then he asked, "Who will I be calling, and what will be the cost and the reward for their discipleship?"

The Holy Spirit answered, "I will show you the men I have chosen."

God added, "First, you must see their reward. They will be among the twenty-four."

The Holy Spirit pulled back the veil that separates Earth's present from its future.

At once, Jesus looked into the throne room of heaven. He saw himself sitting on the right side of the Eternal Father. An emerald rainbow encircled the Father's throne, and twenty-four royal courtiers sat on smaller thrones surrounding the large white throne. Each courtier was dressed in white and had on his head a golden crown.

"I see them!" Jesus exclaimed. "Peter the fisherman and Andrew, his brother. I also see my cousins James and John, the sons of Zebedee. I see Philip and Nathanael who now wants to be called Bartholomew. And look!" Jesus started to laugh. "Tax collectors can go to heaven! There is Matthew. Father, he gave me a wonderful banquet tonight. Bless him for his kindness." Jesus studied the faces some more. They looked a little different without the stress of Earthly life. "I believe I see Thomas and James the son of Alphaeus. Oh, and there is my friend from childhood, Simon the Zealot, also Thaddaeus."

"These are your disciples," God announced.

"There should be one more," Jesus stated.

"Judas will not be among the twenty-four who sit on heavenly thrones," God responded, "but call him to be one of your twelve."

"Why—" Jesus started to ask.

But God interrupted, "You asked about the reward for discipleship. For those who choose to go all the way, there is a crown and a place next to the throne. Not everyone will be willing to pay the price to go all the way."

"I see." Jesus understood. Judas would not go all the way. "And the price?" Jesus asked again. "What does it mean to go all the way for the kingdom?"

A map of the Roman Empire seemed to open in the night sky, and Jesus saw each man traveling to a different destination. Suddenly, a sword flashed in Jerusalem, and Jesus saw his cousin James fall on the stone floor of Herod's dungeon. Then, in Ethiopia, another sword flashed and Matthew crumpled to the ground, surrounded by a clamoring mob. In Greece, a man was being whipped and then tied to an X-shaped cross. Jesus groaned, "Oh Andrew, what am I doing to you?"

Spears flew through the air in India, and Thomas fell in a pool of blood. In Syria, Philip was nailed to a cross. And in Armenia, Bartholomew was also beaten and placed on a cross.

"The good news of our kingdom will be preached in Rome. The emperor will have the opportunity to welcome or reject your gift of eternal life," God informed.

As Jesus watched, a cross was erected in Rome. Peter was stretched across its wooden beams, his feet in the air and his head nearly touching the ground.

Tears were streaming down Jesus's face as he asked, "Will anyone die a natural death?"

"There will be one," God answered. "He will be the final eyewitness. He will pen your last official message to our kingdom on Earth."

Then Jesus saw the disciple who would outlive every other disciple, John the son of Zebedee. He was an old man, sitting alone on a rocky island overlooking the Great Sea.

Overcome, Jesus dropped to the ground next to the boulder where he had been sitting and he began to cry, "Father, how can I ask these men to enter into this future? I think about my own death, and my body recoils. I have seen a man die on a cross. I know it is my future, but how can I call others into that same future?"

God answered, "My son, Yeshua, I make this promise to you. If anyone will follow you and deny himself even to the point of death, I will reward him. The kingdom of heaven is not like the kingdoms of Earth or the kingdom that Satan plans to set up. For in the kingdom of heaven, whoever wants to preserve his life and his possessions will lose both, but whoever loses everything to spread the good news will receive eternity with us. *What good will it be for a man if he gains the whole world, yet forfeits his soul? Or what can a man give in exchange for his soul? For the Son of Man is going to come in his Father's glory with his angels, and then he will reward each person according to what he has done.*"[3]

"Oh, Father, these men we are calling are ordinary working men. They view the world through simple eyes. Teach them. Fill them with your Spirit. Protect them from the Evil One."

Throughout the night, Jesus continued to plead for the men he was about to bring more fully into his ministry.

When the sun rose over the eastern hills and briefly turned the surface of the Sea of Galilee into shimmering gold, Jesus felt the prayer burden lift. He stood and brushed the dirt from his robe. Then he walked down to the sea to wash.

Coming up out of the water, he saw a crowd was gathering. With graciousness, Jesus slowly walked among them, touching those who were ill, blessing all who were discouraged, and sending demons into dry and distant places. Gradually, his new disciples arrived. Tearing himself away from the growing crowd, Jesus walked back up the mountain with the twelve who were chosen.

When they arrived at the boulders, Jesus turned and said, "Many of you call me rabbi, teacher, or even master. Now, I would like to call you disciples."

"You mean we are disciples like the men who follow Rabbi Gamaliel and Rabbi Nicodemus?" Peter asked.

"Yes," Jesus answered. "We're going to get some respect in the academic arena of the Temple."

The men looked at each other and nodded their agreement.

Andrew glanced down the hillside toward the sea. "Master, the crowd is growing, and the people are pushing up toward us."

Jesus nodded. "The crowds will cause many in high positions to pay attention to my teaching." Without another word, Jesus led his twelve special disciples back down the mountain.

He led them to a place near the water's edge where fishing boats had been moored. With his back to the sea, Jesus began to heal and cast out demons. Power from his hand hit each person, driving out illness and demons before he physically touched them.

When he had healed every illness and rebuked every demon, Jesus turned and looked at those men he had just named to be his closest companions. Then he gestured toward the crowd covering the hillside and the flat plain down to the water's edge. "All of these are my followers, my disciples—men, women, even children. The Kingdom of God with all its benefits belongs to every person you see."

Then Jesus spoke to the crowd. It was a message he often repeated, but each time he gave that message, it seemed fresh and more powerful than the last time. His voice rang out in the natural amphitheater of the Galilean hills. *"Blessed are you who are poor, for yours is the Kingdom of God. Blessed are you who hunger now, for you will be satisfied. Blessed are you who weep now, for you will laugh."*[4]

Turning from the crowd, Jesus spoke again to his newly chosen twelve. It was a special, intimate moment. He made eye contact with each individual. *"Blessed are you when men hate you, when they exclude you and insult you and reject your name as evil, because of the Son of Man. Rejoice in that day and leap for joy, because great is your reward in heaven. For that is how their fathers treated the prophets."*[5]

Jesus then turned back to the people and continued his general instruction, but the disciples barely heard the things he was saying. The words he had spoken directly to them carried such Holy Spirit power that they sat stunned as if they had been struck by lightning.

James was the first to find his voice. "When I think about his words, rejoicing during persecution, they make no sense. But I feel like everything he said makes perfect sense, and that is the way it will be."

His brother John nodded. The others agreed and then turned their attention back to the teaching of their master.

Chapter 11

Teach Us to Pray

A good man brings good things out of the good stored up in his heart, and an evil man brings evil things out of the evil stored up in his heart. For the mouth speaks what the heart is full of.

—Luke 6:45

John hoisted the odd-looking chair over his shoulders while Peter broke a path through the masses of people that were slowly ascending or descending the steps leading to the Beautiful Gate at the Temple. On the stone platform, close to the ornate brass doors Peter stopped, and John placed the chair beside the crippled beggar who usually sat in this place.

"Are you Ichabod?" Peter asked. His thick Galilean accent nearly overpowered his question.

The beggar who was sitting in a similar but very worn out chair nodded.

"Our master said to bring you this chair and to dispose of your old one," John added.

"Your master?" Ichabod questioned. "You men must be from Galilee." Then the beggar looked at the chair. "Your master must be Jesus, the carpenter from Nazareth." A big smile crossed the beggar's face. "That young man made my first chair, and he has given me a new chair every few years since he was just a youth."

"He's not doing carpentry work anymore," Peter informed. "He's a teacher, a master of the scriptures."

John pointed toward the Mount of Olives. "See that crowd of people? Right now, they are listening to Jesus."

"I wish I could hear him." Ichabod sighed a little.

"These steps are too small for the crowds," Peter stated. "Huge crowds follow him everywhere."

Then John said, "Jesus does more than teach. He heals the sick and he casts out demons."

"I've seen lame men get up and walk," Peter stated. Then he gave one of the carrying poles on the new chair a sturdy shake. "See if you can get a couple of men to carry you to where Jesus is teaching. If you can get to him, you can be healed."

A strange look came across the beggar's face; hope mixed with incredulous disbelief.

A little apologetically, John added, "We would offer to take you to him now, but we have several other places to go and things to purchase before we return to the place where Jesus is teaching." Bending over, John placed a few coins in the beggar's pot. Before more could be said, both men were on their way back down the steps and into the crowded streets of Jerusalem.

Ichabod looked at the departing men. Both were in a hurry. One was carrying his old chair. He hardly knew what to think. A few more coins were dropped into his pot. He looked up to see the captain of the Temple guard standing with the high priest, Caiaphas. The men seemed agitated.

"Look at the crowd!" Caiaphas pointed. "They are covering one whole side of the mountain!"

"I am surprised the commander of the fortress has not sent me a complaint," the captain responded.

"I know why you haven't received a complaint," the high priest growled. "The wife of the governor of Judea and one of her friends have gone over to the mountain to hear this new teacher."

Caiaphas pointed to a couple of sedan chairs and a small detail of soldiers not far from where Jesus was teaching.

Standing on a flat rock near the summit of the mount, Jesus could see the Temple on the other side of the valley. Tall and white, it gleamed in the afternoon sunlight. All around him, people sat or stood in interested clusters. Hardly a bare patch of ground was visible. Prompted by the Holy Spirit, Jesus scanned the crowd. With unwavering directness, he made eye contact with various men as the Spirit highlighted them. Then he spoke with a divine authority that shot his words like arrows directly to their intended targets.

"You have heard the law of Moses. It says do not murder. But I am here to tell you God will condemn you not just for the act of murder, but also for thoughts of murder. In the eyes of God, *anyone who is angry with his brother will be subject to judgment.*[1]

It has been fifty days since we gathered in this city to remember Passover. If during those fifty weeks you have broken your relationship with your brother or your neighbor, now is the time to mend that relationship. You cannot ask to draw near to God while you hold another human being at a distance from yourself.

When you men bring a lamb into the Court of the Israelites, the priest stands before you holding a silver basin and a sharp knife. At that time, you place your hands on the head of the lamb. You confess your sins, and then you reach into the silver basin and pick up the knife. If at that point, you *remember that your brother has something against you,* do not proceed with your sacrifice. *Leave your gift there in front of the altar. First go and be reconciled to your brother; then come and offer your gift.*"[2]

Procila, the wife of Pilate, turned away from Jesus for a moment and commented to her friend, Susanna. "I am so glad you brought me to hear this teacher. When I sat with you and studied all the laws that pertain to your God, your belief system seemed to be just a hard and regulated life, like the Roman military. But this man applies your beliefs in a way that is deeply relational, person to person and person to God. I feel drawn to learn more."

Susanna responded, "I am also drawn to this man's teaching. I have heard him several times in Galilee."

"My husband will be interested," Procila added as she turned her attention back to the teacher.

The teacher was looking directly at the group of soldiers who had accompanied Procila and Susanna. "*You have heard that it was said, 'Do not commit adultery.' But I tell you that anyone who looks at a woman lustfully has already committed adultery with her in his heart.*"

Several soldiers shifted uncomfortably.

Jesus continued to make eye contact. "*If your right eye causes you to sin, gouge it out and throw it away. It is better for you to lose one part of your body than for your whole body to be thrown into hell.*"

He turned to another group of men, obviously men of the Temple. "*And if your right hand causes you to sin, cut it off and throw it away. It is better for you to lose one part of your body than for your whole body to go into hell.*"[3]

"He is fearless," Susanna commented.

"It seems he knows the secrets of every man and speaks directly to them," Procila stated with obvious appreciation for the spiritual keenness Jesus possessed.

It was nighttime. Jesus led his band of twelve around the numerous camp sites that covered the Mount of Olives, up to a grove of olive trees surrounding an enclosed garden. There was enough room for all twelve to stretch out and sleep. They made a small fire from twigs, ate some flat bread and dried fish, and then the men threw their cloaks on the ground, preparing for the night.

For a few moments, Jesus watched his disciples. Then he took several steps away from the resting men, further into the cluster of twisted olive trunks and gnarled limbs.

James called after him, "Master? Aren't you going to sleep?"

Jesus paused. "I'm going to pray."

James sat up, interested. "Teach us to pray," he eagerly responded.

The other disciples also sat up, their faces turned expectantly toward their teacher.

"Yes," Peter agreed. "Teach us to pray."

Thoughtfully, Jesus walked back into the firelight. He squatted down beside the dying flames and said, "*And when you pray, do not be like the hypocrites, for they love to pray standing in the synagogues and on the street corners to be seen by men. I tell you the truth, they have received their reward in full.*"[4]

Peter nodded his head and commented, "Today, they were all over the Temple, standing in the most prominent places, davening and shouting toward heaven like God is deaf."

"What is their full reward?" Andrew asked.

Jesus answered, "Their full reward is the admiration of men. It is worthless. *But when you pray, go into your room, close the door and pray to your Father, who is unseen. Then your Father, who sees what is done in secret, will reward you.*"[5]

"Our prayers and our deeds are all recorded in the books of heaven," Philip stated. Then he looked to Jesus for confirmation.

Jesus nodded affirmatively.

"And those books will be opened in the Day of Judgment," John added.

Jesus nodded again, and then he continued, "*And when you pray, do not keep on babbling like pagans, for they think they will be heard because of their many words. Do not be like them, for your Father knows what you need before you ask him.*"[6]

Thomas spoke up, "If we don't need to keep repeating our request, what should we say?"

Jesus answered, "*This, then, is how you should pray. Our Father in heaven, hallowed be your name, your kingdom come, your will be done on earth as it is in heaven. Give us today our daily bread. Forgive us our debts, as we also have forgiven our debtors. And lead us not into temptation, but deliver us from the evil one.*[7] We honor you, God. Every kingdom on Earth is yours. You have the power to create and to destroy. We look forward to seeing every manifestation of your limitless glory, now and in the kingdom to come. Amen."

There was silence around the little campfire. Thoughtfully, each man watched the flames turn into golden coals. Finally, John asked, "Is forgiveness conditional?"

At first, Jesus gave the simple response. "Yes." Then he looked at each face and knew these men needed a more complete answer. "*If you forgive men when they sin against you, your heavenly Father will also forgive you. But if you do not forgive men their sins, your Father will not forgive your sins.*"[8]

Andrew put his hand firmly on Peter's shoulder. "Guess you are going to have to forgive Matthew and his friends for putting a hole in your roof."

Peter spluttered, "It rained the next day! It rained for three whole days, and then it took another four days to repair the roof and clean the mud out of the room."

"Forgive, brother," Andrew lightly teased.

"Jesus?" Peter pleaded for a reprieve.

With a light chuckle, Jesus responded, "Forgive and forget about it. Do not hold any man to a debt."

Matthew spoke up, "Peter, that means you cannot mention the incident to me again! It is finished!"

"Neither can you suggest that Matthew owes you some labor or favors," John added.

All the men laughed because they knew how many times Peter had reminded Matthew of his debt.

"All right, all right," Peter groused. Abruptly, he rose to his feet and strode over to the fire. Only a few coals glowed among the ashes. Peter quickly tossed a handful of dirt on the fire, signaling that the discussion, like the fire, had come to an end.

Quietly, Jesus slipped away from his disciples and moved further into the seclusion of the clustered olive trees.

"My Father..."

It was a warm night in Jerusalem. In the royal apartments of the Antonia Fortress, Pilate and Procila rested in their bed, hot and sleepless. The lightest Egyptian linen was too heavy and a cooling breeze from the open windows seemed an unattainable goal.

Pilate sighed and turned to his wife. "I met with Antipas today. He and Herodias are at his father's palace for the duration of this festival."

Procila, always interested in the politics of their position, asked, "What is the Old Fox up to?"

Pilate answered, "First, he is making sure all the people see that he comes to Jerusalem for every feast. He wants them to think he is one of them."

"You can't fault him for that!" Procila commented.

"He's heard from Rome," Pilate continued.

Procila sat up.

"Sejanus has managed to kill off almost every successor to the throne of Tiberius, and now, Sejanus has arranged a marriage for himself that will bring him into the royal family," Pilate informed.

"He was always very ambitious," Procila commented. "Sejanus was the one who gave you this appointment, so in the eyes of the emperor, you remain connected with every move he makes."

Pilate sat up and shrugged. "I have no control over the things that happen in Rome."

Procila continued her thoughtful commentary. "I remember when you were a young centurion, riding beside Sejanus as the Praetorian Guard paraded through the streets of Rome."

Pilate sighed. "Sejanus was making himself visible and indispensible to the emperor, while I was making myself indispensible to Sejanus." Hanging his head a little, Pilate recalled. "I did some things for that man that no one else would do." Pilate hesitated and then he confessed, "Procila, there is blood on my hands. I don't like how it feels to remember the shedding of innocent blood. So that one man can rise to political power, men, woman, even children 'accidently' die."

"That is the way of Rome," Procila pragmatically admitted. Then she moved closer to her husband. She put her hand on his bare chest and laid her head on his shoulder. "You have a sense of justice that I admire."

"I have to balance that with self-preservation and the interests of the empire," Pilate replied with heaviness in his voice. "There are times when I have to throw right and wrong on the dung heap." He covered his wife's hand with his own.

Procila changed the subject. "Did Herod mention the prophet he is holding in his dungeon?"

"The desert man with the long hair?" Pilate asked.

"Yes."

"He is still in the bowels of Herod's desert fortress," Pilate answered. As a matter of fact, Antipas said we might hear him speak when we come to celebrate his birthday."

"Do we have to attend?" Procila moaned her question.

"We will get an official invitation after the Fall Feasts," Pilate answered as he assured his wife with an affirmative nod of his head that it was the politically correct thing to do. "Antipas has a fascination for these charismatic Jewish teachers. He was asking me about a new teacher who is drawing large crowds. He is reported to be a healer, maybe the next Messiah."

"You mean Rabbi Jesus?" Procila replied. "I heard him today. He was on the Mount of Olives. The man is the most amazing teacher! He is no threat to Rome. He tells the people to be good from the inside to the outside. He says they should become masters of their own thoughts, not allowing themselves to even consider hatred and resentment. He speaks very practically to the people." Procila paused to remember. "One thing that he said was, '*Settle matters quickly with your adversary who is taking you to court. Do it while you are still with him on the way, or he may hand you over to the judge, and the judge may hand you over to the officer, and you may be thrown into prison. I tell you the truth, you will not get out until you have paid the last penny.*'"[9]

"I can't say that I disagree." Pilate left the bed and walked over to the open window. Stars filled the Jerusalem sky. From the corner of the fortress that housed the royal apartments, he silently surveyed the dark walls and buildings spread out before him. "Rome expects me to keep the peace and to allow the citizens of this city complete freedom of worship while making sure the authority of Rome is never compromised.

I warned Antipas today. He had better settle his differences with the king of the Nabataeans. They are building war machines and amassing an army to attack him."

"Over the wife he divorced to marry Herodias?" Procila shook her head. "This is not going to turn out well for Antipas."

"I think he believes some silly superstition that so long as he keeps the prophet called John the Baptist in his dungeon, he will be safe."

Procila shook her head negatively. "Once you displease the god of the land, no one can save you."

"I think he is wondering if this new teacher, with his powers to heal, can help him." Pilate looked questioningly at his wife.

"I saw some healings today. A little crippled girl jumped up and ran up and down the mountain, but I don't think this teacher is trying to get the attention of the rulers and important people. The mountain was filled with ordinary people, and he seemed to just love them."

"Longinus gave me a report from Hadrien, a centurion who supervises the region of Galilee." Pilate moved to the lampstand.

With a flint, he lit several wicks. Then he went to the table and picked up a rolled parchment. "Hadrien wrote a complete report." Pilate unrolled the parchment and began to read to his wife. "For two days, I watched the road, waiting and hoping that Jesus would return to Capernaum before it was too late. When I saw him walking down the road surrounded by friends and followers, I hurried to him.

"Obviously, those who were with him were disturbed, but the healer welcomed me and listened respectfully. I told him a servant on my estate was confined to bed and suffering terribly.

"It was true. A paralysis had suddenly come upon his entire right side. He could not move his arm or his leg on that side, and his speech was badly garbled. In addition, my servant could not eat or drink. This man was my personal servant. Because of his loyalty to me and my family, he had traveled from Rome to serve me in this foreign land.

"On several occasions, I had observed this Jewish teacher. I had seen him heal, but I had only seen him heal Jewish people.

"When Jesus said to me, 'I will go to your home and heal your servant,' I was amazed. I knew it was culturally impossible for this man to enter my house, yet I could see in his eyes and hear in his voice that the need of my servant was greater than his need to be ritually pure.

"Quickly, I responded, 'Healer, I recognize your authority. It is like the authority of my own rank. I do not run here and there. I just give an order, and it is obeyed. Just speak the healing word. You do not need to enter my home.'

"Jesus then turned to his close followers and said, 'This Roman has greater faith than the sons of Abraham! He is one of the first fruits of the gentiles who will stream into the Kingdom of God.'

"Then Jesus said to me, 'Go home, your servant has been healed. This happened because you believed.'

"As I walked back to my estate, there was a certainty in my heart. I could not even force an anxious thought to enter my mind. I knew I would find my servant totally restored to health. When I arrived at my home, my servant was waiting at the gate. He said power had rolled like waves through his body, and he then leaped from his bed. This happened at the very hour Jesus had spoken with me." Pilate looked up at his wife, waiting for her reaction.

Excitedly, she exclaimed, "That is an amazing report! Will you send it on to Rome? To Sejanus?"

"I don't know. Sejanus would either try to use Jesus for his own amusement—"

"That's what Antipas wants to do!" Procila interjected.

"Or Jesus would become an expendable player in his power games." Pilate slowly shook his head. "Rome is not the only place where power games are played. The captain of the Temple guard wanted Longinus to disperse the crowd today. It seems the Temple authorities do not like this teacher's popularity."

"Longinus joined me for part of the afternoon," Procila informed.

"I know. It pleased him to deny their request," Pilate smugly replied. Slowly, he walked over to where his wife sat on their bed. He took her by both hands and drew her up to stand facing him. "You are the one who reads omens and understands dreams. Tell me why I feel so uneasy about Sejanus in Rome and this Jesus in Jerusalem?"

"They are very different men," Procila replied. "Sejanus will stop at nothing to elevate himself, and Jesus, I believe, would give everything for just one poor suffering individual. Each man is powerful, but the source of each power is different. In Jewish thinking, there is only one God. He is good and powerful. Jesus gets his power from that God. There is also an Evil One who is the source of all that is wicked in the Earth. I believe Sejanus gets his power from the Evil One." With sudden realization and alarm in her voice, Procila added, "Distance yourself from Sejanus!"

Pilate did not respond verbally. He just nodded his head to let his wife know he had listened to everything she had said, and he would consider her words seriously.

A little breeze fluttered through the room, promising a cooling trend for the rest of the night. Mutual affection and tenderness overpowered the pressures of politics and government. Pilate pulled his wife into his arms. Then they shared the pleasures God had given to all men and women who are united in marriage.

Chapter 12

A Funeral Interrupted

Soon afterward, Jesus went to a town called Nain, and his disciples and a large crowd went along with him.

—Luke 7:11

It was late afternoon as Jesus, with his disciples, continued his return journey from Jerusalem into the region of Galilee. A curious crowd was walking with them and behind them. Everyone wanted to hear the teacher, touch the teacher, and be close to the teacher. Peter, James, and Andrew led the way, forming a front guard so no one blocked their forward progress toward Capernaum.

Ahead, they could see the gate and the rustic wall surrounding the crowded houses and crooked streets of the village of Nain. The narrow gate was filled with people streaming out behind a covered body, laid flat on planks of wood and carried high on the shoulders of strong young men. High-pitched wailing, shrieks and sobs filled the space between the two groups.

For a moment Peter, James, and Andrew hesitated. Peter turned back to Jesus. "Master, the road is narrow. There is not enough room for our followers and the funeral procession to pass each other."

"And we must not trample the wheat!" James cautioned as he gestured toward the ripening fields on both sides of the road.

"Oh, Jesus," Philip hurried forward and spoke with concern. "We must somehow make space between our party and theirs. If we do not move and the body brushes against someone, that person will immediately become unclean."

Without replying, Jesus gestured to the three disciples leading the way. "Proceed toward the village gate."

They did not travel far before both groups met, facing each other, uncertain of the way around. Then Jesus stepped forward. Walking right up to the men who carried the corpse on their shoulders, he asked, "Who has died?"

"The only son of a widow," one of the men answered.

Jesus then looked around until he saw an older woman, bent over and brokenheartedly sobbing. It was a memory relived in the present, like seeing his own mother as she wept over the body of Joseph, her husband. Her tears touched his heart, and he spoke as the Holy Spirit directed, "Don't cry, dear woman."

Jesus turned back and faced the men who were still making slow progress through the crowd. He could see the Holy Spirit hovering above the dead body, beckoning him to approach and speak recreative words of life. Those words burned in his heart. He had to say them. He could not wait another moment.

Eagerly, Jesus pressed forward until he reached up and touched the coffin.

A horrified gasp rolled through the onlookers. People whispered, "Unclean!" But Jesus ignored everyone. He pointed to the ground, and the bearers laid their sad burden down in the middle of the road.

Curiosity seemed to overtake everyone. The mourners stopped their wailing, and every eye became fixed on the man who could not be intimidated by Death. They watched as Jesus knelt beside the bier. Gently, he removed the small square cloth that covered the face of a handsome young man.

Another audible gasp rolled through the crowd. Someone exclaimed, "He is touching the body!"

Unmoved by the comments that flew around him, Jesus continued to kneel by the bier, looking tenderly into the expressionless young face. After a long moment, he stood up. His eyes moved past the bearers, past his disciples, past the curious who had been following him. On the dirt road, he could see the spirit of Early Death waiting for the funeral procession to continue. Jesus looked hard at this evil agent. Then at the top of his voice, he announced, "Not today! There will not be a burial today!"

Early Death. shivered and then slunk away.

Jesus turned back to the lifeless body. In a commanding voice, he said, "Young man, get up!"

At first, the young man's eyelids barely fluttered. Then, they opened. He took a few shuddering breaths. Then he sat up and began to speak. Jesus put one arm around the man's shoulders, and with his other arm, he arranged the burial shroud so the man would not appear exposed.

Peter and Andrew raced forward, sweeping the widow off her feet and literally carrying her to her son. Joyfully, Jesus returned the son to his mother.

At the entrance to the village of Nain, excitement erupted. "Praise God! He has come to help us!" the people shouted. Others exclaimed, "A prophet is among us."

In the village of Nazareth, James and Simon pulled and pushed their two-man saw back and forth through the length of a hardwood log while their youngest brother, Jude, steadied the unwieldy piece of timber. Suddenly, the door to the carpentry shop flew open. Work immediately came to a halt as all three brothers looked up to see Chebar and Lemuel standing in the doorway.

"Have you heard about your brother, Jesus?" Chebar abruptly asked.

Before anyone could respond, Lemuel added, "He was in Jerusalem for the Feast of Weeks. The Temple. authorities are very concerned. They are asking questions about Jesus and about Nazareth!"

James straightened up from his work and leveled a no-nonsense gaze at both men. "Look around this shop. Do you see Jesus here?" James paused and then he added, "Since you don't see him sweating with the three of us, you can be sure he has nothing to do with us."

At that moment, the heavy wooden door that separated the carpentry shop from the living quarters opened, and Mary stepped into the shop. She looked quickly from face to face, easily reading each hostile or annoyed expression. "What is the problem?" With her sharp tone and her steady gaze, Joseph's widow demanded a clear response.

"It's your son, Jesus!" Chebar was quick to answer.

"Jesus is in Capernaum," Mary responded. "What business does he have with you or with Nazareth?"

"During this last feast, more than two thousand people gathered on the Mount of Olives to hear him teach," Lemuel asserted. "The captain of the Temple. guard reported the incident to the Romans."

Jude interrupted, "How did the Romans respond?"

"They did nothing, but I was called before the Sanhedrin and questioned," Chebar added.

Simon asked, "Why don't they just go listen to his teaching?"

"They are listening to his teaching," Lemuel responded. "Men from the Temple. are following him and questioning every word he speaks."

"This is the second time the officers of the Temple. have questioned me," Chebar complained. "During the Feast of Esther, I was standing before Caiaphas. Again, before I left Jerusalem after the Feast of Weeks, I was called to answer questions directly from the high priest. He wants to know about Jesus of Nazareth!"

Mary left the doorway and took a confrontational stance in front of the president of Nazareth's synagogue. "And what did you tell him?"

Chebar took a few steps back from the angry little woman who had three strapping sons to back her up. Then with a less aggressive tone, he said, "I told them that Jesus was a troublemaker."

James picked up a rag and wiped the sweat from his face and neck, and then with a disgusted toss, he threw the rag onto the workbench. "Can't this family just work and live without the problems Jesus brings into our lives? He is more than two days' journey from this place, and it is like he is here."

Taking a fatherly tone, Lemuel approached Mary. "I've seen good men on Roman crosses. All they did was gather a small crowd and quote the scriptures."

"And innocent people died with them," Chebar added, "people who were only associated by a name."

Mary was ready to defend her son. The words were on the tip of her tongue, but a memory held her back. She remembered the words of Simeon, the old man at the Temple., who had held baby Jesus in his arms. "*This child is destined to cause the falling and rising of many in Israel, and to be a sign that will be spoken against, so that the thoughts of many hearts will be revealed. And a sword will pierce your own soul too.*"[1]

Was it his destiny to cause the kind of problems that cost men their lives? Mary remembered the babies that had died in Bethlehem. Her own hands begin to tremble, so she quickly clasped them together and pulled them under the folds of her robe. With a determined glint in her eye, she approached the president of the synagogue. "My sons and I will go to Capernaum. We will find out the truth regarding your accusations."

"We will deal with Jesus," James growled. Then under his breath he added, "As best we can."

"Shalom!" Mary, along with her three sons James, Simon, and Jude stood at the gate of her sister's home in Capernaum. "Shalom!" they called again, but no one answered in the home of Zebedee and Salome.

Jude began to look around. He wandered away from his uncle's home near the sea only to come running back exclaiming, "The whole town has gathered at an estate, not far from here! The street is filled with people. Men have climbed on the walls. So many are sitting on top of the compound walls, I believe they could collapse!"

"Let's go see!" Simon urged.

"Yes," James responded. "I believe we may find our brother at the center of that crowd." He sighed and shook his head as he said, "Mother, Chebar and Lemuel were not making up stories about Jesus. Somehow, he always managed to be the focus of attention while he was growing up, but now, he has gone too far."

As Mary and her sons approached the elaborate home, James asked a man on the street, "Whose home is this?"

"This estate belongs to Matthew the tax collector."

"Tax collector?" James repeated with a hint of disdain.

"Well, he's not a tax collector any more. He has become a disciple of Rabbi Jesus."

"Rabbi Jesus?" James repeated. "Jesus has disciples?"

"Oh, yes!"

Mary and her other sons joined the conversation.

James asked, "Where is this Rabbi Jesus from? Is he from Jerusalem?"

"Oh no," the man answered. "He is one of us. His family lives in Nazareth."

"Let me guess," James continued incredulously. "He used to practice the trade of carpentry."

"That's right!" the man exclaimed. "You must know him!"

"I am his brother." James gestured toward Mary. "His mother has also come. Could you get a message to him? Tell him that his mother and brothers have come to see him."

Inside the house, the table filled with uneaten food had been pushed back against a far wall. Pharisees from the region as well as scholars from the Temple. were crowded into one corner of the courtyard. They were dissecting every word and gesture. The disciples filled the area directly in front of Jesus. They controlled the press of the crowd, allowing only one person at a time to come forward for a healing touch.

Andrew led a demon-possessed man to Jesus. The man was both blind and mute. Word passed from person to person, "They have brought a deaf-mute to Jesus."

Mary and his brothers heard this and James remarked, "What is my brother going to do with such a man?"

"Heal him!" A bystander excitedly supplied the answer.

"Heal him?" the brothers echoed, but Mary remained silent, full of memories and wonder.

Suddenly, an amazed roar, like a swelling cheer, started within the house and rolled through the crowd.

"He hears! He speaks!" All the people were excited and said, "Could this Jesus be the One we have been waiting for?

When James heard what the people were saying, he said to his mother, "This is dangerous talk. This is the reason Chebar was so upset. We need to get Jesus and bring him home where we can control him."

Simon interrupted his older brother, "You cannot control Jesus."

"We'll see." James began forcing a path through the crowd. "Make way! Jesus's mother and brothers have come to see him." Together, they moved through the gate, managing to get close enough to hear but not close enough to see and speak to Jesus.

"It is only by the power of the Evil One that this healer drives out demons." Yonaton, the leading scholar for the region of Galilee made the damning proclamation.

It was easy for Mary to hear the other Pharisees and scholars as they concurred, congratulating each other on their superior analysis of the amazing event.

"Such a horrifying accusation!" Mary gasped.

James also heard and he turned decisively to his brothers. "We must take Jesus home with us and keep him there. He has been declared insane!"

Jesus quickly responded to his main accuser, "Yonaton, if Satan casts out Satan, he is fighting against himself. How can he be victorious? And if I use evil incantations to cast out demons, how do the religious leaders in the Temple cast them out? Let me clarify for you and those you will report to. I drive out demons by the Spirit of God so you will know that the Kingdom of God is now among you."

"What does he mean?" Speculations like the bees in a disturbed nest flew from one mouth to the other.

Jesus confronted Yonaton and his fellow Pharisees again. "Why are you so confused?" he asked. Don't you know that every plant is identified by its fruit?" Pointing his finger firmly in their faces, he loudly declared, "You nest of poisonous snakes, how can you judge between good and evil?"

"Jesus?" John made his way close to Jesus. "Your mother and brothers are waiting outside. They want to speak to you."

Immediately by the Spirit, Jesus knew the thoughts of the family members who had come from Nazareth. Jesus replied to him, "My mother? My brothers?" Pointing to his disciples, he said, "You are my family. Whoever hears and obeys the one sent from above is a member of the family of God."

"That does it!" James exclaimed. "We're going back to Nazareth! If the Temple. authorities stone him, they stone him.

If the Romans arrest him, then he will die like a traitor. I am through with my brother!"

"You go," Mary agreed. "All three of you go back to the carpentry shop. But I will stay." Mary pointed across the courtyard. "Salome and Zebedee are here. They do not seem disturbed by the things Jesus is saying and doing. I will hear the complete story from them, and I will speak to Jesus myself."

Soon after this event, Jesus began another teaching trip in the region of Galilee. The twelve disciples, along with some women of means, traveled with him. Walking from village to village, they helped with the crowds, provided and cooked the food, and shared their personal testimonies of healing and deliverance, so the good news of the Kingdom of God advanced.

Mary, the mother of Jesus, traveled with the women, hearing their stories and helping to prepare food for the men. In every town, she listened to her son teach, and she watched as sad and broken people instantly became joyous and healthy.

Finally, the mystery of this special son was coming together in Mary's mind. And one night around the fire, she began to talk with the other women. "I was only fourteen and betrothed to Joseph the carpenter. An angel visited me. He said that I would have a son…," she started.

The men overhead snatches of the story, and they moved closer.

"'How will this be,' I *asked the angel, 'since I am a virgin?'"*

"How could it be?" the ladies chorused in amazement.

"The angel said, *'The Holy Spirit will come upon you, and the power of the Most High will overshadow you. So the holy one to be born will be called the Son of God.'"*[2] .

"What? How?" The women were wide-eyed and stumbling to ask, but not to ask improperly.

"The glory of God filled me," Mary stated. Her face glowed with the memory. "Joseph and I did not come together as husband

and wife until after Jesus was born. Joseph knew Jesus was not his son."

Mary from Magdela asked, "But wouldn't Joseph suspect another man was the father?"

"Oh, he did suspect that for several months." Mary slowly shook her head as she remembered the stress of those days. "He was planning to divorce me, but an angel came to him in a dream. Then Joseph knew I was telling the truth."

"Jesus is the son of God because the Holy Spirit is his Father, and he is the son of man because you are his mother," Susanna stated as she looked at Mary for confirmation.

"Yes." There was a little mystery in Mary's smile. There were precious memories she was not yet ready to share. For tonight, she had told enough of the story.

Chapter 13

John's Disciples Come to Jesus

I tell you the truth: Among those born of women there has not risen anyone greater than John the Baptist.

—Matthew 11:11

In the dark, dry dungeon of the fortress-palace called Machaerus, John the Nazirite prophet, sat on the hard stone floor of his cramped cell. In the corner, a pile of straw was his bed. He only had the proper nourishment because his few remaining disciples saw to it. They made sure he received the food that would allow him to be faithful to his lifelong vow.

Sunlight suddenly streamed into the dark cell. John covered his eyes, blocking the intense glare until the outside door was shut again. Then he looked up to see two of his disciples. Geber, his oldest and most faithful friend, embraced him. The other man placed a basket of food in the storage box that prevented the rodent population of the prison from devouring it.

"How long have I been locked up in this prison?" John asked.

"More than a year," Geber replied.

"I did not think it would be so long." John walked slowly over to a jar that held water. He took a drink. "Have you seen Jesus? What is he doing?"

John turned back to his disciples and waited for an answer.

Geber responded, "He teaches, mostly in the area of Capernaum. We have heard he heals the sick and casts out demons."

The other disciple added, "His disciples baptize people for the forgiveness of sins, just like you taught us." His voice trailed off and the three men stood in awkward silence.

"Has he been to Jerusalem?" John asked.

"For the feasts," Geber answered.

"And he has caused a commotion each time," the other disciple added.

John tugged thoughtfully at his knee-length beard, contemplating every word he had ever heard from the Holy Spirit regarding the Messiah. Obviously puzzled, he said, "I know the Holy Spirit told me that Jesus is the Messiah. I saw the dove. I heard the voice. I gave him my blessing as he moved on to begin his own ministry. I thought—"

Geber finished his sentence. "He would confront the Temple. authorities. Maybe he would even somehow gather an army and run the Romans out of this land."

"I have to know what he is doing," John emphatically stated. "I sit alone in the darkness of this dungeon for most of every day, and I begin to wonder, to question."

"The Evil One is testing you," Geber responded. "He is the one putting doubts in your mind, but"—Geber gestured toward his companion disciple—"we will go and find Jesus. We will see what he is doing, and we will bring you back a complete report."

"I want to know everything." John could hear the guard approaching. "I also want to know what the Holy Spirit is doing. I want to be sure Jesus is following his directions."

The guard stood at the door. Once more, the brilliant desert sun was streaming into the gloomy prison cell. Geber and John embraced. John shielded his eyes by burying his face in his friend's shoulder. Urgently, he whispered, "If Jesus is following the directions of the Holy Spirit, if his life is a fulfillment of the scriptures, then I can be at peace in this place. Herod is a fool who thinks he is holding the God of the universe prisoner just because he keeps me in a cell."

"I'll return," Geber assured as he broke away. John quickly covered his eyes again. The door to his prison cell closed one more time, and John was alone in the darkness.

Jesus sat on one of the smooth boulders near the summit of the large hill near Capernaum, fondly called "The Mount." He looked out over the crowd that had gathered to hear him teach, to see him heal and cast out demons. He sensed the Holy Spirit was stirring, moving back and forth over the restless people. With spiritually-heightened eyes, Jesus followed the golden waves of holiness.

Suddenly, Jesus noticed that the Spirit had highlighted two men. He looked closely. Those two men were picking their way through the clumps of sitting and standing people, steadily moving toward the place where Jesus and his disciples prepared to minister. Interested, Jesus stood and took a few steps toward the approaching men. He recognized them, old friends from the time he had spent with his cousin, John the Baptist.

As the men neared the boulders, Jesus hurried to meet them. "Geber!" he hugged the older man. "What news have you brought from John?"

"He is still in Herod's dungeon," Geber responded. "It has been a long time. I am afraid he is wondering...," Geber hesitated, and then he said, "Are you the promised One, the Messiah we have been waiting for, or should we expect another man from God?"

"Sit here." Jesus pointed to one of the large rocks. Then he turned to his own disciples, "Andrew, bring some food and water for our friends. See to their needs." Jesus then turned to Andrew's brother. "Peter, begin bringing the sick. Remember, no more than three at a time."

Turning his attention back to the two disciples who had come from John, Jesus took each man by the hand and said, "Today, I want you to recover from your long journey, and I want to put the questions in your mind to rest. Geber"—he focused on the older man—"when I was only a boy, I heard you describe the signs of the Messiah from the prophet Isaiah. Now, you will see and hear with your own eyes and ears those things you taught by faith."

Peter and Philip carried a young man close to Jesus. Grunting and sweating because he was a good-sized man, the two disciples set him on the ground not far from where Jesus was talking with John's disciples.

"Healer!" the man called. "I have not walked for three years."

Jesus turned away from Geber and focused his entire attention on the man. He knelt down and looked deeply into his eyes. "What happened?"

To the crippled man, it seemed he was alone on the mountainside with Jesus. His upper lip quivered and then tears began to fall. He could hardly get his words out. "There was an accident. I was working with the cattle. Somehow, I fell. The animals became frightened, and in the confusion of running hooves, I was trampled. Since that time, I have pulled myself from place to place with my arms, dragging my body behind me."

Compassionately, Jesus examined one of his raw, bleeding elbows. "How far did you drag your body today?" he asked.

"My brother brought me in a wagon," the man answered, "but then there were so many people I had to crawl up this mountain. When your disciples saw me, they hurried to me and carried me the rest of the way."

"They are good men," Jesus responded. "I could not work with such large groups of people if they were not here to assist me." As Jesus talked with the man, he continued to hold his scraped up elbow. Suddenly, the torn skin became like fresh baby skin. Jesus then touched his other elbow and that skin became instantly healthy. "You say a cow trampled your back?" Jesus began to run his hand along the man's spine, feeling each vertebra, then stopping at the place indicated by the Holy Spirit. "Be whole, my son!"

The command sent a slight shudder through the man's body. His back arched. Then suddenly, he sprang to his feet, stomping, leaping, screaming. "I can walk! I can work!"

A couple of disciples grabbed the man's flaying elbows and guided him back down the mountain laughing and rejoicing all the way.

Watching, Jesus rocked back on his heels and laughed until he fell over. His disciple James came over and pulled him to his feet to receive the next person who came for healing.

Joanna and Mary of Magdela brought the next person to Jesus, a woman whose hand and arm were wrapped in strips of linen. The lines on her face, the dark circles under her eyes spoke of painful, sleepless nights and agonizing days.

"It is a burn." Mary's eyes locked with the eyes of the man who had changed her life.

Jesus knew that Mary understood the agony of deeply burned flesh better than anyone nearby. He could see the Holy Spirit was allowing her to feel and connect with this woman.

"Help me with this woman." Jesus was looking directly at Mary, and Mary knew he was talking to her.

At first, Mary shrank back, protesting, "I only came to watch. I just wanted to see what you could do."

"Unwrap her arm." Jesus directed.

Mary looked hard at Jesus to make sure she understood, and then she took the woman's arm in both hands.

Geber and his companion stepped forward for a closer look. Even before the strips of cloth were removed, they knew whatever was beneath was foul-smelling and unclean.

Carefully, Mary began to remove the strips of linen. She worked slowly, but in places, the oozing fluids had dried and the linen stuck. With a little tugging, it would suddenly release, painfully pulling off small chunks of dead skin.

"I'm sorry. I'm sorry," Mary apologized over and over again. Soon, both Mary and the woman were weeping as the terrible burn was exposed.

When the last strip of soiled linen had fallen to the ground there was a collective gasp, followed by whispers. "Maggots."

John's disciples leaned in for another close look. "That arm cannot be saved," Geber stated with awed horror in his voice.

Gently, Jesus took the woman's hand in his. Briefly, he glanced at the disgusting wound where flies had laid eggs and larva feasted on decaying flesh.

But most of his attention was for the woman. He looked into her tear-filled eyes, and in an instant, the Holy Spirit showed him she was the mother of six children. "You were preparing a meal for your family." Jesus spoke with total acceptance and affirmation. "The pot tipped—"

The woman's tears fell like a heavy rain. "I need this hand. My husband cannot manage his business and the home without my help. The doctors want to cut it off."

"Mary?" Jesus beckoned for Mary of Magdela to step closer. Carefully, he placed the woman's hand in Mary's hand. "Because the Holy Spirit has opened your heart to weep for this woman, God will heal through you."

Mary gasped. She could not believe healing could come through her tears and her hands.

"Repeat my words." With his eyes, Jesus encouraged both Mary and the woman. "Because the Father loves you, be healed."

Mary kept her eyes on Jesus. She said each word, using the same inflection and intonation. Then she felt a little shiver run through her own body. She looked down at the woman's hand and arm. New, healthy flesh had displaced the infested wound.

The woman saw it too. Her face lit up. She grabbed Mary, hugging her and screaming, "I'm healed! Look! Look! My arm! My hand! They are new! They are good!"

The two women began to dance in a circle, holding hands and screaming.

Geber stopped them. He reached out and grabbed the woman's arm, examining it, turning it and feeling the flesh. Amazed, he released her arm.

The women fell back into their joyous dance. And Jesus looked Geber squarely in the eyes. "Stay all day. Then return to John and tell him everything."

"Healer! Healer!" A frantic voice interrupted their conversation. A woman, dragging a violently cursing boy, struggled to get to Jesus. "My son is possessed. No one can help him!"

"Peter! Philip!" Jesus called for two of his burly fishermen-disciples to take hold of the boy and bring him forward.

Wrestling that boy like a sail in a storm, they carried him to Jesus. Then they dropped him at Jesus's feet, like a sack of dried sardines. The fishermen remained on either side of the boy, ready to pounce if he should decide to run. They glared down at the disobedient child, and the evil spirit within the child glared back.

For a long moment, Jesus studied the defiant boy. He could see the evil that lived within. It stared back at him through unnaturally black eyes. Then Jesus spoke, "I know you. Your name is Rebellion, and I command you to leave this boy!"

Instantly, the boy collapsed. His mother rushed forward, but Jesus held her back with an upraised hand. It wasn't long before the boy sat up on his own. Then Jesus sternly said, "Come and stand before me."

The boy, now in his right mind, got to his feet and stood respectfully before Jesus.

Once again, Jesus looked deeply into his eyes. They had changed from bottomless black to light brown. Then Jesus said, "Young man, you invited that demon into your mind by resisting the authority of your mother. This day, I am telling you to *honor… your mother, so that you may live long in the land the* L*ORD your God is giving you.*[1] If you resist her authority, if you disobey her in your heart or by your actions, the demon called Rebellion will be allowed to return, and he will destroy your life."

Jesus motioned for his disciples to bring the mother forward.

She stood beside her son. "Woman, the Spirit of God has shown me you do not have a husband. I will counsel you to find a trusted relative and allow him to enforce your authority in directing your son's life. *Folly is bound up in the heart of a child, but the rod of discipline will drive it far from him.*"[2]

Then Jesus reached out and placed one hand on the head of the child and one hand on the head of the mother, and he prayed, "*The Lord bless you and keep you; the Lord make his face shine upon you and be gracious to you; the Lord turn his face toward you and give you peace.*"[3]

Both the boy and his mother began weeping. They fell into each other's arms, and the disciples led them away while they wept and hugged.

After that, the crowd surged forward, everyone eager for a healing touch. It took all the strength of his hardworking, well-muscled disciples to control the people so they could bring the most needy to their master a few at a time. The women who followed Jesus went into the crowd, and they brought the women and children forward. The disciples who were not busy holding the people back, brought men forward to be healed.

Even Judas went back and forth, finding those men who were blind, lame, and hopeless. But Judas had an eye for the money bag he carried, and he chose those who were well dressed. After their healing he would say, "Wouldn't you like to give a contribution to the healer?" That way, the bag that hung on his belt became heavy and filled with coins.

Throughout the day, Jesus healed many diseases. He gave sight to the blind and commanded demons to leave. Then as the sun was beginning to set, Jesus turned to Geber and the man who was with him. "My friends, it is time to return to John. Tell him everything you have seen and heard. The blind see. The lame stand and leap for joy. Lepers are cured. Deaf men hear and even the dead return to life. This is the good news. The Kingdom of God is now on Earth! Remind John, 'Do not give up hope.' He can be certain that I am doing the work of my Father."

As John's messengers made their way back to the desert fortress, Jesus began to speak to the crowd. "Why did you go to the springs in the desert? Were you looking for a weak man dressed in fine clothing and living in luxury? No, those who live indulgent lives are in palaces that sit on mountain fortresses. So, why did you flock to the oasis near the Jordan? Were you looking for a prophet? Yes, John is a prophet and much more. In the scriptures, it is written about him. '*I will send my messenger ahead of you, who will prepare your way before you.*'[4] Believe me, there has never been a prophet greater than John. Yet, now that the Kingdom of God is on Earth, each citizen has more authority over the Evil One than John was able to exercise."

Chapter 14

Feast of Trumpets

Come to me, all you who are weary and burdened, and I will give you rest.

—Matthew 11:28

The sky was full of stars, but the moon was in its darkest phase. On a hillside in Capernaum, Jesus sat with his closest followers, the twelve he had chosen. All of the men were silent, studying the night sky, each man hoping to be the first to see the tiny sliver of the new moon. It was Jesus who broke the silence. In a clear baritone, he sang. "*The heavens declare the glory of God; the skies proclaim the work of his hands.*"[1] The disciples joined in.

The fear of the Lord is pure, enduring forever.
The ordinances of the Lord are sure and altogether righteous.
By them is your servant warned;
in keeping them there is great reward.[2]

When the song had ended, Jesus announced, "We will see the new moon tomorrow night while we are walking toward Jerusalem, and we will hear the trumpets of the New Year before we see the city gates." Jesus turned to Peter, "Don't you have relatives who live in Jerusalem?"

Peter responded, "My sister, Miriam, married a merchant. She has a home with a large upper room. She and her husband have always welcomed me."

Jesus nodded, "Then we will stay in her home until it is time to build booths and sleep under the canopy of heaven."

In the storage room behind her husband's perfume shop, Mary, the wife of Jonathan, studied the beautifully carved stone vials that filled one of the shelves. She selected one. It was smooth and oval, carved from translucent alabaster. Rubbing her fingertips over the golden swirls running through the polished stone, she brought it to her husband. "I want your most fragrant ointment put in this container. It is for my childhood friend, Rea."

"Such an expensive gift?" Jonathan questioned. "Is this for Rea, once known as the prostitute of Bethany?"

Incensed, Mary retorted, "Rea has always been a perfectly respectable woman! We have been friends since childhood." Mary took a step back so she could look her husband squarely in the eyes. "I know what happened to Rea. She married when she was thirteen, and the man she married shared her against her will with some of his friends. Then everyone in the town talked. I know how the people of Bethany can talk!"

Jonathan did a little remembering nod with his head, and then he concurred, "My brother Simon told me about her. I believe he may have been one of the men who slept with Rea."

Mary interrupted, "Remember, Rea was not married to her first husband for very long. He suddenly became ill, and he died."

"It was the judgment of God," Jonathan confirmed. "After his death, some of the men, including my brother, became a lot more careful about observing all the laws."

Mary continued, "Then Rea's husband's younger brother, who lived and worked on your brother's estate, took Rea into his home, and she became his wife. Together, they had a son. Her new husband treated her well, and he protected her from the life she had had in her former marriage."

"I have worked with her husband," Jonathan said. "He is a good man, a hard worker. He is very Torah observant."

"But the people of Bethany never forget their gossip," Mary emphatically stated. "They always whisper."

Jonathan thoughtfully agreed.

"I know all about Rea," Mary continued. "For many years, I was her only friend, and she was my only friend. If anyone is at all different, the women of Bethany shut them out. I have experienced it."

"So why the expensive gift?" Jonathan stepped close to his wife and reached for her hand.

As Mary felt her husband's touch and sensed that he was open to understand, she softened. "Martha sent word that Rea's husband was killed in an accident on your brother's estate. Her son was also badly injured." Mary pressed the empty container into her husband's hands. "Fill it with the most precious ointment in the shop. I want her to know I care deeply about what has happened to her. She has no one else who will care. We are traveling back to Bethany after the Days of Awe. We will not open this shop again until the Feast of Booths has ended. Let me take this gift to Rea."

Jonathan nodded. His eyes locked with the eyes of his wife and love flooded his entire being. He could never say no to Mary. He turned away to get the ointment, then he paused and turned back with a playful, yet serious warning. "Do not tell my brother Simon that I allow you to give away all our profits."

Mary agreed, "It's our secret. I do not want to hear another lecture on the value of merchandise."

By the light of a blazing bonfire, Rea strained fresh grape juice from the stomping trough through a loosely woven cloth into one of many jars. Her back ached and her arms were weary from days of hurriedly bringing in the grape harvest on the estate of Simon, the wine producer of Bethany. She turned to pick up a fresh straining cloth and sensed that someone was standing very close behind her. She smelled his perfumed body and felt his warm breath on the back of her neck.

"Rea?"

She heard her name, and she felt the bile rise in her throat.

Forcing a detached tone, Rea responded, "Simon, the harvest is going well. I have filled many jars, and your servants are sealing them efficiently. We will be finished before dawn."

Simon coldly stated, "Your husband's death was unfortunate."

Rea choked back a small sob but continued working.

Simon moved closer. His body was almost pressing against her back. "I've hired a new foreman. He and his family need a home."

Rea's hands stopped moving. A pregnant silence hung in the night air. Then Rea side-stepped and turned to give herself some distance as she faced her husband's employer. "I am working for the right to stay in my home. My son is still recovering from his injuries. He cannot be moved."

"There is a way you can stay in your home." Simon placed his hands on her shoulders.

Rea could feel his eyes traveling over the curves of her body. Both anger and helplessness rose within her—how dare this man take advantage of her circumstances? Yet, how could she defend herself? How could she protect her son?

"I have laid a pallet in the cave where I store my fresh wine. I will be sleeping there tonight. Come to me when you have finished straining the juice." Simon squeezed her shoulders possessively. "Come, and you will never have to be concerned about your home again."

Rea shivered as she held her emotions in check. She wanted to scratch Simon's face, to pull out his beard, to stomp on his manhood! Her husband had been dead less than a month and this man impudently touched her, requested her services, and then threatened her!

"This is not a good night," Rea answered with iron resolve.

"Tomorrow night?" Simon urged. Then he added, "I will personally guard my new wine through the night until the Feast of Booths has come to an end."

Rea picked up a new straining cloth and went back to work. Without turning her head, she spoke with a forced, even tone, "I have no response for you at this time."

Simon turned to leave, and then he paused and added, "I have put my new foreman and his family in a small inadequate structure. I will have to provide them with a better dwelling soon."

Longinus heard the pounding on the door of his barracks quarters. He opened his eyes. The room was dark. Looking out the window, he could see the sun had not yet risen. The pounding continued as the commander of the Antonia Fortress hurried from his bed to determine how this emergency must be dealt with.

A sentry from the gate stood in the corridor.

"What has happened?" Longinus tersely demanded.

"The Temple authorities are at the gate," the sentry replied. "They say the new moon has been sighted, and they must have both sets of garments for their High Priest immediately."

"You woke me because the fanatics of the Temple want the priestly garments in the middle of the night?" Longinus glared at the messenger from the gate.

"During this season, they usually receive the garments for their high priest as soon as a sighting of the new moon is verified. That is always at night." The sentry shifted his weight, obviously uncomfortable with being the messenger who disturbed the commander.

"Give it to them," Longinus growled. "Give it to them item by item. I want a written description of each piece, and each piece is to be signed for. That signature is to be witnessed, and make sure the process takes all night! I'm going back to sleep."

Trumpet blasts suddenly sliced through the silence of the late hour. "What are those people doing?" Longinus rushed to the window that looked down into the Temple courts. Torches were blazing. Trumpets and shofars were blasting both staccato and sustained notes. Horses with riders were galloping toward the city gates, and on the Mount of Olives, torches were lit and waved toward a distant hill where other torches were lit and waved to a hill beyond.

Longinius turned back to the sentry. "Are the Jews going to war?"

"It is the beginning of their Fall Feasts," the sentry respectfully answered. "The first feast is called Trumpets."

The adrenalin that had rushed through his body as he had reacted to the possibility of an uprising, slowly waned and Longinus lowered himself wearily to sit on the edge of his bed. "Yes, now I remember. We had the same disturbance last year. In all of the empire, there is not a people as disruptive and stubborn as these Jews! The demands they make on the government of Rome are insane!"

Longinus heard footsteps in the corridor. He heard sentries snapping to attention. Then Pilate stuck his head in the open door. For an exaggerated moment, both men just looked at each other. They had no words to describe how the ongoing trumpet and shofar blasts irritated every nerve in each of their bodies.

Finally, Pilate said, "My wife usually warns me. She tells me what to expect as we travel from our palace in Caesarea to oversee each major feast in Jerusalem. Evidently, she forgot to mention this feast would begin in the middle of the night!"

More pounding. This time, Gamaliel and Nicodemus were beating on the gate of the walled compound that was the home of Caiaphas, the high priest.

The gate opened quickly. Caiaphas, with his father-in-law Annas, stood ready to leave. They had been expecting these leaders from the Sanhedrin. Both men were prepared to be escorted back to the Temple for ten days of intense instruction, preparation for the most serious duties of the priesthood.

"Mighty blast!" Peter shouted.

Thomas, Andrew, and Philip simultaneously took deep breaths and blew on their ram's horns. Andrew's blast continued after the other two ran out of air.

The rest of the disciples laughed and proclaimed Andrew, the disciple, gifted by God with the greatest volume of wind.

Walking south toward Jerusalem, it was obvious the season of the shofar was upon them. In every village and among the travelers on the road, there were shofars in hand and intermittent blasts were heard throughout each day.

Jesus did not miss this opportunity to teach. "On the sixth day of creation, the Creator knelt in the dirt of Earth, and from its minerals, he made Adam. It was detailed and precise labor. The Creator did not stop until a perfect man lay on the ground."

Jesus stopped talking as the Holy Spirit pulled back the veil and opened to Jesus the memory of Yeshua the Creator. Jesus then continued speaking from his heavenly memory. "Adam was beautiful, a magnificent muscular man, but he was lifeless, like a fallen statue. The Holy Spirit hovered over his body, blessing and warming the flesh that had been made from clay. Then I reached down and took the man in my arms."

The disciples looked at one another quizzically because the familiar story was now being told in such a personal manner as if Jesus himself had participated in the event. As Jesus continued, he had their full attention.

"I pressed my lips against the lips of the first man and blew like Andrew blew into the shofar. I filled his lungs with holy air.

I blew the essence of God into humanity. Every man alive, no matter how wicked, still has some of the essence of God within his being." Jesus paused. A little remembering smile played across his lips. "Adam came alive in my arms. At that moment, I held all of humanity close to my heart."

Jesus stopped talking, and until the men saw the walls of the city of Jerusalem, everyone in their party remained silent and contemplative.

"No!" Rea quickly ducked out of Simon's uninvited embrace. "I am still mourning my husband. Please, have some respect."

"Your husband has no brother to care for you and help you produce an heir, so I can provide this service for you," Simon confidently stated.

"I have a son. I do not need another heir," Rea answered.

"I have heard the physicians' reports," Simon replied. "Your son will never work again. The best you can hope for is that he will be a beggar."

"You cannot say that!" Rea screamed. "My son has not had time to heal."

"Face the facts, woman." Simon was cold. "The wagon rolled over. Your husband's neck was broken, and your son's hips were crushed. It would have been better for your son if he had died also. The one kindness I have to offer you is based on the fact that you are not too old to have another son."

Memories, like demons from the pit, rose up in Rea's mind. Angrily, she pushed them back into their place as she hotly responded, "This is not an offer of kindness; it is just a way to satisfy your own lust!" As the words left her mouth, Rea broke into a run. She ran and she ran until she had left the estate of Simon, the wine producer, and had come to the estate of Lazarus, the elder brother of her childhood friend, Mary.

Oh, how she longed to talk to Mary. Mary was not like the other women, so wrapped up in the traditions of their people that they could not think for themselves. Rea came to the gate ,and she breathlessly called, “Shalom!” It seemed ridiculous to stand here. Mary was in Jerusalem with her husband and Martha. Rea shook her head when she thought about how Martha would react. Martha would tell her to be grateful for Simon’s offer!

A servant opened the gate. Rea stumbled for her words. Then she finally said, “I want to see Mary.”

The servant answered, “We expect Mary and her husband to visit soon. They are planning to spend the fall holidays here.”

Hope rose in Rea’s heart. “Tell her I came. Tell her I need to speak with her.” Rea turned away and began the slow walk back to her home on Simon’s estate.

It was a crisp morning. Just before dawn, Jesus and his disciples were washing in the purification pool in the home that belonged to Peter’s family. John Mark, the boy of the home, stood at the edge of the pool curiously watching the men. Peter came up from ducking beneath the water and said to the boy, “Take off your clothes and come wash.”

John Mark responded, “I was waiting. I didn’t want to be in your way.”

Jesus, who was pulling his tunic over his head said, “Wash quickly, then join us for morning prayers.”

John Mark immediately pulled off his tunic and ran down the stone steps. He threw his body into the water with a splash that soaked the side of Jesus’s robe and brought laughter, like sunshine, into the cold courtyard.

John Mark’s father met the boy as he came out of the pool. His face was silently reprimanding, but Jesus lightly brushed the incident aside as he called all the males together to remember the special relationship they enjoyed with God as a nation and as men created in the image of God.

"We are in the Days of Awe," Jesus said. "The trumpets have sounded a warning. The books of heaven are about to be opened and on the Day of Atonement, judgment will take place. *Hear, O Israel, and be careful to obey so that it may go well with you and that you may increase greatly in a land flowing with milk and honey, just as the Lord, the God of your fathers, promised you.*"[3]

Jesus paused and picked up his fringed prayer shawl. He closed his eyes and kissed the fabric, then the fringes. Holding the plain fringed cloth toward heaven, Jesus led the men as they said, "Blessed are you O, Lord, Creator of the Universe, who wraps our lives in the laws from heaven and allows us to wear these fringes to remind us to always remember your regulations for our lives." With one smooth movement, Jesus laid the cloth across his own shoulders. His disciples, along with the man of the house, repeated his movements.

Jesus could feel the eyes of the boy, John Mark. He knew the young man was studying every part of the morning ritual. Turning to the boy's father, Jesus asked, "Has your son received his own prayer shawl and tefillin?"

"We have prepared a set for him," the man answered, "but we have not had the opportunity to present it to him in the presence of a rabbi."

"Bring the prayer shawl with the tefillin," Jesus directed. Peter's brother-in-law hurried off to get the special piece of fabric and the small leather boxes that symbolized man living under the covering of the laws of God.

When the boy's father returned, Jesus called John Mark to stand in front of him. He showed the boy how to kiss the fabric and the fringes. Then he laid the fabric across the boy's shoulders. Squatting to John Mark's eye level and pulling the cloth so that it hugged the boy's neck, Jesus quoted from the proverbs of Solomon, "*My son, do not forget my teaching, but keep my commands in your heart for they will prolong your life many years and bring you prosperity. Let love and faithfulness never leave you; bind them around your neck, write them on the tablet of your heart.*"[4]

Next, each man took his own small set of leather boxes and straps from a cloth bag that hung from each belt. Jesus put his on first, securing one box over his left bicep and then wrapping his arm seven times with its leather strap. The second box, he tied to his forehead. He quickly finished his left arm by wrapping the ends of the straps around his hand and fingers.

"You do that very fast," John Mark commented with obvious amazement.

Jesus smiled as he replied, "I have done it every weekday morning since I was your age. My father showed me how to lay the boxes and straps, just as your father will now show you."

As Peter's brother-in-law adjusted the boxes that contained miniature copies of the ten commandments and other admonitions from the mouth of God for Israel, Jesus and his disciples began to sway and chant, "*Hear, O Israel: The LORD our God, the LORD is one. Love the LORD your God with all your heart and with all your soul and with all your strength.*"[5]

John Mark and his father joined in, "*These commandments that I give you today are to be upon your hearts. Impress them on your children. Talk about them when you sit at home and when you walk along the road, when you lie down and when you get up. Tie them as symbols on your hands and bind them on your foreheads. Write them on the doorframes of your houses and on your gates.*"[6]

Above all the men, the voice of Jesus rang out, "*Fear the LORD your God, serve him only and take your oaths in his name. Do not follow other gods, the gods of the peoples around you; for the LORD your God, who is among you, is a jealous God and his anger will burn against you, and he will destroy you from the face of the land.*[7] *Be sure to keep the commands of the LORD your God and the stipulations and decrees he has given you. Do what is right and good in the LORD's sight, so that it may go well with you.*"[8]

The sun had fully risen, and the traditional prayers ended. The men began to respectfully remove the leather straps and boxes. Jesus helped John Mark with his, and then he pulled the boy close to him. Placing his hands on the boy's head, Jesus said, "*Blessed are they whose ways are blameless, who walk according to the law of the* Lord. *Blessed are they who keep his statutes and seek him with all their heart. They do nothing wrong; they walk in his ways.*"[9] Jesus then took both of John Mark's hands in his own. "These are the hands of a scribe."

The disciples sensed the prophetic power of the words Jesus was speaking. They stopped to listen. "The Holy Spirit is waiting to dictate to you, and you will write his words."

John Mark bowed his head under the weight of the words that Jesus was speaking over him. "Take your preparations seriously," Jesus admonished. "Work diligently to learn the skills of a scribe."

Speechless and wide-eyed, John Mark could only nod his acceptance of the word.

Turning to the men who were standing around in the courtyard, Jesus said, "In two days, it will be the Day of Atonement. I am going out to the wilderness, to the Cliff of the Azazel. Who would like to go with me?"

Judas spoke first. "It is a hard day without food or water. To be in the desert would only increase the discomfort. I will stay in the city."

Among the twelve, most were nodding affirmatively, agreeing with Judas. But Peter spoke up, "I will go with you."

James and his brother John also quickly offered to walk a full day into the desert.

John Mark then asked, "May I go?"

Peter was quick to respond, "This will be your first day to fully participate in the fast—no water, no food. You should not make it worse by sitting in the desert sun."

"This is not my first time," John Mark protested. "I did the complete fast last year. Let me come with you. I am not a whiney baby."

Jesus intervened, "If your father gives his permission, you are welcome.

Chapter 15

The Day of Atonement

The law is only a shadow of the good things that are coming—not the realities themselves. For this reason it can never, by the same sacrifices repeated endlessly year after year, make perfect those who draw near to worship.

—Hebrews 10:1

Loaded down with poles and branches, water and wineskins, Jesus with Peter, James, John, and John Mark left the city of Jerusalem. They took the road that led into the harsh and rocky Judean Wilderness. Their desert route was marked by men constructing booths at regular intervals. Each time they passed a way station in preparation, the working men waved and shouted the familiar greeting, "May your name be engraved in the Book of Life."

John Mark looked around at the four men he was traveling with. They were all sturdy and confident in this rugged environment. They were comfortable returning the greetings of their countrymen. Everyone seemed to know what this feast was all about except John Mark. After passing the third construction site, John walked up close to his Uncle Peter. "How many more booths will we see on this trip into the desert?"

"There are ten in all," Peter answered. "Each booth is about one Roman mile from the last booth. The scapegoat will be led from booth to booth. At each booth, a new man takes over. We are going out past the tenth booth, to set up our own shelter. We will be about twelve miles from the city."

Jesus added, "I know a spot where we can sink our poles into soft sand and then throw the palm branches across the top so we will have shade. From that place, we will see the scapegoat as it is pushed over the cliff."

John, the youngest of the disciples, spoke up. "I have actually been in the Court of the Israelites during the Day of Atonement. There are many parts to the service, but so many people crowd into the Temple that you cannot really see much of what the high priest and his assistants are doing."

John's older brother James expanded on his brother's comment, "Since very few people want to add more discomfort to this day of fasting, it is easy for anyone willing to spend three days and two nights in the desert to view this unusual Day of Atonement sacrifice."

Jesus turned to John Mark and said, "Your willingness to endure discomfort for the opportunity to see the things of God with your own eyes is a sacrifice that pleases God."

John Mark responded, "My mother didn't want us to experience too much discomfort. She sent food for before and after the fast."

"We do appreciate her kindness," Peter replied while the others heartily agreed.

Longinus and Pilate walked slowly along the top of the wall the Antonia Fortress shared with the Temple. Both men were silent. Their eyes were fixed on the activities below. Coming to a corner tower, they climbed the stone steps together, stopping at a window where they could see the fires on the altar and the steps leading up into the sacred rooms of the Jewish Temple.

Longinus spoke first. "I have been watching all week. The high priest is unusually involved in every aspect of Temple activity.

I wanted to write a report, but I didn't understand what I was seeing so I asked you to come and look for yourself."

Pilate studied the scene below. "Caiaphas has a large group of men with him. I recognize some of them, important Pharisees who have come before me at various times. Who is that man with the purple cloak?"

Longinus thought a moment and then he answered, "I believe that is Joseph of Arimathea, a member of the Sanhedrin. My sources tell me he has business interests with Rome. We spent an evening with him in Herod's palace. He is a wealthy man and a reasonable man with a good reputation in the city."

"I remember him." Pilate considered the information. Then he said, "Invite that man to the fortress to share the noon meal with us. I'm going to ask him to explain this season of feasts and the duties of the high priest. If I am going to successfully govern these people, I have to know what they are doing and, more importantly, why they are doing it."

Longinus agreed, "We can't afford to make any more mistakes. I have heard from Rome. Sejanus, the man who appointed you to this governorship, has been accused of treason and executed. Every appointee is being looked at with suspicion."

Pilate responded, "I used to resent this appointment. I thought I deserved better, a province with greater importance and closer to Rome. Now I am thankful to be in this obscure desert region. Here, I can easily be forgotten."

"The winds of fortune come and go," Longinus commented. "For now, we will make Judea our safe harbor." Longinus saluted Pilate. Then he added, "The winds of fortune will blow on you again. I feel certain your name will not be lost in the obscurity of history."

After walking most of the day, Jesus with John Mark and three of his fishermen-disciples settled in the shade of their simple booth.

Four poles and some twine supported a single layer of palm branches. The men spread their cloaks for a ground covering, and John Mark began to lay out the food for their late afternoon meal. They would not eat or drink again until after sundown of the next day.

Jesus picked up a round piece of flat bread and broke it. He held both pieces toward heaven and began the familiar blessing, "Blessed are you, O Lord, our God, Ruler of the Universe, who brings bread from the earth." John Mark and the disciples said it with him. Then everyone ate the bread, boiled eggs, and sweet figs. They finished the meal, blessing the wine and then passing the wineskin around so each man had a refreshing taste. It was new wine because the harvest had just ended.

Jesus helped John Mark pack the remaining food away, but he paused as he wrapped the remaining loaves of bread in a piece of linen. He began to teach. "Our ancestors left Egypt, and they came to the desert on the other side of the Red Sea. Like the land you see around you, their desert was bleak and harsh. In that deserted place, they received the law, and they were told they could only please God by obeying the law.

While they were in the desert, they also received bread that came down from heaven. That bread represented God's mercy. They gathered it every weekday morning, and miraculously, they did not need to gather it on the Sabbath. Heaven made a way for Israel to meet the requirements of the law.

That is why a jar of manna was placed in the ark next to the law so everyone would know that the bread that comes down from heaven is God's mercy for all who love his laws. Without mercy from heaven, you cannot meet the obligations of the law. Without meeting the obligations of the law, you cannot please God."

The men looked at Jesus. Their mouths were silent, but their eyes shouted confusion. Jesus knew they were puzzled by his teaching. He also knew each man wanted to appear to the others as if he had complete understanding.

Jesus continued, "On this sacred day that is now beginning, we do not eat any bread or drink any water. We stand before God, and his law without mercy from heaven. That is why it is such a solemn day. We are about to be judged. God knows every man's thoughts and deeds. Will any man have his name recorded in the Book of Life? One man, the high priest, goes into the Most Holy Place to stand before God for all the people. He carries the blood of a bull and the blood of a goat."

John, the youngest disciple, interrupted, "In our past, there have been times when the high priest has died before the Lord."

"The man who dares to place blood before God for himself and for all the people must first be sinless," Jesus responded.

"How can that be?" everyone exclaimed. "Surely, Caiaphas is not a sinless man!"

"Aaron and every high priest who has performed the services for this holy day have been symbols of a service that will take place in the holy of holies where God dwells. A sinless high priest will carry his own blood from Earth to heaven. He will enter the Most Holy Place and place that blood on the mercy seat. Then atonement will be made not just for one year but forever for all mankind."

The disciples did not respond because no one was confident that their response would be correct. Jesus said no more, but he knew the men with him were considering every word.

Joseph from the town of Arimathea took a sip of wine. Over the rim of his cup, he studied the faces of the governor of Judea and the commander of the fortress. After a second sip, he matter-of-factly stated, "The most important of all our obligations to our God begins at sundown tonight. I must make preparations very soon, so I will ask directly, "Why have you called me to share this meal with you?"

Pilate answered, "We have been watching the activities in your Temple, and this week, we have observed the high priest has been present and presiding over every function of the Temple."

Longinus asserted, "This is not typical behavior for Caiaphas. An unusual number of men, many from your high court, have accompanied him."

"We want to understand what is happening." Pilate leaned forward. "We want to know what to expect when your holy day begins."

Slightly amazed, Joseph looked at both men. "No representative from Rome has ever inquired."

"We are interested," Pilate urged.

"Well," Joseph answered, "for the past week, the elders of the Sanhedrin have been instructing Caiaphas on the procedures for every sacrifice and priestly duty, because on the Day of Atonement, the high priest performs every priestly function, including some functions that only occur once a year. He must represent the people before God. He must enter the Most Holy part of the sanctuary, once with incense and twice with blood."

Longinus interrupted, "What is in the Most Holy room of the Temple sanctuary?"

Joseph sighed, "In this Temple, there is only a stone slab where the Ark of the Covenant that contains the Law of God should rest."

Pilate then became a little more intense and pressed, "Where is the ark? Do your rabbis know?"

With a shrug of his shoulders, Joseph answered, "It has not been seen since before Nebuchadnezzar destroyed Jerusalem and Solomon's Temple. According to our history, a priest named Jeremiah hid it, along with many of the original Temple furnishings."

"Where?" Longinus asked.

Joseph shrugged again. "Underground, somewhere in the maze of caves and tunnels beneath Mount Moriah. Only God knows and his angels guard that place."

"Will there be unrest in the city tomorrow?" Longinus asked.

"No," Joseph replied with certainty. "The people will gather and fall on their faces before the one true God. They will not eat or drink all day. They will wait for the sign that God has heard their prayers and accepted their sacrifices. They will believe that in heaven their names have been written in the Book of Life for this year."

"What is the sign you are talking about?" Pilate asked.

Joseph answered, "From your tower, you will see a priest attach a piece of crimson wool to the door post of the sanctuary. When it miraculously turns white, atonement has been made for the sins of the people, and as a nation, we can live for one more year under the blessing of God."

"So we should expect a calm day," Longinus emphatically stated as he stood, indicating that the meeting was over.

Joseph also stood, and without further conversation, Longinus escorted him to the gate.

In Bethany, the sun had set. Rea hurriedly slipped into a seat in the women's section of the synagogue. It was time for the opening service that marked the highest holy day on the Jewish calendar. This year, it seemed to Rea that the natural order of Jewish life had been shattered. Her son was unable to attend the service. He was a young man, strong and healthy until…

Rea pulled her mantel over her face and let the tears fall. "God, God, on this day…your day of judgment, remember my son. You can leave my name out of your heavenly Book of Life. Just give his life back to him. Take away his pain and his brokenness. Restore strength and mobility to his legs. Allow him to mature into a man who can work and marry. Above all, do not let him be a cripple who can never enter your Temple or bring an offering before the priest."

The chants began in the section where the men worshiped. Rea looked up through the separating lattice. Most of the men had wrapped themselves in large white sheets of cloth, symbolizing purity and righteousness before the law. She saw Simon in his usual place on the front row of benches. Wearing white from head to toe, he was bowing, swaying, and chanting with the other men. "God, do you see past the white fabric? Do you see into the heart of this man?"

Rea sensed someone had taken the empty seat beside her. She felt an arm around her shoulders. Responding to the encouraging touch, she turned.

"Mary!" Rea whispered her exclamation as she buried her face in her friend's shoulder. The tears flowed. Rea could not hold them back.

Mary wrapped both arms around her friend and rocked her like a child, while in the main part of the building, the men chanted and swayed through the traditional prayers for this service.

When Rea's tears finally ceased, Mary pressed the alabaster vial of expensive perfume into Rea's hands. "This is for you. Keep it, or even sell it if that is your need."

"Oh, Mary!" Rea whispered as she hugged the gift to her breast. "I want to keep it, but I may have to sell it…"

Both women sensed intense disapproval coming from the eyes of the respectable women of the town. Direct, stinging stares signaled that the elder females of Bethany had endured enough disruption from these two young ladies.

Mary turned her head from side to side, boldly making eye contact and returning their intimidating glares. Then she protectively took Rea by the shoulders, guiding her out of the women's area, into the refreshing night air.

The two friends found a bench close to the synagogue. Mary sat Rea down and said, "Tell me, how are you being treated?"

Tears started to flow again as Rea said, "Simon insists he has the right to perform the duties of a kinsman, and if I don't agree to this, he will put both me and my son out of our home."

"What?" Mary gasped. "How does he have the right of the kinsman?"

"My husband has no brothers and no close male relatives. Simon says he has the right because he was my husband's employer," Rea answered.

"I never heard of such a thing!" Mary hotly exclaimed.

"I went to him once," Rea admitted. "It was a secret meeting in the cave where he stores his new wine."

"You didn't?" Mary gasped.

"I had no choice. Simon said he was going to put me out of my home immediately, and I believed him." Rea grabbed Mary's hands. "Please understand. My son's injuries are severe. He cannot be moved until his bones heal. The physicians have told me to keep his body aligned so the bones will grow back together correctly. What else could I do?"

"I always knew Simon was an evil man," Mary stated.

"I feel like I am the evil one. I feel condemnation in the eyes of every person who looks at me," Rea responded. "I know he has told some of the other men on the estate. And they have told their wives. I feel so unclean." Rea lowered her voice and confided, "Simon has a skin condition. It does not look healthy." Rea shuttered. "His skin touched mine. I never want to be near that man again, but he keeps pressuring me. I expect this holy day will be the only reprieve I will get from his threats and advances."

"This is wrong," Mary emphatically stated. "I am going to do something about it!"

"What can you do?" Rea asked. "Your husband is Simon's younger brother. He has no authority over Simon."

Mary leaned close, cautiously revealing information that was only known by Simon's immediate family. "First, I know why Simon is so anxious for you to spend the night with him in the storage cave. His wife will not allow him to touch her body because of the very skin condition you mentioned. He is unclean. My husband has made ointments for him, and he fears Simon may have leprosy. Other family members have thought the same, but each person is remaining silent. Simon has a way of intimidating everyone."

Rea's eyes opened wide in horrified amazement. "He touched me! His unclean flesh was next to my skin! I feel sick." She covered her face with her hands. "After sunset tomorrow, he will still pursue me and threaten me. If my son was not so badly injured, I would just leave. Let him have the house. I don't care."

"I know someone who can help you," Mary stated. "As soon as the Day of Atonement has ended, I will ask my brother, Lazarus, to send a messenger to find Jesus. He is a healer. I know he can heal your son. My brother's bones were crushed, and Jesus touched his body—I saw the miracle."

"When did this happen?" Rea asked.

"Many years ago, when I was becoming of age," Mary answered. "I also want to tell my brother how shamefully Simon is treating you."

"No," Rea protested. "I am already so humiliated. He would tell Martha. You know how proper your sister is. She would consider me a sinful woman."

A thin gray line of light edged the rocky wilderness terrain. John Mark got up and walked a short distance from where the men were sleeping. He relieved himself and then returned to find Jesus sitting up, watching the approaching dawn. Jesus turned his head toward the boy and with one hand, beckoned him to his side.

John Mark sat beside Jesus, and Jesus stretched out one side of his prayer cloth, bringing the boy under the comforting fabric, protectively close to his chest. John sat quietly, receiving the fatherly gesture.

"The Temple gates are just now opening. It takes a whole team of Levites to open each gate." Jesus began telling the boy what the Holy Spirit was showing him. "The sacrifices have been inspected. Each animal is ready. The high priest has washed, and he is now wearing his priestly garments."

"I would like to see that," John Mark wistfully stated.

"The high priest's garments are strikingly beautiful," Jesus agreed. "Aaron, the first high priest, wore them all the time. Crimson, blue, and white with gold and valuable gemstones, those garments were the symbol of his office. But now, the Romans only allow them to be worn on holy days. Before Caiaphas brings the blood into the Most Holy Place, he will remove those beautiful garments, so he for that part of the ceremony, will be wearing only the simple white robes of an ordinary priest."

John Mark nodded as he tried to create a mental picture. Then he continued to listen attentively.

"First, the high priest has to confess his own sins on the head of a bullock," Jesus informed.

Peter, James, and John were now up. They found places to sit close to Jesus and John Mark. Peter commented, "Caiaphas should spend most of the day with his hands on the head of that young bull."

The other two disciples laughed a little as they tried to imagine how long it would take for the current high priest to actually confess each individual sin.

John added, "Caiaphas is more of a political than a spiritual high priest. He has paid a lot of money for that position."

"Even more reason for a long, long confession," Peter restated.

Jesus ignored the sarcasm of his companions. He continued to teach. "Think about it, the sins of a man are placed on sinless flesh. The man who was condemned to die will live, and the animal who never sinned will die in his place."

"After the high priest kills that bull, he takes its blood into the Most Holy Place and sprinkles it in that place where the ark should be," James informed.

"Yes," Jesus agreed. "A time is coming when it will not be the blood of a bull. It will be the blood of a man who, in his flesh, lived a sinless life."

"A man?" James asked.

"The Messiah!" Peter asserted.

"No," John protested. "The Messiah conquers and rules. He doesn't die!"

Jesus did not involve himself in their discussion. He remained silent until John Mark asked, "What about the scapegoat?"

Jesus answered, "About now, the priests are bringing two goats into the Court of the Priests. They are also bringing a small wooden box to Caiaphas. In the box are two pieces of wood overlaid with gold. One bears the words "For the Lord" and the other, "For Azazel."

As Jesus spoke, all the men looked up at the cliff called Azazel.

John continued to describe the ritual. "The high priest puts both hands in the box and pulls out both pieces of wood at the same time. The piece in his right hand is placed on the forehead of the goat that is to his right, and the piece in his left hand is placed on the forehead of the goat on his left."

"So far, throughout history, the goat on the right has always been 'for the Lord,'" Peter stated.

"So far," Jesus restated as if he expected that the phenomena would change in the near future.

"Last year, a friend got me into the entrance of the Court of the Priests. I was standing very close," John related. "I saw Caiaphas kill the goat 'for the Lord" and catch its blood in a golden container. He carried that blood into the Most Holy Place. Everyone fell on their faces, stretched out on the floor stones, waiting, praying, hoping that this sacrifice would be accepted."

"The blood of the goat is for the children of Abraham," Jesus said. "As soon as it comes before God, their sins are forgiven and their names are written in the Book of Life."

"What about the other goat?" Peter asked.

"Forgiveness happens in an instant," Jesus answered. "Every name is recorded in the Book of Life in the blink of an eye. But many sins have long-term effects, emotional and physical. As we walk out our lives, the effects of forgiven sins may walk beside us, like the scapegoat walking beside the man assigned to bring it into the wilderness. On the long trek, the animal loses its strength. Finally, the man and the animal come to a place where the man uses his God-given authority to free himself. He wrestles with that animal and pushes it over the cliff. Then he is completely free."

"So, that is what we have come to the desert to see?" John Mark asked.

"Yes," Jesus answered. "We have come to see what happens beyond applying blood to blot out sins. Every man and woman has a role to play in obtaining freedom. They must take authority over the effects of sin. They must choose to cast away every thought that does not line up with the word of God for their lives. When Moses led the Israelites through the Red Sea, they were free men and women, but it took forty years in the wilderness for them to throw off the thought patterns of slavery."

The sun rose, searing the desert floor and baking the brown rock formations. Beneath the dry palm branch shelter, conversation ceased, and the men stoically endured thirst and hunger, heat and gritty discomfort.

Slowly, slowly the sun, like a ball of fire, moved from its zenith back down toward the desert floor. By now, the men were reclining, sleeping away as much of their discomfort as possible. The sound of approaching footsteps roused them. The men sat up. Then they stood so they could better see the approaching party of priests and prominent men.

Jesus pointed.

With his eyes, John Mark followed the line of the carpenter's hand. The boy could see that one man had stepped away from the group. That man walked alone, the scapegoat at his side. Closer and closer, they came to the edge of the cliff. John Mark felt himself getting nervous.

Jesus reached out and took the boy's hand, pulling him into the strength of his torso.

The man, obviously a priest, was now pushing the animal close to the edge of the precipice.

John Mark held his breath as he watched man and animal engage in a life-and-death dance, where one misstep would send the unfortunate loser over the edge. Suddenly, the struggle ended. The goat lost its footing and sailed over the rock wall. Moments later, it hit the jagged rocks below with a sickening thud. The rest of the men in the escort excitedly hurried forward. They pelted the animal with stones to make sure it had certainly died.

John Mark did not see the end of the animal. As the goat had gone over the cliff, the boy had turned his head into the folds of Jesus's garment. Jesus understood. He kept his arm around the boy, discretely allowing him to hide from the horror of that animal's death while not being exposed to the judgment of men who had lost the tenderness of childhood.

Pilate and Longinius stood at the window in the fortress tower. Their eyes were fixed on the crimson wool that had been attached to the door of the sanctuary.

"Do you believe—" Longinus started to ask.

Before the commander could finish his question, a shout went up from the people in the Temple courts. "*Though your sins are like scarlet, they shall be as white as snow; though they are red as crimson, they shall be like wool.*"[1]

Both Pilate and Longinus leaned out of the tower window. The men could not believe their eyes. The crimson wool now appeared pure white by the light of the setting sun. Immediately, the Levitical choir began to sing. From one of the rooms in the Temple, a procession of priests joyfully brought out several scrolls. With great reverence, they laid them on a table that had been set up on the upper platform of the semi-circular steps at the entrance to the Court of the Israelites. In the Court of the Women, the people stood. Masses of people, they stood shoulder to shoulder, silent, awed, and respectful. They were totally open to hearing the words that Moses had received from God.

Pilate and Longinus watched, amazed at the unified display of devotion. Until the sun set and the first stars could be clearly seen in the night sky, no one sat; no one moved. No one spoke. There was complete attentiveness as the scriptures were read. And throughout the land, no one—man, woman, youth, or animal—broke the fast until night had fallen and the final trumpet signaled the end of the Day of the Covering for Sins.

In the desert, Jesus picked up the wineskin. Holding it toward heaven, he began the traditional chant, "Blessed are you, O Lord our God, Ruler of the Universe who brings forth fruit from the vine." Then he moved from man to man beginning with John Mark, offering each a drink before he enjoyed a few swallows. The men shared another light meal and then they all stretched out to sleep until dawn brought enough light to safely hike back into the city.

Mary hurried into the banquet room where the men of the estate were breaking their fast with a sumptuous feast. She ignored their pointed looks and refused to even glance in the direction of Jonathan, her husband. Going directly to her brother, she took a firm stance in front of him. "Lazarus, I need a servant to go find Jesus. He always comes to Jerusalem for the holy days. I must find him."

For a moment, Lazarus was speechless. Then he asked, "May I inquire about the urgency?"

"A young man in this town is lying on his bed with crushed bones."

A remembering look passed between brother and sister.

Lazarus nodded, and with a beckoning gesture, he placed a servant at Mary's disposal.

Chapter 16

A Tainted Woman at the Banquet

Now one of the Pharisees invited Jesus to have dinner with him, so he went to the Pharisee's house and reclined at the table. When a woman who had lived a sinful life in that town learned that Jesus was eating at the Pharisee's house, she brought an alabaster jar of perfume.

—Luke 7:36–37

Jerusalem was filled with joy and expectation. Every son of Abraham felt certain that his name had been written in the Book of Life for another year, and all were eager to begin the festivities for the Feast of Tabernacles. Up and down the steps to the Beautiful Gate, crowds surged in and out of the Temple.

Ichabod placed his beggar's pot where it could easily be seen. This was a good day for begging. Coins dropped into his pot with a steady clink. Leaning back into the worn leather of his chair, Ichabod picked up bits and pieces of conversations. Often, he heard the name Jesus. He heard about healing and teaching. Then he remembered the young man from Nazareth who had built his first chair and who delivered a new chair every few years. Ichabod's eyes scanned the crowd. He wondered when he would see that man again.

Looking over toward the Mount of Olives, Ichabod could see a crowd was gathering. He heard the passing people speak excitedly about a healer. Suddenly, it seemed everyone was leaving the Temple, hurrying across the bridge, hoping to see a miracle with their own eyes.

Surprised at the sudden emptying of this entrance to the Temple, Ichabod found himself alone, wondering how he could get over the bridge to this healer named Jesus. Maybe when the servants from his father's house came to take him home.

The thought died as Ichabod watched a messenger approach the central figure on the mountain. The crowd dispersed. The man who seemed to be the main attraction, along with a small escort, made his way down the hill to the road that led to Bethany.

"I told my brother that Mary had sent for you," Jonathan explained as he led Jesus to the back of Simon's estate, to the cave where he expected to find his eldest brother labeling and sealing large pottery vats filled with fresh wine. "Simon wants to meet you in private," Jonathan continued to explain.

Jesus nodded, but he was listening more to the Holy Spirit than to Mary's husband. The secret sins of one of the wealthiest and most influential men in Bethany were being revealed.

"Shalom," Jonathan called as they entered the mouth of the cave.

Both men saw the flickering lamplight on the back walls of the cave. They heard soft alarmed voices accompanied by a little scurrying. A few moments later, Simon came out from the semi-darkness of the cave. Smoothing and straightening his robes, he started to say, "I have some workers with me," but when he looked up into the eyes of Jesus, the untruth stuck in his throat.

Pretending he did not notice the awkwardness of the moment, Jonathan turned to Jesus and said, "My brother has a skin condition I have been trying to treat without success. Mary is certain you can heal anything." There was a little question in his voice.

Simon latched on to that question and started to philosophize, "I have heard of the crowds and the miracles. My friends in Jerusalem speak of you often. Do you consider yourself to be in agreement with the Pharisees or the Sadducees, maybe even the Essenes?"

Jesus could see the demonic spirits that had attached themselves to Simon—Dishonesty, Greed, Lust, and Pride. Ignoring Simon's efforts to divert him into meaningless theological debate, Jesus said, "The Holy Spirit has brought me to this place to speak healing to one whose heart has been broken and for another whose bones have been crushed."

In response, all three men heard sudden muffled sobs coming from the depths of the cave.

Without reacting to the source of the sound, Jesus continued, "Because you are present to hear this proclamation of healing, your condition is also healed."

Immediately, Simon trembled from head to toe.

Jesus could see his words had freed Simon from the tormenting spirits that had caused his skin condition.

With warning fire in his eye, Jesus then added, *"This is what the Lord Almighty says: 'Administer true justice; show mercy and compassion to one another. Do not oppress the widow or the fatherless, the alien or the poor. Do not plot evil against each other.'"*[1]

Simon fearfully bowed his head. He could not look this man in the eye. Subtly, he moved his hand under his robe, feeling the area where his skin had been most infected—it was smooth. His body continued to tremble. This Jesus had a power he had never encountered before. Simon could not place it in the category of a particular theology or political alliance. Barely raising his eyes, Simon said, "I would like to hear you teach. In your honor, I will prepare a banquet. My servants will come to the home of Lazarus, where you are staying and call you when it is ready."

"What are we doing here? I cannot believe it!" Mary fumed as Martha placed a bowl of fruit in her arms.

"You are honoring your husband's family by helping with this banquet," Martha admonished. "Do not speak! Serve the men with grace and with downcast eyes. Do not embarrass your brother or your husband."

"But, Martha, you do not understand! Simon is the most disreputable, unclean man in the vicinity of Bethany!" Mary protested.

"I've spoken to his wife," Martha informed. "His skin condition is gone."

"It is more than a skin condition," Mary argued. "He is trying to take advantage of a widow."

Martha waved Mary's argument aside as she directed her toward the banquet room. "I know all about Rea. The whole town knows about Rea. Simon was just being kind."

Mary glared at her older sister.

Martha responded to the expression on Mary's face. "Yes, I will admit Simon was stretching his interpretation of the kinsman's duty. Nevertheless, we will serve Simon and his guests." Martha gave Mary one more directional push and Mary moved into the banquet room.

Mary went to Jesus first. He was reclining in the seat of honor. She offered Jesus the fruit, and he rewarded her with such a personal and beautiful smile that the agitation of a few moments ago disappeared.

Mary then moved to Peter, who dug into the bowl with both hands. Judas was next. Mary could not help but notice that Judas kept mostly to himself. He did not interact well with the other men who were Jesus's disciples.

Suddenly, above the male conversation, Mary caught her sister's voice, shrill and alarmed, "You can't go in there!"

Mary turned to see Rea pushing past Martha. Her mantle had slipped to her shoulders and her hair was falling freely about her tear-streaked face. Rea's eyes were on Jesus. For her, no one else was in the room.

Rea ran directly to where Jesus was stretched out on cushions. For one brief moment, she stood behind him, bending over his feet and sobbing. Then dropping to her knees, she began to wash his feet with her tears, and she dried them with her long dark hair.

Around the room, shocked stares turned into horrified gasps of amazement.

"That woman is kissing his feet!"

"Why hasn't Jesus thrown Rea to the floor?" someone exclaimed. "She should not be allowed to touch him!"

"At least she should not be allowed to touch him in public," a knowing voice sneered.

Suddenly, an aroma filled the air. Mary knew what it was before she saw the open alabaster vial in Rea's hand, and she watched as her friend poured out the expensive perfume. The extravagance of the gesture even took Mary's breath away. Not one drop was spared as Rea bathed Jesus's feet with the only wealth she possessed.

Contemptuously, Simon muttered, "If Jesus were a prophet or even a righteous man, he would recognize that this woman is the worst kind of sinner."

Jesus heard the remark, and in response, he sent Simon a hard leveling stare.

For a moment, Simon looked shocked. What kind of man would rise to the defense of Rea? Without warning, vivid memories of meetings in the cave and the methods he had used to force Rea to comply with his demands suddenly rushed through his mind. Simon's hands began to tremble then Fear gripped his throat.

Jesus never broke eye contact.

Simon had to look away. He managed to take a few sips of water as he fought to gain control of his own thoughts and emotions. Somehow, Jesus knew more about his own actions and motives than about the immorality of the woman who continued to wipe his feet with her hair.

At last, Jesus responded, "Simon, I have a story to tell."

Relieved that words had finally broken the intensity of the healer's accusing look, Simon managed to say, "Tell us, teacher."

Jesus sat up and placed his feet on the floor. Rea was still kneeling by the cushions and the odor of expensive perfume hung heavily in the room.

Every eye was on Jesus. What would this man say to explain his reaction to this sinful woman?

Then, Jesus began, "Two men owed money to a banker. One owed a large sum, five hundred denarii, and the other owed a small sum, fifty denarii. Neither man had the means to meet his debt, so each man approached the banker explaining his circumstance. Now the banker was a good and just man so he forgave each man, canceling both debts. Tell me, Simon. Which man will be more grateful?"

Shrugging his shoulders, Simon replied, "I'm sure the man with the larger debt will be most appreciative."

You have answered correctly," Jesus said. Again, Jesus fixed Simon with a level stare that spoke more than all the words of the Torah.

Simon shifted his weight and looked down at the table.

Jesus then turned toward the woman while he spoke to Simon. "Look at this woman. When I entered your home, you did not supply water for my feet, but she has washed my feet with her tears and dried them with her hair. You did not give me a welcoming kiss, but this woman continues to kiss my feet. Where is the perfumed oil that is usually offered to an honored guest? You did not provide any. But this woman has more than made up for your breech of etiquette. She has poured an entire bottle of nard on my feet, without sparing any for herself. Yes, I know about the laws she has broken, and I know the circumstances." Then with his eyes still fixed on Simon, Jesus added, "The man who believes his debt is small will not value forgiveness, so his display of love will be pitiful."

Then Jesus stood. He took Rea by the hand and brought her to her feet. "Your son?" he kindly asked. "Was he completely recovered when you returned to your home?"

"He is totally well," Rea answered with eyes respectfully downcast.

"Look at me," Jesus said.

Rea looked up into the warmth of eyes that understood. Then in front of everyone, Jesus said to her, "Your sins are forgiven."

Then the other guests began to mutter and comment, "Can this man forgive sins? What is his authority?"

Jesus paid no attention to the men at the banquet or their comments. His concern was for Rea. Turning his head, he saw Mary. Calling her over with a glance and a nod, he placed Rea's hand in hers. But before sending both women away from the critical stares and comments, Jesus said to Rea, "Be at peace. Your faith has saved you and your son."

Jesus then signaled a servant to bring his sandals. Without another word, he walked out of the banquet. His disciples followed with wistful backward glances at the wonderfully prepared food they were leaving behind.

In the grassy pasture behind the estate that was owned by Lazarus of Bethany, Peter and Andrew expertly secured four sturdy limbs in the ground. James and John had already established the four solid supports for their booth. They were attaching a lattice of twine to support their roof. Bartholomew and Philip were tossing leafy branches across their lattice of twine, while Matthew and Thomas sat on their cloaks, resting in the shade of their newly completed booth and critiquing the construction efforts of their companions.

"Hey, Peter," Thomas jestingly called. "You and your brother had better hurry. The sun is going to set. We're going to leave for the Temple, and you will still be throwing branches on your roof!"

"Don't worry about us!" Peter called back. "We'll be ready long before they light the giant torches in the Temple courts. It's Judas who needs some help! At the rate, he's going, he won't be finished before the next Feast of Tabernacles!"

All the men glanced at Judas, working by himself, struggling to keep his supports from falling over. Lightly taunting, masculine laughter rolled across the pasture.

Bartholomew threw the last branch on the roof of his booth, and then he and Philip walked over to where Judas was doggedly trying to prepare his shelter for the next eight nights. Bartholomew slapped him on the back. "Let a couple of fishermen give you a hand."

Judas scowled, but he stepped aside and allowed the assistance.

Thomas turned to Matthew. "Judas did not come from a working family. The only thing he knows to do with his hands is count money."

Matthew nodded. "I'm glad my father made sure I could count money and build a house."

Thomas responded, "That's why Judas doesn't seem to fit in. The rest of us are working men. We are used to using our muscles and our hands. He only knows how to count money and keep records.

"He doesn't keep records," Matthew stated. "Out of the twelve who travel with Jesus, only Judas and I know how to properly keep records of monetary transactions. When I ask him about the money that comes in, he brushes me off. He never gives me a clear factual answer about the cash flow."

Thomas raised his eyebrows and questioned, "Do you think he is putting some aside for himself?"

Matthew nodded his head affirmatively.

"Have you told Jesus?" Thomas asked.

"I have mentioned the possibility to him, but Jesus is totally unconcerned. Jesus told me he has instructed Judas to give all the money away.

The conversation ended when the men saw Jesus standing with Lazarus and Jonathan near the back of the estate. They knew it was time to walk to the Temple to be part of the opening festivities. Late in the night, they would return to sleep in their booths.

Cushions and cloaks were spread on the grass. With the booths in the background, Jesus and his disciples sat around a small fire. Lazarus and Jonathan relaxed with them while Mary and Martha, along with several other women, set up a late afternoon meal. Responding to the alert of the Holy Spirit, Jesus looked down the road.

The Spirit quickly identified Simon, Jonathan's older brother, accompanied by several Pharisee friends. Rebellious and Religious spirits hovered over the little group.

Turning back to Lazarus, Jesus said, "Rise and greet your guests."

Lazarus looked a little surprised. He glanced down the road and then turned back to Jesus. "Are those men coming here? Do I know them?"

Jesus laughed. "Once they get closer, you will recognize the men. They are not really interested in visiting with you. They have come to challenge me."

Together, Jesus and Lazarus walked down the road to meet the men and escort them back to the estate. It was an act of courtesy and respect. Through the eyes of the Spirit, Jesus could see his respectful gesture had thrown the demonic spirits accompanying this group into disarray.

"Come to my house," Lazarus bowed, and then he greeted Simon with the kiss of a kinsman. "My servants have water for your hands and your feet. My sisters are laying out food, and Jesus will teach after the meal."

Simon stepped back out of the brief embrace. "We came to hear Jesus and to question him. We will remain for the meal only if Jesus is planning to stay for the entire meal."

Everyone caught the veiled reference to the fact that Jesus had left Simon's banquet, even before the main course had been served.

With total politeness, Jesus answered, "I come and I go as the Holy Spirit directs. We can both hope I will remain for the entire meal. The women have worked very hard. I know the food will be delicious." Then Jesus gave Simon and his friends a genuinely open smile before turning and leading the way back to the home of Lazarus.

Full and contented, the men leaned back into the cushions that had been carried from the dining hall into the grassy pasture. Simon was the first to speak. He turned to Jesus. "All of us were at the banquet in my home. We heard you say to that woman—"

"Rea," Jesus interrupted to give the woman the dignity of a name.

"Yes—Rea," Simon continued. "We heard you say that her sins were forgiven. Do you have the authority to forgive sins?"

Another Pharisee interrupted, "Teacher, show us an amazing sign, something that will convince us that you are more than just an ordinary man."

Jesus replied, "For you, who are as wicked as the citizens of Nineveh, I only have the sign of the prophet Jonah. As Jonah was three days and three nights in the belly of the great fish, so I will be three days and three nights in the Place of the Dead."

"You insult us!" Several Pharisees picked up stones, but they did not throw them.

Jesus continued, "At the judgment, when all men stand before the throne of God, the men of Nineveh will be rewarded because they heard the preaching of Jonah and repented while the present leadership of this nation will be condemned because someone greater than Jonah came to them and they refused his teaching."

The friends of Simon ground their teeth and shook their fists, but Jesus was not intimidated.

"The Queen of the South, Sheba from Ethiopia, was awed by the wisdom of Solomon. Now, someone greater is teaching in Jerusalem." Jesus pointed toward himself. "And the leaders of the people will not listen."

"Are you saying that you are greater and wiser than King Solomon?" Simon asked.

One of Simon's friends quickly spoke up, "No, he is saying that we, the sons of Abraham, are more demon-possessed than the gentiles of Nineveh and Ethiopia!"

"We are the sons of Abraham!" Simon exclaimed. "As a people, God brought us through the Red Sea and cleansed us by the laws he gave to Moses. We are not like the other nations! Only God can forgive sins."

Jesus pointed to Martha who was scrubbing a cooking pot at the back of the house. "When a pot has been washed it is clean, but it will get dirty again. Without regular cleaning, the filth will actually multiply."

Then Jesus looked directly at Simon.

And Simon felt such discomfort that he had to look down. He knew the words Jesus was about to speak applied directly to him.

"When an unclean spirit comes out at my command, it travels through wilderness places, searching for another home, another person who is welcoming. When it wearies of the search, it often returns to its former dwelling. There it finds a life where evil has been removed, but holiness has not filled the void. Because there is no righteousness in place to resist evil, that demon enters with seven more, and the final condition of that man is worse than before. Beware, many in this generation are in danger."

Evening was coming. Behind the men, Martha moved from booth to booth, placing a lighted lamp on a small sturdy stand in each booth. For a moment, Jesus watched Martha, noticing how careful she was to attend to every need her guests might have. Silently, he said, "Father God, bless Martha with the desires of her heart because her service pleases me."

Then Jesus turned back to the men who were waiting to be taught. "*No one lights a lamp and hides it in a clay jar or puts it under a bed. Instead, they put it on a stand, so that those who come in can see the light.*" Jesus looked around at the men. Once again, he caught Simon's eye, and he continued without breaking eye contact. "*For there is nothing hidden that will not be disclosed, and nothing concealed that will not be known or brought out into the open; therefore, consider carefully how you listen. Whoever has will be given more; whoever does not have, even what they think they have will be taken from them.*"[2]

As Jesus paused at the end of that thought, Simon nodded, signaling to Jesus that he understood the warning.

Then he stood, and those who were with him also stood. They lit their little handheld lamps and began the short walk back to Simon's estate.

The rest of the men were quiet, staring into the fire, each wrapped in his own thoughts. Jesus noticed Mary had brought her kneading bowl, and she had found a place to sit and listen while she prepared the dough so it could rise over night.

The Holy Spirit said, "Always remember the ideas that the Pharisees and the Sadducees project onto the people are their own ideas or the ideas of my enemy. They are like the yeast Mary is now mixing into the dough. At first, she uses no more than a handful, but overnight, it grows and expands until the dough becomes puffed up like a man over impressed with his own thoughts. He fills his head until he has no room for the thoughts of God."

Chapter 17

A Banquet and a Beheading

Now Herod had arrested John and bound him and put him in prison because of Herodias, his brother Philip's wife, for John had been saying to him: "It is not lawful for you to have her." Herod wanted to kill John, but he was afraid of the people, because they considered John a prophet.

—Matthew 12:3–5

Antipas, Cuza, and Manaen stood together at the observation window, high atop the ninety-foot tower at Machaerus. From this tower, built on the walls of a palace-fortress that sat on the upper lip of a dry cone-shaped mountain, the men focused their attention on the desert hills that belonged to the Nabataeans.

Manaen spoke first. "I have been up here every day and every night for the past two weeks. King Arteas is gathering his troops on the other side of that last ridge. At night, I can see their campfires, and during the day, I can sometimes see the glint of their shields or smoke from their cooking area."

Antipas leaned out the window, staring as hard as he could. "Maybe I see a little smoke." He turned back to Manaen. "Have you sent scouts?"

"Yes, they estimate ten thousand foot soldiers and more are arriving," Manaen answered.

"Do you think they are going to attack this fortress?" Antipas asked incredulously. "My father made it impregnable."

Cuza responded, "We believe it would be prudent to bring reinforcements and weapons to the fortress so we can protect the villages at the base of this mountain as well as the palace."

Herod Antipas nodded in agreement. "Put patrols on the road from Jerusalem to this place. Important men and women are coming for my birthday celebration. I do not want anyone abducted or attacked."

Cuza agreed. Then he asked, "Should we contact the commander of all the Roman armies stationed in Syria and this region of the world?"

"No!" Antipas exploded. "I want to handle this myself, without involving Rome. If I call for help, I will be seen as weak and troublesome. If I end this dispute without violence, I will be considered an asset to the empire. If I must go to war and I win, I will also win respect in Rome. Whatever I do, I must do it myself!"

"Then what is your next move?" Manaen asked.

"Send envoys," Antipas responded. "I will try reason."

There was a brief moment of contemplation. Antipas got a little quizzical expression on his face and then he said to Manaen, "I want to speak to the prophet in my dungeon. Clean him up and bring him to my chambers for a private audience."

Antipas looked up from his afternoon meal as the prophet known to the people as John the Baptist was escorted into his living chambers. The prisoner was seated a short distance from the king. Antipas nodded to the others in the room as he said, "Leave us."

When the room had emptied, Antipas coldly looked John up and down. Then he said, "My nose tells me that you have washed, but my eyes see that you are still as unkempt as ever. Wouldn't you like to cut your hair and shave your beard?"

John casually responded, using the words of Sampson, *"I have been a Nazirite dedicated to God from my mother's womb.*[1] Unlike

Sampson, who had no regard for the symbols of his connection with God, I know this uncut hair is the physical evidence of the anointing that is on my life. I have no desire to have it cut or shaved."

Antipas nodded as he swallowed a bite and took a sip of wine. "I know you also do not eat or drink any form of grape, so I will not offer."

John shrugged a little and waited to hear what the monarch had on his mind.

"Prophet, what has the Lord spoken to you regarding my kingdom?" Antipas had stopped eating and was looking directly at John.

"Humble yourself. Repent and restore Herodias to the husband of her youth. Then you can expect the favor of God to rest upon you," John answered.

"Some things cannot be reversed," Antipas replied.

"The word of the Lord does not change with our circumstances," John countered. "Through the prophet Ezekiel, God speaks clearly, *'But if a wicked man turns away from all the sins he has committed and keeps all my decrees and does what is just and right, he will surely live; he will not die. None of the offenses he has committed will be remembered against him. Because of the righteous things he has done, he will live. Do I take any pleasure in the death of the wicked? declares the Sovereign Lord. Rather, am I not pleased when they turn from their ways and live?'*"[2]

"There is an army gathering in the desert on my border!" Antipas shouted. "How will the Lord help me?"

Very calmly, John responded. "You are the offspring of an Edomite and a Samaritan. It is very presumptuous of you to expect help from the God of the Jews. Yet you live in our promised land and you rule over the descendants of Abraham. Our history is very clear. When our kings are faithful to God and when they have removed the things that offend our God, then God fights for them and turns back great armies. But when the leadership of the nation continues to trample the laws of God, then God fights against them."

Antipas shook his spoon toward John. "You have nothing to offer me! I can see you will be no help with the threat that is gathering not far from this fortress."

Again, John gave a slight shrug as he said, "I am not a warrior. I only speak the words of the Lord as they are written in the scriptures and as they are given to me by the Spirit of God."

"You're a prophet, aren't you?" Antipas growled.

"Some call me a prophet."

Don't prophets tell what will happen in the future?"

"Sometimes," John cautiously answered.

"Tomorrow night is my fiftieth birthday celebration. The food will be wonderful. I have hired a dance troop from Syria. I want my guests to never forget the evening. I would like you to come and speak of future events for my guests—you know—tell what will happen to them. I would especially like to hear what God has told you about Pontius Pilate."

John held up a cautioning hand. "God does not give prophetic words for entertainment. If you bring me to your celebration, then I will be there. But no matter what, I will speak only those things that God tells me to speak, and it might turn the celebration into an unpleasant event."

Antipas pushed himself away from his table. "I'm through! You've ruined my meal, and now you threaten to ruin my birthday! Guard! Guard!"

The prison warden and his assistant hurried into the room.

Antipas pointed toward John. "Take this man back to his cell."

As John was being escorted from the room, Antipas called after him, "I fear your God."

John's escorts stopped, allowing John to respond, "You do not fear God enough to obey him."

"Grungy desert man. You only live because I also fear the people of this land."

"*Wisdom's instruction is to fear the* Lord, *and humility comes before honor.*"[3]

"Why do I call you to my chambers and engage in these pointless discussions?" Antipas raged.

"The Spirit of God has not given up on you," John kindly replied. "It is God himself appealing to your heart. That is the reason I am here." John then turned and followed his escorts back to his cell.

Once again, Jesus was in Capernaum. A crowd gathered near the waterfront. It became so large that, once again, Jesus stepped into one of the fishing boats. From there, with a small expanse of water separating him from the people, he began to teach, illustrating his points with parables.

"A farmer prepared his field and then went out to scatter his seed. As he paced back and forth across the turned earth, the farmer broadcast his seed as widely as possible. Some fell beyond the freshly turned dirt. It landed on the hard path. Birds quickly swooped in, devouring each kernel.

Some of the seed also fell in the places where rocks had been tossed in the process of clearing the field. There, the soil was thin. Seeds did take root and spring up quickly, but they could not survive the heat of the growing season.

Other seeds fell beyond the plowed field, landing in the thorny brush. Choked by hardy weeds, the seedlings sprouted but could not produce grain.

Still, most of the seed fell on the well-prepared soil. It took root, grew, and produced a mighty harvest."

Then Jesus said, "This is a story for every man and woman who makes a home in the land that God gave to Abraham. It is for both rich and poor, ruler and peasant. Consider this parable and understand."

Later, when the people had returned to their homes, Jesus sat with his disciples. Philip asked, "Teacher, tell us the meaning of the parables."

"Don't you know?" Jesus responded as his gaze moved from face to face. "The keys to understanding the secrets of the Kingdom of God have been given to you. But to those who remain outside the kingdom, no understanding is offered."

Then Jesus began to explain. "The farmer is sowing the word of God. Some people are like the hard ground of the path. They stand in the crowd and hear my teaching, but they only hear with their ears. Before my words can reach their minds and their hearts, agents of Satan swoop in, destroying truth and leaving nothing.

"Others in the crowd are like the rocky places. They hear my teaching, and they are filled with brief excitement. Ridicule or just the problems of life can quickly kill their excitement.

"There are others who hear me speak. Their minds are like patches of tangled thorns, filled with the ideas of men and the concerns of life. Since they never distinguish between fruitful and unfruitful growth, their lives remain unchanged, unproductive, worthless.

"This is a story full of hope because most people who hear my teachings will accept them. Their lives will be transformed and the transformation of each life will cause other lives to be transformed. So in the harvest of the last day, many will enter into everlasting life with the Messiah.

In the fortress-palace of Machaerus, Cuza and Manaen walked briskly into the banquet hall to oversee the seating arrangements for the evening. The room was filled with activity—furniture was being moved, draperies were being hung, the dance troop from Syria was rehearsing, and six-year-old Salome was underfoot. Cuza, heading toward one of the tables, his arms loaded with name placards, nearly tripped over the child as she darted in front of him waving a sheer veil she had snatched from one of the dancers.

With very little patience, Cuza glanced around the room, looking for the nanny who usually accompanied the little girl. He found her. "Do something," he directed. "This is not her playroom!"

The nanny let loose her own pent-up frustrations. "Antipas has ordered that she have the run of the palace. Salome's joy is not to be curtailed in any way. Even Herodias, her own mother, can say or do very little to discipline this child."

Cuza started to respond, "Antipas is an old—"

But before fool left his lips, Manaen interrupted, "Tell one of the performers to teach Salome a little dance to present this evening."

The nanny quickly agreed, "The child is young enough that it will not be improper."

"And," Cuza added, "Antipas is so smitten by the child that he will consider it the greatest moment of the evening."

Pilate smiled insincerely as he raised his wine-filled goblet and proclaimed, "A toast to Herod Antipas, ruler of Galilee and Perea, may he live and rule another fifty years for the empire."

Everyone responded by emptying their drinking cups and holding them out for the servants to refill. Antipas clapped his hands and shouted, "Entertainment! Bring on the entertainment."

In the women's section of the banquet hall, gossip ceased, and everyone watched as male and female dancers rushed into the room, flipping, twirling, and swaying to exotic tunes. Suddenly, all the dancers dropped to the floor and one very small veiled dancer stepped out from behind the draperies. She twirled and waved colorful scarves as she wove in and out between the motionless members of the troop. As she approached Antipas, two of the male dancers jumped up. One grabbed her and tossed her high into the air, and the other caught her.

A joyous giggle burst from the dancer. "Again!" she shouted in a childish voice.

The men tossed her again and again as Antipas leaned forward, studying the act with great curiosity.

When the dancer's feet finally touched the floor, her veil slipped from her face and dropped to the mosaic tiles.

"Salome!" Antipas cried.

"Happy birthday, Papa!" Salome broke away from the dance and ran to jump on her stepfather's lap.

"You really surprised me!" Antipas laughed, and everyone in the room laughed with him. Then *the king said to the girl, "Ask me for anything you want, and I'll give it to you." And he promised her with an oath, "Whatever you ask I will give you, up to half my kingdom."*[4]

A look of uncertainty crossed the little girl's face. She looked over at her mother, Herodias, who sat with the other women.

Herodias looked back, briefly locking eyes with her husband instead of her daughter. Beckoning with a slight finger movement, Herodias called her little girl to her side.

With typical six-year-old energy, Salome skipped and danced to her mother's side, perfectly aware that she was the center of attention in the banquet hall. She gave her mother a little bow.

Herodias bent over and whispered in her daughter's ear. Then she said, "Repeat what I have said back into my ear."

Salome whispered in her mother's ear, and Herodias rewarded her with an affirmative nod and a smile.

Once more, Herodias locked eyes with her husband, and then she turned her attention back to her daughter. "Be sure to bow respectfully to your father and speak loudly so everyone in the room will hear," Herodias gave her instructions as she sent the little girl back to Antipas.

"So cute," the women whispered.

"Oh, and that little bow! She was born for the palaces of Rome." Everyone in the room was captivated by the child.

Salome stopped her twirling and dancing. Then she walked with a dignity that mimicked thc adults of the palace. Stopping a few paces from her father's seat of honor, she bowed again.

Antipas, eager to play her game, extended his hand with the royal signet ring and the little girl moved forward. She kissed the ring.

The room broke into applause.

Antipas took Salome by the hand and brought her face up to look squarely into his smiling face. He repeated his offer. "*Ask me for anything you want, and I'll give it to you... Whatever you ask, I will give you, up to half my kingdom.*"[5]

Speaking slowly and clearly, the little girl repeated the words her mother had whispered in her ear. *"I want you to give me right now the head of John the Baptist on a platter."*[6]

A collective gasp filled the room.

Antipas fell back into his chair as if someone had struck him, but the tetrarch recovered quickly. The uncompromising glint in his wife's eye, the curious expectant glances of his guests left him no choice. "As a ruler, I am true to my word." He turned to Manaen. "Call the executioner to remove the head of the prophet called John the Baptist. Do it immediately and bring his head to us."

Stunned that he would be ordered to oversee this royal directive, Manaen quickly removed himself from the banquet room before his face could reveal the horror he felt. Cuza followed him.

Both men paused and looked back in the room.

"We cannot save the prophet," Cuza stated.

"I know." Manaen shook his head regretfully. "Too many important people heard Antipas. If he backed down now, he would look weak."

With the executioner walking between them, Manaen and Cuza entered John's cell.

John looked up. "The Spirit of the Lord has been speaking to me all day. I am ready."

"We are sorry," Manaen said.

John responded, *"Who can live and not see death, or who can escape the power of the grave?"*[7]

"Your early death is not our idea," Cuza added. "It has been ordered by Herod Antipas."

The executioner pulled his sword from its sheath. Cuza gave the man a coin and said, "Make your stroke swift and sure."

John moved his long hair to one side and bowed his head, exposing his neck. The desert prophet began to speak, and Manaen kept a restraining hand on the executioner's arm until the last word had been spoken. *"I know that my redeemer lives, and that in the end he will stand on the earth. And after my skin has been destroyed, yet in my flesh I will see God; I myself will see him with my own eyes—I, and not another. How my heart yearns within me!"*[8]

Manaen removed his hand, and the executioner's sword swiftly struck the prophet's neck. Blood spurted and splashed across the walls of the cell. The banquet garments that had been carefully chosen by Cuza and Manaen were instantly ruined. The men looked down. John's head lay on the floor, his haunting black eyes unnaturally open.

From within the cell, Cuza called, "Bring a covered platter."

Respectfully, the two palace officials arranged John's uncut hair on the oversized plate, like a pillow for his bloody head. As they worked, both men were silent, deep in memories of hours spent at the oasis by the Jordan where this man had been preaching and baptizing.

Manaen wiped the coagulating blood from the outside of the platter, before handing it to the executioner. "Take this bloody head to King Antipas. We are unclean, and we will not be reentering the banquet."

The executioner left, and John's body remained on the floor. As Manaen and Cuza stepped out of the cell, Cuza gave orders to the warden, "Call John's disciples. Give them the body." Then both men left the prison, disgusted with their jobs.

Chapter 18

A Legion of Demons

The Spirit of the Sovereign LORD is on me, because the LORD has anointed me to preach good news to the poor. He has sent me to bind up the brokenhearted, to proclaim freedom for the captives and release from darkness for the prisoners.

—Isaiah 61:1

The fishing boats rocked gently on blue-gray wavelets, their masts like limbless trees against a clear afternoon sky. From the bow of Peter's boat, Jesus looked out over the crowd. The needs of humanity seemed endless. All morning, people with their illnesses and emotional pain had been pressing and pressing, struggling for a touch or a word from the healer. By noon, Jesus's burly fishermen-disciples could not maintain an orderly approach so people could safely come.

That was when Jesus had stepped into Peter's boat and ordered that they push away from the shore. Now most of the people were seated. Separated by a small expanse of water, Jesus could also sit and teach. "How can I explain the Kingdom of God? What parable will describe it?"

Jesus paused and then he said, "I know. The Kingdom of God is like a mustard seed. It is the smallest seed that a farmer can plant. Yet, it grows into the largest of all the garden plants. Birds can perch on its branches!"

On a nearby hill, Satan stood with Raziel, his second-in-command. Both evil angels listened closely. Nothing missed their keen observation.

"The Kingdom of God! The Kingdom of God!" Satan exploded. "Those illiterate fishermen who call themselves disciples don't know what Yeshua-Jesus is talking about, but I do! Once, I lived in the Kingdom of God. I stood outside the throne room while God, Yeshua, and the Holy Spirit planned the creation of this planet. I traveled with the Holy Rulers to this distant corner of the universe, and there I heard the Creator speak. With one word, there was light, then atmosphere. Another word, then dry land with vegetation appeared. Birds, fish, and animals—those disciples do not know about the power that is within the Kingdom of God."

"Adam had power to demand obedience from all the creatures and the forces of nature on this planet," Raziel commented.

"Until I tricked him into giving it to me," Satan sneered. "Dominion over Earth, power over creation—it is the same."

"You know Yeshua-Jesus has come to challenge you over this dominion?" Raziel looked his evil commander dead in the eye while he waited for a response.

"Yeshua-Jesus, he's not so different from me," Satan asserted. "I entered a serpent. Yeshua the Creator somehow entered the womb of a woman and became in part a created being."

Raziel shook his head as if trying to comprehend the mystery of God becoming human.

"It's just a trick," Satan ranted. "It's just a way to bring the Kingdom of God down to Earth. First, the Creator sneaks in. He claims dominion by right of creation and by right of having a body made from the elements of the Earth. Then he gathers more and more followers until he, along with his followers, can challenge me."

With a little smugness, Raziel quoted, "'*Man's fate is like that of the animals; the same fate awaits them both: As one dies, so dies the other. All have the same breath; man has no advantage over the animals...all come from dust, and to dust all return.*'[1] Yeshua-Jesus has become a man, so he will have to die."

"The sooner the better," Satan agreed.

When evening came, Jesus said to the disciples who were with him in the fishing boat, "Haul in the anchor and set the sail. Let's go to the other side of the lake."

Without comment, the men responded. James quickly pulled up the anchor, and John hoisted the square sail. A quick breeze filled the heavy cloth so the boat easily glided out over the calm water, away from the demands of the crowd. Physically exhausted, Jesus immediately curled up on a cushion in the stern of the boat. He was asleep before most of the people who had been listening to him teach realized that his boat was sailing away.

Thomas and Matthew, Philip and Bartholomew kept their eyes on the shore. Some from the crowd hurried to their own boats, intent on following Jesus where ever he might go. But most slowly got to their feet and made their way back to their homes. Peter held the rudder steady.

"Where are you taking us?" Andrew asked his brother.

"Away from all these people," Peter answered.

"Most of the boats are giving up already," John commented.

Peter responded, "Anyone who has a basic knowledge of navigation on this body of water can see that we are headed for the distant shore. If they keep following us, they will not make it back before dark."

"One boat is still coming." Phillip pointed to a vessel with only three occupants.

"I know who's in that boat!" Peter growled. "It's that Pharisee, Yonatan, and his friend from the Temple. "I'm going to anchor this boat someplace where no self-respecting Pharisee will step foot on land."

Judas commented, "We must be going to non-Jewish territory.

"Better than that," Peter responded. He pointed back to the boat that was gaining on their heavily loaded fishing vessel. "If those pious Pharisees want to spy on us, they are going to have to walk over the tombs of the uncircumcised."

"I know the harbor you are headed for," Andrew announced. "It's in the region of the Gerasenes. There is a narrow trail that goes from the beach, past a cliff, and in that cliff are numerous caves where the gentiles bury their dead."

"There's a town nearby," Peter defended his destination. "We can buy food, and then we can make camp on top of the cliff overlooking our boat."

The rest of the disciples responded with satisfied chuckles and taunting glances toward the boat that would soon have to turn back.

With a swish of his mighty wings, Satan rose from the mountainous shore. Raziel followed. Briefly, both evil angels hovered over the center of the Sea of Galilee. Then with a malevolent thought, the Evil One summoned his warriors, the angels who had followed him to Earth to hold positions in his counter-kingdom.

Satan drew his sword and waved it in a circular motion above his head. His wicked angelic army quickly fell into ranks and began to fly in a steady circular pattern, creating new wind currents.

In the black recesses of a shallow cave, Cleon felt himself drawn toward the mouth of the cave that overlooked the sea. On his hands and knees, he crawled to the entrance and looked out to see the glowing streaks of sunset. The golden brightness made him feel like screaming, so he screamed like a frenzied beast.

Cleon then looked down and out across the great expanse of light gray water. Two distant fishing boats seemed to be approaching. The thought of approaching people sent dread and emotional pain swirling through every cell in his body. Shivering and crouching, he dug his claw-like fingernails into the grass. The wind began to pick up. Cleon sniffed the circling breeze. Naked and wary as a wild animal, every nerve in his body was on alert. In his head, his familiar voices began again—relentless, snarling voices. They shouted to their counterparts in the sky. Today, Cleon did not understand the words they said. For him, it was all swirling chaos and dark torment. He screamed again and again. The ever-increasing wind whipped his anguished cries away

Desperate, Cleon picked up a sharp stone. He drew its jagged edge across the scarred flesh of his left arm and watched as his blood filled the cut and then ran down his forearm to drip off his fingertips onto the rocky ground. "A blood sacrifice! Here is my blood. Now, stop tormenting me!" Cleon shrieked again.

The next time he looked up, he saw several herdsmen staring curiously at him. He knew they had been caring for the pigs that were foraging nearby.

Attack! It was a command from the legions within Cleon's mind.

With the jagged rock as his weapon, Cleon charged the closest man, smashing the rock into his face again and again. There was no thought of restraint. The voices in his head were demanding, "Kill! Kill!"

At first, the other herdsmen jumped on Cleon, beating him with their rods, but the demonized man seemed impervious to physical pain. Alas, all the intervening herdsmen could do was to drag their injured companion away from the wild man. Beaten and bruised, they carried their friend away hoping his injuries were not serious, and they all could make it to shelter before the atmospheric turbulence turned into a full-blown storm.

In the boat, all the fishermen-disciples sensed the mood of the sea was changing. Light conversation ceased. Peter focused on keeping his balance while holding the steering oar against the changing currents. The boat dipped and climbed over the wind-whipped whitecaps. Peter flexed his knees and shifted his weight as he anticipated each plunge and lift. Judas and Matthew scooted nervously toward the center of the boat while Peter growled at them. "We don't need any additional movement on this vessel."

The two non-fishermen hunkered down close to the mast, shivering as the wind blew fine spray into their faces.

A large wave smacked the boat broadside. The steering oar flew from Peter's hands. His brother Andrew caught the oar just before it fell overboard.

Again, Peter grabbed the long oar and thrust it into the rough water, fighting to point the bow into the waves, but the wind kept picking up, blowing violently and erratically.

"I think we should head for the nearest harbor," Judas shouted his opinion over the wind.

Peter answered with an edge to his voice that revealed his disdain, "All the fishermen on this boat know there is no close harbor. We are in the center of the sea." He pulled the long oar that served as a rudder out of the raging waves. "We're going to have to ride this out and go wherever the wind and the waves take us."

Black clouds darkened the sky. Suddenly, rain fell in sheets.

"Stop hugging the mast and bail!" James threw a bucket at Judas. Matthew had already put his back into scooping water from the bottom of the vessel.

Complete darkness quickly overtook the wind-battered boat. Philip and Andrew groped with their experienced hands, feeling the mast and the ropes as they wrestled to lower the sail. Each man was doing something to save the boat, to save their lives.

John was the first to look around for Jesus. Had their teacher been swept overboard? "Where's Jesus?" He hollered above the wind.

For a moment, everyone paused.

Then the shouting began. "Jesus? Jesus?"

Without a torch, they could not see. Each man only felt the bodies of the men closest to him.

"I found him!" Andrew called back. "Jesus is asleep on the cushions."

Andrew shook him roughly. The others called his name.

Finally, Jesus sat up.

Frantic and somewhat angry, his disciples shouted over the shrieking wind, "How can you sleep? Don't you care that we are all about to drown?"

Still sitting on the water-soaked cushion, Jesus looked around, briefly studying the emergency situation and getting his directions from the Holy Spirit. Then in one defiant movement, Jesus threw off his water-soaked cloak and took a wide stance in the stern of the violently rocking boat. A large wave washed over the bow. The men scrambled to bail.

Over the wind, Peter yelled in alarm, "Master! Sit down!"

The others added their concerned cries. "Get down! You'll be swept away!"

Unmoved, Jesus stared at the roaring elements, seeing past them to the source of the turbulence. Then he spoke in a firm, commanding voice, "I command peace! Rotating winds, cease! Raging waves, be still!"

The swirling black clouds of evil angels came to an abrupt halt. Satan lowered his sword, and Raziel spread his wings. The ranks of evil then flew to the distant hills. Their Creator had spoken.

Immediately, the wind diminished to a soft breeze, and the water became smooth as glass.

Wet and overwhelmingly weary, the disciples slumped to the floor of the fishing boat, but their eyes remained fixed on their teacher who stood in the stern with his eyes fixed on the distant shore.

"Thank you, Father God. Today, you have shown my followers the prophetic fulfillment of the words your servant Moses used to proclaim each time he moved Israel to a new location. The Ark of the Covenant, like this wooden boat, carried the Word on tablets of stone. At the beginning of each journey, Moses would declare, *'Rise up, Lord! May your enemies be scattered; may your foes flee before you.'*"[2]

Then Jesus turned to the men in the boat. "Why were you so afraid? Don't you trust your Father and the plans he has for your life? Where is your faith?"

The disciples had no direct response for their master. Overcome with amazement, they could only look at each other and exclaim, "He commands the wind and the water, then they obey! What other man has such authority?"

"Raise the sail. Set the rudder." Jesus issued the orders that sent his fishermen-disciples back to the tasks they understood best. Looking at Peter, Jesus added, "Make way for the harbor where you had planned to set the anchor. The Holy Spirit is calling me to that place."

Peter looked at the stars, now clear and bright against the night sky. The moon reflected softly on the calm water. Peter put the long steering oar into the water and took his place, standing in the stern of the boat.

It was dawn when Cleon heard men's voices.

"Take a rope and haul the bow closer to shore. Throw the anchor."

"Let's build a fire as soon as we can get ashore. We need to dry off!"

"If we throw a net, do you think we could catch some fish for breakfast?"

Curious but wary, Cleon crawled past a pile of human bones to peer out the cave. The old iron fetters from previous attempts to chain him clanked and scraped against the stone floor. At the mouth of the cave, he crouched and observed.

A fishing boat filled with men had anchored in the little cove beneath the cliff. He counted the men. There were thirteen strong working men. Cleon reached for a weapon, something he could use to protect himself. He grabbed a human thighbone, and he waited to see if the men would approach.

Some gathered wood. Others cast a net. It wasn't long before the men were standing around a fire, roasting fish and making light conversation.

That was when the voices began again, moaning voices, screaming voices. "We know who you are. Stay away! Stay away!"

Cleon put both hands to his head, pressing on his own skull, in a futile effort to squeeze the voices out. When that didn't work, Cleon added his own screams to the frenzied voices within his head.

Peter looked up from the half-eaten fish in his hands. "Oh, Master, is that some kind of wild animal? That shrieking makes the hair on the back of my neck stand up."

Jesus looked up toward the top of the cliff. Then he responded, "That is not the cry of an animal. It is a child of God."

"Did some heathen mother leave an infant to die?" Andrew asked.

"No." Jesus rose to his feet and walked briskly to the trail that zigzagged across the face of the cliff. There was urgency in each hurried step.

The disciples followed.

Cleon saw the men coming. He wanted to run away. He wanted to hide. He wanted to fight, but his eyes locked with the deep brown eyes of the man in the lead. At first, Cleon could not move, and then he sensed a presence in his heart. It compelled him to leap to his feet and start running. As he ran to meet the men, Cleon shouted, "Why have you come? Jesus, Son of the God of Abraham, have you come to punish me?"

"Be careful, Master," Peter warned as he tried to hurry forward and make himself a buffer between Jesus and the mad man. But the trail was narrow and Peter could not get around Jesus.

From behind, Andrew added his own warning, "We've heard about this man." But the rest of his cautionary words died on his lips when he saw the deranged man stop and fall pathetically to his knees in front of Jesus.

Immediately, Jesus also dropped to his knees. He reached out and firmly took the naked, trembling man by the shoulders, lifting him up so he could look into his eyes.

The closest disciples cringed. The smell, the filth that covered this man's naked body. How could their master touch—it was worse than leprosy!

"Fear not. I see your problem," Jesus reassured, but the man seemed unable to comprehend. Again, Jesus looked deeply into his eyes, and then Jesus said, "I command the evil within this man to leave!"

The disciples watched the man shudder. His eyeballs rolled back into his head, like a man about to die.

Jesus kept his firm grip. Still holding the man upright, Jesus demanded, "Evil, tell me your name."

Without moving his lips, the man responded in an unnatural guttural voice, "My name is Legion for we are a mighty segment of the army of Satan."

Suddenly, a chorus of demonic voices shrieked, "What will you do with us, Yeshua-Jesus? We know you have come from the Most High. Do not send us to the place of torture before our appointed time. We beg you. We beg you. We beg you."

"Where would you go?" Jesus asked.

"We must inhabit flesh and blood," they chorused. "Send us into the pigs."

The disciples looked around, and for the first time, noticed a herd of pigs foraging on the plateau that was the top of the cliff.

"Go!" With one word, Jesus granted their request.

Immediately, there were frantic squeals and grunts followed by running hooves. Amazed, the disciples watched forty swine rush headlong over the cliff, plummeting onto the rocks and waves below.

When they turned back from that horrific sight, they saw Jesus embracing the naked, filth-encrusted man, and the man was in his right mind.

Jesus stepped out of the embrace and looked at his disciples. "This is Cleon," he introduced the delivered man.

It did not take long for the men to lead Cleon to the placid water beside their boat. Cleon washed, and Peter baptized him. James found some extra clothing. The tunic had a little fishy smell, but Cleon was thrilled to be dressed and normal.

For the next few days, Jesus and his disciples camped near the cove. Michael set an angelic guard so Jesus could teach without disturbances. The men sat around the fire, and Jesus exposed his enemy, Satan. He described his strategies and the hierarchy of his evil kingdom.

Cleon, especially, was totally amazed, totally grateful to be a captive who had been set free.

The morning came when the fishermen-disciples began to ready their boat. Cleon was preparing to go with them, but Jesus took him aside. "My friend, you cannot go where we go. Our friends and our families will not accept a non-Jewish person. Return to your own family. Show them what the God of Israel has done for you and know that his love extends to you and to many others who are not descendants of Abraham."

Chapter 19

More Miracles in Capernaum

When Jesus had again crossed over by boat to the other side of the lake, a large crowd gathered around him while he was by the lake.

—Mark 5:21

Jairus stood in the doorway of the synagogue of Capernaum. From there, he could see the waterfront and the crowds restlessly milling about. Rabbi Yonatan joined him. For a brief time, both men watched the people. Then Yonatan asked, "Is Jesus the Healer in town?"

"No." Jairus's answer was unusually short.

"He might be dead," the rabbi offered.

Slightly alarmed, Jairus quickly turned and asked, "Why would you think he is dead?"

"Peter's boat is not at its mooring, and the last time I saw Jesus, he was in Peter's boat when a violent storm overpowered them."

"Peter and his friends have weathered storms before," Jairus replied. "That idea is just your own wishful thinking."

"Storms follow that man on land and on the sea. Jesus is very dangerous because he draws unsuspecting people into his turbulence," Yonatan protested. Then he added, "I know, I nearly drowned in the squall that overtook us last week."

"Bless the Holy One, for he spared both of your boats!" Jairus suddenly became excited. "I see Peter's boat! It's coming in. I'm going to tell my wife." Before the last word left his lips, the president of the synagogue at Capernaum was running down the path.

Yonatan felt extreme annoyance bubbling up within, like a little spring quickly becoming a mighty river. How can this man who has no official education and no connection with any school of rabbinical teaching set himself up to be the teacher for both Galilee and Jerusalem? In front of everyone, I'm going to expose his ignorance! Before the thought was complete, Rabbi Yonatan was hurrying toward the waterfront with plans to meet that boat and challenge Jesus as soon as he set foot on shore.

Jairus rushed into his house, "Shira?" He called his little girl's name as he hurried to her bedside.

His wife looked up, dry-eyed and drawn. "The fever still rages in her body, and she only speaks a few confused words as if her mind is separating from her body."

"The Healer has returned." Jairus placed a reassuring hand on his wife's shoulder. "Peter's boat is coming in, and I know Jesus is with him. I will bring him back."

Jairus ran from the room, nearly knocking down a servant who was bringing a fresh basin of water so they could continue sponging the feverish child.

Jesus picked up a mooring line and tossed it to John, who jumped into the water pulling the boat to its anchorage. Immediately, the rest of the disciples leapt from the boat, forming a human barricade between Jesus and the surging crowd. Most of the people responded to their instructions, "Sit down. Our master will speak to each one. Be patient!"

Rabbi Yonatan had no time for directions from fishermen. He pushed forward, using his name and title to get past Judas.

"Rabbi? Rabbi Jesus? I have a question for you."

Jesus looked down at the pompous, pushy man so filled with self-righteousness. Then he looked out at the crowd so beaten by the evil Satan had unleashed upon the world. Jesus sighed.

And the Holy Spirit directed, "Deal with this man quickly. There are more pressing matters."

"Yes?" Jesus refocused on the rabbi, acknowledging that Yonatan had his attention.

"It is the fifth day of the week, a fast day for all the truly observant. Do you and your disciples fast every second and fifth day?"

Jesus laughed a little at the absurdity of the question, and then he answered. "I'm still picking little bits of fresh fish from between my teeth. We had a good catch this morning and a good meal."

Then Jesus became serious and spoke the words the Holy Spirit put on his lips. "You are asking if my disciples are like the disciples that follow the other rabbis in Jerusalem. The answer is no!" He pointed to the muscular men who were organizing the crowd. "They are working men, and working men eat every day. They are laborers in the Kingdom of God."

Yonatan sneeringly repeated, "Working men, common laborers."

Jesus ignored his rudeness. "It is a new thing that God is doing. He is preserving all the words he spoke to Moses, but he is sweeping away the traditions of the rabbis. Those traditions, such as fasting every second and fifth day, are works of men, and they cannot hold the weight of what God is now doing. *No one tears a patch from a new garment and sews it on an old one. If he does, he will have torn the new garment, and the patch from the new will not match the old. And no one pours new wine into old wineskins. If he does, the new wine will burst the skins, the wine will run out and the wineskins will be ruined. No, new wine must be poured into new wineskins.*"[1]

Then Jairus, the president of the synagogue at Capernaum, hurried forward. Frantically pushing his way between Rabbi

Yonatan and Jesus, he dropped to his knees before Jesus. "My daughter, my beautiful Shira, is dying. Please come. Touch her and speak healing words so she will live." Immediately, Jesus went with him.

The crowd groaned in disappointment as they watched Jesus leave. Then, breaking through the wall of disciples, the people followed and crowded around him until walking became slow and difficult.

Desperately, Jairus pushed and shoved, trying to make a way. Peter and some of the other disciples put their shoulders and commanding voices into moving the people who were right in front of their master. From behind, a little woman threaded her way between the crushing bodies.

She had heard of the healer, and he was her last hope. For twelve years, she had been unclean, discharging blood every day instead of just a few days each month. Her husband could not touch her. She could not wash in the purification pool, visit the home of a friend, or enter a house of worship. Because she was a woman of means, the physicians had come with their tormenting instruments and bitter-tasting remedies. Nothing helped. A quiet divorce and a life of seclusion loomed on the horizon of her life.

But she wouldn't slip into oblivion that easily. She was going to fight for the life God meant for her to have. Tenaciously, she wormed her way closer and closer. Obviously, the healer had another mission. He was walking away with an important man. She was just an unclean woman.

Her mind said, Give up.

Her heart said, *If I just touch his clothes, I will be healed.*[2]

Following her heart, the woman stretched until her fingertips barely brushed the fringes of his prayer shawl. At the moment of contact, a jolt of power rolled through her body, igniting a fire inside her womb—it burned intensely. *Immediately her bleeding stopped and she felt in her body that she was freed from her suffering.*

At once Jesus realized that power had gone out from him. He turned around in the crowd and asked, "Who touched my clothes?"[3]

"Master?" Peter was incredulous. He looked around at the pressing crowd. How can you ask, *'Who touched my clothes?'*"[4]

"Hurry! Hurry!" Jairus urged. "My little Shira is so ill."

Still Jesus remained immovable and looking around.

Then the woman, realizing that a miracle had taken place in her body, stepped forward. Timidly, she told her story.

Reassuringly, Jesus smiled. "Daughter of Abraham, your persistent faith initiated your healing. Now go home. Live in peace and happiness with your husband."

While Jesus was blessing the woman and sending her back to her home, some servants arrived from the home of Jairus. "Do not spend more time running after the healer. Shira has taken her last breath, and your wife said for you to return as quickly as possible."

"Too late! It is too late!" Jairus wailed as he dropped to his knees in the dust of the road.

"No, no," Jesus reassured as he indicated that Peter, who was closest to the man, should bring him up to his feet. Then Jesus looked directly into the eyes of the synagogue ruler. "Don't despair; just believe."

Jesus looked at Andrew and sternly directed, "Keep the people here." Then he motioned for Peter, James, and John to come with him. Breaking free of the crowd, Jairus led the men to his home.

When they entered the house, Jesus could see the professional mourners had already arrived, such an unholy commotion filled the room—shrieks and wails, flutes and drums.

Standing in the entrance, Jesus firmly announced, "All this is unnecessary. The child is not dead. She sleeps."

The parents had no response. They just stared at Jesus, mute with grief and confusion. But the mourners loudly laughed at his statement. It was taunting laughter, demons jeering through the open mouths and yellowed teeth of old women. Behind the women, Premature Death gloated.

Righteous anger welled within the Messiah, and Jesus leveled a fiery glare at both the women and their demons. "Get out!" It was a command that could not be ignored.

Immediately, the three disciples who had accompanied Jesus moved to propel and assist the women, carrying their stools and musical instruments out the door, efficiently depositing everything on the dusty road.

After the house had been cleared, Jesus took Jairus by the elbow, guiding both parents into the room where the child lay. His three disciples followed, standing by the wall and watching as Jesus approached the bed.

"Little girl?" Jesus bent so his breath blew softly across her face as he spoke. "Shira? Get up." The fringes of his prayer shawl brushed across the girl's body as Jesus took her by the hand. "Come, Shira, touch the fringes of my prayer shawl." Jesus moved again so the fringes brushed across her hand one more time.

Immediately, the girl sat up. Then she stood and walked around, smiling shyly at the strangers in her room as she found a safe place between her parents.

At this, everyone in the room was completely astonished, overwhelmed and amazed. "Now I believe," Jairus stated. "You are the One we have been waiting for."

Then Jesus spoke very seriously. "I have many enemies. You know some of them. Please, do not tell what has happened here. It will only be twisted against you and against me." Then Jesus bent down and smiled at Shira, "Are you hungry? I think you have not eaten in some time." Jesus looked up at her mother, "Feed this child. Her fever is gone, and it will not return."

By the time Jesus, along with Peter, James, and John, left the home of Jairus, darkness had driven most of the people back to their homes or campsites. Peter glanced at the night sky. There was no moon, and a heavy cloud cover hid the stars. The fisherman shrugged. In his hometown of Capernaum, he did not need to see the paths to make his way around. Confidently, he began leading the way back to his home.

Jesus and his friends were close to Peter's home when they heard shuffling footsteps on the path behind them and voices calling out, "Son of David, pity us. Have mercy."

"Hurry," Peter urged. "Once we are in my courtyard, I will lock the gate and send these men away so we can rest."

"No," Jesus replied. "Bring them in and I will meet their needs before I rest." Then with Holy Spirit insight, Jesus directed James and John, "Give these men assistance. They are blind."

Inside Peter's house, Jesus sat comfortably watching and giving silent approval as James and John assisted the two blind men. Water for washing hands and water for drinking, a little food, and the comfort of cushions, the men were treated like welcome guests.

When all had been done, Jesus approached the men. "Why have you come?"

One man answered, "We have heard that you are a healer sent from God. Restore our sight."

"Do you believe I have the authority to perform such a miracle?" Jesus asked.

Both men immediately replied, "Yes, Lord."

"Every time you have been in town, we have gathered with the crowd, listening to all you have said and listening to what others have said. We believe!"

Then Jesus reached out with both hands, touching the eyes of each man. "Because you have come to this place proclaiming your faith, be restored!"

At that moment, sight returned to both men, and they screamed and danced wildly around the room. When they had calmed, Jesus warned, "Do not tell what I have done this night. Please understand, I have powerful enemies. When they cannot touch me, they will turn on you."

The men did not need to be led to the door. They could see, but Peter accompanied them, asking questions, trying to really understand the depth of their need and the magnitude of the miracle.

Peter did not return to Jesus alone. A drooling, wild-eyed man was with him.

Jesus looked up to see a Mute spirit frantically trying to evade the sinless gaze that was now fixed on him.

"Enough!" That one word from the lips of Jesus brought complete calmness to the possessed man. Then Jesus called him over and indicated that he should sit on the cushion beside him.

"How long have you been this way?" Jesus asked. And then Jesus added, "It's all right. You can speak. The demon is gone, and he will not torment you again."

Jesus turned to Peter. "Bring some food and water. I want to visit with this man."

When Peter returned to serve the man, he looked at Jesus and said, "A crowd is gathering again. I hear everyone talking about the two blind men who were just healed. They must have told every relative and acquaintance. Even Rabbi Yonatan is out there gathering information and telling everyone that you can only cast out demons because you are empowered by the Prince of Demons."

Jesus shrugged off Yonatan's statements. Then he said, "Tomorrow, we will begin another teaching tour. We will start in Nazareth."

Chapter 20

A Cold Reception in Nazareth

A man's enemies will be the members of his own household.

—Matthew 10:36

Enos, the eldest son of James was the first to hear the commotion on the road. He left his father at the workbench and ran to the door. Looking out on the road that led into Nazareth, he joyfully announced, "Jesus is coming."

With a disgusted grunt, James set his hammer on the bench and walked to the door. He saw his older brother flanked by fishermen, tax collectors, peasants, even women. "The rabbi with his followers," James sarcastically commented. "He always brings trouble to town. Then he leaves, and I have to restore the family name." James turned away from the scene, but Enos ran down the road to meet his favorite uncle.

Jesus saw the young man coming and swooped him into a big embrace. Then he stepped back and looked his nephew up and down. "I believe you are taller than I am."

Enos laughed and quickly responded, "Grandmother says I look like Grandfather Joseph. I remind her of when he was a young man, and they were betrothed." Then in a quieter voice, Enos added, "She told me the story. She told me about the angel, about your birth, the shepherds and the wise men."

"How is your father?" Jesus changed the subject.

"He's working, saving money so I can get a wife in a year or two," Enos answered

"A wife?" Jesus looked at his nephew again. "I guess you are getting old enough. "I will ask my Father to find the right girl for you."

"Your Father? You're not talking about Grandfather Joseph, are you? Grandmother told me. God is your father."

"You are correct," Jesus answered. "But I don't speak of this to many people—they don't understand."

"The people understand miracles." With his arm, Enos made a sweeping gesture that said, Look at all those who are following you!

"Everywhere I go, the people have needs," Jesus replied.

Enos responded eagerly, "Grandmother Mary told me about the healings and casting out demons. She saw it with her own eyes. I want to see those things too!"

"Stay with me, Enos. We will see what my Father tells me to do." Jesus reached up and playfully tugged at the scraggly hairs of his nephew's new beard. "It seems like you have become a man overnight."

Behind Jesus, the disciples began to take charge of the crowd. Enos could hear Peter's voice above all the others. "There are camping places in the pastures just outside of town. Spring water is in the middle of the town, and there is a market."

Jesus spoke to Enos again, "I will be bringing my twelve disciples to stay with me at the family home. I want you to go with Judas." Jesus called the disciple who carried his money forward. "Take Judas to the market and purchase enough food for the family and for my friends, so we can all eat for several days. We do not want to be a burden on the family."

Enos nodded and then set out, eagerly leading Judas into town.

By Sabbath morning, James wore a scowl like an impending thunderstorm. The only man in the synagogue with a darker scowl was Chebar. By popular demand, he was being pressured to call Jesus, the son of Joseph, up to the bema to read and comment on the Torah.

That morning in the Synagogue of Nazareth, every bench was filling quickly. No one had a good excuse to stay home. Jesus, the son of Joseph, was in town. Stories were passing from man to man, rumors from Jerusalem as well as accounts of healings within their own town of Nazareth.

It was whispered that Alon the cheesemaker had visited in the home of Mary. Everyone knew Alon had become terribly hunched and had to lean heavily on a walking stick. Today, his back was straight, and there was a knowing smile on his face.

The men looked around for someone who could confirm the story. Mary's grandson, Enos, grinned and nodded. "Yes, Jesus had touched Alon's back."

In the women's section, the ladies were also sitting shoulder to shoulder, whispering and wondering if they would see an amazing healing. Ruth, Mary's oldest daughter, mentioned that Salmon had brought his granddaughter, heavy with her first child, to visit Jesus. The whole family had been so concerned because the child in the girl's womb had not moved in weeks. Ruth said that she saw Jesus take the fringes of his prayer shawl and touch both sides of the girl's extended belly. Suddenly, the babe within her began moving and kicking so much that the belly underneath the girl's robes bounced from side to side. The women laughed when they heard that story.

Then Moshe showed everyone the tooth that had been abscessed. It was now completely well since he had visited Jesus in his boyhood home and accepted a cup of water from his hand.

Speculation and opinion moved from group to group and controlled the room until Jesus walked in with his family and his disciples. All eyes turned to the healer. For a moment, there was contemplative silence. He looked like such an ordinary man, a familiar face in the community until just a few years ago.

Jesus found a seat with his disciples. James motioned for his son to stand with him by the door.

Then conversations picked up again. Some asked, *"What's this wisdom that has been given him, that he even does miracles?"*

Others said, *"Isn't this the carpenter? Isn't this Mary's son and the brother of James, Joseph, Judas, and Simon? Aren't his sisters here with us?"*[1]

James spoke to Enos, "Do you hear what the men are saying? They are implying that my brother is a fraud. They are suggesting he is pretending to be more than he is."

"But, Father," Enos protested. "You saw the miracles. Some happened right in our courtyard."

"Chebar told me that some scholars believe Jesus does miracles through the power of the Evil One," James growled.

"No!" Enos disagreed. "Jesus is a righteous man. His Father is God."

"My mother shouldn't have told you that story." James crossed his arms and glared across the room at his brother.

The service began with the Sabbath morning chants and the opening of the wooden case that held the sacred scrolls. Chebar lifted the scroll of the fourth book of Moses. He kissed it and carried it over his heart to the reader's table. Following the protocol for that day, the scroll was opened, and Jesus was called. "Jesus, son of Joseph the deceased carpenter of Nazareth, come forward."

Respectfully, Jesus stood and took his place behind the table. He covered his head with his prayer shawl. Taking the fringes in his fingers, he touched the Hebrew script, and then he kissed the fringes. Following the characters from right to left, he began to read, "*Miriam and Aaron began to talk against Moses because of his Cushite wife, for he had married a Cushite. 'Has the Lord spoken only through Moses?' they asked. 'Hasn't he also spoken through us?' And the LORD heard this.*"[2]

Jesus glanced up. He saw the faces of his neighbors and his relatives. Instantly, he knew the thoughts of the people because the Holy Spirit revealed them to him. He saw the spirits of Doubt and Mockery hovering in the room.

That pause was brief. Jesus returned his attention to the scroll. "The Lord came down in a cloud and God *said, 'Listen to my words: "When a prophet of the LORD is among you, I reveal myself to him in visions, I speak to him in dreams. But this is not true of my servant Moses; he is faithful in all my house. With him I speak face to face, clearly and not in riddles; he sees the form of the LORD. Why then were you not afraid to speak against my servant Moses?*"'"[3]

Jesus stepped back from the reader's table. His eyes met the eyes of men he had known all his life. "You came to this place today like Romans running to the hippodrome, intent on being entertained. You planned to pass judgment on what you saw. In other towns, I have spent time, and when I left, not one illness or deformity remained in the town, but I am in my hometown. Here I am a prophet without honor. I will not entertain you. After today, you will rarely see me here again."

In the morning, Jesus said good-bye to his mother. Enos wanted to go with him, but James refused to allow his son to attach himself to the crowd that followed his older brother.

So Jesus left. He continued traveling in the region of Galilee, healing and proclaiming the Kingdom of God on Earth. And each Sabbath, he was welcomed into a synagogue and invited to the bema to teach.

Chapter 21

Twelve Are Sent Out

When he saw the crowds, he had compassion on them, because they were harassed and helpless, like sheep without a shepherd.

—Matthew 9:36

The day had been long. Peter's fishing boat glided easily over the water toward its home anchorage at Capernaum. Jesus settled himself in the bow of Peter's boat. The rest of the twelve who had worked with him all day found places to relax. The men began passing around loaves of fresh flat bread, a provision from Peter's wife. Matthew produced a wine skin, and James pulled a sack of dried sardines from behind the nets.

Jesus took a handful of dried fish and asked, "Have you noticed? You are no longer working at your professions, but we are never without adequate food, clothes, and shelter." Then he looked each man in the eye. "Are you willing to take a greater step of faith?"

Peter was the first to respond. "I know we can do anything with you."

"What about doing things without me?" Jesus challenged. "What about splitting up and traveling in different directions?" He pointed to Peter. "You lay hands on the sick." He pointed to Peter's brother, Andrew. "You cast out demons in my name." To John, he said, "Touch the leper." And to John's brother James, he said, "Heal the blind."

Jesus stood, easily balancing with the gentle movements of the boat. Every eye was fixed on his face. "Judas."

The treasurer for the band of twelve looked up with a "who, me?" expression on his face.

"Leave the money bag with me and set out with nothing but your staff and your sandals. Do you have faith to believe God has someone to take you in, to give you food and shelter? Matthew, will you go in my name and tell people the things you have heard me say? Simon?" Jesus pointed to the disciple often called the Zealot. "Are you afraid of the radical Jews in the synagogues? You know some will arrest you and beat you."

Jesus turned to Philip. "Others will tell lies about you and run you out of town. When this happens, you are to shake the dust of that town from your sandals and move on to another place. My Father who sees and knows all will deal with them at the judgment."

With a little smile on his face, Jesus pointed to another young man. "Thaddaeus, you have been very quiet. Are you hoping I would overlook you? I might overlook you, but the Holy Spirit has a word for you, '*Do not be afraid of those who kill the body but cannot kill the soul. Rather, be afraid of the One who can destroy both soul and body in hell. Are not two sparrows sold for a penny? Yet not one of them will fall to the ground apart from the will of your Father. And even the very hairs of your head are all numbered. So don't be afraid; you are worth more than many sparrows.*'"[1]

Thomas looked up at Jesus. A little hesitantly, he began his question. "How will we get the people to gather to hear us?"

Jesus answered, "Go into the center of town, or to the market and say, 'Bring me all your deaf. When the deaf arrive put a finger in each ear. Speak my name, and when you remove your fingers, they will hear."

"When will we go?" Bartholomew asked.

"In the morning," Jesus answered. "Now, when we have docked, go to your homes. Return to me at dawn. I will be in this boat. My Father and I have much to discuss tonight."

Soon after sunrise, Jesus saw his disciples coming, one by one, dressed for travel. On the dock near Peter's boat, he gathered them around him, each man standing close enough to touch. And he said, *"Do not go among the Gentiles or enter any town of the Samaritans.*[2] I am sending you to your own people. *Whatever town or village you enter, search for some worthy person there and stay at his house until you leave.* [3] In every town and city, there are some who hate me, so *be as shrewd as snakes and as innocent as doves. Be on your guard against men; they will hand you over to the local councils and flog you in their synagogues."*[4]

Jesus paused and looked at the serious faces before him. "I know you are concerned. *But when they arrest you, do not worry about what to say or how to say it. At that time you will be given what to say, for it will not be you speaking, but the Spirit of your Father speaking through you.*[5] I have this promise for you. *'Whoever acknowledges me before men, I will also acknowledge him before my Father in heaven. But whoever disowns me,* the one who came from heaven to Earth…*I will disown him before my Father in heaven.'"*[6]

Then Jesus moved from man to man. He laid both hands on the head of each man and said, "Receive power from on high."

Each man felt wonderful waves of energy surge through the core of his body.

Then Jesus took the fringes of his prayer shawl. He kissed the fringes and placed the fringes on the lips of each man. As he did this, he said, "Speak the words I have given you."

At that moment, the words of the Holy Spirit were ready to explode from their mouths.

Then, holding each face with both hands, he blew his warm breath on each man and said, "Receive the Spirit that heals and gives life."

That one little puff of air knocked each man to his knees.

Then Jesus raised his arms, and all the men stood. All twelve were quiet and introspective, overcome with their new infilling of the Spirit.

Jesus walked among them, placing the men in pairs. Then Jesus said, "Go. Come back to me in two weeks so I can hear about your journey. Remember, anyone *who receives you receives me, and he who receives me receives the one who sent me…* He *will receive a righteous man's reward.*"[7]

Two weeks passed. Jesus waited on the hill overlooking the road that ran through Capernaum. From a distance, he saw his disciples returning, excitedly meeting up and exchanging stories. They came to him, running and leaping, everyone speaking at once.

The sick had been healed. The lame had walked. The deaf heard and spoke. A dead man came to life, and many lepers were totally cured. Best of all, demons had fled from their victims.

"What about persecution?" Jesus asked.

The men shrugged it off.

"Thomas was beaten," Thaddaeus offered.

"Judas and I spend several nights without a roof over our heads," Matthew added.

"We spent a night chained to the synagogue wall," James and John informed. "But it was nothing. In the morning, we healed the magistrate. He had a serious bowel problem. We were blessed and sent on our way."

"You are worthy followers," Jesus said. "You took up your cross. You risked your lives. It will always be that way for my true followers."

Jesus looked out from the top of the hill. He saw a man walking slowly into town. The Holy Spirit whispered the name Geber. And Jesus quickly dispatched Peter to meet him.

As Geber came within speaking distance, Jesus knew the news was not good. "John?" he asked.

"Herod took his head," Geber responded.

All of the men dropped to their knees, mourning. For every man there had been touched by John. Most had received his baptism. Some had been with him as disciples.

When the men had recovered from their first wave of sorrow, Geber spoke to Jesus again. "An official in the court of King Herod told me that you healed his little boy. He gave me this message for you, 'Herod Antipas has heard about all you are doing. Right now, the ruler of Galilee is fearful. The Nabataean army has attacked and taken several of his towns. The people are saying, "Herod Antipas has suffered defeat because he killed John, the prophet of the desert." The king's behavior has become erratic and unpredictable. Stories about the healer have reached him. He *is perplexed, because some* are *saying that John* has *been raised from the dead, others that Elijah* has *appeared, and still others that one of the prophets of long ago* has *come back to life*.... At night, Herod is pacing the halls of the palace muttering to himself, *"I beheaded John. Who, then, is this I hear such things about?"*[8] Herod Antipas wants to see you, but this official fears that he will imprison you, and your fate will be the same as John's."

Jesus nodded thoughtfully. Then he responded, "I know the man you are speaking of. His name is Cuza, and Capernaum is his hometown. We will leave the towns and populated areas for a while." He embraced Geber as he spoke into his ear. "Old friend, you have been so loyal to John. Where will you go and what will you do now?"

Geber replied, "I will go back to my brothers who are mourning. I will stay with them and comfort them."

Jesus nodded and embraced him again. "My Father will not allow the death of his servant John to go unpunished. Neither will the life of John go unrewarded. Tell his disciples, '*I tell you the truth: Among those born of women there has not risen anyone greater than John the Baptist...From the days of John the Baptist until now, the kingdom of heaven has been forcefully advancing, and forceful men lay hold of it. For all the Prophets and the Law prophesied until John. And if you are willing to accept it, he is the Elijah who was to come.*[9]'"

Walking down the mountain, Jesus and his disciples got into Peter's boat, but not before someone shouted, "There is Jesus the Healer!"

Immediately, a crowd began to gather. The disciples jumped into the boat and quickly pushed off. Andrew raised the sail, and Peter stood at the steering oar. Jesus and the other disciples watched as a crowd gathered on shore. The people did not just stay in one place. They began to hurry along the road that followed the shoreline of the lake.

"These people will not let us get away!" James exclaimed.

Across the water, Jesus could hear them calling. "Healer! Healer! Help us!"

When it became obvious that the people were not going to return to their towns, Jesus instructed Peter to find an anchorage so he could minister to them.

"Jesus," Philip protested, "we haven't even eaten, today."

Andrew added, "Couldn't we sail to a nearby town, buy some bread, and then return to these people?"

Jesus answered, "The needs of these people are greater than your need to eat." Jesus pointed toward the growing mass of people. They filled the road as far as the disciples could see.

Obediently, Peter steered; a gusty breeze carried the fishing boat past the people into a little cove. Jesus and his disciples got out of the boat and quickly hiked to the top of a nearby hill. They knew from experience that they could control the crowd best from a hilltop.

The people began to come begging for relief from the physical and spiritual torments of life. The disciples took their places, forcing an orderly approach to their master. There was a little lull. In that one quiet moment, Andrew's stomach growled. It was a distressed cry for food that each disciple identified with—all the men were hungry.

Jesus bowed his head, listening to directions from the Holy Spirit. When he looked up, he saw the vast crowd, and the Spirit of God overshadowing that mass of humanity.

Turning to Philip, Jesus asked, "Where can we purchase food for all these people?"

Philip's mouth dropped open. He looked at Jesus. He looked back at the massive crowd. "Master, I can't even begin to estimate how many people are in this place. They are covering the entire mountainside down to the water. They extend along the road further than I can see. "We could all work for eight months, and our total wages would not buy even a bite for each person!"

Peter overheard the exchange and turned to his brother, Andrew. "We're hungry. Jesus must be very hungry. Probably, he has been fasting since we ate with him yesterday afternoon."

Andrew responded, "I know I'm hungry. We were in such a hurry to escape this crowd that we did not bring any food." Then with a little shame, he added, "I saw a boy with a basket containing five small loaves and two dried fish. I wanted to take it."

Jesus overhead and said to Andrew, "Bring the boy to me." To the rest of the disciples, he said, "There is plenty of grass here. Have the people sit and prepare for a meal."

Obediently, the disciples went out among the people seating them in groups, ten men with their families in each group.

At the top of the hill, Jesus was in conversation with the boy. "Where are you from, and why did you come with this crowd?" Jesus asked.

"I came to see miracles," the boy answered.

Jesus's eyes twinkled as he asked, "Would you like to see what my Father in heaven can do with the bread and fish in your basket?"

"Oh yes!" The boy quickly handed his small basket to Jesus.

Jesus then took the loaves, all five of them in his hands. He held them up while he chanted the typical blessing, "Blessed are you, O Lord our God who gives us bread from the earth."

All over the mountainside, conversations ceased. In Jewish culture, that blessing was followed by bread, broken, and distributed by the head of the family. Even the disciples, most of whom were out among the people seating them in groups, stopped. James said to his brother, "Look, Jesus is breaking the bread."

John responded, "There are only five little loaves."

The brothers held their breath and counted as Jesus broke the first loaf, then the second, the third. "That's a very small pile of bread," James commented.

"The fourth," John continued counting. But as Jesus broke the fifth loaf, something unusual happened. There was always another piece to break off.

James was the first to realize what was happening. At the top of his lungs, he directed, "We want one person from each group to bring a basket to the top of the hill."

When the little boy's basket was almost filled with bread, Jesus then picked up the fish and broke them into pieces. The first fish broke normally, but the second fish, like the bread, always had another piece ready to break off. "Take this basket to your family," Jesus instructed. "And share with those around you."

For the rest of the afternoon, Jesus broke bread and fish. The disciples continued to go among the people, keeping them in orderly groups and patient lines. As the sun set, Jesus gathered his disciples. "I must remove myself from this crowd. There is a spirit moving among them that desires to force me into a kingship that has not be ordained by my Father. Now go out, gather the pieces of bread and fish that are left over so nothing is wasted. Give the leftovers to the poor. Then get in the boat and go over to the other side of the lake. I will send these people to their homes, and then I will slip away into the hills where they cannot follow me."

So the disciples gathered and filled twelve baskets with broken barley loaves and pieces of fish. As the sun dropped toward the horizon, the disciples went down to the lake. They climbed into their boat and set sail for Capernaum.

Chapter 22

Jesus Walks on the Water

By now it was dark, and Jesus had not yet joined them. A strong wind was blowing and the waters grew rough.

—John 6:17–18

Jesus walked for several hours in the darkness, over deserted, rocky hillsides. He stopped when he came to a grove of trees. There, he settled with his back against the rough bark, waiting to hear his Father call him by his heavenly name, Yeshua. There was a slight rustling. Jesus knew a night predator was near, but that knowledge did not disturb the way he listened for the voice of his Father.

A moment later, Jesus felt a swirling warmth. Then he found himself engulfed in brilliant white light.

"Yeshua!"

Jesus heard his eternal name, like glorious music. He looked up and joyfully greeted his old friend.

"Moses!"

The heavenly visitor sat down beside him. "I watched you with all those hungry people today. It reminded me of those days when the entire camp of Israel came to me for food. They were ready to kill me, but it was not God's time for my life to end."

"I gave bread and fish to more than five thousand," Jesus said, "but it did not turn their hearts to God. It just made them greedy for more. The people wanted to make me king so I could heal them and feed them. They did not want to live in righteousness."

"People have not changed," Moses agreed. "Our friend Solomon said it well, '*What has been will be again, what has been done will be done again; there is nothing new under the sun.*'[1] It will takc an act of love so outrageous that every human being will be forced to stop and choose between self-centeredness and sacrifice."

"I know," Jesus spoke sadly. "I must give them this human body, striped and pierced, like a piece of unleavened bread. I must be baked in the oven of persecution so I can be digested by the people."

"And your blood," Moses added. "I wrote, '*The life of a creature is in the blood, and I have given it to you to make atonement for yourselves on the altar; it is the blood that makes atonement for one's life.*'"[2]

Jesus responded, "The third cup of the Passover Seder represents the blood of the Passover lambs. I know it is my blood. The time approaches when my life will pour out of my body like a drink for the world."

"Don't be discouraged," Moses admonished, "your Father God has directed his Holy Spirit to speak to the hearts of men, to draw them to your great sacrifice. As you are raised up, all mankind will be drawn to you."

With that reassurance, Jesus laid his head on Moses's chest. For a long time, Moses held his friend, whispering encouraging words. Then Moses suddenly sat up, and with a little alarm, he warned, "Your disciples are in danger."

Immediately in the Spirit, Jesus could see Peter and the others, struggling against the wind, dropping their sail and ineffectively pulling on the oars. Enabled by the Holy Spirit, Jesus was instantly transported to the edge of the water. It was nearly dawn when he went to them, walking across the lake. A smooth path opened between the angry waves, and he glided along that path, his feet barely touching the water.

To the disciples, exhausted but struggling to point the bow into each wave, it seemed that a ghostly light had suddenly come upon them.

Thomas shouted, "It is a spirit from Sheol. We're going to die! I know it!"

James hotly disagreed, "No! The apparition is passing us by."

"There must be another boat that is about to sink," Andrew declared.

At that moment, their boat suddenly turned, hit broadside by a mighty wave. Instantly, the light was beside them, no longer indistinct. It had the definite form of a man. The disciples screamed in terror.

Then from within the light, they heard a familiar voice. "Fear not! I am coming to you."

"Jesus! It's Jesus!" John exclaimed.

"It can't be." Thomas protested.

Jesus repeated, "Fear not! I am coming."

Peter was the first to respond. "Jesus? If it is you, say the words that will allow me to walk on the water also." Peter then moved to step over the side of the boat.

"No, Peter!" Andrew tried to hold his brother back. "We will never be able to fish you out of these waves."

Over the roar of the whipping wind, Jesus called, "Peter, come to me."

And Peter, knowing the voice of Jesus, threw Andrew off his shoulder and climbed out of the boat. He stepped on the water, tentatively at first. Discovering that the waves held his weight, Peter moved forward toward Jesus, away from the boat.

The wind whipped his beard, and the waves crested at shoulder-height. Ahead, Peter could see Jesus, still beckoning with his outstretched arm. At one point, Peter turned to look back at the boat. The waves had pushed it further away.

Suddenly, a cold wave slapped him in the face, and Peter realized his friends were too far away to attempt a rescue. Panic washed over him. Another wave rose and crested. Jesus was no longer in sight!

Then Peter felt his body sinking into the trough of the wave. "Help me! Jesus?"

Before Peter could cry again, a firm hand grasped his forearm, and he found himself once again standing on top of the water. Jesus was beside him.

"Your faith became too shaky to support your actions. Why did you allow yourself to doubt?" Jesus gently reprimanded.

Peter felt the strength of the hand that held him. It supported him so he stood on top of the water again. Around them, the waves now capped at their waists, while the boat bobbed wildly nearby.

Peter locked eyes with Jesus. "I'm sorry, Master. I should have known that you would never ask me to do something I cannot do." Both men then moved across the water together. And when they climbed into the boat, the wind died down.

As the disciples looked around, they were amazed to find they had been supernaturally transported to a cove on the other side of the lake. Peter was the first to recognize the place. "These are the cliffs where the pigs fell into the sea!" he exclaimed.

Then wet and weary, overcome by the awesomeness of their experience, the disciples dropped to their knees, worshipping Jesus and saying, "Only the Son of God could do these things!"

As soon as they anchored their boat, people recognized Jesus. Quickly, the word spread. "The healer has returned!"

Then from every direction, people came to the lakeshore, carrying their sick on mats. Cleon was one of the first to run into their camp. "I have told everyone how you spoke to the demons, and they left me. The herdsmen told everyone what happened to the pigs. We have been waiting for you to return."

So while Jesus was in that Gentile section of Galilee, Cleon accompanied him. Wherever Jesus went, all were healed.

Jesus and his disciples then left that region of Galilee. They traveled to Tyre on the coast of the Great Sea. On this journey, they did not invite large crowds, and they slept in homes where they were not recognized.

Flanked by his twelve disciples, Jesus led the way over the large paving stones that made the broad busy streets of the seaport city. Past the hippodrome, alongside the massive arches of the aqueduct system, the men were enthusiastically taking in the sights. Thomas, Philip, and Matthew stopped to watch the glass blowing. Thaddaeus and Andrew exclaimed over the vivid purple fabric that was coming out of the dye pots. Peter spotted the Roman bathhouse and was totally amazed to see men using a public toilet that looked like a long stone bench built over a trough. A closer look revealed sticks with sponges attached for completing the process.

"Ah, Master," Peter said as he returned to where Jesus was waiting for his wandering and curious disciples, "there aren't any sights like these in Galilee.

Jesus laughed. "Let's go down to the water's edge. I'm sure there will be sights there that you can relate to."

Lightheartedly, the men followed their teacher. They picked up the scent of salt water and fish. It quickened their steps and put their senses on alert for new experiences. For all of Jesus's followers, it was their first time to venture beyond Galilee, Samaria, and Judea, into the heart of a bustling Gentile city.

Arriving at the stone breakwater, Jesus stopped allowing his followers to take in the vastness of the Great Sea. He could tell by the looks on their faces that the size of everything nearly took their breath away.

"Well, they've got fishermen and nets." James pointed to where the fishermen were stretching enormous nets over large areas of smooth bare rock.

Jesus directed everyone's attention to the rocky causeway that extended far out into the sea."Through the prophet Ezekiel, God declared the destruction of this city, '*I am against you, O Tyre, and I will bring many nations against you, like the sea casting up its waves. They will destroy the walls of Tyre and pull down her towers; I will scrape away her rubble and make her a bare rock. Out in the sea she will become a place to spread fishnets.*'"[3]

John looked around and commented, "Down here by the water and all along that path into the sea that's all I see, bare rocks covered with fish nets."

"Once, the old city of Tyre," Jesus affirmed his observation.

Matthew read the inscription on a nearby monument. "Alexander the Great leveled this port city and threw all the rubble into the sea to create this causeway so his troops could reach the inhabitants who had taken refuge on the island that is just off this coast,"

Jesus added, "And now, this place has become a refuge where we can escape the crowds and rest."

Philip commented, "There aren't many Jews in this city. Probably, no one knows about the crowds that follow you in the region of Galilee."

Looking around, Matthew added, "We are quite removed from the little fishing businesses of Galilee."

"Let's take a closer look at this great body of water." Peter walked to a low spot on the stone breakwater. He got down on his knees and reached over the edge, bringing up a handful of water. He smelled it. Then he tasted it, quickly spitting it back into the sea. "These fish must be salted before they are caught!" he exclaimed. Peter stood again, staring at the Great Sea with a fisherman's eye. "There is no land to the right or to the left. This water seems to go on and on to the end of the Earth."

Jesus looked hard at all twelve of his followers, and then he spoke prophetically, "Each of you will cross this Great Sea one day,"

The men stared back at him, unable to imagine themselves taking such a journey, unable to formulate a response.

Finally, Thomas broke the silence. "I'm hungry,"

Matthew suggested, "We could buy some fish and take it back for the lady of the house to prepare for us."

Andrew responded, "I'd like to taste fish from this salty water."

James and John began drifting away from the group, moving toward the fishing boats that were tied along the shore. "These are sturdier and larger than our boats," James commented. The brothers curiously examined the catch that was piled up by various boats—sponges, trumpet-like shellfish.

Matthew joined them. "I've heard about these shellfish. Inside each shell is a small part of the animal that produces a purple dye."

"We passed the dye pots on the way to the wharf," John added.

"Look at this fish!" Peter called from another section of the dock. "I've never seen a fish this size. It's as big as a man."

"Look closely, brother." Andrew was peering over his shoulder. "These fish are not for eating. They do not have scales."

"I can see that," Peter responded as he bent over to examine the strange sea creature more closely. "This fish has a hole on the top of its head, and its mouth is more like the fleshy beak of a bird than the mouth of a fish." Peter opened the mouth of the dead animal, carefully examining its tongue and sharp teeth.

"It is an unusual creature, I will admit," Andrew responded.

Suddenly feeling alone, Peter and Andrew glanced around to see that Jesus and the rest of their group had moved on to the fresh fish market. Both men lifted their robes and ran to catch up. When they got there, Philip was holding a fish that was as long as his arm and as fat as a man's thigh. Judas was aggressively negotiating the price.

Comfortably full, the disciples leaned back into their cushions. A clean large fish skeleton waited to be cleared from the table.

"Master?"

Jesus looked up, ready to hear John's question. "Why have we come to this place without purposely gathering a crowd and teaching about the kingdom of heaven?"

Jesus answered, "The promise of the kingdom is for the family of the king."

"How do we know who is in the king's family?" James asked.

Jesus replied, "In the beginning, all the privileges of the kingdom belonged to Adam and Eve. They were deceived, and they gave their rights away. But a promise was given to them that a Deliverer would be born. He would restore to mankind all the rights to the kingdom." Jesus looked at his followers. Everyone was listening intently. Jesus continued, "The promise and the seed were passed from generation to generation. Noah carried it on the ark, and out of his three sons, the line of Shem was chosen. Later, the promise was repeated to Abraham. Isaac and his descendants were singled out as guardians of the promise and caretakers of the seed. For that, they have been greatly persecuted."

Just then, there was an urgent knock at the door. Before anyone could open it, a woman burst into the room where the men were resting. "Healer! Healer! I know you are the healer." She ran to Jesus and fell at his feet.

"This is not a Jewish woman!" Judas protested.

Jesus raised a silencing hand and then asked the woman, "What do you need?"

"My daughter is possessed by a demon." The woman lifted her tear-stained face to beg with her eyes. "It shakes her and throws her to the ground. It takes her speech and her good sense. I have heard that demons obey you, and they flee when you command them to go. Please, please, command the demons," she pleaded.

"But woman," Jesus responded, "you are not a daughter of Abraham. *It is not right to take the children's bread and toss it to their dogs."*

"Yes, Lord," she replied, "but even the dogs under the table eat the children's crumbs."

Then Jesus told her, "For such a reply, you may go; the demon has left your daughter."[4]

Jumping to her feet, the woman left as quickly as she had come, and Jesus turned back to his disciples. "The crumbs of my teaching are falling everywhere, and you will find many Gentiles have the faith that is required to lick up those crumbs. Their faith entitles them to the same kingdom benefits as the children of Abraham. Do not deny those who believe."

Then Jesus left the coast of the Great Sea and traveled eastward, to the Sea of Galilee and over into the region of the Decapolis.

James was the first to notice they were being followed. Nudging his brother and then nodding toward the steadily increasing press of people, he said, "I believe Jesus has been recognized."

"Healer! Healer!" the people began to call out to Jesus.

In the middle of the road, Jesus stopped and turned to face the crowd. A confused man was pushed forward. Stumbling through the press of clamoring bodies, he frantically waved his extended arms and unintelligibly stammered, "Make way. Let me through."

Andrew was the closest disciple. He grabbed the man by the shoulders and guided him to Jesus while the onlookers began to chant, "Heal him! Heal him!"

Frantic and shaking, the man sensed he was standing in front of the healer, but in his nervous state, he could not explain his need. Instead of words, only stuttering came from his mouth.

Compassionately, Jesus put one arm around the deaf man's shoulders, carefully leading him away from the crowd. The disciples knew what to do. They formed a barrier with their bodies, giving Jesus the privacy he needed with this man.

Slightly removed from the curious spectators, Jesus stopped and put both hands on the man's face, running his fingers across the man's cheekbones, touching his temples, moving out to both ears. With his fingertips, he searched for the demons who had made this man's body their home. When he touched the man's ears, he suddenly paused and then abruptly put a finger in each ear. "I have found you! You must leave and allow this man to hear."

As Jesus removed his fingers, the man uttered an amazed sound, but it was not a word.

Jesus then moved both hands to the man's mouth. He opened it wide and looked in. "I see you!" Then suddenly, he spit on his own fingertips, and with that saliva, he touched the man's tongue. "Be opened and speak clearly!"

As if exhausted by the effort, Jesus sighed audibly. Then the man began to shout, calling to his neighbors and friends, laughing as he heard and responded.

When Jesus brought the man back to the crowd, their amazement could not be contained. Jesus firmly directed all that were present not to tell anyone about the miracle they had witnessed. But he could not silence them. The people were overwhelmed with amazement, and they could not stop talking.

Chapter 23

The Bread of Life

For the bread of God is he who comes down from heaven and gives life to the world.

—John 6:33

Early in the morning Peter, James, and John stood near the top of a hill and looked at the vast crowd camped in family groups as far as they could see. "These people have been here with us for three days," James stated.

"Don't they have homes and animals to care for?" Peter asked.

"They must be running out of food," John remarked.

"We're running out of food," James added.

"It's time to send these people home," Peter emphatically stated. "I'm going to talk with Jesus." Then he looked at James and John. "You'll come with me, won't you?"

Sitting by the morning fire, Jesus saw his closest disciples approach. He beckoned to them, indicating with his hand that they should sit with him and enjoy the warmth of the fire. Before the men could say what was on their minds, Jesus spoke like he had been part of their previous conversation. *"I have compassion for these people; they have already been with me three days and have nothing to eat. If I send them home hungry, they will collapse on the way, because some of them have come a long distance."*[1]

Peter responded, "They should go home. We cannot feed them."

James looked around. "Haven't you noticed? There is no town in sight, not even a few homes. Where could we get bread for so many?"

"Aren't there a few loaves in the boat?" Jesus asked.

Peter, James, and John exchanged worried glances. "Seven," they replied. "That means we have about a half a loaf for each of us, and then we will go hungry."

"Bring me the bread," Jesus directed as he stood. Moving closer to the summit, he raised his hands to get the attention of the people.

The three disciples were already on their way to bring the loaves to Jesus when they stopped and looked back. Jesus was speaking. His voice was carrying from the top of the hill. "Sit in your family groups. We are going to have breakfast before you return to your homes. I will need each group to send one person with a basket. My disciples will help you make an orderly line."

Peter urged James and John to hurry. "We had better get our bread into the master's hands quickly. This crowd wants to eat. If these people start running up the hill before there is food…," Peter's words trailed off, but his friends knew the pressures and dangers that were part of ministering to large groups of desperate people. They quickened their pace.

It wasn't long before Peter, James, and John were back at the top of the hill, handing Jesus seven large flat loaves of bread. John also produced a handful of small fish. Jesus placed it all in one basket and lifted that basket toward heaven. "Blessed are you, O Lord our God who supplies our daily bread."

All over the mountainside and extending along the road, the people joined in chanting the traditional thanks to God for their sustenance. The sound of four thousand male voices, at least another four thousand females, and two children for every adult reached the throne room.

In heaven, every angel paused to hear the refreshing sound of gratitude swelling from Earth. Led by Gabriel, the angel choirs then raised their own song of praise and adoration for God the Eternal Father, Yeshua the Creator who was now Jesus on Earth, and the Holy Spirit whose mission it was to connect man with God.

"Feed them." The command came directly from the throne room in heaven. Jesus heard it.

Confidently, he passed two loaves to Peter, two to James, and two to John. Then, he gave each man one little dried fish. "Feed the people," he directed.

The three disciples looked at their hands full of food and then at the people. Their eyes met the eyes of their master again. The unwavering confidence that emanated from his brown eyes to theirs suddenly grabbed them, and they began breaking the bread.

Piece after piece, the bread did not end until they had filled more baskets than they could count. And that one little fish that each of the three disciples had, each time they broke the fish in half, a whole fish remained.

By midmorning, the people were obviously satisfied. The disciples could see them relaxing and visiting. Following the directions of their teacher, they walked among the people, gathering the leftovers, then giving those to the poorest in the crowd. When that task was complete, Jesus sent his men to Peter's boat. Then from the top of the hill, he blessed the people. "Your ancestors, during the time of Moses, ate bread from heaven. Today, you have also eaten bread that was miraculously provided by your loving Father. Return to your homes in the strength you have received from eating this bread."

Then Jesus walked down the hillside and got into the boat.

Rabbi Yonatan, Chebar, and Lemuel walked slowly down the main street of Capernaum. They wanted to speak with Jairus before the Friday evening service in the synagogue. He must be informed that the Sanhedrin had commissioned them to bring back a full report on what Jesus was doing and saying. He must understand the urgency of their mission and the importance of his cooperation.

Chebar was the first to see Jairus unlocking the main entrance to the place where the town would soon be gathering for evening and morning Sabbath services

The three men picked up their pace, calling before they were close enough for normal conversation. "Is Jesus in town? Will he be called to read and comment on the scriptures?"

Before answering, Jairus glanced at the docks. "Peter's boat is at its mooring. That usually means Jesus is in town."

The men came into conversational range. "When was the last time Jesus taught in your synagogue? What else has he been doing? Has he said anything that would alarm the Romans or the Temple authorities?"

Jairus looked each man in the eye, and like a revelation, he recognized the evil behind each question. He remembered Jesus's warning after restoring his daughter to life. "Do not tell what has happened today."

Carefully, Jairus answered, "Some time ago, Jesus with some of his disciples entered my home, and I have been a blessed man since that day."

"Jesus is just a man," Rabbi Yonatan huffily responded. "Only God can leave a blessing."

Jairus glanced at the docks again. He studied Peter's boat for a moment, wondering if he should hurry to Peter's house to leave a warning for the healer. Then he looked down the road—he was too late. He saw Jesus, with his twelve disciples, approaching. A large crowd was also following.

Chebar and Lemuel turned. They also saw Jesus. Turning back to Jairus, they said, "Call Jesus to the bema."

Yonatan added, "We have come to hear him teach.

The crowd that followed Jesus filled the road, pushing and trying to get around his disciples. Various voices called out, "Healer, feed us. Perform a miracle."

When it became obvious that they were not going to allow Jesus to quietly enter the synagogue, he turned and spoke to them. "I know why you are clamoring after me. It is not because you saw miracles. It is not because you want to live a life that is pleasing to God. It is because I filled your bellies, and you did not have to work for that food. So foolish! So foolish!" Jesus shook his head and then he shook his finger at them. "This is my Father's admonition, 'Do not expend your energy producing food that spoils after a day or two. Instead, look for the food that has eternal life.' The Promised One who is the seed of Adam is bringing that bread to you. His Father, God, has blessed that bread and with that bread, he will feed the world."

Standing by the synagogue door, Yonatan, Chebar, and Lemuel heard this and asked, "What is this man talking about?"

Jairus responded, "He fed a crowd of more than five thousand men with just a few loaves of bread and a handful of fish. Everyone ate. He did it again just two days ago."

With a little more urgency, the three Pharisees moved away from the entrance to the synagogue so they could see the face of the healer. They found themselves in the middle of a heated dialog between the Jesus and the people.

"What is God asking us to do?"

Jesus answered, "God only has one request. You are to believe that the Promised One has been sent to you."

Within the crowd various men responded. "We need a sign!"

"An amazing and miraculous sign!"

"How will you convince us?"

Jesus replied, "In the days of Moses, manna came down from heaven and the people ate. They were nourished and lived."

In a demanding tone, the people responded, "Yes, Give us bread every day!"

Then Jesus declared, "I am the bread that came down from heaven. If a person believes this, he will never hunger. He will never thirst."

Jesus looked at the faces around him. "I have told you. You have heard me and seen the miracles, but still, you do not believe." Again, Jesus shook his head. "The things I am saying are not my own ideas. I have come from heaven to speak the words of my Father and to do the works he commands. It is my Father's plan for everyone who believes in the Promised One to be raised from their grave in the last day and to then have everlasting life with him."

"What is this man talking about?" Chebar spluttered. "Bringing the dead back to life?"

"Is he trying to tell us that God is his Father?" Lemuel exclaimed.

"That would mean that this man"—Yonatan pointed—"is claiming divinity!"

"Blasphemy!" Chebar yelled.

In a very loud voice, Lemuel protested, *"Is this not Jesus, the son of Joseph, whose father and mother we know?"*

Rabbi Yonatan added, *"How can he now say, 'I came down from heaven'?"*[2]

Jesus could hear others as they began to speak up and question the words he had just spoken. *"Stop grumbling among yourselves!"*[3] Jesus shouted above the confusion of their voices. "Look, I am standing here, and I am the bread that comes down from heaven. The manna in the wilderness was a symbol of who I am and the work I am doing. Eat me and live! My flesh is this bread, and I will give my flesh so the people of the world can have eternal life."

"Eat his flesh? What is this crazy man talking about?" Lemuel was the first to shout this objection, but others soon took it up like a chant.

With fire in his eyes, Jesus turned to face the three Pharisees with whom he had had many encounters. *Jesus said to them* clearly and directly, *"I tell you the truth, unless you eat the flesh of the Son of*

Man and drink his blood, you have no life in you. Whoever eats my flesh and drinks my blood has eternal life, and I will raise him up at the last day. For my flesh is real food and my blood is real drink .[4] This is the bread that came down from heaven. Your forefathers ate manna and died, but he who feeds on this bread will live forever."[5]

On hearing it, many of his disciples said, "This is a hard teaching. Who can accept it?"[6]

Jesus let his eyes scan the crowd. There were many that he knew by name. Some he had healed, others he had delivered from demons, and others who had just shared in his life. Although they were not his close twelve, he considered all of them to be his disciples. Jesus could see the Lying spirits of his enemy moving from person to person, whispering, "The man is insane. Do not follow him. Do not listen to his mad teaching."

Aware that the twelve who traveled and worked with him were also hearing the demonic voices, Jesus turned to them and asked, "Eat my flesh; drink my blood. Does this idea offend you? Are you willing to remain with me until you see me return to my Father in heaven?" He paused, studying their faces. "If you will just stay with me until that event, then you will understand the words I have spoken. Most believe that food gives life, but I am telling you, life comes from the words I speak. My words are not the ideas of men. They are thoughts from the Spirit of God." Jesus looked directly at Judas as he completed his statement. Then he added, "Still, some of you do not believe."

Again, Jesus looked at the crowd. He could see the Lying spirits had had some success. Faces that had been open to him were now closed. Men who had once clung to every word now pushed past Jesus and entered the synagogue. Jesus turned once more to his twelve. "Do you want to leave me also?"

Peter answered, "Rabbi Jesus, who else could we follow? You have taught us the words of eternal life, and we are convinced that you are the Holy One of God."

Then Jesus responded, "Yes, I have chosen you twelve to be my disciples. But one of you is a son of Satan!"

Uncomfortably, the men looked at each other. Who could Jesus be talking about?

Judas broke the worried mood. "Come, let's go into the synagogue and take our seats. The prayers are beginning." With that, Judas led them through the door, and the three Pharisees followed, never taking their eyes from Jesus.

Later in the week, additional men arrived from Jerusalem. They joined Yonatan, Chebar, and Lemuel, showing up whenever Jesus appeared in public and questioning various citizens in private.

All morning, Jesus had been enjoying the privacy of Peter's home, teaching the twelve until he heard their stomachs growl for a meal. Then Jesus brought his disciples to the market of Capernaum, instructing them to buy food and eat. Judas purchased bread and figs for the group. Peter talked a friend into giving them a basket of dried fish. Other disciples went in various directions to acquire their contribution to the meal.

On the grass beneath a shady tree, Thaddaeus spread his cloak. The disciples gathered around, sitting comfortably on the ground and tossing their contributions to the meal on the cloak. James and John had purchased a cheese. Philip offered a small flask of honey, while Matthew laid out a skin of wine from his family's wine cellar.

Without concern for the food, Jesus stepped away. With his hand, he signaled that his disciples should go on and eat the meal without him. Judas was still holding the fresh loaves. Peter quickly snatched one off the stack and led the men in a quick blessing. Before he had finished saying amen, he was breaking the bread and passing the fish. Each man dove into the meal, while Jesus walked back toward the market, toward the men who had been following him since the beginning of last Sabbath.

Without hesitation, Jesus approached them.

Chebar was the first to notice that Jesus was coming toward them. He took a little fearful step backward.

Jesus could easily see the man reacting to the quaking of the Religious spirits that were always at his side. Jesus knew his proximity was greatly disturbing to those spirits whose assignment was to control people through rigid laws that were nothing more than twisted interpretations of the instructions God had given to Moses.

Confidently, Jesus welcomed the men who had just arrived from Jerusalem, "I am honored that you have walked so far to hear me teach and to observe my ministry."

Regaining his composure, Chebar snapped, "You know we are here because the Temple authorities are very concerned. You may be stirring up trouble."

"What kind of trouble?" Jesus asked. "Have I spoken against the authorities?"

"We have not heard those reports," Rabbi Yonatan answered. "But you allow your disciples to set a poor example for the people."

Lemuel jumped in, "Look, your disciples are eating, and they have not followed the washing protocol of the devout! Their hands are unclean so their food has also become unclean

Jesus calmly answered, "The tradition of the elders is not the same as those laws that God spoke to Moses, the ones Moses then wrote for all of Israel. Why do you ignore the words that came from the mouth of God while making an issue out of regulations devised by men?"

"What are you talking about?" Yonatan challenged. "Give us an example."

Jesus replied, "You ignore simple commands such as 'Honor your father and mother' by giving extravagant gifts to the Temple while letting your aging parents do without."

The Holy Spirit pricked the well-known Galilean Pharisee. His own parents were living in poverty while the Temple authorities were praising Yonatan for his generous contributions to the treasury.

Rabbi Yonatan's gaze dropped to the ground. At that moment, he could not look any man in the eye.

Jesus looked around at the people in the market place. Then he beckoned them to gather around. "You came to hear me teach, so you will hear me. *Listen to me, everyone, and understand this. Nothing outside a man can make him 'unclean' by going into him. Rather, it is what comes out of a man that makes him 'unclean.'*"[7]

In that instant, the Holy Spirit spoke again. This time, each man who had come to examine and confront Jesus suddenly saw the pollution that was a part of his own life. Like a nightmare from which they could not escape, relentless visions of wrongdoing pushed to the forefront of their thought processes. At first, the visiting men were speechless. Then they sheepishly turned away and quickly returned to the home where they were staying. The people also drifted back to their buying and selling. Jesus then stood in the road, alone.

When his disciples joined him, Peter asked, "Master, what was all that about?"

"You men ate without first pouring water over your hands," Jesus replied.

"We did not know that that was a requirement for working men," Peter replied with a little amazement.

Jesus gave Peter a good-natured slap on the back. "It's good to wash, but it is not God's requirement for anyone."

One by one, the disciples joined them, and together, the men walked back to Peter's house. Once the gate was closed, Jesus sat with his disciples and seriously explained, "Understand this, the food you eat does not make you unclean. It just goes into your stomach and then out of your body. You need to be concerned with thoughts that enter the heart and mind of a man and then produce actions. *For it is from within, out of a person's heart, that evil thoughts come—sexual immorality, theft, murder, adultery, greed, malice, deceit, lewdness, envy, slander, arrogance and folly. All these evils come from inside and make a man unclean."*[8]

Then Jesus said, "It is time to leave these pesky Pharisees and go where no one will bother us for a few days. In the morning, we will sail to Magdela. I know a woman who will open her home to us. No one will approach us there, and we can rest.

James and John looked questioningly at Jesus. Then, John asked, "Are we going to the home of the sailmaker?"

James added, "The one you healed and delivered from seven demons?"

Jesus answered, "Yes, Mary of Magdela who owns the sailmaker's shop will gladly serve us."

Andrew remarked, "We can be certain no one will disturb us while we remain in her home. She can be a formidable woman!"

The other fishermen-disciples laughed at that understatement. They had all, at one time or another, done business with her establishment.

Jesus just smiled at his disciples. "You will see, now that the demons no longer have access to her mind, she has the heart of a faithful servant."

Chapter 24

Deep in Gentile Territory

Jesus and his disciples went on to the villages around Caesarea Philippi. On the way he asked them, "Who do people say I am?"

—Mark 8:27

Mary of Magdela walked with Jesus from her home to the place where Peter's boat was docked. With a trained eye, she looked at the sail as Andrew prepared for departing. Then she turned to Peter. "Next time you come, I will have a new sail ready for your boat. Jesus must have everything he needs to travel from port to port on this body of water." Her eyes returned to Jesus as she added, "The people need you so much."

It seemed that Mary forgot the other disciples as she continued speaking to Jesus. "Now I know what a miserable life I was leading. You changed everything. Where are you going now? Who will you help?" As she spoke, Mary pressed a large bag of coins into Jesus's hands.

Casually, Jesus passed the bag over to Judas. "We are sailing to Bethsaida. From there, we are walking north to Caesarea Philippi."

Mary gasped, "No other rabbi would set foot in such a godless city! I have heard there is a statue of a Greek god on every corner. And"—she lowered her voice to a secretive whisper—"when they are ready to plant their crops, they go to a big rock just outside the city, and they have sexual relations with goats!"

Jesus nodded. "That may be true, but I get my directions from Father God." Then he lightly added, "I have been informed that it is better to be in the territory of Herod Philip than in the territory of Herod Antipas."

Mary nodded. "I have customers from Tiberias where Antipas maintains most of his governmental offices. They tell me the ruler of Galilee has been like a madman since several of his towns have been taken by the Nabataean army. Rome is sending reinforcements to deal with the Nabataeans. Antipas is raising taxes to cover the expenses, and anyone who speaks a word that might sound treasonous is put in prison."

"Do not be concerned for me," Jesus responded. "No man can touch me unless my Father in heaven declares that it is time."

"Time?" Mary repeated with concern.

"A time will come, Mary. The prophetic songs of my ancestor, David, speak clearly, '*From birth I was cast upon you; from my mother's womb you have been my God. Do not be far from me, for trouble is near and there is no one to help.*'"[1]

"What kind of trouble?" Mary asked.

Jesus took Mary aside, away from his disciples who were preparing the boat. "The prophet Isaiah wrote about me. He wrote what you have witnessed, and he also wrote about those things that are still in the future. God has given me *an instructed tongue, to know the word that sustains the weary.* [2] You have seen the crowds that come to be healed and taught. You also know about those men who come from Jerusalem. They follow me looking for a way to destroy me. One day, I will offer *my back to those who beat me, my cheeks to those who* pull *out my beard; I* will *not hide my face from mocking and spitting.*"[3]

"No, no. This cannot happen to you." Mary was wiping a few tears from her eyes.

"Every Passover, you have heard the story of how God brought Israel out of Egypt *by miraculous signs and wonders, by war, by a mighty hand and an outstretched arm.*[4] Now, all of mankind must be freed from slavery to the Evil One. It can only happen when my arms are stretched out in death, *when all my bones are out of joint...and my tongue sticks to the roof of my mouth.* At that time, *you* will be there to *lay me in the dust of death.*"[5]

"I cannot imagine it. My heart is breaking." Mary's tears flowed freely.

"Believe me, Mary, the prophets also have encouraging words, 'After suffering, the Messiah *will see the light of life and be satisfied.* God *will give him a portion among the great, and he will divide the spoils with the strong, because he poured out his life unto death.*'[6] Death can only hold me for a short time, like Jonah in the belly of the great fish—just three days."

"Why are you telling me these things?" Mary asked between quiet sobs.

"You will be there." Jesus answered. He took Mary's hand as he continued. "I want you to be strong. I want you to have hope. I want you to remember my words and believe the things I have said and not the things you will see with your eyes." Jesus looked over at his disciples who were waiting for him. "On this trip, I will be preparing my close followers for those things that I have just told you. When my time comes, they may forget everything I have said. They may be overwhelmed by fear, but I know you will help them. You will not let their hope die." Jesus looked deeply into Mary's eyes. "I have chosen you."

Mary returned his steady gaze. She willed her tears to stop, and she responded with a level tone. "You can count on me." The tough business woman sealed her commitment with her word. Then she firmly stated her expectation that Jesus keep his part of the contract. "You will come to me after three days."

"I will not let you down," Jesus responded as he gave her hand a reassuring squeeze.

The water was choppy. The breeze was brisk, and Peter's boat flew like a giant brown gull, skimming the wavelets, headed for Bethsaida. The men in the boat were relaxed and jovial until Peter, from his usual post at the steering oar, called, "How about passing a little bread up here?"

"Bread?"

The disciples looked from one to the other, hoping someone had thought to bring some loaves. All eyes stopped on Judas, the keeper of the money.

Andrew roughly demanded, "Didn't you purchase bread at the market just before we embarked?"

Judas glared back at Peter's brother as he responded, "I saw Jesus talking with the woman, Mary of Magdela. She gave him money. I thought she would also give him food for this journey so I did not buy anything."

Thomas responded, "How much would it have cost to have a few extra loaves of bread?"

James looked sternly at the man who seemed to have so little to offer Jesus and his group of followers. "You can't do anything to keep this boat seaworthy, and you cast a net like a school boy."

John interrupted his brother to add his own accusations. "You do very little to manage the crowds, or to help Jesus. All you do is carry a bag of money."

"Is it too much to expect that you would regularly buy us some bread?" Thomas resentfully asked.

"Be thankful you are not required to account for every coin." Matthew was taking advantage of this moment to bring up his own pet peeve. "No one has asked you how much you have or how it is spent. We just want to eat regularly."

"I'm hungry up here!" Peter growled. "Isn't there any food on this boat?"

There was a little rummaging through the rough linen sacks in the storage bin. Philip produced one stale loaf, and he passed it up to Peter with the consoling comment, "I didn't see any mold on it."

Peter took the hard loaf in one hand, feeling the toughness of bread that had probably come from his wife's oven nearly a week ago. "I'll be chewing this all the way to Bethsaida," he remarked before biting off a hard chunk."

Jesus had been deliberately ignoring his disciples, but now, he interjected himself into their conversation. *"Be careful," Jesus warned them. "Watch out for the yeast of the Pharisees and that of Herod."*[7]

Immediately, the disciples began talking among themselves. Everyone except Judas was concerned about the implication of Jesus's words. Was he commending them, or was he pointing out their shortcomings?

Sitting close to the mast, Judas watched his fellow disciples worriedly discuss and speculate. Judas felt that he did not need to engage in their corporate soul-searching. In his heart, he was certain Jesus had just defended him. Judas looked up to catch Jesus looking intently at his face. Their eyes locked, and Judas could not pull his gaze away from those compelling brown eyes. Jesus seemed to be looking though him, reading his soul like an open scroll.

Judas heard one of the disciples say, "We forgot to buy bread. That is why Jesus is displeased with us."

Then Jesus asked, "Why are you talking about a lack of food? Have you forgotten that five loaves fed five thousand and seven loaves fed four thousand with basketsful left over? By now, you should know that I often teach with metaphors. The teaching of the Pharisees and the Sadducees is like the yeast that goes into bread. It is hypocrisy. Do not mix their teachings with my teachings."

Once again, Jesus looked directly at Judas, but he spoke for all the disciples to hear. *There is nothing concealed that will not be disclosed, or hidden that will not be made known. What you have said in the dark will be heard in the daylight, and what you have whispered in the ear in the inner rooms will be proclaimed from the roofs.*"[8]

Judas suddenly felt uncomfortable. He looked away from Jesus as he shifted in his place. Could this man who healed and created food know everything that happened in the land? Like a living memory, a scene from their last trip to Jerusalem ran through his mind, an evening in his family home, a discussion with the head of the Temple guard. He thought no one knew.

He looked back at Jesus, carefully listening and contemplating his words.

"I am telling you these things first, before I teach them to the crowds. *My friends, do not be afraid of those who kill the body and after that can do no more. But I will show you whom you should fear: Fear him who, after your body has been killed, has authority to throw you into hell. Yes, I tell you, fear him,* the one called the Prince of Demons. But he is not greater than my Father who is also your Father. *Are not five sparrows sold for two pennies? Yet not one of them is forgotten by God. Indeed, the very hairs of your head are all numbered. Don't be afraid; you are worth more than many sparrows.*[9] I am telling you this because you will need to remember these things.

"The authorities in Jerusalem are asking questions about me. Those men who have been appointed by Rome to oversee the land are also asking questions. How will you answer?"

Judas felt like he wanted to jump out of the boat and swim to shore. He could take these lowlife fishermen complaining that he had not purchased bread, but he did not want Jesus to know he had spoken like a Sadducee just because he was dining with them. He had not defended his teacher. He had agreed. Jesus might be a troublemaker who had to be eliminated. How could Jesus know?

The voice of Jesus suddenly broke through his thoughts. *I tell you, whoever publicly acknowledges me before others, the Son of*

Man will also acknowledge before the angels of God. But whoever disowns me before others will be disowned before the angels of God. And everyone who speaks a word against the Son of Man will be forgiven, but anyone who blasphemes against the Holy Spirit will not be forgiven.[10]

A warning chill raced along Judas's spine. He dropped his head behind his folded arms and did not look up again until the boat was tied alongside many other fishing boats in the harbor of Bethsaida.

Jesus and his disciples were recognized before they could step from the boat to the stone dock. A small crowd hurried toward them, roughly propelling a blind man.

Jesus could see that the man, so carelessly jostled by the eager crowd, would most likely fall. Quickly stepping forward, Jesus took the man by the hand.

The disciples could see Jesus wanted to separate the man from the people, so they moved between them, holding the crowd back while Jesus guided the man to the outskirts of the village.

At first, the people clamored to follow, but when they saw Jesus had stopped, they became silent, straining to hear and see. An audible gasp rolled through the crowd when they saw Jesus use two fingers to open one eye and then move close and spit in that eye. He did the same with the other eye.

Only the man could hear Jesus say, "You, foul demon of Blindness, I spit on you and cast you out of this man's body. It has been your home for too long! Return to your father, Satan, and tell him the Son of Man is here to take back what Adam lost."

Then Jesus placed a hand over each eye and said, "Be restored!" Jesus then removed his hands and asked, "Can you see anything?"

The man looked around. "I see people, like trees, walking around."

Jesus then placed both hands on the man's eyes again. "Spirit of Distortion, you must also return to your father, Satan. Tell him his lies will no longer be tolerated. I have brought truth to the Earth. Men will no longer be fooled. They will see accurately from this moment on."

Then the man's sight was restored, and he saw all things clearly. Jesus sent him home, cautioning, "Don't enter the village. People will ask too many questions, and they will not understand the things you will tell them. Men will come from Jerusalem to question you. Just go home, live quietly, and enjoy your new freedom."

From Bethsaida, Jesus and his disciples traveled north stopping at Jewish villages, teaching and healing. Within a few days, they left the last Jewish village behind and entered the region of Caesarea Philippi, an area ruled by Herod Philip and occupied by those who worshipped the Greek gods. As they walked across the lush plain at the foot of snow-capped Mount Hermon, the walls of Philip's capital city came into sight. It was built at the foot of the mountain, near a cliff. Both Jesus and his disciples approached in silence, taking in the amazing scenery, so different from Jerusalem or the shores of Galilee.

Jesus broke the silence. He *asked his disciples, "Who do people say the Son of Man is?"*

Andrew answered, "*Some say John the Baptist.*"

Philip quickly added, "*Others say Elijah.*"

Thomas said, "S*till others* say, *Jeremiah or one of the prophets.*"[11]

Jesus nodded affirmatively. Then he walked off the road, stopping at a place where a wide stream of clear water flowed from a cave in the rock wall. His disciples followed.

"What place is this?" John asked.

Jesus answered, "The men of this city believe this spring is the gateway to the underworld. They call it the Gates of Hell. Each year, before planting time, they come to this place and submit themselves to the spirits."

Jesus looked around. His spiritual sense told him that demons named Lust, Bestiality, and False Gods lurked behind every rock.

Jesus turned to the three disciples who were closest to him. For a moment, he looked each man in the eye—Peter, James, and John. *"But what about you?" he asked. "Who do you say I am?"*

Without hesitating, *Simon Peter answered, "You are the Messiah, the Son of the living God."*[12]

Jesus felt the tremor that went through the evil spirits in that place. He knew it would not be long before his enemy received the message that the Son of Man now had followers who recognized his divinity and his mission.

"Say it again, Peter." Jesus wanted this statement of faith to be heard in the demonic underworld.

Emphatically, Peter repeated, *"You are the Messiah, the Son of the living God."*

Then Jesus *replied, "Blessed are you, Simon* Peter *son of Jonah, for this was not revealed to you by man, but by my Father in heaven."*[13] Jesus moved closer to the cliff. He put his hand on the dark rock.

Afraid to place their hands on such an evil monument, the disciples stood back and studied the massive rock wall from a safe distance. They could see the stream that bubbled from the cave at the base of the cliff and the places that had been carved out where pagans would leave their sacrifices. There was even an image, half-goat and half-man.

Peter looked at it and said, "Master, truly this is an evil and blasphemous place. I can easily believe it is the entrance to the home of the Evil One."

Jesus stepped back and stood with his disciples. He looked at the stone image and man-made niches for offerings. "This rock has many imperfections, things that are an abomination to God. Still, it stands, restricting the amount of evil that can flow from Satan's kingdom." Jesus turned to Peter. "But *I tell you that you are Peter, and on* a rock like *this rock I will build my church, and the gates of Hades will not overcome it.*[14] When you see imperfections in yourself, in my followers, and in the structure that will be my kingdom on Earth, do not become discouraged. Just like the side of this cliff is greater than its man-made imperfections, so the Kingdom of God on Earth is greater than the problems it will encounter."

Jesus pointed to the idolatrous carvings. "Over time, God will bring ever-increasing pressure against this rock. You can be sure every monument to evil will be erased from its hard surface.

Daniel spoke of a rock that smashed the kingdoms of this Earth and became the Kingdom of God. It filled the whole Earth. Isaiah referred to me when he spoke of *a stone that causes men to stumble and a rock that makes them fall.*"[15]

Jesus then turned to all the men who were with him. "*I will give you* authority like *the keys of the kingdom of heaven.* When you speak in my name, *whatever you bind on earth will be bound in heaven, and whatever you loose on earth will be loosed in heaven.*[16] For now, do not share what we have discussed. A time will come when you will tell everyone that I am the promised Messiah. But do not speak of this now."

Jesus turned away from the spring and the rock wall. He walked back to the road that led to the city. His disciples followed him, silent and contemplative. When they reached the road, Jesus said, "Come, we will walk through this heathen city. For you, it will be the first of many godless cities."

The men exchanged amazed and slightly horrified glances. All their lives, they had lived as conservative Jewish men, avoiding those areas of their land where pagan worship practices were prevalent.

With many questions running through their minds, they began walking, following Jesus toward a city that stretched their worldview beyond fishing, beyond religious festivals, beyond anything they had ever imagined.

Jesus began teaching. "God spoke to our ancestor, Abraham. He said, 'Walk through this idolatrous land. Go north, south, east, and west. *All the land that you see I will give to you and your offspring forever.*'"[17]

As Jesus spoke, another tremor rolled through the Realm of Evil. Satan heard the proclamation of the expanding Kingdom of God.

He clinched his fist and shouted, "I will stop them!"

Jesus ignored the response of the Evil One. He continued teaching, "Like Abraham was called to leave his home and travel to a godless place, so you are called to leave your homes, to live in pagan lands, to call the people of those lands into the Kingdom of God. You will begin in Jerusalem. You will tell the Jews that I am their Messiah. A time will come when you will leave Jerusalem. You will travel through Samaria. You will find yourselves in many different cities throughout the empire. Everywhere you go, you will stand against the forces of the Evil One."

Looking to the left and to the right, the men followed Jesus through the city gate. There were pagan Temples and statues of Pan, the god of the city.

Jesus continued his teaching, "God spoke to Joshua, and I speak the same words to you, '*I will give you every place where you set your foot.*[18] *I will be with you; I will never leave you nor forsake you. Be strong and very courageous.*[19] *Do not be terrified;* do *not be discouraged, for the* Lord *your God will be with you wherever you go.*'"[20]

Chapter 25

A Hard Truth

"Listen carefully to what I am about to tell you: The Son of Man is going to be betrayed into the hands of men." But they did not understand what this meant. It was hidden from them, so that they did not grasp it, and they were afraid to ask him about it.

—Luke 9:44–45

Leaving the area of Caesarea Philippi, Jesus continued to teach his disciples as they started back toward the region of Galilee. "I brought you on this journey so we would have time without the press of the crowds. I want you to be prepared for the things that will happen. I *must go to Jerusalem and suffer many things at the hands of the elders, chief priests and teachers of the law.*"[1]

Philip gave a little shrug. "It seems there is no way to win them over. I expect the authorities in Jerusalem will always remain against you. They are so jealous of your popularity."

Thomas cautioned, "They can be dangerous men."

Jesus nodded. "They will cause me to be killed."

The disciples all exchanged alarmed glances.

Jesus did not miss the looks that passed from man to man. "As I have told you before, I *must be killed and on the third day be raised to life.*"[2]

Among themselves, the men started discussing the statement Jesus had made, trying to comprehend how it could possibly happen. Peter stepped away from the others. He took a few quick paces and came to Jesus's side. Firmly catching Jesus by the elbow, he steered him ahead of the talking men so he could have a word in private. "Master, why do you say such things? It alarms everyone, and it undermines their confidence in your kingdom." Peter gestured toward the men who were so engrossed in their own discussions that they had dropped behind, slowing their pace to concentrate on this intense topic. "See how disturbed the men are. You are the promised Messiah, the One we have waited for and now believe in. *Never, Lord!' he said. 'This shall never happen to you!'*"[3]

Suddenly, Jesus planted his feet on the packed-surface of the road. He whipped around to squarely face Peter. Jesus took such a confrontational stance that the other disciples immediately stopped and focused on the scene just ahead of them.

Jesus stood like a man ready to fight. *"Get behind me, Satan! You are a stumbling block to me; you do not have in mind the things of God, but the things of men."*[4]

The anger and harsh tone of Jesus's words shocked the other men who were standing on the road.

"I am not your enemy," Peter protested. "And certainly I am not Satan!"

"You are allowing my enemy to put his thoughts into your mind. And those thoughts are coming out of your mouth. Where is your discernment? Can't you distinguish between those thoughts that are inspired by the Holy Spirit and those that come from the Evil One?"

Then Jesus turned to the rest of his disciples. He could see they were dumbfounded. Their minds were spinning with confusion. "You have seen men forced to carry the crossbeam of their cross to the place of execution. They do not want to die, but they have no choice. I have a choice. I have chosen to carry the crossbeam in place of every man, woman, and child who deserves death."

The disciples had now gathered around Jesus, seriously trying to understand. Jesus looked into the face of each man. His heart was drawn to each one, so he continued with a tone of gentle understanding. "True disciples watch their teacher. They learn from their teacher, and they carry on the teachings of their teacher by doing the same things their teacher did. You are my disciples, so you must understand. *If anyone would come after me, he must deny himself and take up his cross and follow me. For whoever wants to save his life will lose it, but whoever loses his life for me will find it. What good will it be for a man if he gains the whole world, yet forfeits his soul? Or what can a man give in exchange for his soul?*[5] Do not let thoughts of my death frighten you. I promise that one day, after these things have passed, *the Son of Man is going to come in his Father's glory with his angels, and then he will reward each person according to what he has done.*"[6]

Once more, Jesus looked into the faces of his closest friends. Twelve bewildered pairs of eyes stared back at him. "I will pray to my Father for you that he will send his Spirit to teach you the things I have said." Then Jesus turned, setting a brisk pace. A moment passed, and he looked over his shoulder.

The men were still standing in the road.

Jesus gestured with his arm. "Come, we must hurry."

Day after day, the men walked, moving together in unbroken rhythmic strides. From sunup to sundown, they walked without pausing to rest. Every evening as twilight turned into darkness, the disciples built a fire and passed the simple staples they carried for nourishment. Meanwhile, Jesus would slip away. His disciples knew he was praying, and they wondered if they were the subject of his intense petitions, but they were afraid to ask.

Conversation fell into well-worn patterns of speculation—the kingdom of their Messiah Jesus and the positions each disciple might fill.

Six days after leaving Caesarea Philippi, the men entered a small village at the base of Mount Tabor. They purchased food in the market, while Judas went from house to house until he found lodging for the group.

As the men were entering the house where they would spend several days, Peter pulled Jesus aside. "Master, I have been very disturbed since we spoke on the road. I want to apologize for my clumsy words. I did not mean to say the wrong thing. I spoke from my heart, but somehow, I was wrong."

Jesus put an arm around Peter's shoulders. "I know your words came from your human mind and your human love. That part of me that is flesh recoils from the things that must take place. I was fighting the thoughts Satan was throwing at my mind as well as the thoughts he put in your mind."

James and John joined the conversation. "Teach us," they said. "We are also troubled by the things you have said."

Jesus answered, "You have been with me for more than two years now, but you have only seen part of my life. Walk with me to the top of this mountain."

Peter protested, "There is a Roman garrison and a fortress near the top of this mountain."

"We will not take the road," Jesus responded. "We will take the shepherds' path to a remote spot."

Before their journey began, Jesus looked into the courtyard of the home where they were staying. He saw Andrew blessing the owner and laying hands on a child with a bad cough. For a moment, Jesus stood in the doorway, waiting to catch Andrew's eye. When the disciple who was Peter's brother looked up, Jesus directed, "Continue to heal and teach. We will return before sundown."

It was easy to find the shepherds' path. It led from the village sheepfolds up a steady incline, around bushes and boulders.

Jesus led the way, setting an eager pace as if more than a pleasant view waited at the summit. There were no lingering moments or casual conversations. The climb was so intense that at one point Peter commented, "This hike takes more of my breath than running along the seashore."

Never slowing, still matching the determined strides of their teacher, John enthusiastically responded, "But from the top of this mountain, we will be able to see the entire plain spread out like a map drawn on a parchment scroll."

Higher and higher, the men climbed until they stood on the highest ridge with only sky above and the vast panorama of flat fertile land below.

"Wait here," Jesus said as he stepped away and knelt to pray.

Peter, James, and John threw themselves down on the grass, taking deep breaths in the thinner air. For a while they dozed, but suddenly, their senses came alive. All over their bodies, they felt a tingling pressure.

The men sat up. Immediately, they looked around for Jesus. Not far away, they saw him, standing in the place where he had been praying. *His face shone like the sun, and his clothes became as white as the light.*[7] He no longer appeared merely human.

The men stood to get a better look.

Peter whispered to James, "If God were to come down from heaven, he would look like this." While Peter was speaking, two other dazzling men appeared. They stood with Jesus, one on either side, speaking like intimate friends.

The disciples heard Jesus say the names of his visitors.

John repeated those names in an awed whisper, "Moses and Elijah have come from heaven."

Peter's excited response was to shout, *"Lord, it is good for us to be here. If you wish, I will put up three shelters—one for you, one for Moses and one for Elijah."*

While Peter *was still speaking, a bright cloud enveloped them.*[8] The men fell to their knees, unable to stand in the presence of such an awesome heavenly display. Then… *a voice from the cloud said, "This is my Son, whom I love; with him I am well pleased. Listen to him!"*

When the disciples heard this, they fell facedown to the ground, terrified.[9] Time passed, but the three disciples remained overcome and unable to move until *Jesus came and touched them.*

"Get up," he said. "Don't be afraid."

When they looked up, they saw no one except Jesus.[10]

Glancing at the late afternoon sun, Jesus said, "It is time to go back down." He led the way, warning as he walked, "Don't talk about today's experience until after the Son of Man has been raised from the dead. You know that Moses died on Mount Nebo. Yet today, you saw him alive. Have no doubt in the power of God to restore life, life that is eternal and more glorious than any you can imagine. My enemy wants you to believe if you lose your life, you have lost everything. But I say the life that God intended for every human being will be yours. You will look like Moses."

James asked, "You have spoken of Moses. What about Elijah?"

Peter was quick to add, "The rabbis say that Elijah will come and announce the Promised One. Did we just see that manifestation of Elijah?"

Jesus replied, "To be sure, Elijah comes and will restore all things. But I tell you, Elijah has already come, and they did not recognize him, but have done to him everything they wished. In the same way the Son of Man is going to suffer at their hands."[11]

Then each disciple remembered their time with John the Baptist, and they understood Jesus was speaking about the man who had immersed them in water as a sign that their old life of self-centeredness had ended and a new life of commitment to the will of God had begun.

Peter wanted to make sure he understood so he asked, "How are John, the desert prophet, and Elijah the same?"

Jesus explained, "Elijah is not just a man who was a prophet. Elijah is also an assignment from God to restore righteousness in the land. Any man who receives that assignment, receives the mantel of Elijah."

Halfway down the mountain, the men could see a crowd had gathered at the home where they were staying. It spread down the road all the way to the market. Above the crowd, Jesus saw Lying spirits moving from person to person. He said to the disciples who were with him, "Whenever my enemy sees the glory of God on Earth, he attacks."

Immediately, Jesus picked up the pace until all four men were almost running down the mountain. When they arrived at the home where they were staying, they saw the other disciples with a large crowd. Rabbis and teachers from the local synagogues were arguing with them.

Jesus stepped in beside his disciples who could feel the heavenly energy that still enveloped his body. In a diminished way, he still glowed so a*s soon as all the people saw Jesus, they were overwhelmed with wonder and ran to greet him.*[12]

Jesus lifted a restraining hand and the disciples held the people back. Turning to the teachers of the law from the local synagogue, Jesus asked, "Why are you arguing with my disciples?"

"We have heard of you." One of the teachers stepped forward.

Jesus could see the spirit that was propelling him. "And what have you heard?" Jesus asked.

"You are a fraud. You promise to heal and feed the people, but you do not deliver. You raise their hopes and then you disappear."

A frantic man pushed his way forward, boldly stepping between Jesus and the irate teacher. *"Teacher, I brought you my son, who is possessed by a spirit that has robbed him of speech. Whenever it seizes him, it throws him to the ground. He foams at the mouth, gnashes his teeth and becomes rigid. I asked your disciples to drive out the spirit, but they could not."*[13]

Jesus looked at Andrew, who sheepishly hung his head. Then his gaze swept over the other disciples who had remained in the village. He knew their minds had been consumed by Jealousy and Competitiveness. Those two evil spirits had been allowed to dominate their thoughts and rob them of the ability to minister to the people effectively. *"O unbelieving generation," Jesus replied, "how long shall I stay with you? How long shall I put up with you? Bring the boy to me."*[14]

Thomas and Matthew were the first to move, going with the father to carry his son through the people to Jesus. The men set the boy down in the dirt of the road.

Jesus got down on one knee so he could look deeply into the boy's eyes. When he looked, his eyes locked with pure evil.

The spirit who lived inside the boy looked out and saw Jesus. Immediately it threw the boy into a convulsion. The boy fell to the ground, rolling around and foaming at the mouth.

With horrified gasps, the onlookers stepped back, but Jesus did not move. He looked up at the father and with true compassion asked, "How long has your son been so possessed?"

"From childhood," the man answered. The father dropped to his knees and tried to steady his son, holding his shoulders. With pleading eyes, he looked back at Jesus. "The spirit *has often thrown him into fire or water to kill him. But if you can do anything, take pity on us and help us."*

"If you can'?" said Jesus. "Everything is possible for him who believes."

Immediately the boy's father exclaimed, "I do believe; help me overcome my unbelief!"[15]

Jesus sensed that the crowd was beginning to press back into the situation. Wasting no more time, *he rebuked the evil spirit. "You deaf and mute spirit," he said, "I command you, come out of him and never enter him again."*

Immediately, *the spirit shrieked, convulsed him violently and came out*[16] like a final gasp.

The boy's body slumped into the dirt and looked so much like a corpse that many who were pressing in for a closer look said, "He's dead. The spirit has killed him."

But Jesus refused to acknowledge those comments. Instead, he stood and took the boy by the hand, guiding him to his feet.

To everyone's amazement, the boy stood.

Then Jesus led him to his father. He placed the boy's hand in his father's hand. "Receive your son. The spirit will not return."

Later, inside the house, Jesus's disciples approached. Andrew asked the question that was on every mind. "Master, *why couldn't we drive it out?*"

Jesus *replied*, "*This kind can come out only by prayer*[17] that is accompanied by fasting. Not just giving up food but putting aside all thoughts of your own success and comfort and focusing on the needs of others." Then Jesus took his disciples out where they could see the mountain rising out of the plain. He pointed toward the summit of the mountain where he had been with Peter, James, and John. "Your faith was too small, your self-centeredness too large. You did not really believe so the spirit was able to resist you. *I tell you the truth, if you have faith as small as a mustard seed, you can say to this mountain, 'Move from here to there' and it will move. Nothing will be impossible for you.*"[18]

Chapter 26

The Temple Tax

Again, I tell you that if two of you on earth agree about anything you ask for, it will be done for you by my Father in heaven.

—Matthew 18:19

All morning, Jairus had been with the tax collectors from the Temple in Jerusalem. Officiously, the men had studied the town records, checking and double-checking to be sure every adult male in Capernaum had paid their half-shekel tax.

"Cuza? He has an estate close to town." One of the officials looked up at Jairus. "Has he paid?"

Jairus sighed before repeating information he had already given. "I made a notation by his name. He is an official in the court of our king, Herod Antipas. He is seldom in town, but he will pay when he comes to Jerusalem."

The official squinted while trying to find the notation the president of the synagogue had mentioned. Then because it was within their power, both tax collectors started once again at the top of the list. "Household of Alphaeus, last year, they paid for six males. This year, they paid for five." Again, the officials looked up at Jairus, waiting for an explanation.

In a controlled tone, Jairus responded. "When you arrived, I gave you the list of births and deaths for the past year. The oldest male in that household died during the summer."

The officials returned to the scroll that listed all the households of Capernaum, pointing and reading down the list. "House of Zebedee, paid; household of Jonas, one son has not paid. His name is Simon Peter." Once again, the officials turned to Jairus with an accusatory look.

"His home is near the synagogue," Jairus suggested. "We can take care of that matter, now." In defense of his friend, Jairus added, "Peter is faithful to his heritage, but he goes out of town a lot. I'm sure this matter just slipped his mind."

"Let's go. Nothing less than one hundred percent is acceptable." One official picked up his money bag, while the other carried the small scroll where he recorded each transaction.

As they walked, one official asked Jairus, "I have heard of a man named Jesus of Nazareth. I believe he stays in your town. Does he pay the Temple tax?"

"He does not own property or belong to a family in town so he is not on our list, but Peter will know the answer to that question," Jairus replied.

Peter was in front of his house when Jairus approached with the tax collector.

Jairus immediately stated their business. "It is time to finish collecting the half-shekel Temple tax."

Peter nodded and turned to go into his house.

"Wait."

Peter turned back to see the tax collectors had more to say. "Are you a disciple of that new man who is so popular? They say he is a healer called Jesus of Nazareth?"

"Yes." Peter waited for a response.

"Does your teacher pay his Temple tax?"

The man's tone was accusatory, but Peter chose to ignore that. "Yes, of course," he replied. "Jesus is in my home now. I will get his coin for you."

When Peter walked through the door, Jesus immediately asked, "Peter, do the rulers of Rome collect taxes from their own citizens or from those who live in their conquered lands?"

"From the conquered," Peter replied. "Caesar sends his troops out to annex foreign lands. Everyone who lives in those annexed territories must pay taxes, but the citizens of Rome are not asked to pay."

"We are citizens in the Kingdom of God. More than that, we are the sons of the King of the Universe. The sons of the king are exempt," Jesus said to him. "But we do not want to offend those men from the Temple so hurry to the lake and throw out your fishing line into the water. Take the first fish you catch. When you open its mouth, you will find a four-drachma coin. Give that coin to the men from the Temple. It will be payment for my tax and yours. My Father has declared that our taxes are to be paid from the treasury of heaven."

"I have the coins in a hole in the wall of my sleeping chamber," Peter declared.

Jesus shook his head. "My Father speaks to you through the prophet Isaiah. 'You have spent yourself *in behalf of the hungry and* satisfied *the needs of the oppressed;* therefore, *the Lord will guide you always; he will satisfy your needs in a sun-scorched land.*'[1] I will go out and speak with the officials while you are bringing in the money God has provided." With a quick gesture, Jesus waved Peter on his way. "Hurry!"

Suddenly excited, Peter burst through his front door. He grabbed the fishing line that was always hanging on the outside wall of his house. He called to the startled officials, "I'll be back shortly!"

They watched Peter sprint toward the waterfront. Jesus came up behind both officials. Casually, he placed a hand on each man's shoulder as he said, "You are watching a man who has been stirred by the Spirit. God has sent him to fetch the Temple tax from the mouth of a fish."

Both men swung around, studying the face of Jesus while their minds tried to make sense of the words he had spoken.

Jairus caught the twinkle in Jesus's eye. A little anticipatory thrill ran along his spine. He knew to expect the unexpected from Jesus, and he knew it was always good. Jairus then glanced at one of the tax collectors, a little man with a big job. Jairus could see he was beginning to puff up.

The tax collector took a step away from Jesus, turning so he could squarely face him. "I am from the Temple, commissioned by the Sanhedrin. This tax must be paid in coins, not fish."

Jairus chuckled. He just couldn't help himself. This tax collector had been so annoying, so vexing, and now, he was the one being vexed.

The other tax collector stepped out from under the friendly arm Jesus had placed on his shoulder. He thrust himself toward Jairus. "As president of the synagogue, you are required to assist us in collecting these taxes."

Just then, the men heard running feet, the pounding of sandals on the hard dirt road. "I've got the fish!"

All the men turned to see Peter running back from the lake. In one hand, he held his line. In the other hand, he held a flopping fish.

The first tax collector spluttered, "What kind of games are you men from Capernaum playing?"

Peter hurried into their little group. He dropped his line on the ground and took the fish with both hands. Opening its wide mouth, he reached in and extracted a coin, which he held out to the closest tax collector.

Shocked, both tax collectors took a step backward.

Jairus spoke up. "Take the coin. It is the tax for both Peter and Jesus."

"It came from a fish!" The tax collectors were spluttering again.

"It's a clean eatable fish," Peter stated. He stuck the freshly caught fish under one man's nose. "See, it has both scales and fins. My wife will cook it for supper."

Jesus took the coin from Peter. He wiped it off with a piece of cloth that he pulled from his belt. Then he placed the coin in one of the tax collector's hands. "Tell your authorities at the Temple that the Creator of the Universe commands the fish to provide the half-shekel tax for Jesus and his friend."

Unable to formulate a response, the tax collector deliberately closed his fist around the coin and turned to Jairus. "We are finished in Capernaum. We will leave town in the morning."

Filled with indignation and self-importance, both men turned abruptly and started down the road that led away from Peter's house. A group of boys, focused on their own game, kicked their wooden barrel down the road. It rolled in front of one of the Temple officials, who stumbled and nearly fell. Immediately, both men raised their fists and their voices, venting all their frustrations on the children.

Respectfully, the boys stopped their game and stood contritely before their elders, receiving their tongue-lashing offering apologies as best they could. Finally, one of the men picked up the barrel and angrily tossed it off the road. His gesture indicated that the game had ended by order of the Temple authorities. Then with a satisfied swagger, both tax officials continued down the road away from Peter's home.

Jesus, who had watched the scene from a bench in front of Peter's house, quickly got up and fetched the wooden barrel. It was lightweight and empty, just right for a game of running and kicking. Jesus could see the boys were slowly starting to leave. He called to them.

They turned to see that Jesus had kicked the barrel toward them and was now running to catch it. The oldest boy stopped it with one foot and then sent it rolling down the street again.

Jesus ran with the boys up and down the street, laughing, getting a kick in here and there, and enjoying the workout.

From the game, Jesus could see his disciples beginning to gather in front of Peter's house. He caught their curious looks. He knew they were wondering about his dignity.

After a few more sprints up and down the street, Jesus stepped out of the game, waving to the boys as he settled on the bench. Peter had walked Jairus back to the synagogue, but the other disciples were there, spreading their cloaks on the ground and sitting down to hear what Jesus would teach.

They looked expectantly into the face of their rabbi, and he looked back at them, peering deeply into each set of eyes. James and John found themselves unable to return that penetrating look. Thomas, Matthew, and Philip shifted their sitting positions, and Judas dropped his head.

Finally, Jesus broke the uncomfortable silence. "What were you arguing about while we were walking back from the gentile cities?

"Arguing," James evasively repeated.

No one else spoke, but the Holy Spirit had given each man the correct answer. They all knew they had argued about who was worthy of the greatest positions in the Messiah's new kingdom. Mile marker after mile marker, the debate had raged.

Jesus then said, "If anyone wants to be important, he must become the very last and the servant to everyone." The children were still playing in the street in front of Peter's house, running back and forth. Jesus called to one, the smallest of the boys.

The boy came over and Jesus *had him stand among them. Taking him in his arms, he said to them, "Whoever welcomes one of these little children in my name welcomes me; and whoever welcomes me does not welcome me but the one who sent me.*[2] Focus on the needs of those who are least in society. That is the only way to greatness in my Father's kingdom."

John then spoke up, "Jesus, did you know another man in this town has been driving out demons in your name?"

James quickly added, "We stopped him and made sure he understood that you would not approve."

"But I do approve," Jesus countered. "In his heart, that man is one of us. Anyone who has enough faith to use my name should be encouraged, and you can be sure my Father has a reward for him." Jesus chuckled to himself as he added, "So few are really for us. Be thankful for the one who believes and acts on his belief. In a short time, I will be calling for more disciples. I will be sending them out to heal and cast out demons in my name. Do not think the miracles you have seen and performed belong to you. They are gifts given by my Father to people who are willing to serve others."

Peter had returned to his home, and he joined the group of disciples gathered around Jesus. Coming in on the end of the last teaching, Peter asked, "What actions are we to stand against?"

Several of the twelve nodded in agreement with Peter's question.

Jesus answered, "To my Father, it is a very serious offense if one man leads another into sin." Jesus once again brought the playing children into his illustration. *"And if anyone causes one of these little ones who believe in me to sin, it would be better for him to be thrown into the sea with a large millstone tied around his neck."*[3]

Jesus stood and looked sternly at each man because he knew each heart. The Holy Spirit had revealed each man to him. His gaze stopped on Judas as he said, *"If your hand causes you to sin, cut it off. It is better for you to enter life maimed than with two hands to go into hell, where the fire never goes out."* Jesus nudged Peter's sandaled foot with his own foot. *"And if your foot causes you to sin, cut it off. It is better for you to enter life crippled than to have two feet and be thrown into hell."* Jesus took a deliberate step so that he stood in front of Judas. *"And if your eye causes you to sin, pluck it out. It is better for you to enter the Kingdom of God with one eye than to have two eyes and be thrown into hell, where their worm does not die, and the fire is not quenched."*[4]

Jesus looked around at the twelve. He could see several little smirks, and he knew some were pleased to see that Judas was the object of his stern comments. Jesus turned a hard gaze on Andrew and Thaddaeus. Then he gave equally hard looks to Matthew and Thomas. "Because you are my disciples, each of you will be tempted to put yourself before others. You will be tempted to deny you ever knew me. Don't you know because you are my students, each of you will become a sacrifice? But remember, before a sacrifice is brought to the altar in the Temple, it is sprinkled with salt." Jesus turned to Andrew and asked, "What is the purpose of salt in the fishing industry?"

Andrew answered, "It is a preservative. We salt the fish and put them in barrels so they can be eaten later."

"Well said." Jesus nodded and paced a little as he continued teaching. "Each of you will be tested with fire, but first, my Father will prepare you, like salted fish. Salt is tasty and useful, but if it loses its flavor, it becomes worthless. You are to be like salt—tasty, a useful preservative, and one who unifies diverse flavors."

Again, Jesus looked at the men who were most loyal to him. Their faces were serious but not serious enough. "Let me be very clear about my teaching this afternoon," Jesus said. "No man here is of greater importance than any other man. Do not think you are so elevated that you can look down on another man. I know typical social norms give you the right to look down on non-Jews, on outcasts, on women, and especially children, but in the Kingdom of God all are equally important."

The barrel that the children had been kicking back and forth on the road's hard surface rolled through the group of men and stopped near Jesus. Jesus gave it a little kick that sent it back into the game. Then he said, *"See that you do not look down on one of these little ones. For I tell you that their angels in heaven always see the face of my Father in heaven."*[5]

Immediately after he said that, Jesus sat down, and with a remembering look in his eye, he began a story. "When I was a boy, we had a good shepherd in Nazareth. One rainy night, he left the flock to find one lost ewe. That night, he fought a lion. He saved the ewe but lost his life. "Now tell me, what will a faithful shepherd do if he loses one out of one hundred sheep?"

Jesus waited for a response, but none of his disciples offered one, so he continued, "The shepherd will leave the ninety-nine in a sheltered place. Then he will go out into the rugged countryside, searching for that lost animal. He will face harsh weather and wild beasts just for the joy of finding that one wayward sheep."

Jesus paused again. Then he said, "I am like the good shepherd, willing to risk everything for just one sheep. To the good shepherd, each life is more valuable than his own."

At that moment, Peter's wife opened the gate, and the smell of freshly baked bread and roasted fish filled the air. She didn't need to say anything. The men just followed their noses and took their usual places on cushions around a low table. Jesus was the last to come in to the meal. At the entrance to the room, he paused and took both of Peter's wife's hands into his own. Looking deeply into her eyes, Jesus said, "Your service is as great as the service that these men do for me."

Peter's wife felt the heat that flowed from the hands of Jesus into her own hands. It moved quickly through her arms and flowed like warm liquid throughout her body.

"From this day forward, each time you serve others, it will be recorded in the books of heaven that you have served me. In my Father's kingdom, every act of kindness is noted. Nothing is overlooked."

Jesus looked up and saw Peter watching.

Jesus responded to his curious look. "Peter, you have *a wife of noble character... She is worth far more than rubies.*[6] And she is equally my disciple because she serves." A shadow of sadness crossed Jesus's face.

Peter saw it. And in a concerned tone, he asked, "What is it?"

In response, Jesus beckoned Peter to stand beside his wife. Jesus took both their hands and held them. "The Spirit of God tells me you will represent me as partners. Peter, my Father has given you a wife who is spiritually wise." Jesus's voice caught a little as he added, "She will share the path you will travel, and the end of your life will be the end of her life also." Then Jesus gave them both a reassuring smile. "You have a long path to travel together." With both arms, Jesus pulled them forward and kissed each on the top of their head.

Peter's wife glanced at the table where the other disciples were waiting for their meal. Jesus caught her eye movement. He understood she felt the pull of serving. Peter also glanced back at the other disciples. Jesus followed his eye movements. It did not take an eye that could see into the spirit realm to know every face was filled with envious speculation. With a little nod of his head, Jesus sent both back to the meal.

After the meal, Jesus and his disciples continued to recline on the cushions. And once again, Jesus began to teach. "Has one of your fellow disciples done something that is bothering you? Do you feel you have been wronged?" Jesus looked at each face, and by the Holy Spirit, he knew that resentments had been building between his disciples. "First, you should go to your brother and speak with him privately. If he hears your heart and embraces the moment to reconcile, then you have strengthened your relationship. But if he rejects your words, then come to him another time with two or three wise companions who will act as mediators and witnesses. If you receive no satisfaction and the witnesses see there is merit to your complaint, then you may bring the complaint to everyone." With his hand, Jesus indicated all of his followers who were in the room.

"What can your followers do if that person is clearly in the wrong but will not accept correction?" James asked.

"Treat him as you would a pagan or a tax collector,"[7] Jesus answered. "I have already told you my followers have great

authority. Heaven listens and enforces the declarations that come from the citizens of my kingdom. *Again, I tell you that if two of you on earth agree about anything you ask for, it will be done for you by my Father in heaven. For where two or three come together in my name, there am I with them."*[8]

Chapter 27

Preparations for the Feast of Tabernacles

After this, Jesus went around in Galilee, purposely staying away from Judea because the Jews there were waiting to take his life. But when the Jewish Feast of Tabernacles was near.

—John 7:1–2

"Nazareth is the next town on this road." Peter made the comment to see how Jesus would respond. Both men knew the leadership of the synagogue in that town led the Galilean opposition to Jesus, and they both knew Jesus's brothers wanted nothing to do with his ministry.

"I must give them another opportunity," Jesus answered. "After all, I grew up in that town."

"Master!" Peter exclaimed, "they have treated you badly. They even tried to stone you."

Jesus shrugged. "That is the past. They are forgiven."

"Forgiven?" Peter repeated the word. Then he walked in silence, deep in his own thoughts. After a time, he spoke to Jesus again. *"Lord, how many times shall I forgive my brother when he sins against me? Up to seven times?"*[1]

Jesus answered, "If you are counting, then do not consider holding your brother hostage to a misdeed, a misspoken word, or any other kind of affront until you have already forgiven him seventy times seven."

"Seventy times seven!" Peter repeated as he tried to do the mental math.

Matthew, who was walking nearby, quickly supplied the number, "Four hundred ninety!"

"That is a huge number!" Peter exclaimed.

The rest of the disciples pressed forward to get in on the conversation.

Jesus began a story.

"Once there was a king who desired to settle the financial affairs of his kingdom. The records were laid out before him and all who had borrowed money were called in to pay their debts.

"A man who owed ten thousand talents came before the king. To meet that debt, the man with his family would have to be sold into slavery and all of his property would then go on the market. Forgetting his pride, the man dropped to his knees and begged for mercy. The king was filled with compassion and forgave the debt.

"But as the forgiven man was leaving the palace, he met a man who owed him a small sum of money, a hundred denarii. 'Pay me!' he demanded. 'Pay now or go to debtor's prison!'

"The man could not pay so he begged for mercy. But the man who had been forgiven a great debt refused to have compassion. The authorities were called, and official charges were made. For just one hundred denarii, the other man went to prison.

"This story spread throughout the kingdom. It reached the palace. When the king heard the story, he called the forgiven debtor into his presence. 'You are a wicked man!' he raged. 'When you begged for mercy, I forgave your enormous debt. But you could not pass that mercy along to another man who owed you a very small sum. Because you did not forgive, I will not forgive your debt.' Turning to his guards, the king gave an order. 'Imprison this man. Allow him to be tortured until he repays in full.'"

Jesus stopped walking and looked at the men who were with him. "This is how my Father administers justice in his kingdom. All of you have been forgiven much; therefore, you must forgive each other, your families, and everyone who has ever wronged you."

"Mother!" James, the younger brother of Jesus, threw his arms in the air in an exasperated gesture of despair. "Why did you send a message to Jesus? Why did you ask him to come before the feast?"

"James!" Mary responded sharply. "Jesus is my son. This is his home as much as it is yours. Your brother is totally misunderstood by this town. He should not be misunderstood in his own family."

"Jesus causes trouble for this family," James retorted. "When he comes to town, we lose business. When he comes to town, Chebar starts threatening to put our family out of the synagogue."

"Chebar doesn't intimidate me!" Mary responded heatedly. "I remember when Chebar was just one more little kid playing in the streets of Nazareth. He still resents the fact that Jesus was recognized as an exceptional student in the synagogue school and he was not!"

"Mother!" James tried to assert himself as the male head of their extended family. "Childhood resentments are over. Jesus is a man, and he has become a dangerous person. The Romans arrest and crucify men who gather crowds much smaller than the ones that gather around Jesus. You were in Jerusalem during the last feast. Remember *the Galileans whose blood Pilate…mixed with their sacrifices.*[2] I have to protect this family."

Fire flashed from Mary's eyes as she responded, "Just what are you protecting us from? When you brother comes, every sickness leaves this house. When your brother is present, we have every provision. Do you remember when he turned water into wine?"

"Mother, I heard the story, but I did not see it happen," James replied.

"Well, Jesus will be here so our family can go to the synagogue on the Day of Atonement and then walk to Jerusalem for the Feast of Tabernacles together!" Mary made her final statement. Then she quickly turned her back and left the carpentry shop, slamming the heavy wooden door to punctuate her words with finality.

James threw his hands in the air again and spoke with mock sincerity toward heaven. "Why does the great Jewish healer and teacher have to come from this family?"

Longinus met Pilate on the ramparts that overlooked the Temple courts. Both men watched as the Day of Atonement came to an end. They did not speak. Both men just stared at the scarlet cloth that was attached to the door of the sanctuary. For a moment, they glanced away, and when they looked again, the scarlet cloth was white.

Below them, the worshipers began to chant, *"Though your sins are like scarlet, they shall be as white as snow; though they are red as crimson, they shall be like wool."*[3]

"How many times have we watched the scarlet cloth become white?" Longinus asked.

"Several," Pilate answered. "Each year, we stand here wondering how it happens."

"And why it happens," Longinus completed the governor's thought.

Pilate responded, "My wife tells me it is the sign that their God is willing to overlook their sins for one more year."

"Are we included in this forgiveness?" Longinus asked. "Does their God see every man we crucify each year? Does he expunge our record?"

Pilate did not answer. He just stood there, remembering all the faces of all the men who had died by his order or by his sword.

Finally, he said, "I believe it is wise to live in the present while hoping for the best regarding the past."

Longinus nodded. He often dealt with his own procession of dead men. As the commander of the Fortress of Antonio, he could never admit there were nights when tortured faces stole his sleep.

Pilate stepped away. Longinus followed him into the officers' barracks, where an insignificant soldier poured each man a cup of wine.

Pilate raised his cup. "I believe it is safe to break the fast now."

Longinus turned to one of his soldiers. "Feed the men." Looking back at the governor, he said, "The men were a little resentful. They did not think they should be forced to endure the Jewish fast."

Pilate replied, "My wife always says, 'It is best to respect the god of the land.'"

"Yes"—Longinus sipped his wine—"and hope that the god of this land will keep us safe from the blood bath Tiberius has ordered throughout the empire."

Pilate looked over the rim of his cup. "My sources in Rome assure me that my name has not been mentioned. I am a forgotten man in this desert outpost."

"As long as the Jewish leaders have no reason to complain to Tiberius, you will be safe," Longinus agreed.

"That is the real reason I directed the soldiers who were in the city to respect the Jewish day of fasting," Pilate admitted.

The commander of the fortress confirmed the wisdom of that decision with an affirmative nod.

Jesus led the donkey out of the shed and hitched her to the wagon. Mary carried a basket full of fresh bread from the kitchen, and James threw some tools and twine into the corner of the wagon. Each member of Mary's family brought something to the wagon—blankets, cooking utensils, and fresh fruits and vegetables. Jesus placed a few waterskins on top and then stepped back to study the way the wagon had been loaded.

Mary took a few determined steps and squarely faced her eldest son. "I don't understand why you will not walk with us to Jerusalem."

"Mother." Jesus looked down at the woman who meant more to him than any other. "When I was just twelve years old, I told you I had to be about my Father's business. Nothing has changed except I have moved into greater and greater levels of trust. My Father has not directed me to begin the journey to Jerusalem. I am waiting until I receive his directions."

"Are you sure this is not about your brothers?" Mary challenged. "James can be very critical and difficult."

Jesus gave his mother a reassuring smile. "I love James. My Father has amazing plans for him. One day, he will defend the words I say and the deeds I do with his life."

A confounded expression settled on Mary's face, and for a few moments, she was without words.

Jesus laughed a little. "If I had not heard what I just told you from God himself, I would not believe it either." Then Jesus pointed to his brother, who was obviously impatient. "Don't make James wait. He's ready to leave."

James responded to overhearing his brother's directions with an insincere nod of appreciation.

Jesus opened the gate and watched his family as they started the five-day journey to Jerusalem.

Curiously, James paused and looked back over his shoulder. He called to his brother, "You're not coming?"

Jesus gave a negative shake of his head.

Sarcastically, James responded, "If you really are the great Healer and teacher, then you have to go to Jerusalem. Nothing happens in Nazareth."

The twelve disciples who stood with Jesus looked at their master, waiting for his response.

Jesus said nothing. He just smiled and waved, watching his family until they disappeared over the hill. Then Jesus turned to those who were with him. "Let's go into the hills. We will camp near the Shepherds' Cave and wait for the next directive from heaven."

At the Beautiful Gate, Ichabod studied the crowds that climbed the steps to bring their First Fruits offerings into the Temple. The first wine of the harvest, the first olive oil, it arrived in large vats and in handheld jars. For rich and poor, this was the most joyous season of thanksgiving. The harvest cycle was now complete.

The experienced beggar leaned back into the soft leather of his chair. He picked up snatches of conversations as people passed. Often he heard the name Jesus from Nazareth, and he remembered the young man who had constructed his first chair. He remembered the man who faithfully presented him a new chair every few years. But he had not spoken to that man in several years. The chair had arrived, but not the man. Was this kind and faithful man the one most people referred to as the healer?

Like everyone else in Jerusalem, Ichabod wondered if the healer would come to this annual festival. He wondered how he could get someone to carry him to wherever this healer was teaching. He hoped that the healer would be teaching outside the Temple, because as a cripple, he was not allowed inside the gates.

The clink of heavy coins falling into his beggar's bowl pulled Ichabod's attention back to the present. He looked up, somewhat startled to see Caiaphas, the high priest, standing with the captain of the Temple guard.

"Have you seen the healer from Galilee?" Caiaphas gruffly asked.

The captain of the guard replied, "My men have been waiting along the road most Galileans use. I have men, disguised as ordinary travelers, waiting at each camping place. Jesus from Nazareth has not been seen."

Ichabod watched Caiaphas clinch and unclench his fists. The high priest lowered his voice, but Ichabod listened closely while he watched the way Caiaphas moved his lips. "I don't want that man to get through the city gates. Once he is inside Jerusalem, we will not be able to get to him because of the crowds."

Confidently, the captain responded, "My men at the gates are prepared. Every Galilean is being stopped and questioned."

"I want him taken quickly and quietly," Caiaphas directed. "Stone him in some deserted place."

"What about his students?" The Temple official asked. "They are always with him. One of them might report it to the commander of the fortress."

"Men can be bought," Caiaphas stated.

"If not?"

"Stone them too!" Caiaphas was both cold and emphatic.

"Stone him?" Ichabod could not believe his ears. Why would anyone want to eliminate such a compassionate man?

Chapter 28

The Water-Pouring Ceremony

However, after his brothers had left for the Feast, he went also, not publicly, but in secret. Now at the Feast, the Jews were watching for him and asking, "Where is that man?"

—John 7:10–11

It was early morning. The disciples were sitting around a fire sharing the bread they had carried with them. Jesus stepped out of the Shepherds' Cave. He looked at his students, and they looked back at him expectantly.

"Let's go to Jerusalem!" Jesus announced. "My Father has said we are to travel through Samaria."

The men quickly cleaned up their camp and then set a steady pace toward Jerusalem. As they walked, the banter among the disciples was typical. Only Judas was quiet. Jesus studied his body language and demeanor. He could see the Critical spirits that hovered around his head, filling his thoughts with accusations and resentments.

Several times, Jesus walked beside Judas, trying to open a dialog, but Judas refused to allow himself to become engaged in conversation.

On the fourth day of the festival, the men saw the city of Jerusalem shrouded in predawn gloom. The road to the city ran through a deep valley full of willows, then up to the mountain top that was covered with homes and official buildings. As the men walked toward the city, the rising sun suddenly threw its golden rays on the limestone walls. The gates swung open to welcome another day of celebration. A group of priests hurried through the gates, exuberantly singing. They entered a grove of willows where they began cutting and gathering the long boughs that would be placed around the altar in the Temple for this day.

From the city and the countryside, men and women lined the road from the willows to the city. They waved branches and cheered. Jesus and his disciples joined the cheering crowd. Waving their own fists full of branches, they fell into step behind the rows of priests that shared the burden of long bundles of willows, swaying and marching to a rhythmic chant.

> *You will go out in joy and be led forth in peace;*
> *the mountains and hills will burst into song before you,*
> *and all the trees of the field will clap their hands.*[1]

In that way, Jesus entered the city and the Temple courts unchallenged.

All the way, through the Court of the Women and the Court of the Israelites, Jesus and his disciples followed the procession of willow limbs. Trumpet blasts filled the courts. Once again, the people cheered as the fresh green boughs were placed upright around the large altar that stood in the Court of the Priests. The leafy tops of the branches extended well above the fires on the altar. The priests began their procession around the altar, waving shorter branches and chanting, "O Lord save us and grant us success."

Watching with his disciples, Jesus could feel the insincerity of their chanted petition, and it tired him. With a few quick gestures, Jesus led his disciples away from the altar toward the outer courts.

Once they were away from that area of the Temple that was so packed with officials, Peter took the initiative and walked up beside Jesus. In a cautious tone, he said, "As we entered the gate,

I heard men talking. The Temple authorities are looking for you. They have offered silver. It will be given to the man who brings you to them."

Jesus gave Peter an acknowledging nod as he replied, "Let's stand here and listen to what the people are saying."

Jesus found a spot near one of the tall cauldrons of oil that would be lit in the evening. His disciples stood casually around him, watching the people. Each man held a fist full of cut branches in his right hand and a yellow citrus fruit in his left hand. The leaves on the branches rustled like the words of the people, pressed in around them, each carrying their own lulav of branches.

Among the people, there was widespread speculation about the healer. Some said, "The healer is a good man, a prophet sent from God."

Many cautiously asked, "Have you seen the healer? I was hoping to find him."

Others replied, "No, he has not come to this feast. That is good because he deceives the people."

Several Pharisees walked by. They stopped and piously waved their branches while chanting a brief prayer for rain. After their prayer, the men stayed a few minutes, conversing about the festival.

All the disciples clearly heard one Pharisee say, "Has that troublemaker shown his face in Jerusalem?"

Most comments were soft and secretive because everyone knew the Temple leadership had denounced the rabbi from Nazareth. Still, the whispers were everywhere. They demanded a response, but Jesus remained silent until the Holy Spirit put the words in his mouth. It was the Song of Moses, the song Moses had written and taught the people just before his death.

Listen, O heavens, and I will speak; hear,
O earth, the words of my mouth.
Let my teaching fall like rain.[2]

The musical cadence of the words soared above the people.

I will proclaim the name of the Lord*...*
He is the Rock, his works are perfect...
upright and just is he.[3]

A crowd quickly gathered, called by the Spirit, inspired by the words.

You deserted the Rock, who fathered you;
you forgot the God who gave you birth.[4]

On and on, Jesus sang, never forgetting one word of the lengthy poem.

"The Lord *will judge his people*
and have compassion on his servants
when he sees their strength is gone.[5]

Responding to the song, the people began to press forward. The disciples took their positions, protecting Jesus from the crush of those who were too eager.

There was a ring of authority in Jesus's voice, a power no one could define.

"See now that I myself am He!
There is no god besides me.
I put to death and I bring to life."[6]

"Is this man singing about himself?" Peter overheard the comment. "Is he saying that he is God?"

"No, no," another replied. "It is just the words of the Song of Moses."

The Sadducees and Pharisees who were nearby became increasingly amazed. The song drew them and the people. It tugged at their hearts and challenged their minds. Among themselves, they asked, "How did this man from Nazareth become such a powerful teacher?"

As the song ended, Jesus responded to their comments, *"My teaching is not my own. It comes from him who sent me."*[7] He looked at the sea of faces before him. "Most men speak to honor themselves, but I speak to honor God. He is the one who sent me."

The people suddenly began to question and comment on his last remark. They became increasingly agitated and loud.

Jesus could see the demonic spirits of Confusion and Mob Mentality swirling through the crowd.

Judas stepped to the side, quietly disassociating himself from Jesus and the rest of the disciples. The rest of the disciples closed ranks, moving shoulder-to-shoulder, standing between Jesus and the people. Over their shoulders, Jesus could see one of the assistants to the high priest. Dramatically pointing toward the man, Jesus shouted, "*Why are you trying to kill me?*"[8]

"What are you talking about?" the priest responded with hostility. The priest did not wait for a response. He turned and hurried away to report the incident.

From within the crowd, accusations were being thrown like stones. *"You are demon-possessed! Who is trying to kill you?"*[9]

Jesus answered with his own question. "What is all this hostility about? I heal a man on the Sabbath, and you decide that I have no respect for the Law of Moses? But you break the Law of Moses any time it is convenient. You just make up a new law to circumvent the old law."

"There's trouble in the Court of the Women."

Both Pilate and Longinus looked up from the scroll that was spread on the table in front of them.

A guard from the wall presented a proper salute. Then he quickly responded to the silent but expectant faces of his superiors. Their stern expressions demanded specific details. "A crowd has gathered. It fills more than half of that court. They are pushing and yelling. I don't know what they are saying. I expect stones to start flying at any moment."

Turning to Longinus, Pilate commented, "The Jews have their own guards who maintain order." Pilate then waited for his commander's response.

"Is the Temple guard present?" the Roman commander asked the messenger. "Have they been overwhelmed? Do they need assistance?"

"I did not see any Temple guards," the soldier answered.

"Continue watching," Longinus directed. "We will not interfere unless you see that the Temple guard has arrived, and they cannot contain the people."

Pilate concurred, "We want to remain as uninvolved as possible. Let them handle their own problems, short of putting a man to death."

"But if stones start flying, a man could die quickly," Longinus cautioned.

"Stones?" Pilate chuckled to himself. "What about the hard yellow citrus fruit that each man carries? When I was preparing to come to this post, I heard that once one of their priests did not do a ritual correctly, and the people stoned him with the fruit. The commander of this fortress had to come to his rescue, and he nearly died in the shower of fruit!"

Longinus pushed his chair back from the table. "I think I should go have a look at the situation for myself."

Pilate nodded and pushed his chair back also. "We'll both have a look."

The governor and his commander quickly strode to the walkway atop the wall that overlooked the Temple courts. From there, it was easy to see the large agitated crowd. They could tell everyone was focused on one man, but they did not know who the man was.

"Maybe we should step in before things get out of hand," Longinus suggested.

Pilate put a lightly restraining hand on his commander's arm and then pointed. "The Temple guard has arrived. Let's see how they handle the situation."

The governor and his commander observed as the Temple guards pushed their way through the crowd, coming right up to the disciples. Their presence seemed to have a calming effect on the people. The clamor of voices died.

The man who was speaking could now be clearly heard and understood. "I did not come here to speak to you because I wanted you to recognize that I am a great rabbi. I came because my Father sent me. You think you know my ancestry and the town where I grew up, but you know nothing. *You do not know* my Father *but I know him because I am from him and he sent me.*"[10]

The Temple guards stood immovably, transfixed by the authoritative words. After listening and briefly taking in the mood of the people, the guards melted into the crowd and then walked away.

Pilate and Longinus exchanged puzzled glances. Then Pilate pointed toward the steps where Caiaphas stood with the captain of the Temple guard. It was obvious. Both men were quite frustrated because the teacher was not being confronted and then roughly carried away for punishment.

The governor and his commander then enjoyed a little smug laughter at the expense of the Temple establishment. When they looked back, the man and those with him were nowhere to be seen. The crowd began breaking up. Bits and pieces of their conversations drifted up to the wall of the fortress. "Isn't this the man the Temple authorities are looking for?"

"He seems to have gotten away," Pilate snidely observed.

"I hope they don't ask me to use any manpower to look for him." Longinus added. "This is nothing more than a Temple power struggle. It has to do with their religious disputes. It has nothing to do with governing this region for Rome."

Pilate agreed, and the two men returned to their business.

That evening, Jesus secluded himself in prayer. The disciples, with the exception of Judas, built three booths in a grove of trees not far from the Pool of Siloam. For a while, Judas observed their efforts, then he got up and went into the city. No one spoke to him. No one inquired about his plans. At last, Peter threw palm branches on top of each structure. Their shelters were complete. Andrew and James gathered dry sticks and got a fire going. Soon, the men were sitting and sharing their evening meal.

Matthew casually commented on the fact that Judas was not with them. No one responded. Jesus joined them. He was unusually quiet. By the firelight, the lines of his face appeared harsh, and when he spoke, his voice seemed stressed.

Out of the evening shadows, two men stepped into their circle of their firelight. Everyone looked up to see James and Simon, the brothers of Jesus. Both men moved to stand directly in front of their oldest brother.

James spoke first. His tone was harsh and uncompromising. "You wouldn't come with us, but you came. You couldn't come quietly and just enjoy the celebration. You had to create a spectacle in the Court of the Women."

"How did you know where to find me?" Jesus calmly responded with his own question.

"We happened to see your follower, Judas," James answered. "He is at the Temple with his father and his brothers."

"Do you want me to accompany you to the Temple to watch the festivities tonight?" Jesus asked with a slightly curious inflection.

Simon answered, "We want you to stop breaking our mother's heart. She is very worried."

James interrupted his younger brother. "Your name is on everyone's lips. Some hate you. Some love you."

"The people who hate you are powerful." Simon cut in. "For mother, stay away from the Temple. You have satisfied the requirements of Moses. Now you can return to Galilee and let things calm down in Jerusalem."

With genuine warmth, Jesus answered, "I am touched by your concern. Believe me. I am not purposely distressing my family. Tell my mother that I honor my Father by following his instructions. She will understand."

"Our father? Our father, Joseph the carpenter?" Simon repeated.

"Go back to your booth and ask mother to tell you about my Father and the events surrounding my birth," Jesus replied. "Then you will understand."

James threw his hands in the air and heatedly exclaimed, "I've heard this story! I heard our parents talk about it when we were children. I did not believe it then, and I refuse to believe it now. You are an ordinary man, a carpenter, and that is all!"

Immediately, Peter stood up and protested, "James, you have not been with us. You have not seen the things your brother does. He is the Messiah! If we did not believe that, we would not be with him now."

Before James could reply, Simon warned, "Messiahs die! That is why mother is so worried. She does not want to see you at the end of a Roman spear or nailed to a cross."

"Neither does she want to find you under a pile of stones," James added. "Roman soldiers do not move swiftly to save Jews who are being stoned by their own people."

"Those things will have to be my Father's concern," Jesus answered. "My life is in his hands."

Both brothers threw their hands in the air again. Then with shaking heads, they turned and walked back to their own family camp.

With joy you will draw water from the wells of salvation![11]

Jesus and his disciples woke to the sound of singing.

"It's the water pouring ceremony!" Peter announced.

"And it's the last day," John reminded everyone.

"Then let's make the most of it and join the crowd," Peter urged.

Jesus had no objection, and everyone was eager. They laced up their sandals and hurried to the Pool of Siloam, arriving just in time to watch a priest fill his golden flask with pure water.

Again, the people came from everywhere to fall in behind the procession and swell the song.

> *Come, let us go up to the mountain of the LORD,*
> *to the house of the God of Jacob.*[12]

The officiating priest then led both priests and people back up the hill, through the Temple courts to the foot of the altar where the morning sacrifice was now burning.

With great dignity, two priests began to slowly ascend the ramp that led to the top of the altar. One carried the golden flask of water and the other carried a silver flask of wine. When they reached the top, the people called to them with one loud voice, "Hold up your hands!"

Both priests responded, raising their vessels high so the people could see the streams of wine and water as they were simultaneously poured into the proper funnels on the side of the altar.

The music began again. The Levitical choir was singing.

> *Surely God is my salvation;*
> *I will trust and not be afraid.*
> *The LORD, the LORD, is my strength and my song;*
> *he has become my salvation.*[13]

"Yeshua!" Jesus heard his Father calling him by his heavenly name. "Yeshua, your name means salvation. You are their salvation. Let the people know. Let them know that you are the water of eternal life."

The chant continued, "Yeshua—salvation. The Lord has become salvation." Jesus listened and the words throbbed in his veins like the beat of his own heart.

Then the music stopped, and in that brief moment of silence, Jesus cried out so that everyone could hear, *"If anyone is thirsty, let him come to me and drink. Whoever believes in me, as the Scripture has said, streams of living water will flow from within him."*[14]

All around people turned to find the man who so identified with the wine and the water poured upon the altar that he would offer something that could only come from God. Some of the people said, "This man must be a prophet!"

Others dared to offer their own hopeful suggestion. "He is the Messiah."

Still others questioned, "How can the Messiah come from Nazareth? He must be from the family of David and the town of Bethlehem."

Some in the crowd seethed with anger. They wanted to throw him to the ground and end his life by stoning. But no one had the courage to act.

The Temple guards were dispatched again, this time, with orders to deal firmly with this troublemaker. But again, they could not approach much less lay hands on the man. Without accomplishing their mission, they returned to the chief priests and Pharisees.

"Why didn't you bind his hands and bring him to us for interrogation and punishment?" the Temple leadership demanded.

"We have never faced a man who speaks like this man," the guards replied.

"So, you are also deceived?" the Pharisees retorted. "You're no better than this mob of peasants—they are fools who know nothing about the law"

Nicodemus, who had often defended Rabbi Jesus, stepped into the conversation. "I know the law, and I want to remind you that it does not condemn a man without a hearing."

With a mocking sneer, one of the chief priests responded, "Did you study in Galilee at the school of the fishermen?"

Around Nicodemus, the Jewish leadership chortled. One of the Pharisees then admonished, "Go to the Temple library and study the prophecies of the Messiah. He will not come from Galilee."

The Pharisees and Temple authorities turned their backs and walked away. Only Nicodemus stayed, listening to Jesus teach. After some time, Joseph of Arimathea joined him.

When evening came, Jesus left his disciples and went to the Mount of Olives to spend the night with his family.

Chapter 29

An Adulterous Woman

In your own Law it is written that the testimony of two men is valid. I am one who testifies for myself; my other witness is the Father, who sent me.

—John 8:17–18

In the valley and covering the rolling slopes of the Mount of Olives, countless families had built their booths. As twilight turned into darkness, little fires were kindled until the hillside appeared to be ablaze. Jesus walked confidently among the campers, knowing where the people from Nazareth always set up their booths. When he saw a woman bent over her fire preparing a savory stew, he knew it was his mother, and he hurried to her. "Mother?"

Mary looked up. "Jesus!" She ran to him and they embraced. "I have been so worried," Mary whispered into his chest.

Jesus pushed his mother away so he could look into her face. "Don't you remember what I told you on that Passover when I was twelve?"

"I have never forgotten," Mary replied. Then in a soft, remembering tone she recalled, *"Didn't you know I had to be in my Father's house?"*[1]

"That statement is truer today than it was when I was a child. My Father has called me to represent him in the Temple." Jesus sat by the fire and his mother sat with him.

"What you are doing is so dangerous," Mary replied. "I know you are a well-respected rabbi, but you have insulted and enraged the most powerful of the Temple authorities."

"Wasn't it dangerous for you to be pregnant by the Holy Spirit? Not yet married?" Jesus countered.

Mary shook her head as she thought back over the years. "Once, I saw a disgraced girl pulled from her parent's home and stoned at the cliff just outside of Nazareth. I know that could have been me."

Jesus continued, "Even after you were married and living in Bethlehem, Herod tried to kill our family."

"But the angel of the Lord warned Joseph and stayed with us as we traveled to Egypt," Mary responded.

Jesus looked directly into his mother's eyes. "You know that my Father speaks to me every day. I do nothing unless I have heard his directions."

Mary nodded.

Jesus said, "That will probably place me in danger just like it placed you in danger."

Mary nodded again, this time with a little resigned sigh.

Jesus continued, "I want you to be certain. Nothing can happen to me unless my Father allows it. He will only allow me to fall into the hands of evil men for his glorious purpose." Jesus softened his tone, and he took his mother's hand. "I expect to die, but my Father has assured me. After three days, I will return to life."

Jesus could see the tears pooling in his mother's eyes. He reached out and touched her cheek. "My time has not come. I will return to Galilee after this feast." He squeezed his mother's hand.

And Mary forced a little relieved smile. Then she fell easily into her maternal role. "The stew is ready. Eat something. Your brothers will be here soon. Speak kindly to them. They mean well."

Jesus took the food his mother offered. He began scooping the meat and seasoned lentils into his mouth with pieces of flat bread. He watched his mother's face light up as she saw he appreciated her cooking. Hearing footsteps, he knew his brothers were coming.

A shadow of concern passed over his mother's face.

Jesus immediately responded, "Mother, I will spend the night here, and it will be well with my brothers."

It was a warm night. Pilate, with his wife Procila, left the governor's apartments to walk along the top of the fortress wall and look out over the city. Side-by-side, they strolled past the guard. Slipping quietly into the privacy of one of the towers, Pilate took his wife's hand, and together, they climbed the stairs to the highest platform. From there, they could see the city.

"It's been a little more than three years since I brought you to this desert land," Pilate commented.

"I'm glad we came," Procila replied. "This part of the world is so much more exciting than Rome. The women of Roman nobility, their gossip, the politics—I don't miss it at all."

Pilate looked at his wife, thoughtfully studying her. "I think you are becoming more like the Jewish women who have become your friends."

Procila nodded. "I do appreciate their food, their customs. Their religion—just one god is a very fascinating concept. And look at their city! This is my favorite time in Jerusalem. Today, I took a tour around the city just looking at all the different booths that have been constructed. The people are so joyous!"

A quick movement in the street below caught the couple's attention. Someone was running— being chased! A small mob ran through the twisted street shouting and thrusting lit torches into dark corners. Pilate hurried to the base of the tower, quickly dispatching a few soldiers to investigate.

When he returned to his wife's side, she reported that someone had been apprehended by the mob, surrounded and restrained.

Pilate responded, "We will see if this is a matter for my office or a matter the Jews must deal with."

Together, the couple returned to their apartment. It wasn't long before a guard reported. A woman had left her husband's side. She had been found in another man's booth. Both would be held for the remainder of the night. In the morning, they would be brought to the Temple authorities.

Procila moved to stand beside her husband. She offered her council. "I have studied their laws concerning such matters. *If a man commits adultery with another man's wife—with the wife of his neighbor—both the adulterer and the adulteress must be put to death.*"[2]

Pilate then said to the messenger, "Make sure the Jews who will deal with this case know that no man can be executed except by my order. And I will not order the death penalty for marital unfaithfulness. They may whip him."

"What about the woman?" Procila asked.

"Under Roman law, the woman is the property of her husband. He can have her killed," Pilate answered.

Procila responded, "Under Jewish law, the husband does not have a choice. They will stone her, with or without his consent."

"If the man speaks up and desires protection for his property, I will intervene." Pilate turned back to the messenger. "Did you get all of that?"

The soldier saluted, fist to chest. "Yes."

"Then deliver my orders. I want to hear the resolution of the matter in the morning."

At dawn, a silver trumpet sounded and teams of Levites pushed the gates of the Temple open. It was the additional day of celebration called the Joy of the Torah. On the Mount of Olives, Jesus kissed his mother and promised to see her again in Nazareth. With a wave for his brothers, he moved with all the other people to the Temple where he knew a few of his disciples would meet him.

Jesus found a place near the offering boxes where the rabbis sat and taught. John, Judas, and Matthew found him there. The people gathered expectantly around him. He began to teach.

On the periphery of his vision, he caught the agitation of a group of Pharisees and teachers of the law. They were arguing—Roman law versus Mosaic law. Their opposing opinions reached a volume that could not be ignored.

Finally, those men brought their dispute to Jesus. They roughly forced the object of their dispute through the crowd that surrounded Jesus. With one hard shove, they knocked a disheveled woman across the paving stones to land at the feet of the rabbi from Nazareth.

A collective gasp rose from the crowd. The woman was exposed, her clothing torn, her mantle missing. Dark tangled hair fell loosely across her terrified and tear-streaked face.

Three Pharisees stepped forward.

"They seem too confident," Matthew remarked to Judas.

One of the men pulled the woman roughly to her feet. "Stand before your accusers," he demanded.

The woman stood, weak and trembling. Her eyes remained on the dust-covered pavement, and with her hands, she pulled at the pieces of fabric that hung on her body, trying to minimize her exposure.

Immediately, Jesus felt his Father's heart of mercy for this daughter of Eve.

Another of the Pharisees approached Jesus with a condescending bow. "You are the rabbi who can recite all the laws Moses wrote so we have brought this case to you. We want to hear your judgment."

Immediately, Judas became very interested and focused on the exchange. Then he spoke to Matthew who was beside him. "This is a time for Jesus to be cautious. I know these men. They have been waiting for an opportunity to catch Jesus in a legal trap."

John moved to get a better view.

The oldest Pharisee, a senior member of the Council of Seventy, repeated his query, "Rabbi, we know you are a master of the Torah. Witnesses observed this woman in the act of adultery. The law that Moses received on Sinai says she must be stoned. How would you dispatch this case?"

In that moment, the Holy Spirit revealed everything to Jesus—the name of each person, their involvement, their motives, their secrets. Jesus knew these men cared little for his opinion. They were hoping that his heart of mercy would lead him to err in the application of the law. Then the woman would be forgotten while he was denounced and accused.

Every eye was now focused on the scene as Jesus leveled a piercing look at this prominent Pharisee, the one who had made the accusation. Jesus left his seat. Briefly, he studied the woman. Then he wet the tip of his index finger, and he bent to write in the dust. First, the name of the Pharisee and then the name of his first wife, the one he had dishonestly divorced. Next, Jesus wrote the name of the teacher of the law who stood beside the Pharisee, and he wrote the fact that this teacher had forced his wife to be intimate, even when she was ceremonially unclean.

At first, the men paid no attention to the things Jesus was writing. They just kept demanding that he pass judgment. Then Jesus straightened up and pointedly said, "According to the protocol of our courts, the witnesses are the first to be examined. Which of you has not sinned? That man may throw the first stone."

Jesus glanced compassionately at the woman, and again, he bent over and wrote on the ground.

The morning sunshine came out from behind the clouds, illuminating the words in the dust and drawing the attention of the Pharisees to the messages from the Rabbi of Nazareth. Now the Pharisees began to read the things Jesus had written.

The crowd could hear their shocked gasps. "Has this man been in my sleeping chamber?"

Jesus continued to write. He wrote the name of the man who had pulled this woman into an adulterous relationship. It was the son of one of her accusers. Again, Jesus looked up. "Can you read? Shall I read for you?"

A soft ripple of laughter passed through the onlookers.

The accusers then began to move away one by one, until only Jesus remained beside the trembling woman. He turned his full attention on the woman and asked, "Where are the men who accused you?"

With wonder in her voice, the woman answered, "They are no longer here."

"Their accusation has been dropped, and I will not bring it forward," Jesus stated. Then Jesus declared. "Return to your husband and live without sin. Your husband will take you back."

Slowly, Jesus took his seat again. He did not speak right away because he was listening to the Holy Spirit.

After a few moments, he addressed those who had been watching. "The law that God gave to Moses is harsh, yet every man and woman will be judged and condemned by it unless one man lives without offending the law, and that man becomes the sacrifice for all who have offended the law."

Jesus began to teach again. The sun was like a ball of fire sitting atop the eastern hills. Jesus pointed to it. *"I am the light of the world. Whoever follows me will never walk in darkness, but will have the light of life."*

Other Pharisees and members of the Sanhedrin who were among the onlookers heard his statement and hotly exclaimed, "The man talks like he is God!"

They challenged Jesus. "Who are you to tell us that you are as important as the sun in the sky?"

"Is there someone else who can verify your greatness?"

"Do you have a witness to substantiate your claims?"

"We would like to examine your witnesses!"

Jesus answered them, *"My testimony is valid, for I know where I came from and where I am going. But you have no idea where I come from or where I am going."*[3]

Another accusing voice rose above the crowd of onlookers. "You did not judge that woman according to the law."

With a ring of authority in his voice, Jesus answered, "Your statement is merely a human opinion. It does not even apply because I did not make a judgment on this case. When I do pass judgment, I will stand with my Father and our decisions will be right!"

"Who is your father?" The question came from a group of Pharisees.

"My Father?" Jesus replied, "I represent my Father, doing the things he would do, saying the things he would say. So if you know me, you know my Father."

Mary of Bethany with her husband, Jonathan, slipped in among those who were listening to this exchange. Mary whispered to her husband, "Once Jesus told me about his Father. He is not the son of Joseph. He is not the son of any man. God is his father."

"Mary!" Jonathan spoke with alarm. "Do not speak such things in this place. Your words are blasphemy!"

Mary shrugged. "Jesus is telling them what I just said."

Mary and Jonathan turned their attention to the heated exchange between Jesus and the Pharisees.

Jesus stood, confronting them, *"You are from below; I am from above. You are of this world; I am not of this world."*[4]

"See." Mary nudged her husband. "He is telling them that he is from heaven."

"They don't understand him," Jonathan replied. "Listen!"

"Who are you?" they asked again.

"I am the one I have claimed to be all along," Jesus answered. "You saw. I judged the witnesses who brought the fallen woman. I will also judge you. I am the one who has been given that authority. My authority is not from this world. The One who sent me is trustworthy. The things I have heard from him I tell the world."

"They still do not understand. He is claiming to be from heaven, to be the Anointed One." Jonathan looked at his wife. "Those men would kill him. They would stone him on the spot if they understood his claim."

"But the Romans…," Mary quietly protested.

"There are some things that the Romans have to deal with after the fact," Jonathan softly countered. Then both turned their attention back to Jesus.

"When you have succeeded and placed me on a Roman cross, then you will know who I am and that I always do the things that please my Father."

All around, Mary and Jonathan heard the comments of the people.

"This is the Messiah!"

"Do you hear his sincerity? He is willing to die!"

Jesus heard their comments also, and he turned to the people and he *said, "If you hold to my teaching, you are really my disciples. Then you will know the truth, and the truth will set you free."*[5]

The Pharisees who were waiting for another chance to argue shouted their objection. "Set us free? What are you talking about?"

Jesus answered, "Every man and woman is bound by the chains of sin." He looked over the crowd. He could see their demons. He looked around this area of the Temple. It was the place where the people brought their monetary gifts. Greed and Pride, Dishonesty, and Religious Bondage lurked around the offering boxes.

Jesus sat down again and began speaking to the people, "Let me give an illustration. A household slave may be sold to another master, but the son in the household can never be sold. If the son of the household gives a slave his freedom, then the slave is free, and no one can change that decree."

"That story has nothing to do with us!" one of the Pharisees announced. "We are the children of Abraham. We are the sons, not the slaves!"

"If you were Abraham's children," said Jesus, "then you would do the things Abraham did. As it is, you are determined to kill me, a man who has told you the truth that I heard from God. Abraham did not do such things. You are doing the things your own father does.[6] You are illegitimate children. Your father is the Evil One."

"We are not illegitimate children," they protested. "The only Father we have is God himself."[7]

Jesus answered, "My Father is pleased with me. *Before Abraham was born, I am!*"[8]

"I am? I am!" Several Pharisees screamed and tore their clothes.

Jonathan looked around anxiously. "Mary, this is going to get ugly!" He took his wife by the elbow and began to steer her out of the crowd.

Amazed whispers spread from person to person. "He took the holy name of God and made it his own!"

"Blasphemy!"

"Stone him!"

Longinus looked up as one of his sentries rushed in to report, "Another disturbance in the Temple near the offering boxes. The Pharisees are pulling stones out of their pockets."

"Those Jews!" Longinus exclaimed. "They can't settle their problems with words. They have to resort to stones!" He grabbed his sword and hurried to the stairway that led down into the Temple courts. With a few men behind him, he rushed into the center of the disturbance.

A mob was milling about shouting, "Where is the teacher?"

"Lay hands on the rabbi from Nazareth. Bring him to us!"

"The healer spoke blasphemy! He must die!"

Longinus shouldered his way through the angry men. In the center of the mob, he stopped and looked around. His presence caused every Jewish man to stop in his tracks. At the top of his voice, Longinus shouted, "Where is the man who caused this outrage?"

"We cannot find him!" one red-face Pharisee exclaimed.

Longinus stepped up to the Pharisee who had answered. He snatched a stone from the man's hand. "And what were you going to do if you found the man?"

For a moment, there was silence except for the sound of stones casually dropping onto the pavement.

Longinus glared at the man he was confronting. "The death penalty requires a trial. You may hold your own trial, but we must also judge the man. Execution can only be carried out by Roman soldiers with orders from the governor. Save your stones for building."

Longinus strode back to the stairway leading up to the fortress. His men fell into formation behind him. Once on the stairway, he looked back over the groups of people who wandered about in the massive Court of the Women. His eye rested on a man who wore the white robes of a teacher. He was casually walking toward one of the exits. There was something about that man. He held the attention of the commander of the Antonio Fortress until he disappeared through the gate.

Jesus, along with Matthew, John, and Judas left the city of Jerusalem and walked to the town of Bethany to the estate of his friend Lazarus. They stayed several days, visiting with the family. Mary and Jonathan were also there.

On the last night of their visit, the women served food to the men as this was proper in Jewish families. The meal ended and the men reclined on their cushions as Jesus began to teach.

From the cooking area, Mary heard his voice. It drew her to the entrance of the room. She saw the remains of the meal spread across the table, and she knew it was her responsibility to clear it away. But Jesus was telling a story.

"Once there was a wealthy man. He dressed in purple and fine imported linen. Every day, the man lived in luxury. In the shadow of all that wealth, a poor beggar named Lazarus made his home. During the day, Lazarus scrambled for a few crumbs from the rich man's table, and at night, the dogs came and licked the sores that covered his body."

Mary slipped into the room full of men. She did not look at her husband. She did not want to see his face or hear his whispered direction to return to the women's area. Her eyes were on Jesus. Her ears were focused on every word.

"Malnutrition and illness took the life of the beggar, and God sent angels to carry the poor man to rest at Abraham's side. The wealthy man also died. He was buried in a fine tomb, but angels did not escort him to Paradise. Instead, he went to the dark side of Sheol; and there, he was tormented, day and night.

"From his place of torment, the wealthy man looked up, and he saw Lazarus far away, resting comfortably in the arms of Abraham. Frantically, he called across the deep gorge, hoping his voice would carry to that part of Sheol called Paradise. "Father Abraham, send Lazarus to me with some water. I am suffering in this hot place."

Mary saw a cushion that had fallen on the floor not far from the feet of Jesus. She quickly moved to that place, scrunching down and making herself small so she could remain among the men.

She knew Jesus saw her. He smiled and gave her a little wink as he moved his story along.

"From across the gorge, Abraham answered, 'Sir, you have had your lifetime of luxury while Lazarus experienced unbelievable misery. Now Lazarus is receiving the comfort he deserves.'

"In the place of torment, the wealthy man groaned and pleaded.

"Then Abraham responded, 'I cannot help you. There is a great gorge between us, and no one can cross to the other side.'"

Behind her, Mary heard the dishes rattling. She knew her older sister, Martha, was clearing the table, and she felt a little tug of conscience. It was her duty to help, but the words of Jesus were so compelling. She had to hear the end of the story.

"The rich man responded, 'Please, Father Abraham, send Lazarus to my five brothers with a warning so they will change their ways and avoid the fate that is mine.'"

At that moment, Mary heard her sister clear her throat. It was a not so subtle signal that Mary had been seen and she should quickly excuse herself.

But Mary remained scrunched down on the cushion, pretending to be deaf to everything except the words of Jesus.

"Abraham answered, 'Your brothers have the writings of Moses and the prophets. That is enough.'"

Remembering the confrontation in the Temple, Mary understood that the brothers in the story represented the Pharisees who manipulated the writings of Moses and the prophets for their own benefit but never applied the principles of righteousness to their own lives.

"Again, the wealthy man pleaded. 'If someone comes to my brothers from the Place of the Dead, they will listen and repent.'"

Jonathan suddenly interrupted the story. "Those Pharisees at the Temple, they are like this rich man. They will never accept your teaching even though your instruction is straight from the scriptures!"

Mary felt a little satisfaction that she had a husband who could make an intelligent comment.

Jesus nodded and finished, "Father Abraham answered the wealthy man, 'If your brothers are not following the teachings of Moses and the prophets, they will not change, even if a man comes to them from the grave.'"

The next moment, Mary felt an angry presence hovering close to her back, and she heard a familiar fretful voice. "Teacher, are you going to allow my sister to rest while I do all the work? Tell Mary she has a responsibility to fulfill."

Jesus looked at both women. Then he spoke to Martha. *"Martha, Martha…you are worried and upset about many things, but only one thing is needed. Mary has chosen what is better, and it will not be taken away from her."*[9] Jesus tossed another cushion on the floor. "There will always be dirty dishes. They can wait. Sit here with your sister. Call the servants in the morning; they will clean up."

The next morning, Jesus and his disciples began their journey back to Capernaum.

Chapter 30

A Softened Heart

Therefore Jesus said again, "I tell you the truth, I am the gate for the sheep."

—John 10:7

"His name shall be Heli, son of James the carpenter of Nazareth!"

Jesus, along with his disciples and the friends of his family, all cheered as the newly circumcised infant was passed back to his mother. They congratulated the father and thanked the mohel. Tables overflowed with food and wine. Neighbors laughed and talked.

Mary sighed contentedly. "I am a grandmother again. And it is so fitting that this child has been named after my father." She went over to run her fingers over the smooth dark hair of the eight-day-old babe who still trembled in his mother's arms.

Salmon, the old olive grower, approached Jesus. He was steering Chebar by the elbow. "Jesus, it is so good to have you back in your hometown."

Jesus could see Salmon was sincere, but Chebar wanted nothing to do with this conversation.

Salmon continued, "I have convinced Chebar that when you are in town, you should be asked to teach in our synagogue."

Jesus saw Salmon give Chebar a hard nudge.

The president of the synagogue of Nazareth cleared his throat, and with great effort, said, "Could you teach on the Torah portion for this Sabbath? That is, if you are staying with us that long?" His last question sounded slightly hopeful.

Jesus heard the Holy Spirit. "Yes," so he repeated the affirmative answer for both men. Chebar's face fell, and the men turned back to the food table.

James stepped over to Jesus. "What was that conversation about?"

"Chebar asked me to come to the bema for the Torah portion," Jesus answered.

James raised a surprised eyebrow. "Salmon has given some very large contributions, so Chebar feels indebted." Then James cautioned, "Remember, after you leave town, your family must still live with these people." For the first time in a long time, James gave his older brother a genuine smile. "And thank you for coming. If you stay out of trouble, I'll name my next son after you."

Jesus laughed and both brothers hugged.

That Sabbath, Jesus with his brothers went to the synagogue. The men filed into their section and the women into the area reserved for the females. James came with his family. His wife's mother slowly followed. She was a widow, bent over, supporting herself with two walking sticks. For eighteen years, James had watched his mother-in-law struggle with life. He knew her to be a woman bound by spirits of Rigidness and Anger. Now, exhausted from her effort, she made her awkward way to a seat not far from the door.

Jesus also found a seat. He chose a place where he could observe the people and allow the Holy Spirit to reveal the needs he was to minister to as well as the demons he might confront. The presence of God was sweet that morning. The Holy Spirit draped himself over Jesus like the prayer shawl that covered his head.

The traditional chants began. Men stood and swayed to the cadence of the words.

> Lord, King of heaven and earth,
> You are mighty forever.
> You raise the dead. You heal the sick.
> You set free those who are in bondage,
> And you have abundant mercy for the living.
> You are mighty to save.

The last chant ended, and James, the carpenter of Nazareth, was honored because of the birth of his son. Chebar called him forward to read a small portion.

James read, "*Worship the* *Lord* *your God, and his blessing will be on your food and water. I will take away sickness from among you, and none will miscarry or be barren in your land. I will give you a full life span.*"[1]

James took his seat, and Chebar intoned the call for the next reader. Jesus stood and came forward.

The scroll was open before him. He found the place where his brother had read. He touched it with the fringes of his prayer shawl and then brought the fringes to his lips. He placed the pointer. Then he looked up at the expectant worshipers.

His eye caught a little movement in the women's section. The Spirit directed his vision toward the woman who was sitting close to the door and leaning heavily on her two walking sticks. Jesus knew the woman was his brother's mother-in-law. He also knew that heaven was highlighting her, singling her out from every other person in the building.

Without reading or teaching, Jesus stepped away from the Torah table. He stretched his arm toward the women's section. With his fingers still entangled in the fringes of his prayer shawl, his outstretched arm resembled a bird's wing. "Woman!" he called.

All heads turned. All eyes were now on the woman who sat close to the door.

"Come forward," Jesus directed.

"Come forward?" several people whispered.

"Women don't come to the bema."

"Women don't enter the men's section."

Jesus ignored the critical comments as he watched the woman who was a kinsman by marriage struggle to her feet. Each step was slow. Each movement filled with shaky effort. But with his eyes, Jesus urged her on.

She reached his outstretched hand, and in front of everyone, Jesus loudly declared, *"Woman, you are set free from your infirmity." Then he put his hands on her, and immediately she straightened up and praised God.*[2]

The spirit of Indignation rolled through the room. Chebar hurried to the bema to denounce the event. Over the voices of his commenting congregants he shouted, *"There are six days for work. So come and be healed on those days, not on the Sabbath."*[3]

Jesus quickly turned and responded to both the president of the synagogue and those who were criticizing from their seats. *"You hypocrites! Doesn't each of you on the Sabbath untie his ox or donkey from the stall and lead it out to give it water? Then should not this woman, a daughter of Abraham, whom Satan has kept bound for eighteen long years, be set free on the Sabbath day from what bound her?"*[4]

The Holy Spirit then struck each critical person with a sense of shame, and silence filled the room. As Jesus glanced around the quiet room, he could see some were thoughtful and many were delighted that a miracle had taken place. Jesus looked at the place where his brothers were seated, and he saw on the face of James open amazement.

At that moment, the brothers locked eyes. Jesus smiled. And the Holy Spirit united them, heart-to-heart.

It was winter, time for the Feast of Dedication. Jesus, with his disciples, had traveled to Jerusalem, staying in the home of Peter's sister, the mother of John Mark. It was evening, and the men were resting after a long day of teaching and healing.

There was a quiet knock on the gate, and moments later, John Mark brought two men in to see Jesus.

Jesus looked up, surprised to see his visitors, even more surprised when they removed the hoods that were attached to their cloaks and exposed their faces. "Nicodemus?" Jesus remembered the man who had spoken to him privately several years ago.

"This is Joseph of Arimathea," Nicodemus introduced his companion.

Joseph immediately began speaking. "We came to warn you. Your name is on the lips of every important man in the city. Caiaphas went in person to speak with Herod Antipas while he was at his Jerusalem palace. He has convinced Herod that you should die for the good of the nation."

Nicodemus interrupted, "Leave Jerusalem. Find a safer place to teach and heal."

Jesus looked steadily at the two men. He appreciated the risk they were taking. "I have said many times that I do not choose where I go, who I heal, or what I say. I only follow the directions of my Father, and those directions come to me from above. Herod Antipas, that old fox, cannot touch me unless my Father permits it. So, *go tell that fox, 'I will drive out demons and heal people today and tomorrow, and on the third day I will reach my goal.'* After that I will leave the city…*for surely no prophet can die outside Jerusalem!*"[5]

Jesus stood and walked over to the window that looked out on the city street. Speaking introspectively, he said, *"O Jerusalem, Jerusalem, you who kill the prophets and stone those sent to you, how often I have longed to gather your children together, as a hen gathers her chicks under her wings, but you were not willing! Look, your house is left to you desolate. I tell you, you will not see me again until you say, 'Blessed is he who comes in the name of the Lord.'*"[6]

Two days later, while walking on the Sabbath day, Jesus and his disciples saw a beggar, a man blind from birth. His disciples asked, "Rabbi, is this man blind because of his own sin or because of the sin of his parents?"

"His blindness was allowed so my Father could display his good work on Earth."

Then Jesus walked over to the man who lifted his unseeing eyes and held his beggar's bowl in the general direction of the sounds he was hearing.

Jesus knelt on one knee, level with the man's face. "Do you know me?" He asked.

"No," the beggar responded.

"I am the one who has come to bring light into your darkness," Jesus stated. "May I touch your eyes?"

"If you can bring light into my darkness, please touch my eyes." The beggar dropped his bowl and reached with both hands to identify the man who was in front of him, to run his hands over Jesus's robe and to feel the compassionate contours of his face.

With one hand, Jesus scooped a little dirt from the ground. He spit into his hand and then stirred the muddy mixture with his finger.

Very gently, Jesus lifted one eyelid. He applied the mud directly to the man's eyeball, all the while softly speaking, "In the beginning *the LORD God formed the man from the dust of the ground.*[7] With dust, I will create again." He moved to the other eyeball, applying more of the dirt mixed with saliva.

"Now go," Jesus was very close to the beggar's face, and he breathed on the man as he spoke. "Wash the mud from your eyes in the Pool of Siloam"

Jesus signaled two men who were nearby and requested that they lead the man to the fresh water reservoir. So the man went. He washed and came home seeing clearly.

His friends and those who had formerly seen him begging asked, "Is this the blind man who used to sit and beg?"

Some claimed that he was the same man.

Others said, "No, he only resembles the blind beggar."

But the former blind man stood up and insisted, "I am the man who was blind, the one who begged for coins."

"How was your sight restored?" they demanded.

He replied, "The man called Jesus the Healer put mud in my eyes. He told me to go to the Pool of Siloam and wash. So I did, and now, I can see."

"Where is this healer?" everyone asked.

"I don't know," he answered

Excited, amazed, curious beyond words, neighbors surrounded the former blind man, propelling him down the street to the Temple authorities. "A priest must see this miracle and declare you a whole man," they exclaimed.

Another friend shouted, "You are now an Israelite without blemish who can rightfully enter the Temple!"

When the authorities at the Temple heard the man's story, some were horrified and said, "The healer has broken the Sabbath commandments again. He is not doing the works of God!"

But those who were standing nearby talked among themselves and said, "Only a man of God could do this miracle."

Once again, the Temple authorities focused on the man who had been blind. "Tell us about this healer."

The man answered, "I am certain he is a prophet."

Immediately, the Pharisees and priests became very agitated. "Witnesses! Witnesses! We must have two who can verify this man's story."

"Send for this man's parents," someone suggested. "Surly, they know whether or not this man has been blind from birth."

So a messenger was dispatched. And the parents came, elderly and frightened. They were pushed forward so they stood nervously before the Temple authorities.

The questioning began. "Is this your son? Has he been blind from birth? How then can he see?"

Nervously, the parents answered, "We know this is our son, and he was born blind. But we do not know what has happened to him. He is not a child, so you must ask him for the answers."

Once more, the Pharisees turned to the man who had been healed. "Tell us now, how did this healer break the Sabbath? What work did he do? He is a sinner, and he must be brought to trial for his sins."

Looking at the angry, demanding faces that confronted him, the man felt a sudden boldness. "Sinner? I do not know. But one thing I do know. I lived in darkness, but now, I see in the light!"

The Pharisees pressed forward as if they intended to lay hands on this man and haul him to the whipping post. "What did the healer say to you? What did he do to open your eyes?"

With a little impudence the former blind man answered, "Weren't you listening? I have already answered these questions. Why must I say it again? Do you want to become disciples of the healer?"

Oaths and insults filled the air. Hotly, the men from the Temple protested. "We are the disciples of the teachings of Moses, and we want to have nothing to do with this healer. We don't even know where he comes from!"

Enjoying the heated exchange, the former blind man taunted, "How little you know! Even I am certain that the healer is a man from God. Who else could do this miracle?"

"You are not educated so you cannot lecture us!" the authorities retorted. "Your name and the names of your parents are from this moment on removed from the synagogue rolls. You many not enter any synagogue in this city!"

The man who had been healed laughed at the tirade that was on display for everyone to see. "I have never entered a synagogue so I guess I will never know what I am missing." With that, he turned and walked away, joyously turning from side to side to catch every sight.

Judas brought the news to Jesus. "The blind beggar that you sent to wash in the Pool of Siloam has been banned from every synagogue in the city."

Jesus shook his head. "There are many blind men in this city who think they can see." Turning to his other disciples, Jesus said, "We must find this man again."

Judas offered, "He was last seen walking toward the bridge that goes over to the Mount of Olives."

On the bridge, it was easy to find the man who stood peering intently over the valley that stretched into the distance.

"Friend?" Jesus approached the man. "I hear something amazing happened to you today."

The man turned and replied, "All my life I have been in darkness, but today, a man touched my eyes, and now, I can see."

For a moment, Jesus just shared his happiness, and then he asked, "Do you believe in the descendent of Adam who is the Promised One?"

"I do not know," the man answered. "But tell me more about him so that I can recognize him if I see him.

Jesus then said, "You are looking at him and speaking to him now."

Sudden recognition crossed the man's face. He knew this voice. It was the voice of the man who had touched his eyes. Immediately, he dropped to his knees and began to worship. "I believe you are the Promised One."

Passing Pharisees stopped, aghast that one man would worship another. They heard Jesus respond, *"For judgment I have come into this world, so that the blind will see and those who see will become blind."*[8]

Indignantly, they confronted Jesus, "What are you saying? Do you dare to infer that we are the blind ones?"

Jesus answered, *"If you were blind, you would not be guilty of sin; but now that you claim you can see, your guilt remains."*[9]

Jesus did not wait for their rebuttal. He turned and walked back toward the Temple, his disciples following and creating a barrier between their rabbi and the angry Pharisees behind them.

In the Temple, Jesus and his disciples walked along the corridor known as Solomon's Colonnade. Suddenly, a group of Jews surrounded them, saying, "Tell us now. Say it plainly. Are you the Messiah?"

Jesus looked at those who were confronting him. He saw the people mouthing the words of the demons who had been sent to watch him and mock him. His answer was for the demons who would report back to his enemy, Satan. "I have told you. The miracles that I do in my Father's name confirm. I am the one. I am like a good shepherd. *My sheep listen to my voice; I know them, and they follow me. I give them eternal life, and they shall never perish; no one can snatch them out of my hand. My Father, who has given them to me, is greater than all; no one can snatch them out of my Father's hand. I and the Father are one."*[10]

With his spiritual ear, Jesus heard the demons shriek. He saw several speed away to report his proclamation to their evil leader. Jesus then saw the first stone sail through the air and fall short, like it had struck an invisible barrier. Several men lunged forward to lay hands on him, but they could not touch him.

In his heart, Jesus heard his Father's voice. *"Because he loves me…I will rescue him; I will protect him, for he acknowledges my name… I will be with him in trouble. I will deliver him and honor him."*[11]

Gesturing for his disciples to move with him, Jesus turned and quietly walked away, leaving the confused, stone-throwing mob behind.

After this, Jesus left the city.

Chapter 31

Seventy New Disciples Plus Two

Then Jesus went back across the Jordan to the place where John had been baptizing in the early days. Here he stayed.

—John 10:40

Manaen and Cuza pulled their horses to a stop on the ridge overlooking the oasis east of the Jordan. Both men were momentarily speechless.

Finally, Manaen said, "This place looks like it did when the desert prophet was here. Look at all these people!"

"Where have they come from?" Cuza wondered aloud.

"More importantly, why have they come?" Manaen kicked the flanks of his horse and headed toward the oasis. Cuza followed.

Beside a pool of spring water, Jesus stood on a small grassy knoll. He looked at the faces of the men and some women who were seated on the ground, filling the area all the way back to the hill. With a loud voice, Jesus asked, "What does it mean to be my disciple? Have you counted the cost?"

As he spoke, Jesus walked along the edge of the crowd. "If you are not willing to be hated, even disowned by your family, then you should not desire to be my disciple. If you are not willing to endure criticism, whippings, and persecution, you should not desire to be my disciple. A disciple is one who learns from his teacher and then does the same thing his teacher does. I will go to a Roman cross. Can you go to the cross also?"

For a long moment, Jesus paused. His twelve disciples were sitting in a semicircle so close that he could reach out and touch each man. One by one, Jesus looked into their faces. He knew who would go to the cross, and it pained him.

The two officials from the Court of Herod Antipas dismounted at the top of the hill. Jesus recognized them, and he waved.

They waved back.

"Does he know he is a wanted man?" Manaen wondered aloud.

"I will not tell our king where he is," Cuza responded.

Both men tied their horses and then found a place in the shade of a date palm to listen. "What if a man wants to build a tower? Won't he first estimate the cost of labor and materials? He does not want to become a man who is ridiculed by his neighbors for starting a project he cannot complete."

A ripple of agreement spread through the people.

Jesus continued, "What if a king prepares to go to war? Won't he first consider the size of his own army and the size of the troop that will oppose him? If his own forces are insufficient, he will send the diplomats to arrange a treaty."

Manaen commented to Cuza, "Antipas should have come to Jesus for advice before taking on the Nabataean army."

Cuza nodded but remained focused on Jesus's next statement. "In the same way, any man who desires to be called by my name, to be identified as my disciple, he must first count the cost. I deceive no one. My enemy is a deceiver, but I tell you what to expect."

Then Jesus began to tell a story. "While I was walking along the road, a man came to me. He said, *'I will follow you wherever you go.'* But I said to him, *'Foxes have holes and birds of the air have nests, but the Son of Man has no place to lay his head.'*[1] That man returned to his own home."

Jesus looked around. The countryside was barren except for the vegetation that grew around the spring. "It is winter. We will not have another grain crop until spring. Still, I see a harvest that is ready for the workers. People are waiting to be healed, to be freed from demons, to know that God has not forgotten them. Are there workers here? Who will go in my name? Who will teach what I have taught? Who will boldly speak words of healing and freedom?"

Men started moving. Even some women came forward.

"I will lay hands on you, and you will receive all the power you need."

On the dry hill behind him, Jesus sensed an evil stirring. He knew his enemy was present, observing the formation of his first kingdom army.

Two by two, men and women came to Jesus. They knelt at his feet, while Jesus placed a hand on each head. Like mighty surges of liquid power, the Holy Spirit rolled through Jesus, filling each pair until they reeled like drunks. The disciples had to help each person to their feet, supporting them until they recovered from their overwhelming experience with the Spirit of God.

Cuza and Manaen watched. They felt the pull of the Holy Spirit. They wanted to go forward. But what would be the cost? Their positions in the court of Herod Antipas? Their personal wealth? Both men remembered the day the prophet of the desert had been executed. Could his fate become theirs?

Seventy were standing or sitting around Jesus and his disciples. Seventy had answered the call. Jesus began to instruct them. "I am sending you into extreme danger. It is like sending lambs among the wolves. Do not take extra money or clothing. Do not waste your time greeting strangers on the road. Enter a town and find a house that is worthy of your blessing. Stay there. Eat what is provided. *Heal the sick who are there and tell them, 'The Kingdom of God is near you.*[2] *He who listens to you listens to me; he who rejects you rejects me; but he who rejects me rejects him who sent me.*[3] And if you are met with resistance and persecution, leave that town. Shake the dust from your sandals and move on to the next place."

While Jesus was still speaking, Manaen and Cuza got to their feet. Both men came forward.

Jesus saw them coming, and he seriously examined their faces as they approached. When they were face-to-face, he asked, "Have you counted the cost?"

Cuza, the man of finances and ledgers, replied, "The cost is minimal. The profit is far greater than any man can calculate."

Jesus placed a hand on the head of each man.

Both felt fantastic surges, like the waves of the Great Sea roll through their beings. Every doubt, every fear vanished, and they knew their place in the Kingdom of God.

At that moment, the Holy Spirit drew back the veil that separates the earthly from the spiritual realms.

And Jesus saw Satan, like a streak of lightning, falling from his position in the Counsel of Heaven where he had taken Adam's seat as the representative from Earth. No longer could the tempter speak for Earth and all its inhabitants. The sons of Adam were now taking a stand against him.

Like a mighty king sending his troops into battle, Jesus stood in front of the seventy-two. *"I have given you authority to trample on snakes and scorpions and to overcome all the power of the enemy; nothing will harm you.*[4] Now, go! Do the works that I do. Teach the things I have taught you. Spread my name and my message throughout the land and then return to me."

As the seventy-two broke camp and headed for the road, Jesus turned to the twelve who remained with him. "The blessing of God has been with you for the time you have been with me. With your eyes and your ears, you have experienced what prophets and kings only saw in dreams. You are now seeing the formation of the army of the Lord on Earth. These warriors are setting out to engage heaven's enemy.

An unexpected cold wind whipped down from the barren hills that surrounded the springs. Jesus turned. With his physical and his spiritual eyes, he scanned the rugged terrain.

"Inside the cave." The Holy Spirit directed his vision.

There, Jesus saw his enemy, Satan, furiously pacing and shaking his fist toward heaven.

Speaking to the Holy Spirit, Jesus said, "I can see. My enemy is *like a roaring lion looking for someone to devour.*[5] My army will need more protection. Double their angel guards!"

Instantly, the sky was filled with warring angels. Jesus watched as they joined each pair of disciples on the road. Satan saw them too. He saw that all those who carried the truth of the Kingdom of God were heavily guarded. Only Jesus stood without angelic protection.

Satan then fixed his angry eyes on Jesus. With a snarl that was heard throughout the spirit realm, the Evil One shouted, "Once you were Yeshua the Creator, eternal God. But you chose to become flesh and blood. I promise. Flesh and blood will not live to enjoy victory over me."

Index of Characters

Biblical Characters

Abraham	The father of the Jewish race (Genesis 11–50)
Adam	The first man. He was created by God and placed in the Garden of Eden. (Genesis 2–4)
God	God the Father, used interchangeably with God, Abba, Lord, and the Eternal One
Andrew	Brother of Peter, son of Jona, fisherman, one of the twelve disciples of Jesus, later an apostle (John 1:42)
Annas	High priest during the life of Jesus (Luke 3:1–3)
Bartholomew	One of the twelve disciples also named Nathanael (Matthew 10:3, Mark 3:18, Luke 6:14, Acts 1:13)

Beggar at the Beautiful Gate	Fictionalized as Ichabod the crippled son of Asa the Temple perfumer (Acts 3)
Caiaphas	High priest during the life of Jesus (Lukc 3:1–3)
Canaan	Son of Ham, Grandson of Noah (Genesis 9:22)
Cornelius	Roman centurion (Acts.10:1)
Cuza	Officer in the court of Herod, manager of Herod's household, husband to Joanna (Luke 8:3)
David	A king of Israel and ancestor of Jesus (1 Samuel 16–2, Samuel 24, 1 Chronicles 11–29)
Dinah	Daughter of Jacob and Leah (Genesis 34:1–4)
Elijah	Old Testament prophet in Israel who challenged King Ahab and Queen Jezebel (1 Kings 7:2–Kings 2:12)
Elisha	Old Testament prophet who succeeded Elijah and had a double portion of his anointing (1 Kings 19:2–2 Kings 13)

Eve	The first woman. She was created by God from Adam's rib. She was Adam's wife and was the first to fall into sin. (Genesis 2–4)
Gamaliel	Important member of Sanhedrin, grandson of Hillel (Acts 5:34, 22:3)
Ham	One of the three sons of Noah (Genesis 9:22)
Satan	Once a heavenly angel, he rebelled against God. He is referred to in scriptures as the devil and Satan. In this series, he is also called the enemy and the Evil One. (Job 1–2)
Heli	Grandfather of Jesus (Luke 3:23) (One theory is that the genealogy in Luke is actually the genealogy of Mary.)
Herod Antipas	The Son of Herod the Great and ruler of Galilee (Matthew 14:1–11, Luke 23:6–12)
Herod the Great	The King Herod who killed the babies in Bethlehem, hoping to kill Jesus (Matthew 2:1–9)

Herodias	The second wife of Herod Antipas, formerly the wife of his half-brother, Phillip (Matthew 14:1–12, Mark 6:14–29, Luke 3:19–20)
Holy Spirit	Third person of the Godhead
Isaiah	An Old Testament prophet (2 Kings 19–20, 2 Chronicles 26–32, Isaiah)
Jacob	The son of Isaac who was tricked into marrying the wrong woman; father of twelve tribes of Israel (Genesis 29:23–25)
Jairus	A leader of the synagogue in Capernaum, Jesus raised his daughter from the dead (Mark 5 and Luke 8)
James Son of Alphaeus	One of the twelve disciples (Matthew 10:2)
James son of Joseph and Mary	The brother of Jesus, later a leader in the early church and writer of the book of James (Matthew 13:55)

James son of Zebedee	Possibly a cousin of Jesus, one of the twelve disciples, the brother of the disciple John whom Jesus loved, a fisherman, later an apostle (Mark 1:19–20, Mark 9:2–8, Mark 10:35–45)
Jesus	Son of God and Son of Mary, Yeshua in his heavenly person (Gospels of Matthew, Mark, Luke, and John)
Joanna	Wife of Cuza, supporter of Jesus, associated with the court of Herod Antipas (Luke 8:3)
Job	A man who was tested by Satan (Job 1–2)
John Marc	A young man, possibly a relative of Peter who later wrote the Gospel of Mark and went on missionary journeys. (Acts 12:12, 24–25, Acts 15:37)
John son of Zebedee	Possibly a cousin of Jesus, one of the twelve disciples, the brother of the disciple James, a fisherman, later an apostle, writer of the books of John and Revelation (Mark 1:19–

	20, Mark 9:2–8, Mark 14, 32–42)
John son of Zechariah	John the Baptist, a cousin of Jesus, the prophet of the desert (Mark 1:1–11, Luke 1:36–80, Luke 7:18–23, Mark 6:14–29)
Jona	Father of Simon Peter and Andrew, fishing partner with Zebedee (John 1:42, KJV)
Jose	Brother of Jesus, son of Joseph and Mary (Matthew 13:55, KJV)
Joseph	Carpenter of Nazareth, husband of Mary, earthly father of Jesus (Matthew 1:18–24)
Joseph of Arimathea	A wealthy man, member of the Sanhedrin who was able to approach Pilate (Mark 15:43)
Joshua	The leader who replaced Moses and led Israel into the Promised Land (Joshua)
Jude	A brother of Jesus, a son of Mary and Joseph, his name is sometimes spelled Juda or

	Judas. Probably the author of the book of Jude (Jude 1:1, Matthew 13:55, Mark 6:3)
Judas Iscariot	A disciple of Jesus, the one who betrayed him (Acts 1:16–17)
Lazarus	Friend of Jesus who lived in Bethany, fictionalized as the elder brother in the parable of the prodigal son. (John 11)
Lazarus	Rich man in the parable that Jesus told (Luke 16)
Levi	Son of Jacob and Leah, brother of Dinah (Genesis 34)
Manaen	Childhood companion to Herod Antipas, his mother was most likely the wet nurse for Antipas, later an important member of the early Christian community (Acts 13:1)
Martha	The sister of Mary and Lazarus of Bethany (John 11)
Mary	The mother of Jesus, wife of Joseph (Matthew 1–2, Luke 1–2)

Mary	The sister of Lazarus who lives in Bethany (John 11)
Mary of Magdela	A follower of Jesus; he cast seven demons out of her. (Mark 16:9)
Matthew	The tax collector at Capernaum, one of the twelve disciples, author of the Gospel of Matthew (Matthew 9:9)
Michael	A prince of angels who fought the forces of evil to bring a message from God to Daniel (Daniel 10:13)
Moses	A deliverer chosen by God to lead Israel out of Egypt (Exodus, Numbers, Deuteronomy)
Nathanael	One of the twelve disciples; also called Bartholomew (John 1:43–49)
Nicodemus	A rabbi in Jerusalem (John 3)
Noah	An ancestor of Jesus, builder of the ark (Genesis 6–9)
Peter	Simon Peter, son of Jona, brother of Andrew, fisherman, one of the twelve disciples of

	Jesus, later an apostle, writer of First and Second Peter. (John 1:42)
Philip	One of the twelve disciples, later an apostle (John 1:43–49)
Philip the Tetrarch	Son of Herod the Great, half-brother of Herod Antipas, husband of Herodias (Luke 3:1–3)
Pontius Pilate	Governor of Judea, probably appointed by Sejanus (Luke 3:1–3)
Salome	The sister of Mary and the wife of Zebedee (Mark 15:40, Matthew 27:55–56). This relationship is theorized by comparing the two scriptural passages about the women who were with Mary at the cross.
Salome	Daughter of Herodias and her first husband Philip. Her name is recorded in the writings of Josephus. (Matthew 14:6, Mark 6:22)
Sebastian	Fictional name for the paralyzed man who was lowered through the roof for Jesus to heal. (Mark 2:1–12)

Shechem	Son of Hamor, Canaanite who loved Dinah and was killed by Levi and Simeon (Genesis 34)
Shem	A son of Noah, ancestor of Jesus (Genesis 6–9)
Simeon	Son of Jacob and Leah, brother of Dinah (Genesis 34)
Simon the Zealot	One of the twelve disciples of Jesus (Acts 1:12–14) (Fictionalized as a childhood friend of Jesus who moved to Cana)
Simon the Leper	Fictionalized as the older brother of Jonathan who married Mary the sister of Lazarus (Matthew 26:6–7, Mark 14:3)
Simon brother of Jesus	Brother of Jesus, son of Mary and Joseph (Matthew 13:55)
Shira	Fictional name for the daughter of Jairus who was healed by Jesus (Mark 5, Luke 8)
Susanna	A wealthy supporter of the ministry of Jesus (Luke 8:3)

Talmon	Fictional name for the man that Jesus healed at the Pool of Bethesda (John 5)
Thaddaeus	One of the twelve disciples (Matthew 10:3, Mark 3:18)
Thomas	One of the twelve disciples (Matthew 10:3, Mark 3:18)
Yeshua the Creator	Yeshua is the Hebrew name for Jesus. In this story it is used as the heavenly person of Jesus.
Zebedee	A fisherman married to Salome, his sons are James and John, possibly an uncle of Jesus. (Matthew 4:21–22)

Fictional Characters

Abidan	The fictional name of a leper healed by Jesus (Luke 5:12–15)
Ahaz	The son of Moshe the tanner of Nazareth, childhood friend of Jesus
Alon	The father of Deborah the shepherdess who is the bride of Jose.

Asa	The father of Ichobod, perfumer for the Temple
Baruch	Shepherd of Nazareth, grandfather of Deborah, deceased
Casper	Fictional name for the young son of Cuza and Joanna, healed by Jesus
Chebar	President of the synagogue of Nazareth
Cleon	Fictional name for the Demoniac
Deborah	Shepherdess, granddaughter of Baruch, wife of Jose
Enos	Son of James the brother of Jesus, Jesus's nephew
Flavius	Roman Centurion
Geber	An Essene teacher, friend of John the Baptist
Hadrien	Roman Centurion, fictionalized as the one whose servant was healed.
Harim	The son of Moshe the tanner, boyhood friend of Jesus

Ichabod	Fictional name for the beggar by the beautiful gate, later healed by Peter and John
Jessie	Husband to Martha, sister of Lazarus of Bethany
Kheti	Egyptian owner of a trading caravan, Toma and Nodab are his trading partners.
Lemuel	Teacher (rabbi) of the synagogue school in Nazareth
Miriam	Sister of Peter, mother of John Marc, owner of the upper room where Jesus had the Last Supper
Moshe	A tanner in Nazareth, friend of Joseph
Nodab	The fictional name for the prodigal son and fictional younger brother of Lazarus of Bethany, works the trading caravan with Toma and Kheti
Raziel	Fallen angel, second-in-command to Satan
Rea	Woman of Bethany who anointed the head and feet

	of Jesus, childhood friend of Mary the sister of Lazarus
Salmon	The wealthy owner of an olive grove in Nazareth
Sebastian	Fictional name for the paralyzed man who was lowered through the roof for Jesus to heal. (Mark 2)
Shira	Fictional name for the daughter of Jairus who was healed by Jesus. (Mark 5, Luke 8)
Talmon	Fictional name for the man healed at Pool of Bethesda. (John 5)
Toma	Joseph's cousin, co-owner of a trading caravan, lives in Bethlehem. His first family was killed when the infants were slaughtered. He remarried Elishava.

Historical Characters

Antiochus Epiphanes	A Syrian King who tried to force the Greek culture on the Jewish nation about 175 BC

Aretas IV	Nabataean king 9 BC–AD 40, Herod Antipas married his daughter and opened trade relations with his nation. He went to war with Antipas because his daughter had been divorced.
Hillel	A famous rabbi
Judah Maccabee	The hero of Hanukkah who defeated Antiochus Epiphanes
Judith	Jewish heroine who killed a Syrian general
Phasaelis	Some historical information supports this name for the wife of Herod Antipas, daughter of Nabataean king, Aretas IV.
Procila	Wife of Pilate (slightly altered spelling to make pronunciation easier)
Sejanus	Roman ruler under Tiberius. He became too powerful, and he was killed by Tiberius. Then many of those that Sejanus had appointed to government positions were also executed.

Simon	Son of Hillel, head of Sanhedrin about AD 30
Tiberius	Emperor of Rome
Yonatan	A Jewish Rabbi, a student of Hillel, also known as Jonathan ben Uzziel He was from the region of Galilee and his tomb is in that area today.

Traditional Characters

Longinus	Centurion at the crucifixion
Photina	Traditional name for the woman who was at the well

Biblical References

Introduction

1. Matthew 11:28

Chapter 1

1. Joshua 24:2-3
2. Deuteronomy 30:19
3. Deuteronomy 11:26–28
4. John 4:8
5. John 4:9
6. John 4:10
7. John 4:11
8. John 4:12–14
9. John 4:15
10. John 4:16
11. John 4:17–18
12. John 4:19–20
13. John 4:21–23
14. John 4:25–26
15. John 4:27
16. John 4:32–33
17. John 4:34–35
18. John 4:36
19. John 4:37–38

Chapter 3

1. Luke 6:37
2. Luke 6:38
3. Luke 8:17–18

Chapter 4

1. Psalms 67
2. Numbers 10:35
3. Zechariah 4:6
4. Numbers 24:5
5. Psalms 5:7
6. Luke 4:18–19
7. Psalms 91:11–12

Chapter 5

1. Mark 1:17–18
2. Exodus 3:1–3
3. Exodus 3:4–6
4. Exodus 3:7–13
5. Exodus 3:14
6. Exodus 3:15
7. Luke 4:33–34
8. Luke 4:35
9. Numbers 6:24
10. Exodus 31:16
11. Isaiah 29:18–19

Chapter 6

1. Ephesians 6:12
2. Luke 6:27
3. Luke 6:28–29
4. Luke 6:30–31

5. Luke 6:37
6. Luke 3:16–17

Chapter 7

1. Matthew 5:21–22
2. Matthew 5:38
3. Matthew 5:44–45
4. Mark 2:5
5. Matthew 6:19
6. Matthew 6:20–24
7. Matthew 5:3–10

Chapter 8

1. John 5:24–27
2. John 5:39–40
3. John 5:45–47

Chapter 9

1. Psalms 110:51–52
2. Genesis 1:29
3. Mark 2:27–28
4. Matthew 5:17
5. Matthew 5:18
6. Matthew 5:19

Chapter 10

1. Psalms 40:1
2. Psalms 40:7–9
3. Matthew 16:26–27
4. Luke 6:20–21
5. Luke 6:22–23

Chapter 11

1. Matthew 5:22
2. Matthew 5:23–24
3. Matthew 5:27–30
4. Matthew 6:5
5. Matthew 6:6
6. Matthew 6:7
7. Matthew 6:9–13
8. Matthew 6:14–15
9. Matthew 5:25–26

Chapter 12

1. Luke 2:34–35
2. Luke 1:34–35

Chapter 13

1. Exodus 20:12
2. Proverbs 22:15
3. Numbers 6:24–26
4. Luke 7:27

Chapter 14

1. Psalms 19:1
2. Psalms 19:9,11
3. Deuteronomy 6:3
4. Proverbs 3:1–3
5. Deuteronomy 6:4–5
6. Deuteronomy 6:6–9
7. Deuteronomy 6:13–15
8. Deuteronomy 6:17–18
9. Psalms 119:1–3

Chapter 15

1. Isaiah 1:18

Chapter 16

1. Zechariah 7:9–10
2. Luke 8:16–18

Chapter 17

1. Judges 16:17
2. Ezekiel 18:21–23
3. Proverbs 15:33
4. Mark 6:22–23
5. Mark 6:22–23
6. Mark 6:25
7. Psalms 89:48
8. Job 19:25–27

Chapter 18

1. Ecclesiastes 3:19–20
2. Numbers 10:35

Chapter 19

1. Luke 5:36–38
2. Mark 5:28
3. Mark 5:29–30

Chapter 20

1. Mark 6:3
2. Numbers 12:1–2
3. Numbers 12:6–8

Chapter 21

1. Matthew 10:28–31
2. Matthew 10:5
3. Matthew 10:11
4. Matthew 10:16–17
5. Matthew 10:19–20
6. Matthew 10:32–33
7. Matthew 10:40–41
8. Luke 9:7–9
9. Matthew 11:11–14

Chapter 22

1. Ecclesiastes 1:9
2. Leviticus 17:11
3. Ezekiel 26:2–5
4. Mark 7:27–29

Chapter 23

1. Mark 8:2–3
2. John 6:41–42
3. John 6:43
4. John 6:53–55
5. John 6:58
6. John 6:60
7. Mark 7:14–15
8. Mark 7:21–23

Chapter 24

1. Psalms 22:10–11
2. Isaiah 50:4
3. Isaiah 50:6
4. Deuteronomy 4:37

5. Psalms 22:14–15
6. Isaiah 53:11–12
7. Mark 8:15
8. Luke 12:2–3
9. Luke 12:4–7
10. Luke 12:8–10
11. Matthew 16:13–14
12. Matthew 16:15–16
13. Matthew 16:16–17
14. Matthew 16:18
15. Isaiah 8:14
16. Matthew 16:19
17. Genesis 13:15
18. Joshua 1:3
19. Joshua 1:5–6
20. Joshua 1:9

Chapter 25

1. Matthew 16:21
2. Matthew 16:21
3. Matthew 16:22
4. Matthew 16:23
5. Matthew 16:24–26
6. Matthew 16:27
7. Matthew 17:2
8. Matthew 17:4–5
9. Matthew 17:5–6
10. Matthew 17:7–8
11. Matthew 17:11–12
12. Mark 9:15
13. Mark 9:17–18
14. Mark 9:19
15. Mark 9:22–24
16. Mark 9:25–26

17. Mark 9:28–29
18. Matthew 17:20–21

Chapter 26

1. Isaiah 58:10–11
2. Mark 9:36–37
3. Mark 9:42
4. Mark 9:43–48
5. Matthew 18:10
6. Proverbs 31:10
7. Matthew 18:17
8. Matthew 18:19–20

Chapter 27

1. Matthew 18:21
2. Luke 13:1
3. Isaiah 1:18

Chapter 28

1. Isaiah 55:12
2. Deuteronomy 32:1–2
3. Deuteronomy 32:3–4
4. Deuteronomy 32:18
5. Deuteronomy 32:36
6. Deuteronomy 32:39
7. John 7:16
8. John 7:19
9. John 7:20
10. John 7:28–29
11. Isaiah 12:3
12. Isaiah 2:3
13. Isaiah 12:2
14. John 7:37–38

Chapter 29

1. Luke 2:49
2. Leviticus 20:10
3. John 8:14
4. John 8:23
5. John 8:31–32
6. John 8:39–41
7. John 8:41
8. John 8:58
9. Luke 10:41–42

Chapter 30

1. Exodus 23:25–26
2. Luke 13:12–13
3. Luke 13:14
4. Luke 13:15–16
5. Luke 13:32–33
6. Luke 13:34–35
7. Genesis 2:7
8. John 9:39
9. John 9:41
10. John 10:27–30
11. Psalms 91:14–15

Chapter 31

1. Luke 9:57–58
2. Luke 10:9
3. Luke 10:16
4. Luke 10:19
5. 1 Peter 5:8